HAZE

Also by Paula Weston

Shadows

HAZE

THE REPHAIM BOOK 2

PAULA WESTON

Indigo

Originally published in Australia in 2013
by The Text Publishing Company
First published in Great Britain in 2013
by Indigo
An imprint of the Orion Publishing Group Ltd
Orion House
5 Upper St Martin's Lane
London WC2H 9EA

An Hachette UK company

1 3 5 7 9 10 8 6 4 2

The Orion Publishing Group's policy is to use papers
that are natural, renewable and recyclable products and
made from wood grown in sustainable forests. The logging
and manufacturing processes are expected to conform to
the environmental regulations of the country of origin.

A catalogue record for this book is
available from the British Library.

ISBN 978 1 78062 159 3

Typeset by Input Data Services Ltd, Bridgwater, Somerset.

Printed in Great Britain by Clays Ltd, St Ives plc.

FOR FREDDIE

IN THE STILL OF THE NIGHT

I almost wish I still had the blood-soaked dream of the nightclub.

At least then I'd be asleep, not lying here in the dark chasing thoughts I'll never catch. The jacaranda tree outside is still in the warm night; the moon casts a slight shadow of its twisted branches against the wall.

It's the quiet moments like this that get me, when it's impossible to pretend I have a grip on everything that's happened in the past week. In the daylight, in this bungalow, I can fool myself into thinking I still have control over my life. But here in the dark I know that's a lie. And my life already has too many lies. For a year I believed four things: that my twin brother died in a car accident; that nothing in my life would matter as much as that; that my violent dreams are not real; that my memories from before are so faded because I was badly hurt in the accident that killed Jude.

It turns out none of these things is true, and it's the truth that keeps me awake. The biggest truth of all: Jude might be alive.

The shadow shifts on the wall, sharpens, blurs. The ache comes back into my chest. The possibility that I'll see Jude again, the cruel hope of it, never fails to take the breath out of me.

A year of hurting and missing him.

A year of nightmares.

And now the truth. The impossible truth.

My eyes track to the mattress on the floor next to my bed; Rafa's boots are beside it. The TV is on in the lounge room, volume low, blue light flickering under my door. Through the thin walls I can hear Maggie stirring in her room. Jason might be in there with her, but chances are he's on the sofa in the living room, ignoring Rafa or being ignored by Rafa, still thinking of ways to make amends for not telling her he's one of us. Maggie's forgiven me because I didn't know.

How is Maggie sleeping? Is she dreaming of demons? Or of the three Rephaim who held her hostage up the mountain to get to me? I wish I could undo Monday and Tuesday night. I wish I could remember what it is everyone wants me to remember. What Jude and I actually did a year ago. It's not that I don't want to.

I roll over in bed, stare at the silhouette of the old tree outside and the smattering of stars beyond it.

Rafa says we're safe for now, but given that he's sleeping on my floor instead of in his own bed at the shack, he can't really believe that.

Not that he spends all night on the floor.

I turn again, kick the sheet off. Pull it back over me again. God, I need to sleep.

The TV goes quiet in the other room. A few seconds later my door opens and closes, floorboards creak beside the bed.

Silence. I breathe as though I'm sleeping. I can feel him listening. And then a zip slides undone, clothes drop to the floor and Rafa slips under the sheet with me. Warmth radiates from him. His movements are slow, careful. His breath soft on my skin.

Like last night, he doesn't touch me. The night before, Tuesday night – after the attack at the Retreat when we got Maggie back – I leaned against him when he settled behind me. As soon as our bodies touched he went straight back to the mattress on the floor. Shifted from my bed to his. It's one of the more annoying talents of the Rephaim – their ability to be somewhere else in the blink of an eye. He didn't say anything. No explanation. No smartarse comment.

So, since then, we don't touch and we don't talk and he stays. We've slept beside each other before – on the sofa on Patmos, when Rafa told me who I was. *What* I was. Then he was teasing, testing me. This closeness is different. Almost restrained. There's no sign of this Rafa during daylight hours. I know he doesn't want to finish what we started in his bedroom, but why sleep in my bed if he doesn't want the temptation?

He gets comfortable behind me, so close I can almost feel him. Almost. A deep sigh shifts my hair, tickles my neck. I close my eyes.

He knows I'm not asleep; he has to. So is he testing me or himself?

One week. That's how long it's taken to get this complicated. That's how long I've known Rafa. He's known me for a lot longer, but I don't remember it so it doesn't count. I don't remember anything that's true before I woke up in hospital a year ago. I don't remember anything about my life with the Rephaim.

I should roll over, say something. Talk about Jude. Talk about the Rephaim and what their next move will be. Demand to know what happened between Rafa and me – that other version of me – all those years ago. Ask him to tell me again what he knows about the fight that Jude and I had, and why we made up ten years later, and what it was we did a year ago that nearly killed me. But he doesn't have answers and I don't want him to leave my bed. I don't want to be alone with those other thoughts.

'Can you keep it down?' Rafa says. 'I can hear you thinking from here.'

Typical. He even breaks his own rules. Outside the stars disappear behind a bank of clouds.

'Gabe.'

I sigh. How many times do I have to tell him? I swear he calls me that other name just to get a reaction. I pull the sheet over my shoulders to my chin.

'*Gaby*,' he says. 'You can't put it off any longer.' He still doesn't touch me.

'What?' I keep my back to him. I know what's coming next: the one thing guaranteed to keep me awake a while longer.

'Tomorrow we go to Melbourne and start looking for Jude.'

FREEFALLING

'You don't have to do this,' I say to Jude.

'Yeah, I do.' He grins at me and then catches the eye of the girl testing the straps around his legs. She stands up, double-checks the clips and harnesses around his chest and hips. Once, twice. Blushes under his gaze. Honestly, how many backpackers have flirted with her, and still Jude gets a reaction?

Her assistant is calling out as he goes through his equipment and mechanical checklist. Music pounds around us: dirty guitars and fuzzy keyboards thumping out of speakers. The cable car moves under our feet and a breeze pushes the hair from my face. I don't have to look over the edge; I can feel the pull of that gaping space from here. We're up so high there are wispy clouds below us.

My lungs constrict and I don't know if it's because the air is thin or because Jude is about to jump, leaving me here alone. I shouldn't be here, but Jude sweet-talked the jump co-ordinator into bringing me with him.

'You ready?' someone shouts from the other cable car, which is now heading back down. It's the blue-haired Korean guy from the tour group we hung out with in the village last night.

'I was born ready,' Jude calls back. His eyes are bright. 'Hundred-and-forty-metre freefall, baby!'

They salute each other with a fist held out straight, as if they're symbolically bumping knuckles across the empty space.

I knew we shouldn't have come to Switzerland.

'Jude,' I say, forcing his attention back to me. 'What if something happens to you?'

'Princess, nothing's going to happen. Look around; these guys know what they're doing.'

'I mean it.'

There's something in my voice that brings him back to me, overrides his buzz. 'Gaby' – all traces of playfulness have gone – 'if anything ever happens to me, you'll be fine. You're strong enough to look after yourself. I hate to admit it, but you don't need me. Never did.' A smile. 'But listen, nothing is going to happen today. It's all good.'

'Jude, we're high enough up to get a nose bleed.'

'So come with me.'

I blink. 'Fuck off.'

'I mean it. We can do this together.' He raises his eyebrows at the girl who checked his harness. She nods.

I risk looking over the side. There's a river far beneath us. So far down we can't hear it. My entire body goes numb.

'You've got about thirty seconds and then I'm going on my own.'

What a choice: watch my brother jump out of this car or put aside my own fear and go with him. Share the recklessness. Why didn't we go to Paris? We'd be arguing over where to buy cheese right now.

Adrenaline begins to burn through me. 'Screw it.'

Jude breaks into a wide smile. 'Seriously?'

I glance at the yawning space beneath us. 'Hurry up before I change my mind.'

I keep my eyes on Jude while the girl rigs me up, then harnesses me to him. My heart bangs against my ribs. Finally, we're guided, shuffling, to the edge. It's all happening too quickly. But the music, the fear, the pounding of my heart. It's . . . exhilarating.

Jude must see it in my expression. He grins at me. 'Told you.'

I look down again. The bungee cord loops into the thin clouds, swaying. My stomach lurches. The girl positions us: one arm around each other, gripping each other's harness;

my head tucked tight against Jude's neck. We clamp our free hands together.

The countdown starts. 'Five, four—'

Holy shit, I'm really doing this. My pulse is erratic.

'Three, two—'

I'm with Jude. I'm okay. But, God, please don't let that cord break.

'One.'

Gravity pulls us. Undeniable. Irresistible.

'Hang on,' Jude says.

We don't even have to lean forward. We just fall.

I jerk awake. Rafa is still in the bed with me, his breathing slow and deep. I quieten my breath till I can hear the low pounding of the surf from down the hill a block away. Check the clock: four-thirty. Close my eyes again.

These memories of Jude; I cling to them even though I know they're not real.

Someone gave me that memory. Gave me all the memories I have of my fake life and my brother. And that someone wants me to believe Jude and I took a crazy leap together. Stood over an abyss and chose to fall towards a river.

Why?

If Jude is alive, if the impossible really is possible, then other impossible things are true too. Would he take the news as well as I did?

Jude, fallen angels exist.

Jude, we're half-angel bastards. Our father is one of the Fallen. Our mother is long dead. There are more of us out there. The Rephaim. Some of them you'd like, others you'd want to punch. But they're still better than the demons hunting our fathers.

Oh, and Jude? You're meant to be dead.

Me too.

Yeah. It's a little complicated.

It starts to fade – the memory, the rush, Jude's voice. Every part of me aches. How am I supposed to accept the Rephaim's version of my life when I don't remember it? How can I let go of the only thing I have left of Jude? These memories are all I've had this past year. How do I understand who I am, who I *was*, when they all claim to know a different version of me?

I drag my spare pillow close, bury my face in it. Try to hang on to that image of Jude grinning at me, the sky and the unknown behind him and below him.

God, I miss him.

BREAKFAST OF CHAMPIONS

Jason is cooking breakfast: blueberry and ricotta pancakes. He must think he can win Maggie back through her tastebuds. In fairness, it won't harm his chances.

'That smells amazing,' I say. It's so bright in the kitchen I can feel the night receding. On mornings like this it's easy to believe the Pan Beach sun can burn any darkness away. Jason turns briefly, looks at me as if he can see remnants of my night. Whatever he's thinking he keeps to himself.

'Nearly ready,' he says, pouring batter into two pans on the stove, swirling each with practised efficiency. Pretending there's nothing wrong with me and that there's no tension in the room.

I glance at the sofa. Pillow, sheet and blanket neatly stacked at one end. He and Maggie are talking again, awkwardly. Jason has spent his life avoiding the other Rephaim, so she understands why he took so long to tell us what he was, but she's not letting him off the hook quickly, which is the clearest sign yet she's fallen for him. Jason could go back to the resort – Rafa is here every night in case the demons come back to Pan Beach or Nathaniel sends more Rephaim for me or Maggie. But we all know Jason's not going anywhere.

I've known Jason for a week too. Apart from the time I knew him a century or so ago, and our reunion last year before Jude and I did whatever we did. But I don't remember either: more memories lost along with everything else from my old life. With his long blond curls and my dark bird-nest hair, it's hard to believe his mother and mine were cousins. Two Italian peasant girls seduced by fallen angels. I'm still getting my head around that one: that our fathers were among the two hundred Fallen who broke out of hell, spent two days and two nights roaming the earth and then vanished. Selfish pricks.

I can't bear to think about my mother – the woman who gave birth to Jude and me a hundred and thirty-nine years ago. She doesn't feel real. The mother I know – that cold, distant woman always so quick to criticise – feels real, but it turns out she never existed. I can't grieve for either of them, not yet.

Maggie is pretending to be busy revamping a handbag.

The kitchen table is awash with vintage buttons: greys and blues, red and pinks, tipped out from the jar she keeps on top of the fridge.

'What do you think?' She turns the bag around so I can see what she's done so far. 'This one is from a dress Mum wore to the Melbourne Cup in the sixties.' She points to a red button shaped like a flower. 'And this came from my old tweed jacket.' Her blonde hair is tied at the nape of her neck, loose strands framing her face.

'It's very you.'

'Isn't it just.'

She catches my eye and smiles. We're still okay. If I was the hugging type, I'd be hugging her right now for not asking me to move out of the bungalow after what happened this week. For letting three half-angels stay.

The pipes in the wall bang. Rafa is in the bathroom. The fact he's showering here must mean he's hanging around for a while this morning.

I flick on the kettle and drop a tea bag into a coffee-stained mug. Sunlight streams through the window and glares off the sink and bench. Wait – the sink is clean enough to give off glare?

'What time did you get up?' I ask Jason.

He shrugs, not looking around. 'Early.'

I try to catch Maggie's eye, but she's focused on her work

again – or trying hard to look as if she is. Her fingers form perfect loops as she sews.

'What are your plans for today?' She doesn't look up but I know she's talking to me.

'Besides checking in on you?' Maggie bites her lip; she hates the watch we've been keeping on her. 'Mick Butler's getting out of hospital this morning,' I say.

'Are you meeting him out front with flowers?'

'Yep, and then I'm taking him for brunch.'

She laughs, tests the button she's just stitched on.

'Rafa wants us to have a chat with him and Rusty at the Imperial.'

Maggie's slender fingers stall, needle and thread hovering in the air. 'Please tell me you're joking.'

'Sadly, no.'

Mick and Rusty Butler. Pan Beach's finest dope-growers. I bet they're wishing they'd listened to Rafa and not forced their way into the middle of the fight between the Rephaim and two of the demons hunting the Fallen. Especially given Bel and Leon brought along two pet hellions for fun. After being savaged by one, there's a good chance Mick's going to want a beer at the first opportunity.

The kettle boils. I bring my cup to the table.

'There's only one way that's going to end, Gaby.' A line creases Maggie's forehead. 'You don't have to go.'

'Rafa thinks I do.'

'Since when do you worry about what Rafa thinks?' She watches me sit down. 'I thought he was keen to leave town?'

I shrug, avoid her eyes. 'He also wants to make sure Mick and Rusty don't talk about what happened up the mountain.'

'Please don't go to the pub. We're down a waitress this morning – Nicky's not coming in until lunchtime. You could cover for her.'

'I need her more than you do,' Rafa says, coming along the corridor with the newspaper. He walks into the kitchen, pulling on a grey t-shirt. His dark blond hair is damp and sticking up after a rough towel-drying.

'What?' he says in response to Maggie's expression. 'I might need back-up.'

I give a short laugh at the ridiculousness of that statement. Rafa can take care of Mick and his mates without breaking a sweat; he just wants to throw me into a violent situation and see how I react – see how much more my body remembers.

I don't know about before, but I know what it remembers *now*: it remembers Rafa. His bed. His hands. The way he kissed me the other night . . . My body flares in response to him, and then my mind shuts it down, blocks out all the images of his skin, the green of his eyes that night.

He's still keeping things from me about the past. Our past. Violence comes to him as easy as breathing. He's reckless. So why do I still feel safer with him around, even if it means following him into the public bar at the Imperial?

Rafa lifts his shirt to rub a palm across his flat stomach, a lazy gesture. He catches my eye. 'Sleep well?'

'Like a baby.'

We both know I'm lying.

'And you, Margaret?'

'Like a log, thank you, Rafael.'

Rafa comes further into the kitchen and looks over Jason's shoulder. 'If you're trying to score points with me, Goldilocks, you'd do better with bacon and eggs.'

'You don't want any, then?' Jason asks. He tosses a pancake and catches it in the pan. Maggie forgets herself for a second and smiles.

'I didn't say that.' Rafa pulls up a stool at the bench and unfolds the paper. 'So, where did you get to last night?' he asks Jason.

Maggie and I share a quick look and go back to our respective tasks. I dunk my tea bag. Maggie keeps sewing.

'I was on the sofa.'

'No, you weren't. Not until midnight – I heard you get back. Where did you go?'

'I had a few errands to run.'

'Like what?'

'Not everything is your business, Rafa.'

Rafa's hands go still on the paper. 'You're joking, right?'

Jason doesn't respond.

'Like it was none of my business you're one of us? Or that you're the reason Jude and Gabe disappeared last year?'

Jason fusses with the pan, keeps his back to Rafa.

'You came and went all day yesterday, and now you disappear for half the night. Given all the bombshells you've dropped this week—'

'I'm trying to find Dani and Maria.'

Maggie and I look at each other. Is Jason going to tell him the truth?

Rafa already knows Jason's mother survived Nathaniel's round-up of Rephaite babies and that she later had another child, Arianna, a human girl, with *gifts*. Rafa knows Dani is a descendant of Arianna and is also gifted; that she can *see* the Rephaim. He knows it was Dani who told Jason I was still alive, who saw Rafa tracking me through the rainforest when he turned up a week ago. And he knows Dani had a vision that prompted Jason to reach out to Jude and me a year ago. That she then vanished with us and reappeared the following day with no memory of what had happened to us.

What Rafa doesn't know is why Jason is looking for Dani and her mother now.

'And?' Rafa says.

'And nothing. I haven't found them. They still won't take my calls.'

'The kid knows more than she's admitting.'

Jason turns around. 'Dani doesn't remember what happened last year. How many times do I have to tell you?'

Rafa flattens the newspaper. 'They're hiding something and you can't or won't see it. You're blinded by misplaced loyalty.'

'They're not hiding anything.' The pan bangs on the stove. 'Dani's twelve. She has a gift any Rephaite, angel or demon, would exploit in a heartbeat. Maria is protecting her only child.'

I go to the sink on the pretext of putting my tea bag in the bin.

'So, that's what you've been doing when you're not here, looking for them?' Rafa says. 'How do you know where to look if you don't know where they are?'

'Let it go,' I say to Rafa, blocking his view.

'In a minute.' He leans sideways to see around me. 'Are you going to tell me if they call?'

'That depends.'

'On what?'

'When you trust me, I'll trust you.'

Rafa runs his palm over his jaw. They watch each other.

Yeah, that's not happening any time soon.

Jason turns back to the pancakes. 'Not everyone is your enemy, Rafa,' he says, quieter now.

'No,' Rafa mutters, 'just people related to you.'

I catch his eye. '*I'm* related to him.'

Maggie puts her sewing away and I help her scoop the buttons back into the jar. The promise of pancakes, blueberries and maple syrup is enough to get Rafa sitting at the table with us. It's not enough to take the tension from Jason's shoulders.

And for good reason.

What Jason is keeping from Rafa has to come out. Today.

TALKING TO A BRICK WALL

Can you decapitate someone with a pool cue?

I hope not, or I'm in a shitload of trouble. Our chat with Mick and Rusty isn't going well.

Mick's on a stool, propped against the bar, his neck and shoulder heavily bandaged. Half his scruffy beard is missing where medics had to stitch up his throat two nights ago. Anyone else would have tidied up the rest of it, but he's left it hanging down to his chest. He looks strangely frail under the insipid bar lights: the stubble on his head is stark against his pallid scalp. Even the ink on his neck and arms looks tired.

His brother sits beside him. Rusty's beard is intact but his buzz-cropped hair is interrupted by a square, white bandage behind his left ear, held in place with surgical tape.

'Tell me where I can find it,' Mick says for about the fifth time. 'I'm gonna mount its fat head on my wall.'

'You really want to talk about this here?' Rafa asks.

Mick eyeballs him. 'You think I'd hide this from them?' He gestures to the four guys around us. All pierced and tattooed, in threadbare jeans and blue vests. One has three studs in each eyebrow. Woosha. Another, a tattoo of the Southern Cross on his throat. Tank. I don't know the other two. But I don't doubt for a second they could snap the pool cues they're holding in half with their bare hands. We're unarmed. The Imperial might be rough, but someone would have noticed if we'd walked in with katanas.

A week ago, I didn't know what a katana was. Now I'm starting to feel naked without one. Who knew I could get so attached to a sword?

'Let it go,' Rafa says.

'Are you serious?' Mick points an oil-stained finger at his neck. 'That thing fucking *bit* me.'

'And that thing is dead.'

I glance around the bar. It's half ten on a Friday morning and the place is deserted except for us and a couple of old guys nursing pints on faded beer mats. The place reeks of stale beer, cigarettes and regret.

The story going around town is that the Butlers smoked too much of the heavy-duty weed they grow up the mountain and were savaged by feral cats. But Mick and

Rusty know we saw what attacked them.

'So you reckon,' Mick says. 'How do I know you're—'

'I saw its severed head,' I say. 'Trust me, it's dead.'

Mick eyes me. 'Who got it? The one with the scar, or the bloodnut?'

He means Ez – Esther – and Uriel. Two of the Rephaim who'd been fighting each other until the demons and hellions turned up.

'Ez killed it.'

'What about the other one?' Mick presses. 'Someone get that?'

'Not your problem,' Rafa says.

'Pig's arse. Those pricks came into our territory. There's no way someone's not paying.'

Rafa has one boot resting on a barstool. His shoulders are relaxed, but I know how quickly he can explode into violence. And he's been itching for a fight ever since Tuesday—quiet moments in my bed aside.

He meets my eyes briefly and then turns back to Mick. 'Outside.' He moves towards the beer garden before Mick can argue. I'm a step behind.

'Ready?' Rafa says.

'Keep your temper and I won't have to be.' I don't want to fight. I might have held my own when my life and Maggie's depended on it, but I'm not as confident as Rafa that I can switch this stuff on and off.

And this time I don't have a sword.

The beer 'garden' is empty. It's a slab of concrete under a corrugated-iron roof with a few aluminium tables and benches bolted into the ground. Plastic chairs are scattered around. A pool table in the middle looks as though it was dragged out from the bar a few years ago, and has barely a scrap of felt left on it. It's warm out here, the sea breeze blocked by a high wall.

In the nine months I've been in Pan Beach I've never once had the desire to step inside the Imperial. It's the last bastion of the old seaside town Pan Beach once was, a place for the dwindling minority of locals who prefer tap beer, pies and worn carpet over fusion brews, tapas and polished timber. But it's not the menu or the decor that puts me off. It's the clientele. There's almost as much blood spilled here on a Friday night as there is beer.

Mick shuffles into the garden, wincing, but trying to hide how much the bite on his neck hurts. Rusty puts a hand out to support him. Mick waves him away, lowers himself onto a bench.

'I wanna know what bit me.'

Woosha and Tank station themselves at the door. The other two position themselves between us and the gate to the street. Rafa doesn't seem bothered that the gate's padlocked and we're surrounded. I'm not quite so relaxed.

'Those mutants, they're part of a military experiment,

right? Playing around with DNA and that shit?'

I stare at Mick. This is what he's come up with over the past two days? But then a government conspiracy makes more sense than the truth: that he was attacked by a hell-beast. How else to explain the huge creatures with jaundiced eyes and deadly claws? I don't want to lie, but I can't tell them the truth either. Way too hard.

'I can't say.'

Rafa is half-sitting on the edge of a table scarred with graffiti and cigarette burns, enjoying watching me dig myself into a hole.

'Can't or won't?' Mick says.

'Both.'

His eyes narrow. 'I knew it. What did I tell you, Woosha?'

'Who were the freaks with the white hair?' Rusty asks.

The warmth of the day recedes at the mention of Bel and Leon. I remember the fear in Maggie's eyes. The moment where everything around us turned quiet, when the splintered Rephaim stopped fighting each other and turned, shoulder to shoulder, to look at what was coming out of the dark. I can't quite shake Bel's boasting that he put his sword through my neck. Or what he said when I asked what happened to Jude. *Come with us, and we will show you.*

'Had to be government spooks,' Mick says.

'They didn't look government.'

'They're spooks, dickhead, they're not supposed to.'

Rusty gestures at me. 'Why were they so interested in you?'

I pull myself out of the clearing in the forest, rub the chill from my arms. 'I was in the wrong place at the wrong time. Like you.' I shift my hair from my shoulder to show them the hellion bite near my collarbone.

Rusty's breath comes out in a hiss. 'When did that happen?'

'A few months back.' A lie, but it's not as if I can tell him it happened a few nights ago when I gave myself up to Daniel and the Sanctuary to get Maggie back—not given how advanced the healing is. Rusty would notice: he's a bit more of a thinker than his brother.

'It was one of those mutants? Why?'

'They think I'm someone I'm not.' It's close enough to the truth.

Mick spits a wad of phlegm on the concrete at my feet. 'Bullshit.'

Charming.

'Excuse me? You think I did this to myself?'

'No, sweetheart, I think you're full of crap about how it happened. You've done nothing but feed us fairytales since you walked in the door. We *saw* you.'

'Saw us what?' Rafa eases his weight off the table.

'Playing ninjas up there.'

'And?'

'And start talking. Now.' The men surrounding us step closer with their pool cues.

Rafa laughs. 'Listen, moron, this is a courtesy visit. Your fight's done. Let it go. If you get caught up in this, there won't be enough left of any of you to leave a stain.'

I shoot Rafa a warning look, which he ignores.

Mick's face flushes. He'd be throwing punches by now if he wasn't in so much pain. 'You must have a death wish, mate, coming in here like this.'

'I'm trying to save your worthless arse.' Rafa is clear of the table now, flexing his fingers. Our window for a non-violent chat just closed.

Woosha, Tank and the other two close in around Rafa. 'You should've brought your sword,' Mick says as the four men rush Rafa.

They swing at his head and legs with surprising precision. The pool cues smack against his forearms and shins as he blocks each strike. Rafa grabs one and jerks it closer, pulling Woosha off his feet and into the path of another swinging cue, which cracks across Woosha's shoulders. Rafa shoves him at Tank and they sprawl to the ground. Then he king-hits the third guy and throws a chair at the fourth.

A movement at the door catches my eye: the bartender with his white t-shirt stretched across his stomach. The door slams shut and a bolt slides across on the inside.

Rafa stretches his neck from shoulder to shoulder, waiting for Mick's crew to get up. 'You planning on helping out any time today?' he says to me.

I've moved out of the way, my heart rate climbing. Rafa doesn't need me – he can end this whenever he wants to. He's keeping this going because he wants to see what I can do.

Before Rafa came to town I would have run from a bar fight at the Imperial without hesitation. Now I don't know what to do. I'm not the same girl I was a week ago, trying to run through my grief on the rainforest track. But I'm not the other me either. *Gabe*. One of the Rephaim's best fighters. The things Rafa says I'm capable of . . . I've only seen them in fits and starts. I might not be able to die here – unless you really can decapitate someone with a pool cue – but I could still be seriously injured.

What if I can't fight? It's one thing to throw a punch in a split-second of rage. This is something else.

Woosha is up from the ground, pulling a knife from his jeans. Mick's standing now, gripping the side of the pool table. Rusty is watching the fight closely but doesn't step in. Definitely the smarter of the pair.

Woosha feints left and then right, waiting for the others to surround Rafa again. Tank snaps his cue over his thigh and spins the two halves like batons.

'Mick.' I try to sound reasonable. 'You need to end this before they get hurt.'

He doesn't even look at me. 'Shut her up,' he says absently to Rusty.

Rusty snaps his fingers to get my attention and puts his finger to his lips. Then he turns back to the main action, more interested in the promise of Rafa getting stabbed.

Woosha lunges. Rafa catches him by the wrist and spins him around. He uses his body to block another cue strike and then flings him aside. Woosha hits the concrete hard, grunts. Rafa makes short work of the other two, then gestures for Tank to come at him with his busted cue. Tank grazes Rafa's arm before Rafa takes his legs out from under him.

Woosha is circling Rafa again, spinning the knife, waiting for his opening. My breath shortens as he glimpses me over his shoulder and turns, slashing the blade.

I react without thinking. I smash his wrist – the knife clatters to the ground – and then punch him in the face. *Shit*. His head is as hard as concrete. I stagger back, cradling my fist. Woosha takes a few slow steps towards me, moving his jaw from side to side, searching for the knife.

'You want some action, sweetheart?' he says.

I wait for him to telegraph his next move. What do I do if he lunges at me? What if he—

His eyes flick over my shoulder. Before I can look, something smacks into my head and shoulders. I sprawl forward. The ground is unforgiving, but I roll over and bring up my knees and hands defensively. Rusty is standing over me, holding a plastic chair. 'Stay down.'

I try to sit but he puts his worn boot on my chest and pushes me down.

'Don't make me hit you again.' Rusty's voice isn't menacing – this is his idea of chivalry.

'You're wasting your time,' I say to Rusty, trying to catch my breath. 'You're not going to beat Rafa. Look at him.'

Rusty keeps his boot on my chest – not putting his full weight on it, just enough to keep me in place – and watches the scuffle. Tank lands flat on his back not far from us, blood splattering from a split in his cheek. I wince. I should have taken up Maggie's offer to work at the Green Bean. I'm pretty sure nobody's bleeding on the floor over at Pan Beach's favourite cafe.

Mick's guys are all limping. Rafa has barely broken a sweat. When Tank lunges again, Rafa snaps his wrist. Tank howls and drops to his knees.

'Rafa, stop,' I call out.

Rusty puts more weight on my chest.

Rafa lands a couple of good punches on the guy closest to him. 'Get up,' he says, not looking my way.

He'll keep going until Mick calls it quits, someone calls

the cops, or I give him what he's waiting for. I know what he wants. He wants badass Gabe. But he knows badass Gabe isn't here. Just me. And I just proved that I don't know what I'm doing.

'Stay down,' Rusty says again, as if he can see my mind working.

I grit my teeth. What is wrong with me? In the past week I've killed a hell-beast and fought demons, and I'm letting Rusty Butler pin me to the filthy concrete at the Imperial. With one foot. I've got to do something. I need—

Don't think.

I grab Rusty's boot. He has a second to look down at me with vague amusement before I shove him, hard. He hops backwards, arms wheeling as he tries to keep his balance. I spring to my feet, blood pounding at my temples. I can't feel anything now except my heart against my ribs.

Woosha's knife is under the pool table. Too far away. A plastic chair is closer. I grab it with one hand and fling it at Rusty as he comes towards me. He bats it away, giving me time to snatch up a pool cue. I swing it fast; it cracks as it connects with the side of his head. His knees buckle. He slumps to the floor, dazed.

Fingers clamp around the back of my neck. I swing the cue again, try to turn, but Woosha wrenches the cue out of my hand. I keep my balance and use my momentum to slam an elbow into his stomach. He lets go and falls sideways. I bring my fist down on his nose. Blood instantly streams down over his lips. He stumbles towards Rafa.

My hand throbs, but there's so much adrenaline in my system – and whatever else makes me Rephaite – it's almost bearable.

'Had enough yet, *mate*?' Rafa asks Mick. He's holding the knife against Woosha's cheekbone.

Mick has a death grip on the pool table. His face is pinched.

'Good,' Rafa says. 'So we're clear: you keep out of our business and we'll keep out of yours.' Rafa shoves Woosha so hard he sprawls at Mick's feet. Next to him, Rusty gets back up, groans.

'If I hear you've been talking about what happened up the mountain or what just happened here, I'll come back. And next time, there'll be more of us. Got it?'

Mick doesn't answer. His silence is more menacing than a spray of abuse. Wonderful. As well as the Rephaim and fiery-eyed demons, I've now got the Imperial boys to count as a threat.

I watch Mick in pain, Rusty limping out of the way, a fine spatter of blood on the ground. God, what am I doing? Is this who I am now? I've heard so many versions of who I'm meant to be, they're all starting to seep together: the fearless Gabe that Rafa remembers; the Gabe who didn't talk to Jude for a decade, who refused to go when he left the Sanctuary, who hooked up with Daniel of all people; the Gaby who came here on a bus nine months ago, made friends with Maggie, got a job at the library.

Which one am I?

And what sort of chaos have I brought to Pan Beach?

Rafa kicks the gate and the screws holding the latch to the timber give way. It swings open and we step out onto the street. Rafa knocks it shut behind us.

'Now,' he says as he sets off towards the esplanade, 'was that so hard?'

HOT AND COLD

I make it a block before I trust myself to speak.

'That was always going to end in a brawl.'

Rafa glances at me as we walk. His hair looks fairer out here in the sunlight. Right now I'd like to run my fingers through it, get a good handful, and smack his head into the brick wall we're passing.

'I'm not the one who started it,' he says.

'Please. You've been wound up for days.'

His lips twitch. 'You have no idea.'

I ignore the heat climbing my neck. Above us, the morning sky is cloudless, the sun getting warmer.

'Don't tell me you didn't enjoy that,' I say.

'What – dancing around with those arse clowns while you stood and watched?' He looks at me. 'You think that's my idea of fun? You should have jumped straight in.'

He's not quite so playful now.

'When a fight breaks out, Rafa, my first instinct isn't to jump in.'

'Well, it should be.'

'Why?'

He blocks my path, forcing me to stop. 'You're kidding, right?' He's only half a head taller than me, but it's enough to give him an advantage when he wants to stare me down. 'Do you want to find Jude or not?'

My chest tightens. I don't answer. I shouldn't need to.

'I'm serious,' he says. 'We've got the Sanctuary breathing down our necks, demons gunning for us and God knows what else between us and Jude. You need to know what you're capable of and you can only do that if you break a sweat.'

'I thought you were going to train me.'

'Nothing beats the real thing.'

'So that was for my benefit?'

'Trying to keep this shit out of Pan Beach is for your benefit. You know I'd rather be somewhere else. I'm ready to leave right now: just say the word.'

'It's not that simple.'

'It is, and you know it. We could be in Melbourne and back by lunchtime. I don't know why you're dragging your feet. You're the one who keeps finding excuses to be here.'

He watches me and I hope he can't read me as well as he thinks he can. I don't want to explain this uncertainty – I'm not sure I could, even if I wanted to. His eyes flicker in frustration and anger.

'I told you, we have to wait for Taya and Malachi,' I say.

He's more than over that excuse. 'Shit, Gabe, Nathaniel's not sending them to help, he's sending them to spy on us.'

'I realise that.' I'm yet to convince the fallen angel who found and raised the Rephaim – and built them into an army – that I don't know where the rest of the Fallen are. That I don't know what Jude and I did a year ago that left me broken and bloodied. That maybe killed Jude.

'Then let's go before they get here.'

I look past him to the esplanade. It's not as if I have a burning desire to see Nathaniel's head-kickers again. The first time I met Taya she threw me into a tree and broke my ribs. Then Malachi tried to drown me in a bath, on Nathaniel and Daniel's orders. As if a near-death experience was going to jump-start memories from my old life. And they wonder why I'm not racing to move back into Rephaim headquarters in Italy. There's a reason Jude, Rafa, Ez, Zak and nineteen other Rephaim left the so-called Sanctuary a decade ago and became Outcasts. There's also a reason I didn't go with them. I just wish I knew what it was.

'And what do you think Taya and Malachi will do when

they can't find me?' I say. 'They'll scoop up Mags again and we're back where we started – or worse – because next time they will take her to the Sanctuary.'

'How does that change if we wait for them?'

I press my lips together.

'What?'

'Nothing.'

He watches me for a few seconds. I look away.

'This is about Goldilocks, isn't it?'

I watch a line of bull ants scurry over the concrete wall behind him. 'No.'

'Bullshit. You and Maggie didn't bat an eyelid about him being out half the night. He's doing more than running around after the missing kid with the visions. What else is going on?'

I sigh. 'He's trying to help.'

'How?'

'He thinks there might be a way to protect Mags from being forced to shift by Rephaim.'

Rafa stares at me. 'Don't you think I'd know about it if there was?'

'You didn't know about Jason.'

He turns away.

'His life has been different to yours – it stands to reason he might know different things. You keep saying Nathaniel doesn't know everything.'

'But Goldilocks does?'

'Rafa—'

'Does he think his seer is going to know?'

'I don't know.'

'Who else then?'

'*I don't know.*'

He shakes his head. 'I told you there'd be more. He knows too much about the Rephaim for someone who's never been to the Sanctuary.'

The last time Rafa shared that suspicion, I was half-undressed on his bed. For a second I remember the feel of his lips on my skin, my hands in his hair. The need to touch as much of him as possible . . . I cut short the memory before it robs me of focus. Right now all I feel is Rafa's impatience. His distrust of Jason. His hurt that Jude and I met Jason a hundred years ago and allowed him to stay hidden from the Sanctuary and everyone there. Including Rafa. But like everything else about my past, I don't remember it and I can't undo it. In the sunlight, I think I can see how heavy the last year has been on Rafa. Believing Jude was dead. Believing I was dead. I forget sometimes that he's had his own grief to carry. My own frustration fades a little.

'Maybe Jason will talk to you if you stop jumping down his throat every time he opens his mouth.'

'When were you going to let me in on this plan of his?'

'When I knew if he could help or not.'

The muscle in his jaw twitches. 'Just once, I'd like you to trust me enough to tell me what's going on.'

'Rafa, this wasn't about trust. It was about giving Jason time before you started picking him apart again.'

'What does he think he's going to find?'

'I don't know, but isn't it worth a few more hours to find out?'

'We need to be looking for Jude, Gabe. It's only a matter of time before someone else twigs that if you're alive when you're not meant to be, he might be too.' He shakes his head. 'Some days I really wish you remembered all this shit.'

I don't answer because I know full well that most days he's glad I don't.

Rafa sets off again. We don't speak while we cross the road, stopping halfway to wait for an old jeep to pass us.

'Look, I need a bit longer. For Mags. That's all I'm asking. Jason will watch out for her if we're not here, I know that. But if there's something else we can do to protect her from Taya and Malachi, I want to try.'

He turns to me as we walk, lets his breath out. 'A couple more hours. That's it.'

I nod. It's not much of a concession, but I'll take what I can get. We're on the esplanade now. 'Green Bean?' I ask, realising that's where we've been heading.

He shrugs. His sleeve is torn and his arm is still bleeding.

'Bryce won't be impressed if you go in looking like that,' I say. 'Let's go home first, tidy it up.'

Rafa lifts his arm to get a better look. 'A quick shift will fix it.'

'With who, Zak?' My stomach does a small flip. Like it does every time Rafa says he's leaving Pan Beach. If he'd taught me to shift, I could heal him. But it's another one of those things he keeps mentioning but does nothing about.

'How long will you be?'

He looks away.

Rafa has been to Mexico to see Ez and Zak three times already in the last two days. Most times he's only gone an hour or so. Most times I don't provoke him this much before he leaves.

'Maybe they could come here,' I say. I miss Ez. She's always so calm and sensible – and she's the only Rephaite who's given me straight answers this past week.

'And do what? Hang out at my place?' Rafa stops in front of the alley between the bookshop and the juice bar. He gives me a once-over and steps closer. 'Turn around.'

'Why?'

'You've got dirt on you.'

Of course I do – I was lying on the concrete at the Imperial not so long ago.

Rafa holds my shoulder to keep me steady while he

dusts me off. 'All good.' His hand slides down my arm, falls away. He walks into the laneway. I'm ready for him to shift, for the lane to become empty, but he hesitates.

'What?' I ask.

His eyes search my face. A few seconds pass. 'Nothing.'

And then he's gone.

It's only when I'm nearly at the Green Bean that it hits me. He was waiting for me to ask him to stay.

TEA . . . NO SYMPATHY

Maggie is busy inside when I arrive. I order a coffee and find a chair in the sun, overlooking the water. Let the familiarity of Pandanus Beach ground me: the busy esplanade, the endless ocean, the lush mountain rising up behind the town. Even after everything that's happened here, it's still the closest thing I have to a home.

The surf is rough this morning. Only a few diehards brave the water. A guy in a yellow and black wetsuit climbs a wave, then wipes out spectacularly. His board flips in the air, trailing sunlit water, and disappears back into the surf. He emerges in the wash, laughing, unscathed.

I chase thoughts of Jude. Again. Tomorrow is the anniversary of his death. Or at least the death I remember.

The moment that changed everything: squealing tyres, smashing glass, the car crumpling around us. Blood. Dirt. Petrol.

I've known for a week it never happened. So why does it still feel so real?

Of course I want to know if Jude's alive. Of course I want to find him. How could I not? But Rafa talks about it as though it's some easy two-step process: search for Jude, find Jude. But what if we don't find him? What then? Or what if—

'You're going to get premature wrinkles if you don't stop that.' Maggie is at the table with my cappuccino, squinting against the sun. 'I take it Mick wasn't in the mood for talking?'

I dig my fingers into my shoulder, try to make the muscle relax. 'Oh, Mick was talking. Rafa just didn't like what he heard.'

She moves to block out the sun. 'How bad?'

'Stitches and plaster. Not for Rafa, obviously.'

Maggie glances back at the cafe and slips into the chair opposite me. 'Do you think they got the message?'

'They think the hellions are part of a government conspiracy.'

'Who told them that?'

'I sort of let them believe it.'

Maggie's eyes drop to my knuckles, which are still red,

but she doesn't say anything. 'Simon was in earlier.' She changes the subject.

'How's he doing?'

'Better.'

I've seen Simon since Tuesday night. Since he saw the freak show up the mountain and accused me of putting Maggie in harm's way. Since he found out I'm the bastard offspring of a fallen angel. Since he learned enough to regret kissing me the night Maggie was taken. And since I learned how crappy it feels to kiss a nice guy when you don't really mean it. I've seen Simon – but I haven't spoken to him. It's not my fault he won't make eye contact when I go into Rick's Bar.

Maggie studies me. 'What else is going on?'

A week ago, she wouldn't have pushed me. A lot can happen in a week.

I sigh, sip my coffee. It's strong and earthy. 'I had to tell Rafa what Jason's trying to do.'

'Oh . . . How did he take it?'

'He was cool.'

Maggie blinks.

'*Not*.' I dab at cocoa on the rim of the cup. 'He's impatient to go to Melbourne.'

'Why do you have to go south at all? Can't you call the hospital and ask if anyone remembers you?' She gets up and stacks the empty plates on the next table.

'If we can find the nurse who told me Jude was dead, she might know something that will help Rafa work out who changed my memories . . . Maybe give us a lead on what happened to Jude. It's not really a phone conversation.'

Maggie cradles her plates. 'When are you going?'

'Not until Jason gets back. Hopefully he'll find what he's looking for today.'

She readjusts the stack in her arms. 'You don't have to wait. I'll be fine.'

'Yeah, Mags, after shadowing you for the past two days I'm just going to leave you here alone.'

'Do you really think Taya or Malachi will try something?'

'I don't know, but I'd rather have Jason here, especially if he's armed with something that means you can't be forced to shift.'

Maggie presses her lips together; I know how much she hates blink-of-an-eye travel with the Rephaim.

'Taya won't hurt you – she wouldn't be game – but I don't trust her not to take you for leverage again. Or fun. No way are we making it easy for her. Plus' – I give her a meaningful look – 'Jason made me promise we wouldn't leave until he's back in Pan Beach.'

'He still feels guilty about lying to me.'

'You know it's more than that.'

She drops her eyes. Another glance into the cafe. 'Let me know before you go, okay?'

When she's gone, I sit back in my wicker chair and watch the world pass by. Two women in bikinis and matching sarongs cross the esplanade, deep in conversation. They have the same pleasant round face and mousy hair. Mother and daughter. The younger woman uses her hands to demonstrate something and her mother throws her head back, laughs loudly. I swirl the coffee in my cup, catching the froth on the edges. I never had a moment like that with my mother – not even the fake one. The sun loses some of its comfort.

I pick at a piece of willow sticking up on the armrest. My real mother. What would it have been like to know her? To grow up in a coastal village in Italy with Jude, alongside Jason and his mother? The three of us maybe never fully understanding what we were, still having each other. But Nathaniel found Jude and me like he did the other half-angel babies, killed our mother and took us. Jason escaped his notice because he didn't realise two women from the same village fell pregnant to the Fallen. So it was Jason who got to have a mother. Jason who got to be part of a family – a real family. I've never made friends easily, but a big Italian family? That would have been different.

Maggie is already coming back out of the cafe. Her eyes are locked on me, her steps stilted. There's someone behind her, close, as if they're waiting for an opportunity to pass. A flash of black hair.

Shit. Taya.

I push back my chair and stand up.

'Calm down,' she says to me over Maggie's shoulder. 'I didn't come to fight.' Her hair is pulled back in its usual militant ponytail.

'Then step away from Maggie.'

Taya holds up her hands. 'Not even touching.' She doesn't try to stop Maggie hurrying to my side of the table.

Taya is wearing a t-shirt the colour of a murky ocean. It's the first time I've seen her out of black. The dressing on her neck is the only evidence of Tuesday night's hellion attack.

'What are you so twitchy about?' she says. 'You knew I was coming.'

She's right. I should have been paying attention, not sitting here feeling sorry for myself.

'Where's Malachi?'

'Not here. Where's Rafa?'

'Not here,' I mimic. We watch each other for a few seconds. 'If you didn't come here to fight, what do you want?'

'I've ordered a chai latte, so that'll do for a start.' Taya sits down, puts her feet up on the chair opposite. Her shoulders are loose and her face is relaxed – as relaxed as Taya gets, anyway – so maybe she's not looking for trouble. Yet. It can't be much comfort to Maggie. The last time Taya was this close she had a sword at her throat. A night and a day, that's how long Taya, Malachi and Micah had Maggie at the resort up the mountain, using her to get to me. Though, in fairness, Micah wasn't a prick about it. He even seemed happy to see me when I turned up with Rafa, Ez and Zak.

None of them hurt Maggie, not really, but the experience still left scars. I'm looking at the damage right now. Maggie is next to me, fingers pressing into her elbows. Here on the esplanade, under a clear sky, she's afraid. I hate that I've taken the safety of her home from her.

'Can Mags get back to work without having to watch her back?'

'We're not going anywhere today.'

I don't miss the emphasis on the last word. Taya looks out over the ocean, losing interest in our conversation. I only sit back down when Maggie is two tables away.

'So, what, you're going to stalk me now?'

Taya drags her attention back from the water. 'Just following Daniel's orders.'

'Which orders, specifically?'

'To keep you safe.' She gives me an ironic smile.

I laugh. 'I think we both know I'm safer without you around.'

'Maybe. But without me here, you might think you can run off after the Fallen again.'

I let my head fall back in exasperation. There's no point

telling her yet again that I'm not interested in looking for the Fallen. But then I'm not telling her who I *am* looking for either.

'Anyone would think Daniel still cared about you.' She shakes her head in mock regret. 'You should have stayed with him, Gabe. Walking away from him was your first big mistake. But I guess he got his own back in the cage.'

Another piece of my past I can't quite get a handle on: I used to date a member of the Rephaite Council of Five. Maybe it would make more sense if I'd only seen a photo of Daniel – no doubt, he's breathtaking. But there's nothing I've seen about him this last week that explains any old attachment, and that was before he put me in the cage with the hellion.

'So I'll be keeping a close eye on you,' Taya says. 'But don't fret, I know how to keep a low profile. I've got a job.'

I snort. 'Where?'

'With your barman.'

'Since when?'

'About ten minutes ago.'

'Bull. Simon knows what you are. He'd never give you a job. Wait – did you threaten him?'

She shifts in her seat. 'I may have pointed out that he knows things that could get him killed and it would be in his best interests to help me out.'

'Rick won't hire you just because Simon asks him to.'

'Already sorted. Rick took a bit of a shine to me.'

'To you? Doubtful.'

But she's half angel, isn't she? Her eyes are dark and perceptive and beautiful. She's effortlessly graceful. It's not inconceivable that someone who didn't know her might find her attractive.

My new phone rings: Foo Fighters' 'My Hero'. Rafa picked the ringtone – his idea of a joke. I check the screen: Jason. I let it go to voicemail in case it's a conversation I don't want to have in front of Taya.

'Who was that?' she asks.

'None of your business.'

'Was it Simon?'

I settle back in my chair. 'You worried he'll find out you'll be useless come happy hour?'

'Please. I was tending bar before either of those boys were born.'

'When? Before you realised your true calling was kicking heads?'

She gives me a curious look. 'What is it you think we do?'

'I . . .' I stop. 'You search for the Fallen.'

'And how do you think we do that?'

I shrug. 'Enlighten me.' My cappuccino has gone cold. I finish it, feel the coffee slide down my throat, cool and bitter.

Taya smiles but there's nothing friendly about it. 'Who would have thought the day would come when I'd have to explain something to the great Gabriella.'

Oh, fuck off.

'I wonder what Jude would think if he could see you now, all clueless and peace-loving.'

I push the thought aside before it digs in. 'Get on with it.'

'Fine.' She turns back to the surf for a moment and we watch a kestrel wheeling across the sky in an effortless arc. 'Semyaza and the rest of the Fallen are most likely in another dimension, maybe trapped there. Unless of course you and Jude set them free last year.'

I give her a filthy look.

'Come on, what do you *think* you two were doing? What else but the Fallen would have brought you back together after all that time? And why all the secrecy if you weren't doing something wrong?'

Taya waits for me to bite. I don't. It's not hard: we both know I can't remember.

'Anyway,' she says, 'that many supernatural beings couldn't have crossed over without leaving a residual footprint.'

'Like what?'

'Natural disasters, sudden wars—'

'Even after all this time? It's been a hundred and forty years, hasn't it?'

'We're talking about former members of the Angelic Garrison. We know their stint in hell dulled their glory, but they're still angels and that sort of power doesn't disappear. It seeps into everything and everyone.'

'Wouldn't they have a good influence?'

'They were fresh out of the pit. They would have reeked of the place.'

The kestrel loops towards the headland.

'So when something weird or inexplicable happens, we check it out. Look around, chat to the locals, keep an eye out for demons. If pit scum are sniffing around, there's a good chance they're on to something. They have a better nose than us for that stuff.'

She's talking about the surveillance jobs Daisy mentioned when I was at the Sanctuary. I wish it was Daisy sitting here explaining this to me, but she messaged me yesterday to say Daniel had ordered her to Syria to check out a demon sighting. One of the few Rephaim at the Sanctuary who doesn't think I'm the enemy, sent on a sudden mission. Convenient.

'And you work in bars to do that?'

'Every two-horse town in the world has a bar or a coffee house. That's where people talk.'

I pause. 'Is that what I used to do?'

'Only if you thought there was the chance of a fight.'

I turn my empty cup around on its saucer. 'Semyaza was

the ringleader, right? I don't understand how Nathaniel lost contact with him in the first place. Didn't all the Fallen escape hell together?'

'Nathaniel didn't sin again with the rest of them, so the bond they sealed before their fall was broken.'

What the hell were they thinking? Semyaza and two hundred angels get sent to hell thousands of years ago for seducing human women. They finally break out, and do the same thing all over again. Except Nathaniel. And now he and the Rephaim are obsessed with finding Nathaniel's missing brothers.

'Aren't you even a little bit curious about them?'

'No.' She says it quickly, as if even thinking about it is wrong.

'You've never wondered which one is your father?'

Taya's eyes darken. 'This is what hanging out with Outcasts does. It muddies the water. Don't let Rafa fill your head with that crap.'

Maggie is on her way back with Taya's latte. She comes to my side of the table, places the cup down and slides it across with one finger. She forces herself to look at Taya. 'Anything else?'

'I wouldn't mind a chat with your boyfriend.'

Maggie stiffens. 'Why?'

'He needs to understand to keep his mouth shut.'

I hide my surprise. Taya still doesn't know Jason is

Rephaite. Does that mean Micah hasn't told anyone he saw Jason shift with Maggie at the Retreat? Why would he keep that to himself?

'Jason gets it,' I say.

'That doesn't let him off the hook. And what about your idiot tattooed friends?'

'The Butlers? Rafa's taken care of it.'

Maggie clears my cup and goes back inside.

'How's the bite?' I gesture to Taya's neck.

'Sore.' Her eyes fall to my matching scar. Thanks to Rafa, the wound has almost completely healed, but there's nothing I can do about the ugly marks left behind.

Taya blows on her tea. The smell of cloves and cinnamon wafts across the table.

'Why did you do it?'

'Do what?' I know what she's talking about. I want to hear her say it.

'Why did you jump in front of the hell-spawn?' She watches me. It's totally messing with her head that I saved her life on the mountain.

'Let's call it bad judgment.'

She doesn't say anything. We both know it was more complicated than that.

My phone vibrates with a message. It's Jason. He's waiting at the bungalow. I need to go, but I can't look as though I'm in a hurry.

'So, what's Malachi going to do when he gets here? Wash glasses? Be Rick's door bitch?'

'He's got priorities elsewhere for the moment.'

'Something more important than antagonising me? Must be big.' And then it hits me: maybe the Rephaim have a lead on the Fallen. Maybe Daisy's job in Syria is more than an excuse to distract her from what's happening in Pan Beach. My stomach flutters. I have no idea if that's good or bad news.

Taya stands up. 'I need to settle in. Don't go anywhere.'

Settle in? 'Where are you staying?'

'Above the bar.'

Simon and Rick live above the bar.

'I told Rick I hadn't booked anywhere yet. He offered me their spare room until I find my feet.' She grins.

Across the road, a huge wave smashes onto the beach, bringing a cheer from the surfers watching from the sand. Taya living with Simon. I can only imagine how he feels about that.

'You worried about your barman?'

'Leave him alone, Taya. He doesn't care about us. He wants to forget we exist.'

Her eyes sharpen. 'How many humans do you think know about the Rephaim?'

It's a rhetorical question so I don't bother answering.

'Right now, about three dozen, and most of those are

monks at the Sanctuary. That puts your friends here in a very elite group.'

'And whose fault is that? If you and Malachi hadn't turned up, they'd still be oblivious.'

'No, Gabe, if *you* hadn't turned up they'd be oblivious.'

Out past the waves, the kestrel hovers over the water, riding the wind. It beats its wings once, twice, and dives for the surface, disappearing behind the swell.

'Then that makes my friends my responsibility,' I say, measuring my words. 'I'll take care of it.'

Taya laughs. 'Nice try. Daniel's given me the job and, unlike other people at this table, I know how to follow orders. So' – she drains her tea – 'I'll take care of your mess.'

LAST CAT IN THE BAG

'I'm not going anywhere without telling him.'

'Gaby, he can't know.' Jason is standing in the kitchen, his whole body tense. Sunlight streams through the window, turns his hair an even lighter shade of honey.

'What do you think he's going to do when he finds out I've gone somewhere with you? He's already pissed off about what you've been up to.'

Jason shakes his head. 'We need to go now.'

'I have to tell him.'

'Why?'

'Because the last time I went off without him I ended up in a cage with a hellion.' I say it without thinking, and for a brief sickening moment I'm back behind the diamond-shaped wire, lying on blood-soaked sawdust. Jason frowns and I'm guessing he's remembering how torn up I was when he and Rafa found me. He moves to the kitchen window to let in fresh air. The newspaper flutters on the bench where Rafa left it.

'There's only one way to get what I need to protect Maggie and he can't be a part of it,' he says.

We've been arguing about this since I got here five minutes ago. I don't even know what it is Jason wants to do – only that it involves shifting somewhere without telling Rafa. But I know what we agreed to: that someone be with Maggie at all times unless she's at work, and even then we take turns checking on her. I've told him Taya's in town and even that hasn't swayed him.

'At the very least, he can be here to keep an eye on Mags,' I say.

'We'll be gone a few minutes. Maggie will be safe at work and—'

'Jason, do you trust Rafa?'

'This isn't about trusting him.'

'But do you?'

The sea breeze carries through the open window, making Jason's curls sway across his forehead. 'To a point. But what we need to do, where we need to go . . . it's big. I don't know how he'll take it, and I don't trust what he'll do with the information.'

All Jason wants is to keep Maggie safe. But as much as

Rafa is unpredictable – and has secrets of his own – I can't keep this from him. He's annoyed at me enough right now: I don't want to push him any further. Or push him away.

And we're not leaving Maggie alone.

'Gaby, the sooner we do this, the sooner you can look for Jude.' Jason's eyes have softened as though he understands the fear I wrestle with every night. I don't care if he does – there's no way I'm talking about it.

'I'm not going anywhere until I talk to Rafa.'

Jason rubs the back of his neck, sighs. 'I'm not kidding. He's not going to take this well.'

'He doesn't take anything well. But he needs to know and he'll get over it.'

Rafa's number rings four times before he answers. 'What's up?' He sounds out of breath.

'Taya's here.'

Silence.

'And Jason's back.'

'And?'

'He needs me to go somewhere with him and—'

'Where are you now?'

'The bungalow.'

'Where does he want to take you?'

Jason watches me, silhouetted against the sunlit window.

'He won't say. But I thought—'

Rafa materialises in the room, wearing grey jogging

bottoms and a black vest, his phone still to his ear. He's covered in a light sheen of sweat and his hair is messy. He tosses the phone on the table. 'What now, Goldilocks?'

'You could have finished what you were doing,' I say. 'I wasn't going anywhere.'

'I can throw punches here just as well as in Mexico.'

Jason gives me a pointed look. 'Yes, this was a terrific idea.'

I step between them. 'Hey.' I get Rafa's attention. 'I'm trying to keep you in the loop here. Don't make me regret it.'

He eyes me for a moment, stretches one arm across his chest, then the other. The nick on his shoulder is completely gone. 'What's the story?'

'I don't know yet,' I say.

Jason's fingers are splayed on his hips. He stares down at the faded black and white lino floor. We wait. Finally, he lets out a deep, defeated sigh.

'There's a way to keep Mags safe . . .' I prompt him.

He glances at Rafa. 'There are others who know about the Rephaim. A group of women in America.'

'Oh, for fuck's sake,' Rafa says.

Shit. I pull out a chair and sit down. Every time I think I've got a handle on Jason . . .

'I met them in New York, in the summer of 1940—'

'They've known about us for seven fucking decades?'

'I was in Central Park,' Jason says, ignoring Rafa. 'I'd seen these two women before, watching me. I didn't think much of it, even when they approached me. But then they said they knew what I was, that they'd received a revelation from God about the Fallen and their offspring. They knew things about me. They knew Nathaniel was in Italy – I quote – "building his army of bastards".'

'Did they know where the Fallen went?' Rafa asks. 'No? Then what did they want?'

'For me to stay away from Nathaniel. They said the Rephaim were an abomination, but if I kept myself from Nathaniel and the others I might be spared when the final judgment came.'

I look from him to Rafa. Abomination is not the first word that springs to mind. 'You weren't kidding about getting mixed messages about religion.'

A sad smile. 'They knew about Zarael and the Gatekeepers. They hoped the demons would find the Fallen and drag them and Nathaniel back to hell and take their offspring with them.'

Rafa is perfectly still. 'And what did you tell them?'

'Nothing. I didn't tell them my mother survived and had another child, or about her descendants and their visions. They left and I never saw those two again. But about fifteen years later another two women visited me, again in New York. They were daughters of the first two, younger – maybe early thirties. They somehow knew I'd never been to the Sanctuary. They said I'd proven I could be trusted, so they took me to meet the rest of the family. In Iowa.'

'So you weren't searching for Dani and Maria this morning?' Rafa says.

'I'm always looking for them.' There's sadness in his voice, loss. I feel it, but I can't overlook the fact he didn't tell Maggie and me the truth.

'You lied to us?' I ask.

'I wanted to know if the women could help me before I put them in danger. And I did call Dani and Maria again. I asked if they'd ever heard of an object that could protect humans from Rephaim. They didn't return my call.' Jason doesn't add that apart from the phone call where Dani told him I was in Pan Beach, they haven't taken his calls for a year.

Rafa shakes his head. 'So, there's a cult of women who know about us, and they live among the fucking corn in Iowa?'

Jason looks to me, needing me to understand. 'My mother was long gone, none of the girls in the family were having visions at that point . . . I was curious.' He pauses. 'We travelled by bus – I didn't know I could shift with humans back then. I met three generations of the family. All women. They asked me questions about my abilities—'

'Did you tell them about me and Jude?' I ask.

'No, I lied about how I learned to shift.'

'And you're still in contact with them?'

He nods. 'The current generation knows more about the Rephaim than any before them.'

'How? Who are they?'

Jason sits at the table, runs his fingers along the edge. 'There's a strong religious tradition in the family but I haven't been able to pin down what, if any, denomination they follow. There are rules about what they will and won't tell me. The standard response is that I can't know too much in case I fall under Nathaniel's influence.'

'You're a smart guy,' Rafa says. It's not a compliment. 'Why didn't you do your own research?'

'I didn't know how seriously to take the whole "revelation of God" thing. I didn't know if they would find out.'

'Are you shitting me?'

'They knew things, Rafa. I don't know how. I didn't want to risk losing contact with them.' He drums his fingers on the laminate. 'But they've never seemed like farmers. The current matriarch, Virginia, walks and talks like a corporate CEO and her eldest daughter Debra is an architect. They don't come across as religious zealots – until they start talking about the Fallen and the Rephaim.'

'And it's always women you meet?' I ask.

He nods.

'How can they help Mags?'

Jason's eyes stray to a mark on the table. An old candle burn. He doesn't look up. He's really uncomfortable talking to Rafa about this.

'None of them have ever been scared of me. Nervous, yes, but not frightened. They knew about shifting – don't ask me how – so they should be more on edge in my company.' A pause. 'I've had a theory for a while now. I think they wear some kind of trinket that would prevent them from being forced to shift.'

Rafa lets his breath out. 'Not possible.'

'What sort of something?' I ask.

'I don't know.'

'Then how—'

'Hear me out. They all wear a chain around their neck, which they tuck inside their clothes. These women spend a lot of money on jewellery. They flaunt it – they don't hide it.'

'Is that where you went this morning?' I ask. 'Iowa?'

He nods. 'Sophie was on her own. She's Virginia's granddaughter, about sixteen. I asked about her necklace. She was cagey, but she said she'd show me if I brought you to the farm.'

I blink. 'She knows about me?'

'They know about all the Rephaim.'

'But she knew I was alive?'

Jason shakes his head. 'I had to tell her. It was the only

way I could explain why a human was at risk and why I needed her help.'

'She probably already knew,' Rafa says. 'These women have to be in league with Zarael. How else could they know things we don't?'

'No. They'd bear Nathaniel's bastard child before they'd align themselves with a creature from hell. They hate demons even more than they hate the Fallen. '

'God, you're naive.' Rafa shakes his head. 'If you're so convinced a *necklace* could protect Maggie, why didn't you grab it off the girl while you were there?'

'Because I'm not you.' Jason takes a deep breath, calms himself. 'Look, Sophie is still there on her own. We need to go now.'

The tap drips in the sink. Fat drops splashing on scarred stainless steel. What if Rafa's right and these women have contact with the Gatekeeper demons?

'You're not taking Gabe to Iowa,' Rafa says, his voice flat. 'Not without me.'

'Rafa—'

'Who's going to look after Mags?' I interrupt Jason. 'Taya's already paid the cafe a visit today.'

'Did she threaten Maggie?' Rafa asks.

'No, but—'

'As long as Maggie stays at work, she's fine. What time does she finish?'

'Six,' Jason says. 'We'll be back way before then.'

I chew on my lip and then grab Rafa's phone from the table. 'What about Ez or Zak? Can they check up on her while we're gone?'

'Yeah, I'm sure they'd love to cut short training to babysit—' He stops, sees I'm serious. The call is quick. 'They know where to find her,' he says when he hangs up. 'They'll be there in five.'

I nod. Taya won't try anything with two Outcasts there. Not in broad daylight.

Jason runs his hand through his hair. 'And how do I explain you to Sophie?'

'Can she sense Rephaim?' Rafa asks.

'No—'

'Then don't tell her who I am. Tell her . . .' His attention drifts to me for a second. 'Tell her I'm Gaby's boyfriend.'

It takes a second for me to realise he called me Gaby. Not Gabe.

'The family will never forgive me—'

'Who cares?'

'I do. I care. I never would have been able to keep track of what was happening at the Sanctuary – how Gabe and Jude were doing – without them.'

'They know about all of us?'

'Bits and pieces. I picked up enough over the years to understand what the Sanctuary was, and that Gabe and

Jude were still there – and were okay.'

Rafa studies him, a small smile on his lips. 'How many of these women have you slept with?'

Jason goes to the sink, tightens the tap so it stops dripping. Ignores the question. 'This is a bad idea,' he mutters.

'You don't think I know how to be charming, Goldilocks?'

Jason shakes his head. 'Let's just go.'

I meet Rafa in the middle of the room.

'Please don't screw this up for Mags.' I say it quietly enough that only he can hear.

A hand slides around my waist. His lips brush against my ear. 'She's a teenage girl. I've got it covered.'

CHILDREN OF THE CORN

We arrive in a cornfield, in the dark.

Jason controls the shift, so it's warmer and gentler than the chaos of travelling solo with Rafa. No furious wind, no sense of being stretched and compressed, no iciness. No skittery pulse like my first time. But it still takes a few seconds for my stomach to settle. Which is when the cold hits. After the bright Pan Beach morning, the night air here knocks the breath out of me.

Around us the corn whispers. Everything is dry, dusty. My eyes adjust and I realise the towering plants are dead. I run my hands through the leaves. They feel like ancient paper; I half-expect them to disintegrate under my fingertips.

Rafa and I follow Jason, who's already moving down the

cornrow with sure steps. The ground is firm so the going is easy. It's also short. I almost barrel into Jason when he stops.

I don't know what I was expecting – a cute farmhouse with a red roof nestled between cornfields, maybe – but this isn't it. In the middle of the clearing in front of us is a gleaming building that looks like a super-sized shipping container jutting out from the side of a hill.

'What is that?' Rafa is behind me.

'There used to be an old barn here, but they built this place a few years back.' Jason sets off across the clearing.

'Why?' I ask, hesitating. 'It's hideous.'

Rafa puts his hand lightly on my lower back, guides me forward. As we move closer, I work out that the structure is actually in two parts. The base is made of concrete and set into the hill, and on top of it is the huge rectangular building. It's made from galvanised iron and is big enough to park a couple of trucks stacked three high. It glints, even under an inky sky. The front wall is floor-to-ceiling glass, like some sort of new age church, but it's too high up to see inside. We make our way towards two tall doors at ground level. I wrap my jacket tighter around me.

There's no garden, just lawn mown close to the ground that crunches underfoot. A dusty sedan is parked on gravel at the end of a dirt driveway. The main building sits out over the entry, soft light spilling out from the glass above.

'Let me do the talking.' Jason's face is lit by a row of recessed halogen lights. He checks Rafa over. 'Maybe you should lower your hood.'

Rafa gives him a flat look. His hood stays up.

Jason pauses, knocks. A few second later, hurried steps descend an internal staircase.

'Who's there?' The voice is young, confident. East Coast.

'Jason. I've brought Gabriella.'

The door jerks open.

The girl is not what I expect either: her make-up is flawless and natural, her shiny blonde hair cut blunt to her fine jaw. She's wearing a black silk dress cinched at her waist, a cashmere cardigan tied around pale shoulders. Gold bracelets jangle on her slender wrists. If she's wearing a necklace it's hidden by her cardigan.

I look at her. She looks at me.

'Sophie, this is Gabriella,' Jason says.

The breeze carries a strand of hair across her face. It sticks in her lip gloss. Her pale eyes flit to Rafa.

'Who are you?'

'That's Matt, Gaby's boyfriend,' Jason says before either of us can speak.

I've only just managed to hide my surprise that Jason has acquired a New York accent in the last ten seconds when he floors me again by remembering the name I gave Rafa in the short story I entered in an online competition;

the story that brought Rafa to Pan Beach to find me.

'Are you still alone?' Jason asks.

She uses a French-polished fingernail to drag the hair away from her lip. 'Yes.' Another glance at Rafa.

Warmth and a hint of wood smoke seep out from the house, making the temperature outside seem even colder. I shiver.

'Can we come in?' Jason asks.

Sophie's hand comes up to her chest. She hesitates, lets it fall. 'Sure.' She steps aside and we enter.

For a second, I think we've wandered into an art gallery, but one devoid of art. We're in a bright square room with a high ceiling, surrounded by bare walls. Our boots echo on hardwood floors. The only thing down here other than us is a long table lined with high-backed chairs. No bills or newspapers scattered across it, no vase or candles. No personal touches. Nobody lives here.

We climb the stairs to the upper level.

Rafa walks with his hands in his pockets, sizing up the house. He might have joked in Pan Beach about being able to handle Sophie, but now that he's here, I can see the tightness across his shoulders. Jason's too, though there was no tension in his voice. The space on the upper level is bigger again, like a studio apartment. Sophie leads us to the wall of glass overlooking the dark cornfield, not that we can see it. The lights inside have turned the glass to mirrors. There's no hint of the rows of dry husks that surround the house. All I can see is us. Rafa watching Sophie. Of all the places I can imagine him in – bars, pubs, even a mediaeval monastery – this isn't one of them. He doesn't fit. He's like something wild, trapped in this sterile space, wary of the silence and emptiness.

We pass a pot-bellied stove radiating heat. I stop for a second to warm my fingers. Sophie gestures to facing sofas in front of the window. Jason and I take one; Rafa stays standing.

'Please, sit down.' Sophie doesn't take her eyes from him.

'I'm good.' Rafa gives her one of his slow, sexy smiles. It doesn't quite reach his eyes, but her cheeks still turn a delicate shade of pink. I glance at the window, forgetting that I can't see out. My reflection stares at me. My spine is too straight. Breathe.

'What is this place?' I ask.

Sophie sits opposite us, bracelets jangling. 'My aunt Debra is an architect. This is a prototype for a design she's experimenting with.'

'A prototype for what? Are you—'

'You're really Gabriella,' she says. It's not a question. She looks at me the way the Rephaim do when they first see me. As if they're trying to match up the person they knew before I disappeared with the person in front of them. As if they're startled that I look exactly the same. As if they'd be more comfortable if there was a physical difference they could point to. They've all done it: Malachi and Taya, Daniel, even Ez and Zak. Especially Ez and Zak. And now Sophie. But her gaze doesn't shift and after a few seconds I realise I was wrong: she doesn't look at me like them at all. Her eyes travel over my face and body as if she's examining a specimen. She's not seeing *me*. It's not the clothes that are slightly too old for her that make her seem a little off. Or the way she keeps fussing with her bracelets. It's her eyes. There's no light in them. No warmth.

'Have we met before?' I ask.

'No.' Her fingertips press into the leather of the sofa.

'Jason says you can protect our friend,' I say.

Sophie nods. 'For a price.'

'And what price is that?'

'Information.' She pulls one of the bracelets tight against her skin. 'I need to know where Nathaniel is searching for the Fallen.'

'How would I know? I'm not part of the Sanctuary. I don't remember that life.'

She lets the bracelet go, then puts her hand over the red indent it left behind. 'Then tell me what you and your brother did last year.'

'I can't. I don't remember.'

Her pale eyes consider me. 'Then I can't help you.'

I stand up, partly to call her bluff, and partly because I

don't like sitting with all this glass at my back. 'This was a waste of time,' I say to Jason. 'Let's go.'

'No, no, wait.' Sophie springs off the sofa. Her tone is conciliatory, coercing. She's a girl who usually gets her way. 'I could get in serious trouble for letting you in here, right, Jason?' She turns to him. 'I need a little piece of information, something to prove a point to my grandmother. This rule we have of not interacting with' – she catches herself, pauses, takes hold of a bracelet again – 'with *them* is crazy. It's the only way we can know what's going on in that monastery.'

'What happened to your revelations about the Rephaim?' Rafa asks.

Sophie moves the bracelet down to her knuckles, folds her hand as if she's trying to take it off, but it's too small. 'Some things are still—' She stops, forgets herself. 'How do you know about the half-breeds? They usually don't tell humans their true nature.'

'It's called pillow talk. What were you about to say?' Rafa pushes off his hoodie. He's actually more threatening without it.

Sophie looks at him and falters. She glances towards the stairs. 'Nothing.'

'Oh, come on, Sophie, you seem like a clever girl. If you want information, you'll have to give Gaby something in return.'

I'm silent, still startled at how easily she said 'half-breeds', as if the words carry no weight.

'I'm offering a blessed amulet. There is nothing else here for her.' Her voice is tighter now.

Jason clears his throat. 'Maybe we should—'

'How did your family find out about the Fallen and the Rephaim?' Rafa asks, ignoring Jason.

'Our ancestors received a sign from God.'

'What sort of sign?'

She presses her lips together and shakes her head.

'How about *when* did they find out?'

She glances at the back of the room. 'When the bastards were born.' Her tone is careful now, guarded.

'How did they know about that?'

'I can't say.'

'I thought they found out through a revelation of God?'

'They did.'

Rafa pauses, changes tack. 'How old are you?'

'Sixteen.'

A smile. 'You don't really care about this stuff, do you?'

'Of course I do.'

'Why?'

'God has chosen us to protect the world from the Fallen and their bastards.' She says it without irony. She believes it.

'Protect the world how?'

She looks at Rafa, her eyes travelling over his face as though she's memorising him. She swallows.

'I can't say.'

Rafa gestures to the almost empty room around us. 'So, what's this place – the Church of the Righteous Corn Farmers?'

Sophie's eyes flit past him again and I notice a door slightly ajar beyond the stairwell, a sliver of light. Rafa follows her gaze. 'What else is up here?' He moves away from the sofa, towards the door.

'Nothing. *Jason* . . . He can't . . .' She presses her palm against her breastbone, her fingers clutching at something beneath the silk.

'I'll get him.' I pass the pot-bellied stove. Rafa is almost at the door.

'Hey, *Matt*, wait up.'

He doesn't break stride as he enters the room.

'What the hell . . .' he says.

I stop short of running into him. It takes me a second to register what he's staring at. The windowless room has an architect's drawing board against one wall, a stool, a filing cabinet and a lamp. All four walls are plastered with photographs of people. It's odd, but I don't understand Rafa's reaction until he walks over and stabs his finger at one of the images. My breath catches. I've seen it before, on his phone. It's of him and Jude at a football match.

'I don't understand.' I peer at the photos around it, all held up by thumbtacks. There's one of a broad-shouldered man with curly black hair, jogging along a road. It can only be Zak. I run my finger over image after image, faces of people I've met this week: Daisy, Ez, Micah, Uriel, Daniel, even Nathaniel. Most of them have been taken from a distance.

Rafa is still staring at the picture of him and Jude.

'Do you think she recognised you?'

Before he can answer, there are three rapid beeps behind us and a door shuts. Not the door that was open – a sliding door, hidden in the wall cavity. Made of metal. Without a handle. 'Hey!' My fist thuds on the cold surface. It sounds like we're inside a bank vault. I press my ear against the door. 'Jason!'

'If she recognised me, she'd know there's no point shutting us in,' Rafa says. 'Come here.' He signals for me to join him in the middle of the room. 'Enough of this bullshit.'

I put my arm around him and the floor drops away almost immediately. And then my right shoulder explodes with pain, just before we smash into the hard floor.

'Ugh,' I grunt and open my eyes. We're still in the photo room. 'What happened?'

Rafa disentangles himself from me and climbs to his feet. Without speaking, he shifts again, disappearing like a light going out. And just as quickly, he materialises across the room, slamming into the wall and landing heavily.

We can't get out.

THIS HAS NEVER HAPPENED
TO ME BEFORE . . .

'Rafa, what the hell?'

His eyes are blazing. 'It's a trap.'

'What? How?'

Rafa paces the room. 'I don't know, but that prick out there does.' He shifts, and slams into the wall again.

I rub my shoulder. 'Oh, come on, Rafa, he—'

'Wake up,' Rafa snaps. 'He brought us here.'

Shift, crash. At least now he braces for the impact, although it doesn't stop the wind being driven out of him each time.

'I'm going to kill him. I mean it. I'm going to rip his head' – shift, crash – 'off his fucking shoulders.' He doesn't bother standing up before trying again.

Shift – I wait for him to hit the floor, and then I pin him down, gripping his arms, my knees around his hips. 'Stop it. This isn't helping.'

His chest rises and falls beneath me in short, sharp breaths. My own pulse races. Rafa can't shift out of here. *We* can't shift out of here.

'Just stop. We need to work out what's going on.'

He pushes back against me, trying to move me. I tighten my legs around him so he can't. My hair is loose, a curtain that touches his face.

'I know exactly what's going on. That little shit out there betrayed us—'

'You weren't even supposed to be here, Rafa.'

'Which only means he was willing to sell you out.'

'Jason didn't sell anyone out.' I can't accept that. Not after everything we've been through. Not after the risks he's taken for Maggie. For me. Rafa stares at the ceiling, his jaw working. He's barely noticed I'm straddling him.

Oh. I'm straddling Rafa.

I lose focus for a split second and then I land on the hard floor at his side.

'Not everyone is your friend.' He gets to his feet.

'Nobody forced you to come in here,' I say, and sit up. The smooth board of the ceiling feels way too low. The room smells like stale coffee.

'Oh, so this is my fault? Fucking typical.' Rafa is pacing

again. 'It's always me. Never anyone else. Never you.'

His entire being seems to expand and contract with his rage. This space is way too small for him.

'You know,' I say, 'I'm not convinced this is the best time for that argument.'

He prowls the room twice more before finally stopping. I can see he's not coping with being trapped – it's probably the first time in his long life he's experienced the sensation – but taking it out on me isn't helping. And Jason's outside, so we'll be out soon.

'Truce?' I say to Rafa.

He cracks three knuckles and then holds out a hand to me. I let him help me off the floor.

'Thank you.'

I wait for him to say something, but he doesn't. I go to the drawing board. It's covered in floor plans and sketches. I pick up the top sheet; there are more underneath but I can't make out the faint lines in the lamplight. I go back to the door and run my hands over the photos either side of it. There. A switch, hidden under a picture of a woman I don't recognise.

A fluorescent light sputters and comes on. Rafa leafs through the drawings, flipping back and forth. His eyes are constantly straying to the door. 'That's the Sanctuary,' he says without looking at me. I move closer. It's the first time I've seen the Italian monastery from the outside. If these drawings are even remotely to scale, the Rephaite headquarters are seriously impressive. I glance over half a dozen pages, each showing a different angle of the mediaeval compound. Some are technical floor plans, others rough pencil sketches. Piazzas surrounded by cloisters and three-storey wings, dome-roofed chapels, an imposing façade with Corinthian columns. Hand-drawn arrows with scribbled notes beside them: *Nathaniel's private chambers, infirmary, library.*

'And these photos . . .' Rafa moves to the nearest wall. 'Some are surveillance shots of missions. Others are from personal collections.' He taps the photo of him and Jude.

'How's that possible?'

Rafa points to an image not far above his. 'Look.'

The blood drains from my face. It's a photo of me.

I'm somewhere outdoors. I'm wearing leggings and a black vest. My feet are planted apart and I'm holding a katana over my head as though it's the most natural thing in the world. My hair is pulled back in a plait that hangs halfway down my back.

I'm grinning at my training partner. He's blurry, but it looks like Micah – Maggie's guard on the mountain – and his pose matches mine. I'm never going to get used to seeing these photos of myself.

'When was this taken?'

Rafa steps closer. I can feel the heat in his skin. 'It's

hard to tell. No landmarks. Could be two years old, could be thirty. It's not like we age.' He goes to the door again, presses his ear against it.

I pull a few prints down and turn them over. They're all on the same kind of paper, home-printed, without date or brand. None are originals.

'How do you think they got them?'

Rafa looks through the photos I hand him. 'Someone inside the Sanctuary.'

'Seriously?'

'Someone had to access computers, phones and albums to get some of these.' He points to a picture of Ez and Zak sunbaking on a beach. Ez's skin is flawless: the shot was taken before a hellion clawed her face. 'I took that. It's at least a decade old. So are these surveillance shots. All they had to know is where we'd be.' He moves on to a grainy photo of a restaurant, taken from a distance. 'This was about a year before the big split.'

There's a crowd around the table. Rafa, relaxed, beer halfway to his lips. Jude beside him, head thrown back, laughing. Next to him is . . . me. That other me. Watching Jude, grinning. Something stirs in my chest.

The back of someone's head blocks the person next to me, but they've got straight red hair so it's probably Daisy. And then . . . Malachi. He's smiling – and not even in a smartarse way. I'm drawn to a blonde woman at the end of the table with dark kohl-rimmed eyes. At a table filled with beautiful people, she stands out. I tap her face with my finger, not sure if I want to ask the question or not.

'That's Mya,' Rafa says and walks away. His voice sounds deliberately empty.

I look for other images of her. I don't want to, but I can't help it. There's something about her. Wild. Defiant. Alive. In every photo, her long hair is messy, as if she's just woken up. I have a flash of her and Rafa in bed and immediately shut it down.

Whatever happened to tear apart the Rephaim a decade ago, she was in the middle of it. Daisy says she was the reason Rafa and Jude challenged Nathaniel's rule and left the Sanctuary. But Ez says it was Jude who caused the split, though Mya liked to take credit for it.

Shit, this mess never gets any clearer. Even with pictures.

I take down the group photo, look around for others of Jude. But it's not Jude my gaze falls on. It's Nathaniel. The fallen angel is alone with his arms folded, his attention fixed on something in the distance. He's standing among blackened ruins in a forest, his fair hair damp from rain. In real life, his irises flicker icy blue; in the image they simply look odd, glassy. He's in old jeans and a jumper that hints at muscle underneath. Again, the contradiction surprises me: by all accounts the angel who raised the Rephaim is a tough disciplinarian, but he looks more like a footballer.

I lean in closer. The image is crisp. It doesn't look as if it was taken with a zoom lens. How did someone get close enough to take this shot?

'You really think someone at the Sanctuary has been handing over these photos – for years?' I ask Rafa.

He pulls the stool out from under the desk and sits on it, surveys the room. Taps his foot: a quick, impatient beat. 'Why is that so hard to believe? Because everyone there is so obedient?'

'No, I mean – that photo of you and Jude at the footy, how old is that?'

'About eighteen months.'

'Right. So it can't be someone from the Sanctuary. You don't see any of them any more.' I find another shot with Jude in it, add it to my collection. As well as a couple featuring me.

'That's not totally true. Occasionally we follow the same lead on the Gatekeepers – paths cross. And Daniel or Uri try to guilt us into going back. What's to say someone didn't help themselves to my phone when I wasn't paying attention?'

'You wouldn't drop your guard long enough.'

'Obviously I did.'

My shoulder is still throbbing. I lean against the wall for a moment, close my eyes.

'Oh, that's great,' Rafa mutters.

I find him jamming his phone back in his pocket.
'What?'

'No signal.'

I try mine. Typical. I finally get a phone with international roaming and it's still useless in a crisis. I rub the soreness out of my shoulder. Rafa must be aching all over after hitting that wall half a dozen times.

It's been at least ten minutes now. What's Jason doing out there? I take a slow breath. No need to panic. Rafa's here. Just keep busy.

'Maybe there's something useful in here.' I go over to the filing cabinet and open the single drawer. It's empty except for an old leather-bound book held together with fat rubber bands.

'What is that?' Rafa says over my shoulder. 'An old family bible?'

'I don't think so.' The red leather is soft under my fingers, rubbed bare at the corners, the spine flaky like dead skin. There's no writing on the cover. I sit down and take off the rubber bands, careful not to tear the loose pages poking out. A photo drops to the floor.

Rafa picks it up. He frowns and turns it towards me. 'What the . . .?'

A cornfield. Six men, grim-faced in black tailcoats, top hats, cravats and pocket watches. They're standing around a hole that looks like a freshly dug grave. The photo is sepia, antique. It's strange enough to keep Rafa's attention from the door for the moment. He flips it over. A date is scrawled in ink: *1874*.

I gently open the book and find more images of the same scene. In the first, there's something rolled up in a sheet at the men's feet to the side of the hole – something the size of a person – placed on a low stack of logs. A coldness trails up my spine. In the next image, the bundle is in flames. And then the hole is nothing but a mound of dirt, no trace of the bundle or the ashes from the fire. It's beyond creepy.

'Well, that's disturbing.' Rafa does another lap of the room, thumps the door twice as he passes it, as if it might miraculously open.

I can't tear my eyes from the photos; the resolute expressions of the men in each image. I make myself keep flicking through, find handwritten pages of spidery writing. It's a journal.

Carefully, I leaf through notes and diagrams, find more photos tucked between the thick pages. Images of an old wooden church, first in its prime and then burned to its stumps. The cold reaches my neck and face. Every page is crowded with words and it takes me a second to realise why I don't understand them.

'Is that German?' I hold it up for Rafa to see.

He barely glances at the page. 'Looks like it.'

'Can you read it?'

'My German's a little rusty.'

'Give it a go.'

He sighs, creases his forehead in concentration. 'I know a few words: blood, ritual, sacrifice . . . bastards.' He presses a finger to the page. 'Here's a mention of the Fallen and *Verdammt* . . . I think that means damned.'

'I guess Sophie was telling the truth about how long the family's known about the Rephaim.' I rub my eyelid. 'It looks as if the men of the family used to be in charge. I wonder what happened to change that?'

'Burning a body in a cornfield?' Rafa says, only half-joking. He hands me back the journal. 'Ez will be more useful at translating this – if we ever get out of this rat trap.'

'Do you think . . .?' The chill is all through my body now.

'What?'

'Do you seriously believe the family is tied up with demons? With Zarael?' I haven't seen the leader of the Gatekeepers. I never want to. Bel and Leon were bad enough.

Rafa opens his mouth to reply but sees something in my face that makes him pause. He rethinks what he was about to say. 'Look, I don't know what the fuck is going on here, but it's not likely the Gatekeepers are involved.'

'Why?'

'For a start, if they had a place that could trap us, they wouldn't be leaving it unguarded. And trust me, if Zarael or Bel had been here, Little Miss Let's-Do-a-Deal wouldn't be in one piece. Demons aren't renowned for self-control when it comes to humans and confined spaces.'

This place is getting claustrophobic. I'm drawn to the door. 'What do you think this is made of?' I run my palm over the rough surface. 'It doesn't feel like steel. Maybe it's the same thing Sophie's trinket-thingy is made from – something powerful enough to block a Rephaite from shifting.'

'Nothing can do that.'

I give him an even look. He begins to examine the photos again.

'What about iron?'

'No,' he says absently. 'I've shifted into planes and they're full of iron.'

'You shifted into a plane? While it was in the air?'

'Yeah.'

'Did I ever do stuff like that?'

'Frequently.'

I let my hand drop from the door. 'Jason wasn't lying about Sophie having a trinket that protects her. She grabbed something through her dress when you headed for this room.'

Rafa stares at the wall, not seeing and not listening.

Then he grabs a pencil and a scrap of paper.

'What are you doing?'

He peers at an image and writes something down. 'Listing everyone in these photos to see who's missing.'

'Why?'

He meets my eyes, taps the pencil against a photo, then trails it across several others.

'Because, Gaby, I'd like to *talk* to whoever is selling us out to these bitches.'

IRON WILL

'I'm thirsty.'

'Don't think about it.'

'How can I not think about it? I'm thirsty.'

Nearly thirty minutes have passed. It's getting colder, a bone cold that even Rafa is feeling. I can't stop thinking about what's going on outside this room. Where the hell is Jason? Why hasn't he got us out already? Did Sophie do something to him? Has he left us here?

I look through my photographs of Jude. Some I'd seen on Rafa's phone, but there are new ones. Of the two of us jogging side by side on a dirt road next to a field of wheat, of him saying something to a small group of Rephaim in a training room, all of them listening intently. Of him with people I don't recognise.

My throat feels cracked. I swallow.

He could be out there somewhere. And we're here. I see Rafa's eyes flicker to the photos of Jude and I wait for him to say it: that if we were looking for my brother like we were meant to be, we wouldn't be here. But he doesn't. And then I think about the place on Patmos in Greece, the island cottage where Rafa and Jude hung out. It was there Rafa pulled me to him when I was crying over another photo of Jude.

I nearly open my mouth. I nearly tell him what scares me the most, but I can't deal with those thoughts. Not in this tiny space. Not holding these photos from that other life. I put them aside.

'Did you tell Ez and Zak where we were going?' I ask.

'Only vaguely.'

'They'll keep an eye on Mags till we get back, right? They wouldn't leave her?'

'Not unless something came up.'

Not much of a reassurance. My body is shivering. God, I need to get moving. We really have to get out of here.

'You sure you didn't sense demons when we arrived?'

'I told you—'

'I know, I'm just asking.'

He turns away from the wall to face me. 'If they'd shifted here in the last few hours, I'd feel it. So would you.'

I think back to that moment up the mountain when we

rescued Maggie, when we crept through the forest and my stomach dropped so fast I thought I was falling. That's what it feels like when Rephaim shift.

'It's the same with demons?'

'About a thousand time worse.'

I nod. Wet my lips.

'Gaby.' He doesn't come closer, but the quietness in his voice settles my racing pulse. 'I don't like this any more than you do. I hate enclosed spaces. I always take the stairs over a lift.'

I scoff. 'You've never walked a flight of stairs in your life.'

A wry smile. He's trying to make me feel better. 'True. But I meant what I said: there are no pit scum here. Whatever *is* going on, we'll deal with it.'

I pull myself together. 'So, who's missing from the photos?'

'Nobody.'

'You sure?'

'I've counted twice. There are a hundred and eighty-two of us, all up. We're all here.' He tosses the pencil and paper back onto the desk. 'Actually there's a hundred and eighty-three if you count Goldilocks. He's not there.'

'They didn't need his photo. They know what he looks like – and he's never been part of the Sanctuary.'

'Goldilocks could have taken the surveillance shots, but

someone still had to tell him where to be and that person had to be at the Sanctuary.' Rafa picks up the stool by the desk and smashes it into the nearest wall.

'Hey!' My pulse begins to hammer. I thought he was okay. If he's not, how can I be? 'Calm down.'

He gives me a level look. 'I am calm. I thought we should take a closer look at these walls.'

'Oh.' The adrenaline subsides. 'Good idea.'

I stand back while he swings the stool again and then I pry back the busted plasterboard. There's a beaten metal wall underneath. I tap it with my knuckle. It's solid. Rafa throws the stool aside and we tear a bigger hole.

'That has to be iron,' he says. 'I don't get it.'

The surface is covered in intricate marks. Rafa drags the lamp over from the corner, rips off the shade and holds the bare bulb close to the exposed wall. The marks are actually symbols: a recurring icon that looks like a rudimentary set of wings.

'Have you seen anything like this before?'

Rafa traces the symbols with his fingertips. 'Never.' He runs a palm along his jaw. 'This room . . . it changes everything.'

'How could they know how to do this?'

He's still studying the etchings. 'Whoever gave them floor plans and photos could have found something in Nathaniel's library.'

'But that would mean Nathaniel knows it's possible to trap Rephaim.'

Rafa rips another piece of plasterboard from the wall. Photos come loose and flutter to the floor. 'It wouldn't be the first time he's kept something from us, would it?'

We keep pulling the wall apart until one whole side of the room is exposed. The air is thick with plaster dust. We stand back and wait for it to settle.

'Holy shit.'

Up close, the marks were haphazard and random, some deeper and darker than others. But now I see the darker etchings aren't random at all. They create another larger set of wings. Not rudimentary ones like the individual markings, but detailed feathered wings, outstretched so the tip of each extends to the corners of the wall.

I pull out my phone and photograph it. It takes two attempts; my hand isn't steady enough the first time.

There's a heavy thud on the door. We both turn around and take a step back. The impact comes again, shaking more plaster and dust loose.

Rafa nods at me, moves into a fighter's stance. I snatch up the journal and do the same, but it doesn't feel natural. I feel numb, outside myself, unfocused. We're unarmed. Alone. Rafa moves so he's slightly in front of me.

More thumps. Ten of them. Twenty. Then something gives inside the iron door. A few seconds later, it's forced back until there's a gap large enough for someone to fit through.

I feel my pulse in my fingertips, my throat.

And then my heart stutters.

FLY IN THE OINTMENT

'I should leave you in here to rot.'

Mya stands inside the room, katana in hand, pushing long blonde hair from her face. There's no mistaking her. In the photos I couldn't see the colour of her eyes, but it turns out they're blue, iridescent even, smeared with kohl.

'It's been a year, Rafa. And the first I hear from you is when you need help.'

'Nobody here asked for your help.' His voice is tight.

She looks me up and down. 'When were you going to tell me she was alive?'

'Are you here to help or interrogate?' Rafa eyes the opening behind her.

'Both. You pick the order.' And then to me, 'No smartarse comments, Gabe? No critique on our rescue methods?'

'You're wasting your breath. She doesn't know you.'

'So I've been told.' She raises her sculpted eyebrows at me. 'Is that right?'

'Yep,' I say. 'A fact that's making me happier by the second.'

Her eyes drop to the journal. 'What's that?'

'Something we can discuss outside.' Rafa takes my hand and leads me through the narrow opening. We could probably shift now, but I guess he doesn't want to risk hitting the wall. Just in case. He lets go of me as soon as we're clear.

Ez and Zak are waiting. Rafa's closest friends – aside from Jude. The photos in the room don't do either of them justice. Zak is so much bigger than he can ever look on camera and Ez . . . Ez is breathtaking, even with the deep scars down her face and neck. But if they're here, who's watching the cafe?

'Is Mags okay?' My breath is still short.

'She's fine,' Ez says. 'Are you?'

I nod. She and Zak are with an Outcast I haven't met. At their feet is a large, blunt metal pipe with handles.

'Only you could get in this much strife in a couple of hours,' Zak says to Rafa.

Flames still dance behind the grill of the pot-bellied stove. Wind buffets the house. There's no sign of Sophie. Or Jason.

'You used the ram.' Rafa is grinning – giving no hint he was hurling himself at a wall not half an hour ago.

'Yeah, so take it back.' Zak pushes thick black curls out of his eyes.

'I stand corrected: it's not a useless piece of crap. How did you know we were in a jam?'

'Jason found us at the cafe.'

Some of the tension leaves me. Jason's okay. He went for help. He didn't just leave us here.

'Where is he now?' I ask Ez.

'Back in Pan Beach.'

'What about Sophie, the girl who was here?'

'Gone by the time we arrived.'

Behind her, the other Outcast is staring at me as if there's nobody else in the room.

'That's Jones,' Ez says.

Jones nods at his name. His black hair frames a beautiful, angular face that is vaguely familiar from the photos in the room. He only cuts eye contact when Rafa steps into his line of sight. Jones breaks into a wide smile, his almond-shaped eyes crinkling. 'Dude, where have you been?' He pulls Rafa into a hug and slaps him between the shoulders.

I look back into the iron room. Mya has pulled a photo from the wall and is studying it. Her mouth is set in a thin line, her chest rising and falling rapidly. I can't tell if she's furious – or spooked. She sees me watching her, flings the picture aside and comes out.

'What happened last year? How are you alive?'

I glance at Rafa. If he wanted her to know Jude might be alive too, he would have told her already.

'I don't know.'

Her eyes are glittering, darker now. 'How can you just stand here like it's nothing? If Jude hadn't run off with you—'

'Mya.' Rafa's voice is sharp. 'Back off. She doesn't remember.'

'So she gets a free pass? After everything that's happened? What are you doing with her anyway?'

'What Jude would have wanted: keeping her alive.' Rafa's angry now. Really angry. 'Between the Sanctuary and the Gatekeepers—'

'You want me to feel sorry for her? Come on, Rafa. Remember what she's done to us. To you.'

The way she looks at him, it's as if the rest of us have vanished. Ez, Zak, Jones, me. Especially me. They watch each other. The air is charged with their history. I feel strangely exposed standing between them.

'After all,' Mya holds Rafa's eyes, doesn't look at me at all, 'Gabe is the reason Jude is dead.'

Ez stirs beside me. Zak is looking down, tapping his boot against the battering ram. I feel ill.

'Out of curiosity,' I say to Mya, 'did Jude tell you what he and I were going to do?' The words are cotton wool in my mouth but I get them out. Screw this stinging behind my ribs. Screw this guilt. Screw her sanctimonious bullshit. Screw her.

She doesn't answer. She's still looking at Rafa.

'No? Then you might want to shut your mouth.'

Rafa moves, shakes his head, and Mya turns to me.

'Are you threatening me, Gabe?'

'All right,' Ez says. 'Let's dial this back a notch.'

Mya glares at her. 'I can't believe *you* kept this from me. Gabe. Alive.'

'No,' Ez says. 'I can't imagine why I'd hold off giving you that piece of information. A more pressing issue is what we do about that.' She points to the iron room.

Mya looks past Ez. Then she disappears – literally – and reappears inside the room. Just as quickly, she's back with us. 'It's useless now the door's broken.'

'For now,' Rafa says.

'Should we try to break the walls somehow?' I ask, but really all I want is to leave. This place feels hollow, soulless, nothing more than a shell. And we're an easy target here behind the glass. It doesn't matter that Rafa and I aren't alone any more.

'It was hard enough getting through the door,' Zak says and shows me his hands, which look a little raw. 'We'll need something bigger.'

Mya checks me over again, a smile that's not a smile. 'As I said, it's useless now the door's broken.'

'Don't you want to know how they worked out how to do that?' Rafa asks her. 'Aren't you interested in who's feeding them floor plans and happy snaps?'

'And who are you going to ask? Nobody's coming back while we're here.' Mya rests her hands on slender hips. 'And tell me: who's this Jason and how come we've never heard of him? Care to explain, *Gabe*?'

Seriously.

I flex my fingers. 'Nobody knew he was Rephaite until a few days ago. Except the women who live here.'

Something dark passes over her face. 'How long has he known them?'

'A long time.'

'How long?'

'Seventy years.'

It takes her a moment to absorb that. 'I want to talk to him.'

'No,' Rafa says, his voice flat.

'Where is he?' Mya looks to Ez.

'Pandanus Beach.'

Rafa shakes his head. 'You're not coming with us.'

'It's not your call.'

'Stay out of it, Mya,' Rafa says.

Mya runs a tongue across her top lip. 'I can help.'

'Bullshit. You know Nathaniel sent Taya there.' He glances at Ez, who nods.

'So?' Mya says. 'It doesn't have to end in a fight.'

'Spare me. We know exactly how it will end.'

'Since when do you have a problem with that?'

'We don't need any more heat right now.'

'We?' She glances from Rafa to me, back to Rafa. Something flutters under my ribs.

Everyone else is very still, as if a sudden movement might drag them into the firing line. The wind gusts against the house; the fire cracks and pops.

'Haven't you got a job you need to get to? Bad things to kill?' Rafa asks her.

'We do, as a matter of fact. And now that you've resurfaced, I expect you'll be joining us.'

'How about we deal with one pile of shit at a time?'

Mya folds her arms, looks me over again. 'So why haven't you run back to Nathaniel?'

'Oh, I don't know,' I say. 'Maybe because until a few days ago, I didn't know who the hell Nathaniel was. Or maybe because he kidnapped my best friend. Or possibly because he had me thrown in a cage with a hellion and let it feed on me.'

She doesn't look at my neck but there's no way she's missed the bite there.

'And before you throw any more accusations around, I

don't know what Jude and I were doing a year ago and I don't know where the Fallen are. And I swear I am going to take someone's head if I have to explain that again.'

Jones lets out a low whistle. 'Aaaand she's back . . .'

I stare Mya down. She turns away, flicks her fingers at me as if she's shaking off water.

'Someone needs to check the rest of the house.' She strides back through the room and down the stairs, boots echoing on the timber. 'I'll give you all some quality time with Gabe.' She says my name like an insult.

Rafa is watching me now, a muscle twitching in his jaw. I can't meet his gaze. I'm not sure what I'll find there.

Ez sighs. 'Sorry. We called Jones for back-up and Mya was with him. I had to tell her about Gabe. I couldn't have kept it from her much longer anyway.' She points at the journal. 'Anything we should know about?'

'We found it in the room.' I hold it out and she takes it. 'It's in German. Rafa said you might be able to read it?'

'I can take a look.'

'Can we go now?' I ask Rafa. We look at each other properly for the first time since we left the iron room. I need him to remember I'm not the Gabe they all think I am. His eyes are clear, steady, green-flecked. Watching me. Seeing *me*. My shoulders lose some of their tightness.

'Yeah,' he says. 'Time to chat with Goldilocks. Again.'

'Okay.'

He pauses and then nods.

Ez helps Zak lift the battering ram, even though he could probably do it with one hand. 'You know Mya will follow you. She's not going to let up about questioning Jason over this place.'

Jones stands behind her, still studying me.

'Talk her out of it,' Rafa says.

Ez gives a humourless laugh. 'Sure. Right after I stop the tide.'

SAVE YOUR BREATH

We arrive in what passes as the living room of Rafa's shack in Pan Beach. Warmth envelops me. It makes sense we came here – the esplanade is only a street away – but it's a little awkward. The last time I was here Rafa was undressing me on his bed.

I shrug my jacket off and toss it on the lumpy sofa. Rafa unzips his hoodie and does the same. We stand there, watching each other. Sunlight filters through the filthy window. It's only early afternoon here. Rafa looks as though he wants to say something, but instead he shoves his hands in his pockets.

'So, Mya,' I say.

'What?' He doesn't avoid my eyes. His mood has lifted already, between Iowa and here, between the dark night and the bright Pan Beach day.

'You and Mya.' I'm not sure I want to know, but it's out there now.

He shrugs. 'She blamed me when Jude disappeared. Said I should have known there'd be trouble when the two of you started talking again. That I should have forced the issue and found out what was going on.'

'Why didn't you?' And why doesn't he answer the question I'm really asking?

'I did. That's when you broke my nose.'

Oh.

He goes to the fridge, looks inside. Closes it.

'She seemed pretty pissed off that you were with me.'

'You've given her a hard time over the years.'

I carefully word my next question. That look between them. The look she gave him . . . 'A year ago, were you two still . . . together?'

'Who?'

God, he's not making this easy.

'You and Mya.'

Silence.

'Didn't you leave the Sanctuary to be with her?'

He stares at me and then shakes his head slowly. 'More of Daniel's bullshit, I take it?'

I pick up my jacket, find a smattering of dust to brush off. 'He said you were in love with her.'

Another expression I don't understand flickers across his face. 'Yeah, because that's who I'd tell.'

'But—'

'It's ancient history.'

He's in the pantry now, his back to me again. So what is she to him now?

'Does Mya run the Outcasts?'

'Jude always called the shots. But she wishes she did. She co-ordinates our jobs and fires everyone up about our God-given right to slaughter demons.'

'Can she fight?'

'She can hold her own. More cunning than skill. You were never a fan.'

'But you guys all fought together as a team?'

Rafa turns, nudges the pantry door shut with his boot. 'Yeah. And we were good – really good. Then Jude disappeared and it all went to shit. Mya's never got over it.'

I toss my jacket onto the sofa. 'Should we mention the iron room to someone at the Sanctuary?'

His eyes are instantly dark. 'You want to call Daniel?'

'No, I thought maybe the others should know there's a room that can trap them.'

'And what do you think Nathaniel would do about it? He'd overrun the place in a heartbeat and then use it against us.'

'And the Outcasts won't do exactly the same thing?'

'Not if I've got any say in it. I'd like to see that place in ruins.' He goes to the back door and tests the bolt, even though I can see from here it's locked.

'You ready?' he asks.

I guess the discussion's over. 'Where are we going?'

'Green Bean.'

'You promise not to make a scene there?'

'No. It's up to Goldilocks how this goes down.'

I block his path to the front door. 'Don't make a scene. I mean it.'

'Then why are we even bothering?'

'We need to know if he got that trinket from Sophie.' I swallow, test the feel of the next words in my head before I say them. 'Because if he did and it works, we can go to Melbourne.'

His lips finally soften. 'About freaking time.'

On the beach, the breeze has strengthened. Beyond the break, the surf is rough now; even the hardcore board riders have packed up. White caps fleck the ocean.

It's lunchtime, so there are no spare tables at the cafe. We push our way inside to a wall of noise: conversations, a plate falling, the hissing of the espresso machine.

Jason is near the takeaway counter. His eyes flick from me to Rafa. Maggie is heading towards the kitchen with a tray stacked high. As soon as she sees us, she changes direction, dirty dishes and all.

'Are you all right?' she mouths at me.

I nod, hold out my arms to show I'm in one piece. She sees Rafa moving towards Jason and gets between tables to block him. 'He didn't know,' she says when we reach her. 'He told me he didn't know about the room and I believe him.' Nothing like a crisis to dissolve whatever tension was left between her and Jason. She looks from me to Rafa. 'He came straight here and told Zak—'

'Did he bring you anything?' I ask.

'A pendant. Not my style.'

'Show me.'

She checks the counter. 'I have to keep moving.'

'At least wear it,' I say. 'Just in case.'

Someone calls for Maggie from the kitchen. 'I have to go,' she says, and then leans in closer. 'Jason's waiting for you. And don't worry about me.' She turns away before I can ask what she means. A woman wearing leopard print pushes me into Rafa as she jostles her way to the counter. He steadies me without looking.

'Where'd the little fucker go?'

He'd better not mean Maggie.

I check the takeaway counter – Jason's gone – scan the room, find him near the front window.

'There.'

Jason watches us approach, waiting between two tables of noisy families.

'Outside,' Rafa says.

Jason ignores him. 'Are you staying in town a few more hours?' he asks me, and then steps sideways to let a man push his chair out further. 'There's something I need to do. Please, let me make up for what happened in Iowa.'

'Are you shitting me?' Rafa says, incredulous. He earns a filthy look from a mother spoon-feeding a baby next to us. 'I want answers, Goldilocks.'

'So do I,' Jason says.

Diners at both tables are looking at us now, annoyed.

'I'll meet you at the bungalow when Maggie's finished work. I only need a few hours.' His eyes plead with me. 'Do you still trust me?'

Do I? He's trusted me with so much. And he's never looked at me the way the rest of the Rephaim do. As if I'm the enemy.

'Not a chance,' Rafa says.

I hold Jason's gaze. 'Be quick.'

He gives me a grateful nod and ducks out from the tables and into the street. I stop Rafa from following.

'Let him go.'

'Melbourne, Gaby. Unbelievable. How much slack does this guy get?'

I take my time moving outside, feeling his impatience at every step.

'What now then?' he says. 'Are we going to sit here drinking coffee all day?'

Yeah, him, me and his short temper. I don't think so. I need to burn some energy.

'I'm going home and then I'm going for a run,' I say.

'How is that going to—'

'Do you want to come or not?'

He stops. 'You want me to run with you?' He asks me as if it's a trick question.

I shrug. 'It's up to you.'

His lips slowly curl into a smile. 'You're on.'

We jog down from the bungalow and follow the path into the park. A small boy and his mother are eating hot chips at one of the picnic tables. Seagulls dot the grass, waiting for scraps they can't digest. We pass the tree that Taya threw me into when we first met last weekend. It feels longer than six days ago; I wonder if it still has my blood on it.

We run to the esplanade without speaking. And then we're on the boardwalk, shoulder to shoulder, running parallel to the ocean.

'Forest or beach?' I ask.

'Beach.'

We reach the fork and veer right. At least this time I'm

running with Rafa, not from him. I'm ready to tackle the sand when he puts out his arm, forcing me to stop.

'You done already?' I lean over to rest my hands on my knees while I catch my breath. The air is cool, salty.

'In your dreams.' He's hardly broken a sweat. He kicks off his trainers and socks. I do the same.

'Race you to the headland,' he says.

It's about five hundred metres up the empty beach. 'Soft sand or hard?'

'Hard.' He looks amused. All traces of his annoyance in the cafe are gone.

'No shifting.'

He grins. 'I don't need to cheat. You're so out of shape, Maggie's mum could beat you.'

I shove his shoulder and jog down to the water line. A wave breaks violently in the shallows and the wash races up to us. It covers my feet, dragging away the sand beneath me as it recedes. I find firmer ground.

'Ready?' My pulse quickens.

We plant our feet, elbows touching and heads turned towards each other. I'm coiled, ready. A light breeze keeps my hair out of my eyes. I love this feeling.

Rafa grins. He takes off. 'Go,' he calls over his shoulder.

So much for not cheating.

I reach him in four strides, my toes digging into the hard-packed sand. My feet pound to the rhythm of my pulse. Everything jolts – my bad leg, sore ribs, bruised shoulder – but between the adrenaline driving my limbs and the wind cooling the sweat on my skin, I barely notice.

We're about three-quarters of the way to our arbitrary finish line when Rafa starts to pull away. I dig in harder and make up the distance. My chest is about to explode. Muscles are straining in Rafa's neck. He pulls away again and this time I can't catch him.

He reaches the headland about three steps ahead of me, then turns up the beach so he can collapse in softer sand. I follow and drop to my knees. He's on his back, breathing so hard he can't speak. Black spots slide across my vision. I lean forward and take my weight on my hands.

'Not bad.' He takes a big breath, then laughs. 'Not bad at all.'

It's a bit longer before I can speak.

'I didn't realise you were so competitive,' I finally manage, then sit back.

'You've never beaten me in a foot race. I wasn't about to let that change today.' He smiles. A warm, unguarded expression that till now I've only seen in photographs.

'What, never?'

He props himself on his elbows. 'Occasionally, you'd beat me in skills tests with the katana, but I've always been quicker. Always.'

'And humble.'

He lies back with his hands clasped behind his head and closes his eyes. The rise and fall of his rib cage slows to normal. He's ridiculously fit.

'What about Jude? What was he good at?'

'Everything,' Rafa says, without thinking. 'Particularly swords and knives. And he's the smartest guy I know, especially with languages.'

'Which languages?'

Rafa's eyes are still shut, so I poke his side with my bare foot to get him to answer. He grabs my foot without looking.

'All of them.' He massages my instep with his thumb, almost absently. 'We can understand every human language ever spoken – another gift from our fathers. But we're not all great at reading or speaking them or getting the accents right. Jude was a freak. It used to annoy the crap out of Daniel that he was such a natural.'

I'm trying to concentrate on what he's saying, but his fingers are very distracting. I close my eyes and listen to his voice. I still can't place his accent. I'm starting to think the Rephaim have one all of their own.

'Goldilocks has a bit of a talent for it himself, given that New York accent he pulled out of his arse in Iowa,' he says.

'Do I have one?'

Rafa's fingers slide up to my ankle. He's using two hands now. 'You sound vaguely Australian these days. You must have instinctively adapted when you woke up in the hospital.'

I open my eyes. He's sitting up, cradling my foot in his lap, watching me. My pulse forgets itself. How can someone so quick to anger be capable of such tenderness?

'Do you want me to stop?' His hair is damp on his forehead.

'No.'

He leans forward until his face is only centimetres from mine. I don't move away. The last few days recede. That other history between us, the one he won't tell me about, melts away under the warm sun. And then Rafa kisses me, not with the urgency of our last encounter, but softly, thoughtfully. He tastes like oranges. His hands stay on my ankle, restrained. The kiss deepens. I slide my palm up his thigh. He stops me and pulls back. 'You're killing me, you know that?'

'Do you want me to stop?' I mean to sound playful but it comes out breathless.

'No.'

His mouth is on mine again, hands on my hips, drawing me across his lap. I wind my legs and arms around him, pull him to me until there's no space left between us. One of his hands slips under my shirt, climbs my back, the other slides around my waist. My legs tighten around his hips. His breath catches; his fingertips press into my skin. His kisses are still controlled, measured – until I move against him, slowly. The small sound that escapes him sends a thrill of pleasure through me. I need to touch more of him. His t-shirt is coated with sand; I pull at it, hitch it up so I can run my palm over his warm skin. Rafa's touch is stronger. His tongue, his lips, his hands . . . exploring with more purpose. I know there's a reason I'm not supposed to be giving in to this, but I can't remember what it is—

'Yoo hoo!'

It's Mrs Williamson. Her voice whips away in the breeze. She's not normally on the beach this time of the day.

Our kiss slows, our grip on each other eases. I linger for a second, kissing his lower lip while my heart rate steadies.

Mrs Williamson is making her way down the headland track with her husband. She gives a quick wave with an arthritic hand and then goes back to concentrating on where she's putting her feet. Mr Williamson keeps her upright, clutching the handrail as they descend from the dunes.

The last time they saw me here I was running for my life. I'm not sure this is any better. They head straight for us.

'Friends of yours?' Rafa asks, still slightly breathless. His chest rises and falls against mine.

'Yes, so be polite.'

His teeth graze my earlobe, teasing. 'I'm always polite.'

He kisses me again. 'You really need to move or I'm not going to be in any state to stand up.'

By the time he helps me to my feet, the Williamsons have almost reached us. Mrs Williamson is smiling, Mr Williamson, not so much. I once heard he was a career army man. I can see that in him now.

I introduce them and Mr Williamson pumps Rafa's hand like he's trying to get water out of him.

'Walk us back to town, lad,' he says, gruff.

Rafa glances at me. 'Sure.'

We start back up the beach, the men leading the way. Mrs Williamson gestures to Rafa behind his back and pretends to fan herself.

'In my day we didn't kiss respectable girls like that in public,' Mr Williamson says. His shoulders are stooped, but he must have been nearly as tall as Rafa in his prime. We're walking into the wind so his voice carries clearly.

'You think Gaby's respectable?' Rafa grins at me over his shoulder.

'Don't be a smart alec, lad. And yes, I do. It's not like her to take up with your type.'

'Define my "type"?'

'No-hopers who blow in and out of town as though they own the place, bringing nothing but trouble.' Mr Williamson peers at Rafa from under his cap. 'Are you staying long?'

'That's up to Gaby.'

'She's a good girl, a hard worker. Don't go playing games with her. Don't you hurt her.'

I don't catch Rafa's response.

When we reach the boardwalk, the Williamsons continue on to the esplanade and Rafa and I go back to our shoes. I'm strangely touched by Mr Williamson's protectiveness.

'I don't think he likes you,' I say to Rafa.

'If he'd been five minutes later, he would have liked me a lot less.'

With the Williamsons gone I'm thinking that he'll kiss me again. I see him thinking it too. But he doesn't.

I sit down to put on my shoes, hoping the breeze cools the heat in my neck. As usual, I can't really tell what's going on with him. Like when he kissed me the night we met. I thought he wanted me. He thought I was pretending not to know him and was trying to get a reaction.

Or in his bedroom, when he knew I wanted him. He backed off because I'm a virgin – or because I *think* I am – and he doesn't want the fall-out if I ever get my other life back.

'You know that first night at the bar,' I say, knocking sand out of a runner. 'What did you mean about not realising I was that good?'

Rafa gives me a sidelong glance as he joins me on

the ground. 'You thought I was complimenting your technique?' He finishes tying a double-knot and realises I'm waiting for an answer. 'I thought you were faking being into me and I was impressed at your commitment to your cover. That kiss was pretty convincing.'

He can talk.

'What about a year ago – why did I break your nose?'

Rafa gets up and goes to the boardwalk, stretches his calves. 'I found you and Jude on Patmos. I was pissed off he'd taken you there – you hadn't been there before. I questioned your motives in talking to him again. There may have been some mention of "Daniel" and "puppet". And of course we got into it. This . . . volatility between us – it's not new.' He sets off along the boardwalk.

I jam my feet into my runners and jog to catch him.

'That's why you think I'll be pissed off at you if I remember my old life? Because the last time we saw each other we had a fight?'

His eyes are ahead of us, either scanning for threats or avoiding me. Or both. 'It's not so simple but, yeah, something like that.'

DID THE EARTH MOVE FOR YOU?

It's after six when we hear the front door. Maggie and Jason are walking close, hands not quite touching. Maggie is still in her work clothes: a black skirt and white t-shirt, a silver chain tucked beneath.

Rafa is pacing the kitchen. He stops when they come in. It's taking all of his self-control not to pin Jason to the wall.

'Hey you,' I say to Maggie as she leans in for a quick hug, keeping the bench between us.

'How are you, Rafael?' she asks, all politeness.

'I'm very well, Margaret,' he says. 'I'll be better when I hear your boy explain what the hell happened today.'

Jason holds up a hand. 'I swear I had no idea that room

existed or that it was possible to trap Rephaim. All the times I've been there, I—'

'Yeah, yeah. All I care about is what happened today.'

'Sophie worked out you were Rephaim – I don't know how, although all those questions didn't help. Anyway,' he continues before Rafa can jump in again, 'when you went in that room she was straight over to a keypad and the cavity door closed.'

'And then what?'

He takes a breath. 'She accused me of bringing "one of the damned" to the farm. I told her I didn't know who you were. She didn't believe me. She gave me the necklace, but she was so scared.' He drops his gaze, studies the floor.

'Shit, Goldilocks,' Rafa says. 'You didn't hurt a girl, did you?'

'Of course I didn't.' He nods to Maggie. 'Show them.'

She draws the chain out, revealing a flat, round pendant the size of a twenty-cent piece, then takes it off and hands it to me. Both sides are etched with the wing design of the iron room. Rafa leans in so close our heads touch. He smells like he always does after a shower: fresh, earthy.

'Fuck,' he mutters, fixated on the pendant.

Jason frowns. 'I wish I knew how Sophie figured out you were Rephaite.'

'They have photos of all of us.' Rafa lifts his head. 'Except you.'

I show Jason the images on my phone of the photos plastering the room and the iron wall with the giant wings.

He studies them and then leans back against the sink, stares past me. 'I don't understand . . .'

'You still want to cling to the delusion they're not getting information from someone?' Rafa asks.

'They always said—'

'You say "revelation of God" again and I will headbutt you.'

Jason sighs.

'Have you heard from any of them?' I ask.

'I tried to call Sophie, but she wouldn't answer. But I do have something.' He grabs a folded piece of paper from his pocket. 'I researched the family this afternoon. Made an after-hours visit to the Des Moines Public Library and trawled through the local history collection.'

Rafa raises his eyebrows, mocking. 'Seventy years after you met them, and now you go to the library?'

'I know you don't get it, Rafa. You've always been surrounded by Rephaim. I haven't. I've known these women half my life. Other than my mother's family, they've been the only constant. So I respected their wishes—'

'Their threats, you mean.'

Jason sighs. 'It doesn't matter any more. Everything's changed with that room.'

Maggie puts a hand on his arm. 'Tell them what you found.'

Jason flattens the page on the bench. It's covered in neat handwritten notes.

'The library records of the property date back to 1866. It was settled by a German family around 1870. The father was a Lutheran minister and he built a church there along with the original house. But the church was only sanctified for a few years.' Jason turns the page over. 'I found a reference to it in official records in 1876, by which time the church and the family had been cut off from the Iowa Lutheran Synod due to "unorthodox practices and heresy".'

I think about the photo of a human-sized bundle in flames and tell him and Maggie about the journal I gave to Ez: the burial, and the photo of the gutted church.

Jason runs a finger over his notes. 'The church burned down in 1939. A newspaper report called it arson, most likely related to the fact the family was German and the war had started in Europe.'

'Or not,' Rafa says. 'Something's missing here. They start out as Lutheran immigrants and then run off the rails not long after the Fallen do the rounds. They perform weird rituals out in the cornfield and spook someone enough that their church is burned down. And then what? The men just disappear? These iron bitches work out how to protect themselves from being forced to shift? They get floor plans of the Sanctuary, have someone take photos of all of us and suddenly know how to build a room to trap us?' He pushes Jason's notes away. 'There's a leak at the Sanctuary.'

I wait for Jason to argue but he looks thoughtful. 'That would make sense. How else would they know I'd never been there?'

'But can't Nathaniel see into people's thoughts?' I ask. 'Wouldn't he know if someone was betraying him? Wouldn't he know about the women?'

Rafa shrugs. 'Maybe someone found a way to hide it from him.'

I remember waking on the cold bed in the Sanctuary infirmary. Nathaniel's voice: soothing, promising answers. The memory he found of Jude, so beautiful it hurt. And then the angel's unmistakable confusion.

We sit in silence for a moment.

Finally, Rafa points to Maggie's pendant. 'Did you try it out?' He looks at Jason and then answers his own question: 'Of course not. Wouldn't want to frighten any more pretty blondes today, would we? Well, someone has to. No point going through all this crap if it doesn't work.'

'Do we have to?' Maggie asks. 'I'd rather not throw up today.'

'The plan is for you *not* to shift,' I say.

Rafa moves around the bench. 'Come on. I promise I'll

be gentle.' Maggie manages a lopsided smile. 'Don't look so worried, Goldilocks.'

I know Rafa doesn't have to hold Maggie close to shift with her, but for a second I think he will, to annoy Jason. Instead, he stands in front of her and holds out his palms.

She takes a deep breath, puts her hands in his and closes her eyes. Her skirt flutters as if there's a breeze.

Rafa disappears.

Maggie shudders but stays.

She opens one eye. 'Was that it? I could feel the pulling but then . . . It worked!' She claps her hands and turns to Jason. He looks as though he wants to hug her. He doesn't. I guess there's still some hesitancy between them.

Rafa materialises next to me. 'It's nowhere near as effective as the room,' he says, 'but it's strong enough that I couldn't take her with me.'

'So Jason was telling the truth?' I give him a pointed look.

'Jury's still out. But the urge to punch him has eased a little. A drink would help.'

'That's fine,' Jason says. 'Talk about me as though I'm not here.'

Maggie half-skips over to the fridge. There's a lonely beer on the top shelf. 'Maybe it'll have to be Rick's.' She pauses then turns to Jason. 'Do you want to come?'

He smiles at her.

'Sounds like a plan,' I say. 'Just let me get changed.'

'I thought we already had plans,' Rafa says to me, and I can see Maggie watching his reaction. Jason studies me with kind eyes. I look away. I don't want his pity.

'We do,' I say to Rafa and head down the corridor to get changed. 'Melbourne will still be there in an hour. A quick drink isn't going to hurt.'

I close my bedroom door before I hear his response.

WHERE EVERYBODY KNOWS
YOUR NAME

Maggie and I share the mirror in the bathroom. I've changed into a silk t-shirt – a Christmas gift from her – and skinny jeans. She's wearing a little black dress and wedges, her hair straightened and falling softly past her shoulders.

I give up trying to get my hair to sit properly, and tie it back, then try to reposition my top so it covers more of the hellion scar. Maggie is biting her tongue. I know what she wants to say and I know she'll say it, eventually.

She takes over doing my hair, pulls it out of the ponytail and ties another one at the curve of my neck so my hair falls over the scar.

'So are you and Rafa fighting or flirting at the moment?'

'A little bit of both.' I turn away from the mirror so I can't see my skin flush. I keep getting flashbacks to the beach earlier.

'You could go south tonight if you wanted,' she says. 'You don't have to come out if it's going to cause more drama between you.'

'It's fine,' I say, avoiding the real question. 'We need to put in an appearance for Taya anyway.'

Maggie tucks her pendant inside her dress. 'But I'm okay now.'

'Taya can still hurt you, Mags – and she will if she finds out we're gone. Especially if she realises she can't shift with you.'

'But Jason will be with me around the clock—'

'Is he moving into your room?' I tease.

She dips her chin. 'Not . . . no . . . Gaby?'

'What?'

'Why are you putting off looking for Jude?'

My smile fades. 'I'm not.'

She touches my arm, lightly, as if she expects me to pull away. 'Are you worried you won't find him?'

She waits. I run the tap, wash away loose powder clinging to the sides of the mottled basin. I really can't look at my reflection now.

'Oh, babe. I can't imagine what this is like for you.'

Living this past year thinking Jude was dead has

been unbearable. The thought he might be alive and I might never find him . . . I can't even give that feeling a name.

'The nurse is the only lead we've got,' I say quietly. 'What if we can't find her, or she doesn't remember anything?' I focus on a crack in the powder-blue wall.

'But what if she does remember?' Maggie says gently. 'What if she can help?'

My throat constricts. The other fear, the one I can't hide from in the dark, leaches in. What if we find Jude and he hasn't lost his memory? What if he doesn't want to be found? I grit my teeth. I had no idea hope could be this suffocating. 'I didn't think it would feel like this.'

'This isn't exactly a normal situation, Gaby. Maybe you should go a little easier on yourself. I mean it. Don't let Rafa rush you. If Jude's alive – and, God, I hope he is – then taking one more day to feel grounded isn't a bad thing.'

Grounded. When have I ever felt grounded? I use the hand towel to wipe out the basin and then hang it over the edge of the bath to dry.

'Seriously, it won't kill Rafa to show some patience.'

'Yeah, because patience is Rafa's strong suit.' I give her a tight smile. 'He's right to want to get moving: we may not be the only ones looking for him.'

Maggie puts her arms around me, enveloping me in cherry blossom and Chanel No. 5.

'I worry about you.' She squeezes me and then steps back, hands me a tissue.

'We'll go tomorrow,' I say. 'I just need . . . I don't know what I need.'

'Have you told Rafa how you feel? Okay, stupid question.' She pauses, then smiles. 'Here's another one: does he always smell that good?'

I manage to laugh and immediately I can breathe again. I smile at Maggie, push the dark away.

'Yeah,' I say. 'He really does.'

Rafa and Jason are ignoring each other when we come out of the bathroom. I grab my keys and go out of the front door without speaking to either of them.

Rafa's annoyance is palpable as we walk down the hill to the esplanade. Maggie positions herself between him and me and chats with him all the way to the pub. It's a temporary reprieve, but I'm grateful for it.

Rick's is humming when we get there. Surfers, backpackers and locals sit around the wine barrels on the veranda. The air is heady with beer and chargrilled lamb.

Taya is behind the bar. She's wearing a black t-shirt with 'Rick's' stretched across her chest. Her hair isn't tied back as tightly as usual. Make-up softens the sharp lines of her face. Or maybe she looks softer because she's smiling.

'Is she, like, happy?' I say to nobody in particular.

Rafa makes a noise in the back of his throat. 'She's never been happy in her life.'

Taya moves back and forth, pouring beers, uncorking imported wines and mixing cocktails. She wipes the bar down after Rick and he nods his appreciation. Like Simon, Rick's all gym-toned muscle and Japanese tatts, though he's a few years older.

Simon is working alongside them, trying hard to ignore Taya. His cropped tawny hair stands up at odd angles as though he's been repeatedly dragging his fingers through it. He's a good guy. A *nice* guy. He doesn't deserve to have Taya – or any other Rephaite – complicating his life.

'I've seen enough,' Rafa says. 'If we really have to be here, let's drink.' He moves towards the bar.

Simon spots Rafa first and he heads to the other end of the bar. Taya is putting money in the till, her back to us. She turns around and breaks into a wide smile. I guess this is what Rafa means by commitment to cover.

'See, Simon, I told you Gabe cared.'

Simon snaps off the beer tap with force.

Rafa leans on the bar. 'Taya, I've seen Tibetan monks pull beer better than you. See if you can manage four.'

Taya measures him for a moment. 'Coming right up.'

Her first pour is not bad and her second near perfect. She gives Rafa the better of the two. Never let it be said she doesn't rise to a challenge.

'Not too shabby,' I say. 'Maybe it's time you retired those fists and opened up your own place in some seedy corner of the world.'

Taya brushes off the compliment and pours the other two. 'Bigger fish to fry, Gabe.'

Despite the crowd, we manage to get a seat at the window overlooking the street. I position myself so I can keep an eye on the room. Rafa sits close, not touching me, but near enough to make me think about that kiss again.

Simon is mixing an elaborate cocktail, complete with shaker tossing. He empties the flask into a wide glass and pushes it towards a brunette in a low-cut dress. Taya saunters past and ruffles his hair, making him flinch. 'Nice work.' On the way back, she smacks his backside. 'And nice arse.'

The brunette and her friends giggle. Simon smiles, embarrassed.

Rafa knocks his knee against mine. 'Jealous?'

'Disturbed is more like it. I can't believe how well she's pulling this off.'

'She's had a few decades of practice.'

I take a sip of beer and stare out at the streaky purple sky beyond the Poinciana trees. Heavy clouds drift out towards the darkening horizon. I could almost pretend this is a normal Friday afternoon.

Rafa is still a little prickly towards Jason, so when

Maggie offers to shout the next round I get up with her.

'How about you two kiss and make up while we're gone,' I say to Rafa and Jason. Neither finds me funny.

We squeeze into a gap at the bar and wait to be served. Please let Simon reach us before Taya. If he can stand to be around Taya, surely he can serve me a drink? I make a crescent moon in the dregs on the bar, remember the feel of that shape on the nape of Rafa's neck. The mark of the Rephaim. Maybe if I still had mine, I'd feel more of a connection to the Rephaim. All that's on my neck now is a thick scar – made by a demon blade, according to Bel.

'Another round, ladies?' Taya places four bottles of beer in front of us. 'Try these. Italian. Brewed not far from a certain monastery.' She eyes me for a moment and then tips her head to where Simon is pouring a bright blue drink into a row of glasses. 'Your boy's good, Gabe.' She winks at me. *Winks.* 'I understand why you couldn't keep your hands off him.' She takes the money from Maggie without looking at her. 'He seems to have gone off you a bit, though. Must like his women a little more faithful.'

I smile at her, ignoring the crush of drinkers waiting to be served. 'I'm not sure exactly how he likes his women. But if you keep your mouth shut and your fists to yourself, he might overlook the fact that you're a cold hard bitch.' I snatch up the beers and turn away.

I'm walking back to the window, smug, when my

stomach drops. I recognise that feeling. Rephaim have arrived close by. Rafa twists on his stool to look out of the window. By the time I reach him and Jason, the drinkers under the veranda are making low sounds of appreciation.

'Here we go,' Rafa says.

I don't have to look outside to know who's arrived.

LADIES' NIGHT

'What?' Maggie glances around.

'Mya's here.' I set down the drinks.

She stares at me. 'The Outcast you told me about? Do you know her?'

'She was with Ez and Zak when they came to Iowa.'

'And you're only telling me this now?' Maggie strains to see through the crowd. 'Why is she here?'

'To cause a shit-storm,' Rafa says.

Mya walks in, wearing skin-tight jeans and a red silk halter top.

'I hate her,' Maggie says. It comes off like a compliment.

Mya heads straight for us. Jones is with her. The entire bar watches them.

'Good thing we're still in town,' I say to Rafa.

He ignores the comment.

'How did she find us?' I ask.

Rafa watches Mya, his expression unreadable. 'I told Ez and Zak about the bar.'

'Why aren't they with her?'

'Don't you think there's enough of a spectacle in here?'

Taya has seen Mya and Jones. She finds me in the crowd, measures me – she thinks this is my doing. I shake my head. I don't care whether she reads it as 'I'm not involved' or 'Don't even think about starting a fight', as long as she stays on her side of the bar.

Jason steps in front of Maggie protectively. I'm next to him but Mya's not interested in me. I wait for her to fire questions at him. Instead she gives him a slow, sultry smile.

'Jason, I presume?'

'And you are?'

'Mya. This is Jones.'

Jones nods at Jason, checks out Maggie. Glances at me once, twice, as if he's not sure what I'm going to do. Jason doesn't offer his hand or introduce Maggie.

Mya's smile doesn't quite reach her eyes now.

'How often have you been to that farm?' she asks Jason.

'I haven't kept count.'

'How about a guess?'

'A dozen times, maybe.'

Rafa swirls his beer. 'Tell her the story, Goldilocks.

Nobody's getting any peace until she hears it.'

Mya pulls up a stool. She still hasn't looked at me.

Jason puts down his glass, keeps Maggie behind him. When he's ready, he gives Mya an even shorter version of the story he told Rafa and me – minus references to his own family history and my connection to it. And, not surprisingly, he makes no mention of Dani and her visions.

'Did they tell you why they built that room?'

'I didn't know it existed. I would never have set foot there if I had.'

'How many of these women have you met?'

'Over the years? Fourteen.'

Mya taps her finger against her bottom lip. 'How did they know about you? How did they track you down?'

He goes to answer, but suddenly pauses. 'Did they find you too?'

Something passes over her face, something dark and bitter. 'Nobody found me.'

'Nathaniel did. Eventually.'

'What do you know about the Sanctuary?' Mya asks.

'Not as much as you. I managed to stay away.'

I glance at Jason. Is he intentionally baiting her? It shouldn't be a surprise given how strongly he feels about other Rephaim, but it still throws me a little.

'I thought Nathaniel had answers,' Mya says. 'I was wrong.'

They watch each other for a moment. I know nothing about how Mya survived all those decades before Nathaniel found her. How she learned what she was, what she was capable of.

'And all this was about getting some amulet' – she finally looks past Jason to Maggie – 'for her?'

I bristle. Jason steps closer to Mya, blocking her from Maggie. 'Yes.'

'Show me.'

Jason hesitates but steps aside and nods to Maggie. She takes out the pendant and holds it up for Mya to see, but when Mya reaches for it, she quickly tucks it away.

'Does it work?'

'Yes.'

Mya gives Jason a slow once-over. 'Rephaim don't usually care this much about humans.'

'I'm sure you've had your share over the years,' he says.

'I didn't fall in love with any of them.'

Rafa lets out a short laugh. 'Not much of a measuring stick.'

'You can talk.' Mya turns back to Jason. 'I'm guessing you've never experienced your own kind?' This time when her eyes roam over him, they linger in places that make *me* blush, and I'm not his girlfriend. I can only imagine how Maggie's feeling. 'Oh, Jason,' Mya says, 'you have no idea what you're missing.'

Jason couldn't look less interested.

'It's your loss.' Mya nods in Maggie's direction. 'But if you want your girl here to stay safe, Rafa will be coming back to my crew.'

'It's not your crew,' Rafa says. 'And don't threaten Maggie.'

I nearly kiss him right then and there.

'Start back with one job,' Mya says. 'With Gabe.'

My stomach clenches.

Rafa doesn't flinch. 'No.'

'Why not?'

'Because this isn't a game. And that's not Gabe.'

'That's why it's too good an opportunity to pass up. Can you imagine what those self-righteous bastards will think when they hear Gabe has done a job with us? How Daniel will react?'

Something passes between them, some joint history. Different to Iowa, but still something. It reconnects them again for a second. The idea must hold some appeal for Rafa. I preferred it when they were sniping at each other.

'Being blackmailed isn't the same as choosing,' I say.

'Then don't make me blackmail you.'

Rafa sees my face. 'Don't look at me like that. We're not going anywhere with her.'

'It was good enough for Jude,' Mya says to me. 'You still think you're better than him, don't you?'

Before I know it, my hand is around her throat. I shove her to the window, press her face to the sill. 'Don't talk about my brother.' I've got her awkwardly pinned so she can't lash out.

'I see you remember you don't like me,' she says out the side of her mouth.

I put my face close to hers. 'No, this is my opinion based on our time together today.' Her submission is strangely gratifying. 'Don't threaten me or my friends. Ever.' I let go.

She stands up and wipes beer from her face. There's a lull in the bar: drinkers inside and out watch us. Mya gives Jones a black look. 'Thanks for the back-up.'

'You want to take on Gabe, go right ahead,' he says.

Mya straightens her top. 'I see you remember a few moves.'

I stand my ground. 'When pushed.'

'Then let's see what else you've got.' She brushes past me and heads for the bar.

'Ah, crap.' Rafa and Jones exchange a quick look and follow her. I hesitate and then cross the room behind them.

Two guys I recognise from the party where Maggie was snatched are propped against the bar, chatting with Simon. Sun-bleached hair, boardies low on narrow hips. From memory, one is Dane; the other is Tyler. They're both bare-chested, making the most of happy hour before Rick tells them to cover up.

Simon notices Mya and gives her an appreciative once-over. Then he spots Rafa. His eyes flick from Mya to Rafa to me. His mouth forms a hard line and he moves away again.

Dane and Tyler take one look at Mya and make room for her.

'Good evening, boys,' she says. 'What do you recommend?'

'Me,' Dane says.

Tyler laughs. 'Dude, get your hand off it.'

'How about you buy me a drink and I'll decide which of you can take me home.'

Jones has elbowed his way near Tyler; Rafa and I are next to Dane.

'What's she doing?' I ask.

'Starting a fight.' Rafa watches Mya in the mirror behind the bar. 'She'll tease them for a while, draw in a few more suckers and then turn them all on each other.'

'Come on, they might not be brain surgeons but they're not that stupid.'

He glances at me and then checks the mirror again. 'They're human. Of course they're that stupid.'

I catch a whiff of chargrilled lamb from the kitchen. I'd really rather a kebab than a second pub fight today. The floor is cleaner here than at the Imperial, but still.

'Maybe I can stop this before it gets out of hand,' I say.

Rafa raises his eyebrows. 'What are you going to do?

'Run interference.'

'You're going to flirt with those two?'

I give a self-conscious shrug. 'It's not my strongest skill, but it's better than a punch-up.'

Rafa's mouth curves into a slow smile. 'Now this I want to see.'

TONIGHT'S SPECIAL: MOLOTOV COCKTAIL

Mya is laughing at something Tyler said, a hand on his chest.

'Hey guys,' I say. 'Mind if I join you?'

Dane checks me out. 'Sure.' He and Taylor grin at each other. 'Especially if you two are planning on some girl-on-girl action.'

Mya runs a fingernail down his stomach to the top of his boardies. 'Would you like that?'

'I'd like it a *lot*,' Tyler says, and hooks an arm around her.

'I don't think you'd find it sexy if I split her nose all over her face,' I say.

I catch a glimpse of Rafa in the mirror. He's smirking. Oh yeah, I'm a natural.

'Dude, that would be extreme,' Tyler says. 'I was thinking more jelly wrestling.'

'*Dude*,' I say, keeping my tone light, 'think again.'

Dane leans close, breathes beer on me. 'When are you going to start talking to our boy again?' He tips his glass at Simon.

'As soon as he starts talking to me.'

'Man, what you did at the party . . . that was cold.'

Great. He thinks I ditched Simon for Rafa the night Maggie was taken. Well, actually, I did. But not in the way he thinks.

Taya is trying to reach us, but she can't ignore the growing press of drinkers shouting orders at her. She shoves a pink drink with an umbrella in front of Jones by way of insult and then gets sidetracked by a cocktail order.

'Recognise her?' I flick my thumb in Taya's direction.

Dane eyes her up and down. 'Nope. Undoubtedly bangable, though.'

'She was at the party at the falls – made a cameo right before Maggie left. Remember?'

He frowns. 'That's not her. Seriously?'

Tyler looks around for Maggie and finds her at the window with Jason. They're deep in conversation. He checks out Taya again. 'That's Jason's ex?'

Mya turns to me, eyes like granite. 'Jason used to date

Taya? That Jason, over there, who claims he's never been near the Sanctuary?'

'What sanctuary?' Dane asks.

Oh shit. I'm trapped between lies. And here comes Taya, who still doesn't know Jason is Rephaite.

'I hear you've been busy since you hit town,' Mya says to her. She's acting tough but I notice she takes a step back.

Taya looks at me for an explanation.

'She means you breaking up with Jason and taking Maggie away from the party for a chat the other night – in front of these guys.' I gesture to the two surfers.

Taya narrows her eyes. I can almost hear the gears grinding in her head. I don't know what would be worse: if she denies it, raising questions about what really happened at the party, or if she plays along and Mya thinks Jason is connected to Nathaniel.

'You and Jason?' Mya asks.

'Yeah,' Taya says, seeing how much the idea grates on Mya. 'What's it to you?'

Mya tilts her head a fraction. 'It's nothing to me. How did Malachi take it?'

'It's got nothing to do with Malachi.'

Wait. Taya and Malachi had a thing? Seriously? I try to picture Taya flirting with him – or anyone. I can't. Her idea of foreplay probably involves some sort of blood sport.

Around us people are still shouting for their drinks. She quickly pulls two beers.

Mya waits until she's close again and then says to the surfers: 'So Taya wanted Malachi, but then I came along and showed him what a real woman can do between the sheets . . . and against a wall . . . and on top of a car.'

Tyler swallows.

'And still you can't keep a man,' Mya continues, nodding in Jason and Maggie's direction.

Taya slams a glass down on the counter. She's not playing happy bartender any more.

'Let it go,' I say, trying to drag her attention from Mya. 'None of us needs this right now. Think about where you are.'

Her eyes lock on me. 'Did you bring her here?'

'You're joking, right?'

'Oi!' A guy yells for Taya further down the bar. 'Where's my bloody drink?'

Taya ignores him, gets her temper under control.

'Get your bony arse down here and pour me a beer.'

I take a quick look. The guy – who looks as though he'd be more at home at the Imperial – is hoisting his gut on to the bar, trying to reach the row of taps to help himself.

Simon hurries over and tries to push him back. It's as if he's trying to roll a whale into the sea. The guy grabs an empty glass. Taya begins moving but not before he smashes it into the side of Simon's head. Simon staggers back. His hand comes up and finds streaming blood – and then his knees give out.

Taya flies down the bar, lands a brutal kick to the guy's jaw. She drags him over to her side and lets him get to his feet. He snarls and swings at her and she king-hits him back to the sticky bar mat.

Everyone is watching Taya. I use the distraction to push Mya away from the surfers and Rafa grabs her arm. 'Enough of this shit,' he says.

Mya jerks away from him. 'Don't touch me.' She says it loudly enough to distract the surfers from the one-sided fight behind the bar.

'You,' Dane says to Rafa. 'Piss off.'

Rafa gives him a pitying smile. 'Let it go, boys. This is what she does for fun.'

'Don't—' I say, as Dane throws a sloppy punch at Rafa. Rafa catches him by the wrist, wrenches Dane's arm behind him and shoves him at Tyler. They stumble into a pack of drinkers in polo shirts – who shove back, hard.

'Watch it, mate,' someone says.

There's more pushing and sledging. A shirt rips, a glass breaks, another punch is thrown. It's on.

It's not even dark outside.

Behind the bar, Taya is still hammering the guy who hurt Simon.

'Taya,' I call out, 'bigger fish to fry!'

She looks up, blows a stray hair out of her eyes, and registers what else is going on in the room. A second later, she's over the bar, hauling people towards the door.

The brawl spreads out. I lose Rafa as people scurry out of the way, clutching their drinks. A girl with a see-through blouse launches herself onto the back of one of the polo shirts, her skirt hitched up to her hips. She's trying to get him to release Tyler, who's now trapped in a headlock.

It's a shit-storm all right.

I dodge an airborne stool and jump on the bar to get out of the way. More than a dozen guys are now wrestling or punching each other. Everyone else is streaming out onto the street. Not running away, but getting a good spot where they can watch and cheer from a safe distance. Jason has his arm protectively over Maggie's head, guiding her through the mayhem.

Where's Mya?

I scan the room. She's sitting on the cigarette machine, sipping a neon cocktail, watching.

Rafa and Jones are in the middle of the fracas. They're not breaking up fights, just holding their ground like outcrops in a river, letting the chaos flow around them, deflecting bodies and punches.

Simon is back on his feet, a tea towel to his head. I drop down to his side of the bar and check his wound.

'What just happened?' he says.

'Hurricane Mya,' I say, echoing Daisy's description when I first asked about her at the Sanctuary. 'Where's Rick?'

I scan the room, spot him helping Taya thin the crowd.

'He's fine.' I press the tea towel back on his scalp. 'You'll probably need a stitch or two.' A siren sounds further along the esplanade.

'Is this what it's going to be like from now on?' Simon asks. 'What do these people want?'

I breathe out heavily, still holding the cloth to his head. 'Me.'

'I can't deal with this.' Simon leans against the fridge, slides back to the floor.

'I was trying to keep you out of it.' I spot one of the kitchen staff hovering in the doorway and wave for her to take over with the tea towel. 'Make sure he gets an ambulance.'

I jump back up on the bar and wait for Mya to look at me. I point to the alley. Time to end this.

She pushes herself off the cigarette machine and skirts around Taya and Rick, now wrestling a shirtless man with a hairy back. I catch Rafa's eye and make sure he sees Mya leaving. I pick my way around the room, trying not to breathe in the heady cocktail of beer, rum and post-mix cola sloshed over the timber floor. My shoes crunch on glass.

I duck into the alley as the cops pull up; the crowd on the street scatters. The piercing siren goes on for a few more seconds before someone finally kills it. It's quieter out here but smells even worse than the bar.

Mya steps out of the shadows. Flickering blue light from the police car washes over her.

'I can do this every night,' she says, still holding her drink. 'It never gets boring.'

I turn at the sound of footsteps. Rafa and Jones.

'I thought you fought demons?' I say to her.

'We hunt demons. We amuse ourselves in bars.'

'Speak for yourself,' Jones says. 'I came for a quiet drink.'

'Blame Rafa. I didn't throw a punch.'

Another police car pulls up. We move further into the shadows.

'Come with us,' Mya says. 'One job. Open your eyes to what goes on in the real world.'

'No.'

'I'm happy to come back tomorrow night. And the one after. My calendar's free, Gabe.'

I can feel Rafa beside me. His anger.

'I only found out a few days ago that I can use a sword. I'm not a mercenary, Mya. I'd get in the way – or get myself killed.'

She studies me. 'What if I told you I had something of

Jude's? Something you could have if you did this job.'

My breath hitches.

'For fuck's sake,' Rafa says, voice tight. 'Don't get sucked in.'

'Like what?' I ask.

'His laptop.'

For a second, nobody speaks.

'Bullshit,' Rafa says. 'He had it with him.'

'No, he didn't. And I took it.'

'You what?'

'I took it. Come on, we all knew something was going on when he started talking to Gabe again. When he left that last time, I *borrowed* it. And when he didn't come back' – she pauses – 'I kept it.'

'You've had it this whole time?' Rafa's words are measured, loaded.

'I'll give it to you and Gabe if you do this job.'

I swallow. Find my voice again. 'What's on it?'

'You can find that out for yourself.'

Rafa shakes his head. 'There's nothing on it. She wouldn't be offering it up if there was.'

But it's Jude's laptop. The real Jude. Whatever's on there will tell me something about who he was. Maybe something about where he is now. It's another lead, another possibility.

I fold my arms, dig my nails into warm skin. 'If we do

this, will you stay away from here? No more fights? No more threats to Jason or Maggie?'

Rafa steps in front of me. 'You seriously want to go with her?'

'No, I want that laptop.'

He breathes into my ear. 'We need to leave, Gaby.' Searches my face for something he doesn't find. 'Fuck.' He kicks an empty can into the wall. Walks from one side of the alley to the other and back again.

'What is it – a lead on the Fallen or a paying job?' Even in the shadowy alley I can see how coiled he is, how furious.

'Paying job,' Mya says. 'A big one.'

'Where?'

She finishes her drink, puts the glass on a ledge. 'I'm only giving the briefing once. You'll have to turn up like everyone else.'

'Where?'

'The sandbox. Pack light. You've got an hour.'

'What about—' I say, but I'm talking to an empty alley.

Bloody Rephaim and their ability to always get in the last word.

Jones rubs his knuckles. 'I'm sorry it went down like that,' he says to Rafa. 'But I'm not sorry you're coming back. And you,' he says to me. 'It'll make a nice change to be fighting on the same side again.'

And then he's gone too.

I can't bring myself to face Rafa. I'm glad of the distraction of an ambulance pulling up in the street. Its sirens are off, but the lights are flashing, and—

'Shit!' I flinch. Taya is standing in the shadows inside the alley, half her face lit by the streetlight.

'You are *not* joining that whore and her Outcasts.' She's breathless, a black eye already blossoming. Someone got in a lucky shot, but I bet it wasn't so lucky for them a split-second later.

'You're right,' I say. 'I'm not. I'm doing one job.'

'Do you even know what a job with Mya involves?' She looks at Rafa. 'Have you told her?'

He doesn't answer.

'You may as well spit in Nathaniel's face if you do this,' she says to me. 'And your own. If you remembered who you were you would *never* team up with that psychopath.'

'You saw that debacle in there. I don't have a choice.'

'Of course you do. I can have twenty Rephaim here tomorrow night—'

'And turn Pan Beach into a war zone? How many innocent people do you think will get hurt?'

'Not too many innocents in there, Gabe.'

'Of course there are! Have you people completely lost all value for human life?'

'What? No . . .' She frowns. 'Of course we haven't.'

'Then value the people who come here for a few hours to

escape all the other crap they have to deal with.'

'We can take Mya—'

I smack my palm on the bricks. 'I don't want you to take her. There's been enough violence between all of you already.'

'Since when did you care?'

'Since she started thinking like a human,' Rafa says, gruff. I have no idea if that's a compliment or not.

I look from one to the other. 'I'm not screwing anyone over. I'm not taking sides. I'm trying to keep everyone safe. And if you overheard that conversation then you know Mya has Jude's laptop, so there's a chance I can find out more about what was going on a year ago—'

'If Rafa doesn't know what Jude was doing, nobody will,' Taya says.

'What else am I going to do? Wait here until Nathaniel comes up with another plan to torture me?'

She turns away. I want to grab her, shake her. Why can't she get this?

'I am so over being pushed around by you people,' I say. 'All of you. I've been to the Sanctuary and I'm in no hurry to go there again—'

'You can't judge us by that.'

'—so I'm going to find out more about Jude. And then I'm coming back, so don't turn this into an excuse to make me public enemy number one again.'

Taya tests her swollen eye, looks back at the street where a group of girls are huddled together, lighting cigarettes near the ambulance.

'You think I betrayed everyone,' I say. 'But you don't know, not for sure. What if you're wrong?'

'What if I'm right?'

'But what if you're not?'

She fidgets, steps back. Behind her, someone is being lifted into the ambulance.

'You owe me,' I say.

She looks away.

'You threw me to a hellion. I saved you from one.'

No response.

'Give me a day.'

Taya finally meets my gaze. 'You screw me on this—'

'I won't. And you have to lay off Maggie. I mean it.'

She breathes out. 'I'm not going to touch your precious Maggie.' She looks past me, chews on her lip. 'You've got twelve hours.'

I have no idea if that's long enough.

It's going to have to be.

HOT AND BOTHERED

It's warm in the 'sandbox'. Not quite Pan-Beach-in-the-height-of-summer hot, but enough to raise a sweat almost immediately.

'Okay, where are we?'

Rafa watched me pack but wouldn't say where we were going. He wouldn't say much about anything. Now we've arrived in a tiny room with a dirty window and unmade bunk beds jammed against the walls. Stiff towels hang from racks nailed above the upper bunks. The place stinks of fried tomato and body odour. Wherever we are, it's the middle of the day.

'Rafa?'

He ignores me.

The floor is covered in a layer of newspaper. Rafa steps

around a gas burner with a blackened pan on top. A cheap air conditioner sits over the doorway, not running. It's stifling in here. Rafa opens the door and we're greeted by a blast of warm air. The view stops me in my tracks.

We're on the balcony of an apartment block, overlooking rows of crumbling buildings peppered with satellite dishes and washing lines. Beyond them is a forest of gleaming skyscrapers, stretched out in either direction. The world's tallest building rises from the middle of them.

Dubai.

'Is this a labour camp?'

'Yep.'

I have a vague memory of being in this city with Jude, but it was further along the coast at a resort in the shadow of the Burj Al Arab. And, of course, that memory's not real.

'Why?'

Rafa leans on the balcony railing, between threadbare t-shirts drying in the warm air. For a second I think he's not going to answer, then he says, 'Jude had a thing for the disenfranchised.'

'But . . .' I look around at the buildings, which are only a few years old but already sandblasted. The place is unnaturally quiet, the migrant workers long gone to their building sites for the day. 'I thought only men lived in these camps?'

'Would you look for us here?'

I get a flash of the Sanctuary. Aside from the blood spatter in the gymnasium, it had looked comfortable. Luxurious, almost. Nothing like this.

Rafa walks along the balcony to the stairs, his weapons pack on his back. I shrug my duffel bag higher on my shoulder and follow him down two flights, into the bright daylight. Washing flaps above us along the balcony rail, but otherwise the place is a ghost town. I fall into step beside him. Feel strangely disconnected to the barren landscape around me.

'You guys live here?'

'It's a rendezvous point.'

'You don't have a base? A home?'

The idea unsettles me. I always felt slightly adrift when Jude and I were backpacking. We had each other, but there was never a sense of permanence about our lives. Was that based on something real as well?

'Jude and I had the place on Patmos.' Rafa won't look at me when he speaks.

We pass a set of battered cricket stumps jammed into the dirt. Rafa rips one out, flings it ahead of us. It hits the concrete path, bounces twice and rolls to a stop.

'This is so fucked up.'

'Rafa—'

'No, don't.' The anger in his eyes brings me to a standstill.

'I shouldn't have brought you here. It's just wasting more time.' He walks a few steps, comes back. 'Explain to me what we're doing.'

'What we have to do to get Jude's laptop.'

'Bullshit. You're stalling.'

I hold his gaze, my breath shortening. 'I'm not.'

'We should have been gone days ago looking for Jude.'

'I needed Mags to be safer—'

'And now she is and you find another reason not to go to Melbourne. Fuck, Gabe, when are you going to stop punishing me?' His eyes have changed. Only a few hours ago they flared with wanting. There's no sign of that now. He hasn't looked at me like this for a week, not since he thought I was lying about what I remembered. It was bad enough then. Now, after everything we've been through, it's worse. Way worse. The night gets back inside me a bit, hollows me out.

'What are you talking about? Punishing you for what?'

'For everything. That's what you do. That's what you've done for the last ten years—'

'Rafa, that's not fair.'

He stares at me, unflinching. 'Do you have any idea what a mess I've been, thinking Jude's dead? He could be out there alive somewhere, and you're finding every excuse not to look for him. For fuck's sake, he's your brother – what's the problem?'

I close my eyes for a second and see Jude's face before he jumped from the cable car; lit up, full of life.

The problem is that I love the brother I remember. I miss that Jude so much I ache. But the Jude we're going to look for, Rafa's best mate . . . that's not him. My stomach folds in on itself. How can I explain that to Rafa?

I meet his gaze again. Force myself to not look away.

'I thought these people were your friends.'

He scowls at my avoidance. 'They are.'

'Then what's wrong with being with them for a few hours?'

'It's not getting us any closer to finding Jude.'

But it might get me closer to the Jude Rafa knows.

'It's more than that,' I say.

'Don't make this about me.'

'Why don't you want me here?'

His lips harden. 'Because it's wrong, that's why.'

'Why?'

'It just is.'

'Let me guess: I'd understand if I remembered my other life?'

'No, Gaby. Like Taya said, you wouldn't be here if you remembered your other life.'

He cracks a knuckle and sets off again. I follow, but my steps aren't as grounded as they need to be. It hits me then: I'm about to face the Outcasts. Rephaite soldiers who think

I chose the Sanctuary over them. Who've hated me for the past ten years. Who loved Jude.

We cross the road to a path flanked by single-storey flats. There's no clutter, no washing strung between these buildings. We're halfway along when I hear ringing steel. I tilt my head towards the building on my left. 'That's training I can hear, right? Not a demon ambush?'

Rafa swings the weapons bag around and offers me the same sword Zak gave me back in Pan Beach the night we went up the mountain. I take the katana, wrap my fingers around its familiar hilt. He doesn't speak. Doesn't offer any reassurance.

Rafa stays in front as we walk past dirty windows with drawn blinds. The air conditioners in the building are on and the metal boxes hum above every doorway we pass, dripping water. At the fifth door, Rafa rests his fingers on the handle. The fighting is on the other side but I can't work out how that's possible, given the room we came from was barely big enough to swing a sword in. I slide my katana out of its cover and wait. My palms are sweaty.

Rafa pauses, as if he's going to say something, but then the door is yanked open. I duck sideways, slamming into the wall. Rafa doesn't flinch.

'Sloppy, Rafa.' Zak fills the doorway – in every direction. 'A dead hellion would have felt you arrive. Where'd you come in, two doors down?'

Rafa resheathes his katana. 'Just keeping you on your toes.' He grins at Zak and it's as if the argument between us didn't happen. I catch my breath.

Zak looks down at me and shakes his head. I'm not sure if he's surprised I've actually shown up or if it feels wrong to him too. He steps back. 'Come on, before you let all the cool air out.'

I falter when I see how many Outcasts are here. There must be twenty men and women scattered around the room, sparring with swords or bare fists. My heart gives a panicked thump. God, what *am* I doing here?

This part of the building has been completely gutted – no furniture, no light fittings and no walls to separate what were once apartments. Just the air conditioners, bare bulbs overhead and exercise mats on the concrete floor.

'Is this place structurally sound?'

Rafa's laugh is brittle. 'That's what you're worried about? The roof falling in?'

The sparring is frenetic. If I hadn't seen the Rephaim in a serious fight, I'd think these clashes were the real deal.

On the far side of the room, Jones holds up a hand in greeting. I'm pretty sure it's for Rafa so I don't wave back.

Ez is training with Mya, blocking sword strikes and occasionally landing a kick. I've seen enough of Ez in action to know she's going easy on her. They trade a few more blows before Mya signals for a break. She knows we're here but she takes her time acknowledging us, and even then doesn't act like it's a big deal.

But it's a big deal for everyone else. By the time Mya and Ez walk over to us, the rest of the Outcasts are facing me, tensed, ready. Like I'm the threat. I try to steady my breathing. Fail.

Rafa still won't look at me.

I only saw Ez a few hours ago in Iowa, but already it feels like days. How can these people keep changing time zones so easily? How do they keep track of what day it is? What season it is?

'Welcome to the Outcasts,' Ez says.

I resist the urge to point out I'm not actually joining them. It's possibly not the best time for that bit of news, given the number of weapons in the room.

'Everyone here's been told what you do and don't remember,' she says and gives my sword a meaningful look.

Shit. I've walked in here armed. No wonder they're so hostile.

I should hand the sword to Rafa. Instead, I force myself to look each and every one of them in the eye. It's a genetic melting pot: blonde hair and blue eyes, olive skin and brown hair, redheads, shaved heads, bearded and clean-shaven. Everyone toned and fit. Nobody welcoming.

Do they blame me for Jude's death too? Or have I done

things over the years to make them despise me the way Rafa despises Daniel? Either way, there's no love here. Which begs the question: do I really want to go into a fight alongside people who don't trust me? Who look like they'd be happy to see me get hurt? Especially with Rafa in the mood he's in.

'Yeah, she can still fight,' Rafa says, stepping between them and me. 'So I'd think twice about taking her on. And if you still think it's a good idea, you'll have me to deal with as well.'

There's a bit of muttering and shuffling, but nobody makes a move. I let my breath out a little.

'Good.' Rafa keeps his back to me. 'So, what, nobody's happy to see me?'

'It's been so long I forgot what you looked like.' The comment comes from a tall blond guy at the edge of the group.

'Only if you lost that photo you keep of me in your wallet.'

'Fuck you.'

'Not in this lifetime, Seth.'

They laugh. And then they're man-hugging and back-slapping. A few seconds later there's a queue lined up to welcome Rafa home. Ez takes my arm and leads me to the back of the room. It doesn't stop the glares, but at least I'm not the centre of attention.

'They'll work out you're not the enemy—'

'I was the enemy?'

'Not really.' Ez thinks for a few seconds. 'After the split, you were critical of everything we did. And in the early days, there were a few emotionally charged run-ins between your crew and ours. You didn't go easy on any of us.'

I feel my mouth drop. 'Did I . . . Did we . . .?'

'I was smart enough to stay out of your way.'

'What about Jude?' I glance down at my katana. Did I attack my brother with a sword? Did he try to hurt me? The thought makes my chest ache.

'Never.' Ez touches my arm. 'You both managed to avoid it. But you and Rafa . . . that's another story.'

'All right.' Mya claps her hands. 'Let's do this.'

It's not so much that everyone snaps to attention, but they stop talking and move to where she's holding a cardboard tube. I drift closer. Rafa comes over to me but refuses to catch my eye. I notice Ez look quickly at him and then me.

Mya shakes a roll of paper out of the tube and flattens it on the floor. A map of an inner city, maybe. She points to the middle of a grid. 'A nest of Immundi is running a child sex racket in the basement of this building. We're going in to kill the pit scum, grab the kids, and round up any humans involved.'

Rafa leans forward. 'Tell me that's not LA.' His face hardens. 'Tell me that's not the Rhythm Palace.' A murmur spreads through the group.

'It's called the Angels' Den these days. I assume it's meant to be ironic—'

'Are you fucking insane? The last time we were there, thirteen humans were torn apart—'

'And we saved twenty-three girls.'

'It was a massacre, Mya. It was a disaster from start to finish and if Jude and I hadn't turned up when we did, we would have lost Rephaim as well as humans.'

Mya stands, and the map at her feet rolls up on itself. 'That's why we're going in at full strength.'

'No.'

'It's a paying job, Rafa.'

'I don't give a shit. You swore to Jude there'd never be another cock-up like that.'

'It won't be a cock-up. That's why I want you along.' A glance in my direction. 'And she may not be full-strength, but from what I've heard she'll still be useful.'

I'm trying to follow their argument, but my brain is stuck on Rhythm Palace. Rhythm Palace . . .

'Crap.'

'What?' Rafa's glance is annoyed.

'That's the nightclub with the hellions.' The one my short story was based on. The memory of Jude's that I now somehow have. The bloody nightmare of gutted bodies and decapitated hellions.

'The one and only. The biggest screw-up of our mercenary career.'

'Only because we didn't know Bel had half a dozen hell-spawn guarding the place,' Mya says. 'And Bel's not involved this time.'

Rafa is taller than Mya and he's taking advantage of that now, standing over her. 'How do you know that?'

'Because I've got Jess on the inside and she says Immundi are running the trafficking ring.'

'You think it's a coincidence they're in that building?'

Mya waves away the comment. 'The place would still reek of demon from the last infestation. You know they love the smell of their own kind.'

'Who's Jess?' I whisper to Ez.

She answers without taking her eyes off Mya. 'An undercover detective.'

I frown. How did an undercover LA cop get involved with the Rephaim?

'How many Immundi?' Zak asks.

'About a dozen.'

Someone lets out a low whistle.

Mya nods. 'The bottom-feeders are turning up in bigger numbers. We need to thin their ranks.'

There's more murmuring and I lean in to Ez again. 'Who are the Immundi?'

'Demons. Lower on the food chain than Gatekeepers, and not as strong. They manipulate humans, drive them to destruction. It's sport for them and they're very good at it.'

Rafa turns to Zak. 'Did you know about this?'

'No, I did not.' Zak doesn't look happy about it. Nobody does.

'Look.' Mya waits until she has everyone's attention again. 'There are kids no older than ten being used and abused and then sold to the highest bidder. You want to walk away from that?'

Silence.

'I know we have history with that place. That we made mistakes there – but this is our chance to make up for it.'

Jones picks up the map and speaks over the muttering around the group. 'How are we going in?'

Mya lays out her plan. Everyone is slightly less tense by the time she finishes.

'Right. Any questions?'

I've got at least twenty, but I'm not drawing any more attention to myself.

'Good. We'll move out at midnight, local time. Do what you want until then but stay close.'

The group drifts apart. Rafa stands with his hands on his hips for a few seconds. Then, without a glance at me, he crosses the room towards the door. For a second I forget to breathe. He wouldn't leave me here . . . would he?

'Give him a minute,' Zak says. 'Let him blow off steam.'

I nod and then see Mya follow Rafa and close the door behind them. I pretend the sight of her disappearing with him doesn't burn.

'Are you ready?' Ez asks me.

I drag my eyes from the door. 'Is there any chance this thing in LA is a trap?'

'There's always that chance, but the risk is no bigger than usual.'

'You don't seem sold on the idea.'

'I'm as sold as I ever am these days.' Ez's smile is tired.

I check the door. Still closed.

'What happened there last time?'

Zak catches my eye, shakes his head.

'It's all right.' Ez puts her hand on his wrist. 'The job was to rescue girls downstairs. We didn't know Bel and Leon were upstairs. They let five hellions loose and then locked the doors. By the time we worked out what was going on it was a bloodbath.' Her fingers absently trace the scars on her face.

'Is that when . . .?'

Zak reaches for her hand, lifting her fingers from her cheek and kissing them. She gives him a reassuring smile.

'Jude was hurt too,' she says. 'None of us saw it coming. It almost tore us apart.'

Jones calls out to Ez and Zak. 'We'll be back in a moment,' Ez says, and I open my duffel bag and try to look busy, rummaging around. I need to keep occupied until Rafa comes back inside and tells me what I'm supposed to do next. He better come back. I glance up at the sound of footsteps. Mya. She must have shifted back in. I look behind her. Rafa is walking towards Ez, Zak and Jones, his shoulders tight.

I get to my feet – no way is Mya looking down on me.

'What now?'

She folds her arms. 'You have no questions. None at all?'

Rafa looks across at us but makes no move towards me. The room falls silent.

'I may have one or two.'

'Hit me.'

Don't tempt me.

'What's this job got to do with finding the Fallen?'

'Absolutely nothing.'

'Then why—'

'Typical! You don't remember being part of the Sanctuary but you still think like them.'

'Don't give me that crap. Finding the Fallen is all any of you care about.'

'So why would we bother saving a few kids? Is that what you're asking?'

Blood rushes up my neck. 'Don't twist my words. And don't act so self-righteous. Kids are being abused and exploited all over the world. You're only saving this lot because someone's paying.'

'And how many are Nathaniel and his acolytes saving? That's right. None.' Her eyes are piercing. 'And at least we earn our way – we're not taking hand-outs from a disgraced angel.'

'So, everyone here takes hand-outs from you?'

'No, Gabe. Everyone gets an equal share of whatever job we do. Does that surprise you?'

Well, yes, as a matter of fact it does, but I'm not going to give her the satisfaction of seeing she's exceeded my expectations.

'So the Fallen aren't a priority?'

'Of course they are, but why not slaughter a few demons in between? We've got a window of time right now and I'm not wasting it.'

What she means is they have no leads on the Fallen. But the Sanctuary must or Malachi would have been in Pan Beach with Taya.

'We serve a purpose,' she says. 'We don't fight the enemy only when there's a vested interest.'

She can't seriously think I'm buying her Joan of Arc

routine. 'How did you come by this place?' I ask.

Her eyes track around the walls. 'A few years ago we took down a pack of desert jinn stirring up the workers here.'

'Desert what?'

'Jinn . . . demons.' She narrows her eyes as if she's not sure whether I'm playing her. 'The client wanted us to come back regularly, keep the place clean. This building was still empty, so Jude did a deal to turn it into a quasi dojo.'

My heart squeezes at his name.

'As long as we keep our heads down, there's not much chance Nathaniel or the Five will track us here and give us another sermon about our duty to our kind and how imperative it is we rejoin the fold.'

I nod, but I'm not really listening. I'm imagining Jude in this room, laughing and training with these strangers, being closer to them than me.

'What's the story with Jason?' Mya asks.

That snaps me out of it. 'Exactly what he told you.'

'If he's never been to the Sanctuary, how'd he hook up with Taya?'

I could tell her the truth. I go with half.

'They met in Pan Beach. She doesn't know what he is.'

She stares at me, dubious. 'How is that possible?'

'Because I didn't tell her.'

'But—'

'I keep telling you,' Rafa says, walking over. 'She's not Gabe. Deal with it.' He faces me and I can still feel his anger. 'We should get in some training.'

The others are loitering. I am so not sparring with an audience.

Rafa turns to Mya. 'You finished in here?'

She looks between him and me. 'For the moment.'

'Good,' he says. 'We'll need all this space.'

MUSCLE MEMORY

The room clears out and we're alone, except for Ez and Zak.

'Did you know Mya has Jude's laptop?' Rafa asks Ez.

'I thought he took it with him?'

'Apparently not. It's what she dangled in front of Gabe to get us here.'

She frowns. 'How come she's never mentioned it?'

'My point exactly.'

He kicks off his shoes and walks over to the practice mats.

My sword is almost out of the weapons bag when Ez stops me. 'You know what you're doing with that. I hear it's hand-to-hand combat you need a refresher on.'

I put the katana back. It might be slender, but it's enough

to hide behind. Bare fists? I may as well be naked. 'Am I sparring with you?'

'No.' She nods in Rafa's direction.

Crap.

'What are you and Zak going to do?'

'Stay out of the way.'

I join Rafa on the mats, barefoot. He steps back into a fighter's stance, not speaking. I do the same and we circle each other. Neither of us makes the first move. I don't attack him because I'm not sure how. I have no idea what his excuse is.

'What are you waiting for?' Rafa's movements are purposeful, controlled. 'Are you telling me you don't want to hit me?'

I give myself away with a small smile.

'Then come at me.'

'You're not pissing me off right this second.'

'Do you want me to?'

I think about that, keep my feet moving. 'No.'

'You've always fought better with a clear head,' Zak breaks in from somewhere behind me. 'You shouldn't have to get wound up to fight.'

'That's very true, Zachariah,' Rafa says, not taking his eyes from me, 'but our girl here has only fought when she's wound up. Look at her – she doesn't know what to do without that fuel.'

It grates on me, but he's right.

'Then attack her.'

He hesitates for a moment – and I swear I see conflict in his eyes – and then he sweeps my legs out from under me so fast I don't see it coming. I hit the floor hard. Air deserts my lungs.

'Get up,' Zak says.

I spring to my feet. Damn, he's scary when he lowers that voice.

Rafa comes at me again, this time with a lightning roundhouse kick. I lift my forearms to block it, more instinct than premeditation.

'That's it,' Ez says. 'Clear your mind. Trust your body.'

I flick a quick glance at her. She obviously doesn't know my body can't be trusted, especially around Rafa—

BAM.

I'm on the floor again, fire exploding across my ribs. What the hell?

'Fuck, Gabe, are you concentrating or daydreaming?' As if it's my fault he's hurt me.

I get up. 'Sorry,' I say, with as much sarcasm as I can muster. My ribs throb in dull waves.

Rafa comes at me again, rapid-fire kicks and hand strikes. I try to forget it's him and concentrate on blocking and countering. He's pushing me back, but at least I'm protecting myself. We move around the room.

'Attack him,' Zak says.

'How?' I bring my forearms up to stop an elbow to my face.

'Stop thinking.'

I drop and kick out at Rafa's knee with a side strike. He loses his feet. Holy shit, I've knocked Rafa down. It throws me for a second. Long enough for him to roll over and slam his bare foot into my solar plexus. I stumble back into Zak. It's like hitting a brick wall. He steadies me with big hands.

'Focus on your body,' he says.

I take a breath, shift my awareness. Count the beats of my heart against my ribs. Flex my fingers.

And then I feel it: strength, pulsing with each beat. Rephaite strength. I had a taste of it at the Imperial, but I haven't felt it like this since the fight on the mountain. And in the cage.

We go at it again. Rafa attacks faster. I'm vaguely aware of my reflexes ramping up to match his. Punch, block, kick, block, strike, duck. Breathe. Zak gets out of the way.

It's like remembering steps to a dance.

I leap at Rafa, my right knee angled down towards his thigh. He steps back to avoid it, but somehow I knew that's what he'd do and I'm ready for it. Before my feet touch down, I punch him in the jaw. Hard. He staggers back. I wait for the explosion of anger. But he only nods, his skin red where I struck him. 'Better.'

We go again. And again. My t-shirt clings to me. Blood pounds at my temples. But I feel strong, focused. We keep going. Rafa peels off his shirt, wipes his neck with it. His skin glistens.

His attacks get harder; his aggression is building. He's wearing me down. Another kick to the thigh, another elbow between my shoulder blades. I'm vaguely aware of Ez saying something about easing up, but either Rafa doesn't hear or he ignores her, because the onslaught continues. I'm in a world of pain. I fend off a fresh flurry of strikes. My forearms throb, my ribs ache. I can't take this for much longer.

I block a kick, see an opening, and punch Rafa in the jaw as hard as I can. His head snaps back – and then my legs are gone from under me again. I slam onto my back and the air rushes out of my lungs. The bare bulb on the ceiling blurs and then all I see is Rafa, red-faced, sweating. He straddles me, pins my arms and legs.

My chest is heaving. We're both trying to catch our breath. His grip tightens on my arms. His eyes are strangely distant as he stares at me. I can't read his expression and it's freaking me out a little.

'You win,' I manage, between breaths.

A bead of sweat runs from his hairline down the side of his face.

Footsteps cross the mats. 'That'll do,' Zak says. 'Rafa.'

Rafa looks up at Zak and his face clears. He nods and lets go. Then he stands up and goes to Ez, takes the water bottle she offers.

Zak helps me up. 'Not bad,' he says, and I catch a quick glance in Rafa's direction. 'You're a little rusty, but your reflexes are still sharp.'

I cradle my right hand. It throbs and my knuckles are split and bleeding from that last punch.

Rafa screws the lid on the water bottle, turns around and tosses it to me. I catch it with my good hand.

'You'll need those bumps and bruises gone before we get to LA.' Ez checks me over. She turns to Rafa. 'You want me to take care of Gaby, and Zak can fix that?' She gestures to his jaw, which is already discoloured.

He probes the bruise. 'Yep.' He meets my gaze, fleetingly. 'You okay?'

I nod and two seconds later he and Zak are gone. The imprint of their bare feet lingers on the mat.

My legs shake from fatigue. I drop back to the floor, stretch out my hamstrings. The air conditioners rattle in the empty room. The mat sighs beneath me.

What the hell just happened? How did we get from kissing on the beach to beating the crap out of each other in half a day? The adrenaline is fading now, leaving me feeling strangely fragile. Lost.

'Are you sure you're all right?' Ez asks.

I show her my busted knuckles. 'I think I've broken something.'

She frowns. 'That got out of hand. He shouldn't have gone so hard on you.'

'He's pissed off at me for coming here.' I carefully cross my legs, not looking at her.

Ez drops gracefully to the floor next to me. I catch a hint of orange blossom. 'It's a little more complicated than that.'

'What do you mean?'

'Sparring with you. I don't think he was ready for it.'

I try to laugh but it comes out as a rasp.

'I mean it. You haven't trained together for a very long time. For the last decade, any time you two threw punches at each other, you were deadly serious.' She tucks her feet underneath her. 'The problem today was that you were too good.'

'How is that a problem?' I finally look up.

She gives me a sad smile.

'There were moments when you fought like the old Gabe. I think, at the end there, he forgot which version of you he was fighting.'

NOT EVERYTHING COMES CLEAN

We shift to the showers. The communal bathroom is big enough for a small army. One wall is lined with wash basins, the other with shower cubicles; the place reeks of bleach and disinfectant.

By the time I'm peeling off my clothes and getting under the warm water, my muscles have mostly stopped complaining. The water pressure is strong, insistent.

I'm okay.

My throat tightens. God, who am I kidding? I'm not okay. I'm far from okay.

My hands shake when I pick up the shampoo. I drop the bottle as I try to open it. I wash my hair and let the water stream over my face, keeping my lips closed so I don't swallow any of it. Try to settle back into my body. Lazy steam envelops me. Maybe I could stay in here until we go to LA. I'm not sure if I can even look at Rafa right now, and I definitely don't want to talk to any of the others. All I see is that distant look in his eyes. I feel myself hitting him. I feel him hitting me. The beach feels far away.

I turn off the tap when my skin starts to prune. Ez is still under the water two stalls down. I dry myself and put on lightweight tracksuit bottoms and a t-shirt, step out of the cubicle.

Mya is leaning against the nearest basin, waiting.

Perfect.

'Zak tells me your training session wasn't a complete disappointment,' she says, glancing at my knuckles, which are bruised but no longer raw, thanks to the short shift from the training room.

I wring my hair out behind my back and her eyes drift to the scar on my neck. I don't need to check the mirror to know it's bright red, angry: it always is after a shower.

I square my shoulders. Keep it together. Don't let her see how shaky I am.

'Did you come here to gloat?'

She folds her arms. 'About what?'

'You got what you wanted: Rafa back.'

'He's here. He's not back.' She pushes off from the basin, turns on a tap. Water gushes out, splashes over the edge onto the tiles. She wrenches it off again. 'How did you find Jason?'

I take a breath. I don't understand why she's so obsessed with Jason, but it's better than talking about Rafa.

'He turned up in Pan Beach a couple of weeks ago. He didn't let on who he was until Maggie was kidnapped.'

'Where's he been all these years? How did he work out what he was and who taught him to shift?'

'Ask him yourself next time you see him.' My fingers are still trembling, so I dry my hair with the towel to keep them busy. 'How did you work it out?'

'The hard way. How did Jason find you?'

'He read the story I posted online.' It's not a complete lie. He probably did read it at some point.

'It's interesting it was one of Jude's memories you wrote about, not your own. You ever wonder how that's possible?'

It's a stupid question so I don't bother answering.

Mya walks along the row of basins, testing taps as she goes. At the third sink she turns again. 'I can't believe you get to have a clean slate, like nothing you've done counts any more.'

'I didn't ask for any of this. I was doing fine with the life I had.'

I was doing fine. Aside from the gnawing grief for Jude and the nightmares about hell-beasts and the loneliness that threatened to swallow me most nights.

183

'You don't care that you and Jude might have triggered a war?'

The prophesied war between angels and demons.

'Ah, no.'

She tilts her head. 'You don't care about Nathaniel's obsession with winning back favour from the Angelic Garrison?'

'No.'

Her eyebrows go up, mocking me. 'Wow, either you're really not Gabe any more or you've got better at lying.' She runs her fingers through her hair. 'No wonder Rafa's so taken with you.'

I feel a pang at his name and warmth floods my chest. Please don't let it climb my neck.

'Let's face it,' she continues, 'you're all the good bits of Gabe with none of the bad.'

She's baiting me. There's no way I'm biting. There's no way—

'What's that supposed to mean?'

She leans against the mirror. 'You and Rafa were tight back in the day, but you've been gunning for each other since we left the Sanctuary. And not just because he walked away from Nathaniel. I have a theory about what happened between you two. Would you like to hear it?'

'Not particularly.'

The reflection of the side of her face in the mirror is

beautiful. It's the only thing about her that is. She keeps talking as if I haven't spoken.

'You two did everything together, except the obvious. But I think you were in love with him – deeply in denial, of course. You made such a big show about not caring whose legs he was between. Until they were mine.'

'Really.' I try to sound bored but that image is searing into my brain. 'And then, what, I tried to talk him out of being with you – that's what we fought over?'

As soon as Mya laughs I know I've played into her hands. 'No, I think you tried to hook up with him.'

'Yeah, right.' I turn away from the mirror. I hate that I can't argue with her. And what if she's right?

Mya pushes on, sensing – and enjoying – my discomfort. 'And when he knocked you back, you were so humiliated you channelled all that unrequited longing into violence. You two had a massive throw-down just before we left the Sanctuary. What else could it have been about?'

'Could you be any more self-absorbed?'

'It's the only thing that explains why you didn't leave with us. You couldn't stand the thought of seeing him with me.'

The water shuts off in Ez's cubicle. I flinch. I'd forgotten she was still here. From the flush in Mya's cheeks, she had too.

'I'm sure there were more important things going on at

that point than your sex life.' I grab a comb and drag it through my damp hair. It pulls at my scalp.

'You could always ask him . . . *Gaby.*'

I catch glimpses of her in all the mirrors above the basins as she walks out the door.

In the silence, I can hear water dripping in Ez's cubicle.

'You can come out now,' I say.

She steps out in a waft of jasmine, fully dressed and hair combed. She gives a self-conscious shrug. 'I kept the water running to give you privacy.'

'But you heard it all? Explain to me why she's in charge here.'

'She's not in charge. She co-ordinates operations – someone has to.'

'So this influence she has over everyone, it's about the money?'

Ez watches me in the mirror as she plaits her hair. 'She sources jobs that pay well, but it's more than that. She's given us another way to exist as Rephaim.'

'As what – mercenaries?'

'No,' Ez says patiently, 'as something other than Nathaniel's puppets.'

'I can't believe you're defending her.'

'She's not always like this.' Ez's fingers deftly work through her luscious hair. 'Being around you brings the worst out in her. Jude and Rafa, they never got over leaving you. No matter what was said, or how bad things got between the three of you, it ripped their hearts out that you stayed behind. We could all see it. Mya wanted their full attention; she never got it. And then a year ago she lost them both.'

'And she blames me.'

Ez lets her hands drop. 'I know you can't see it, but she's not a bad person. She was on her own for a long time, not knowing who or what she was.'

'Did her mother survive?'

'Of course not; she died like they all did. Mya was raised by her mother's cousins.'

I glance at her. Rafa hasn't told Ez about Jason's mother surviving – or her connection to my mother.

'What did she mean about learning to shift the hard way?'

Ez ties off the end of her plait with a strip of leather. 'Her cousins tried to rape her when she was eighteen. I imagine the trauma of it triggered the shift.'

I open my mouth. Close it. 'That's awful.' Water still dribbles from one of the taps and I turn it off tighter. 'Did I know that . . . before?'

'I doubt it; you two never really clicked.'

'But she and Jude did.'

Ez nods. 'That was the issue between you and her.

You didn't like the way she encouraged him to question Nathaniel.'

I try to imagine a situation when I wouldn't support someone – anyone – questioning authority. I can't.

'You didn't like that he was listening to someone other than you. That hadn't happened before.'

I chew my lip. I have to ask. 'Was she right about me and Rafa?'

'Were you in love with him? I don't know. You never gave much away.'

'What about Mya? Was she – was he . . .?'

Ez gives me a sympathetic smile. 'I can't speak for Mya, but I can tell you that whatever was between Rafa and her, it wasn't about love.'

TUMBLING DOWN THE RABBIT HOLE

Ez takes me to a room not unlike the one Rafa and I arrived in. It's cramped and humid, even with the air conditioner rattling away, but doesn't smell quite so badly of burnt food and sweat. I pick a bunk, fuss with my bag.

Rafa and Zak are already there. I'm so tangled up in my own thoughts I can't look at Rafa so it takes me a while to realise that he's avoiding my eyes as well.

'What's up?' he finally asks.

'Nothing.'

'You've packed that thing three times now.'

Who's asking the question? The Rafa who sets my skin alight, or the one always angry at me? 'I'm no good at sitting still.' I turn away from him. 'Have you had a chance to look at the journal we got in Iowa?' I ask Ez.

She looks from Rafa to me and then nods. 'I had a quick flick – and then I stood in the sun for ten minutes to get the chill out of my bones. There are pages about blood-letting and other rituals involving a baby – I'm not sure I want to read it in detail. And those photos . . .'

'Is it here?'

She shakes her head. 'Mya's got it. She can read German better than me. Between us we'll work out what it says and maybe get some clues about the iron room. Everyone was a little jumpy when we told them about it. I suspect that will be the next job – destroying that farmhouse.'

'That's a given,' Rafa says.

I check my watch. It's still set to Pan Beach where it's ten-thirty in the evening. I'm exhausted. 'What's the time here?'

'A little after four-thirty,' Ez says.

'So, are we going to sit here and stare at each other for the next few hours?' I ask.

'We could go into the city.' Ez looks to Zak. 'We should see Khaled while we're here.'

'Who's Khaled?' I ask.

'A gold seller we met a few years ago. Lovely man.'

Zak gives her a curious look. 'You need more jewellery?'

'Always.' She smiles.

I've never seen Ez wear gold, but that's probably because

the only time I see her she's in combat mode.

'Do you want to come?' she asks.

I shake my head. 'I need to ring Maggie.'

'Rafa?'

He meets my eyes. 'I'll stay with Gabe.'

'You're *where*? I thought Dubai was all luxury hotels and resorts.'

'It is,' I say. 'We're just not staying at any of them.' That's an understatement. The mattress I'm sitting on is tissue-thin.

'What's happening there?' In the background, I can hear a police radio. 'Are you back at the bar?' The last time I saw Maggie was at our place, briefly, when I was throwing clothes into a bag and telling her about Jude's laptop. We didn't have time for much of a chat.

'We came to help Rick clean up. The cops are still taking statements.' A pause. 'Mick and Rusty showed up about ten minutes ago and recognised Taya from the other night. They know she's connected with what happened up the mountain.'

I glance at Rafa. He's sitting cross-legged on the floor with a block of wood, a bucket of water and some sort of whetstone, sharpening a katana with a practised rhythm. His jaw is still slightly discoloured where I hit him.

'What happened?' I ask Maggie.

'The cops had to get between Mick and Taya. He thinks Taya knows where the hellions are, and . . .' She pauses again. I can tell by the repetitive clicking that she's tapping a polished nail on her phone.

'And?'

'Rumour is he's putting together a' – she drops her voice – '*militia* to protect the town.'

'You're kidding.'

Rafa's head comes up. He absently flicks water onto the sword without looking at it. 'What?' he mouths, not breaking his rhythm.

I shake my head. 'I'm sure Rafa will sort it out when we get back.' And by 'sort out', I mean beat the crap out of Mick and his militia.

I wipe the back of my neck with a towel. Shouldn't it be cooler north of the equator this time of year?

I don't want to end the call yet. It's so much easier to talk to her than Rafa right now. 'How's Simon?'

'Still waiting to get stitches. I saw him before he left in the ambulance. He's not happy, but I think he'll be okay.'

My eyes sting. I rub them. 'And things are better with you and Jason?'

'We're getting there.' A tiny sigh. 'Are you sure you're okay there?'

I glance at Rafa and then find a scuff mark on the wall above him to study. I wish I was back in our bathroom, chatting to Maggie in front of the mirror. Privately. Maybe then I'd tell her what Mya said to me. I need to talk about it because it's doing my head in. Is Mya right? Did I humiliate myself? Is that what Rafa's hiding from me?

'I'm fine, Mags.'

A pause. I wait for her to push for a real answer, but instead she asks, 'Do you trust Mya?'

Much easier. 'No. But it's only one job and I want that laptop.'

She doesn't ask what the job is and I don't tell her.

'I was thinking Jason and I could make a few discreet calls while you're gone. You know, to the hospital in Melbourne.'

'Oh . . .' It takes a second for my brain to change gears, and then tears threaten. Even after knowing her for nine months, Maggie's thoughtfulness still catches me by surprise. I'm glad she's not here, but that doesn't stop me wishing she was. I could do with one of her hugs right now.

Rafa has put the sword aside. He's watching me closely, forearms resting on his knees, waiting for me to get off the phone.

I swallow. 'Thanks, Mags. I'll see you soon.'

'Please take care.'

I disconnect the call, feel a pang of loneliness.

Rafa raises his eyebrows at me. 'What am I taking care of?'

I tell him about the Butlers.

'Idiots.'

'They think they're protecting their town.'

'They're trigger-happy morons looking for an excuse to play commando in the forest. With any luck they'll shoot each other and we won't have to worry about them.'

I want to tell him about Maggie and Jason's offer to call the hospital. But he's as likely to be annoyed at Jason's involvement and I don't have the energy for another argument today.

Rafa's phone beeps. He checks the message.

'Zak and Ez will bring dinner when they come back.' He glances at my eyes, and then my pillow. 'Are you tired? You've got time for a quick nap.'

'What are you going to do?'

He holds up his sword, the curved blade still dripping water.

I don't need to be told twice.

I spread my towel over the tatty mattress, lie down and listen to the steady rasp of steel on stone as Rafa returns to sharpening. Metal bars beneath the flimsy mattress cut into my back, but at this point I don't care. I put my arm across my face to block out the light, willing sleep to come.

'. . . Nearly there.'

Jude's nudging me awake.

I open my eyes, yawn, carefully move my shoulders and legs. After nearly twenty-two hours of travel, every muscle in my body feels atrophied.

'How long?' It's still dark out, so all I see are guideposts flashing past my window, reflective squares of red, as we race down the highway.

'About twenty minutes.' Jude stops scratching at the stubble on his chin and grins at me, one hand still on the steering wheel. His face is lit by the green dashboard light. 'By the time the sun's up, I'll be carving that famous right point break.'

'And by the time it sets, I'll be sitting in casualty waiting for you to get stitched up.'

He laughs. 'It hasn't been that long since I've been on a board.'

'It's been long enough.'

'Come on, princess, you'll get to see the sun come up at Bells Beach.'

'I'd rather have seen it from the window of a motel near the airport.'

I turn side-on in my seat, lean my head against the cool glass of the window. Jude's tapping away on the steering wheel to a tune only he can hear, smiling at the road. Where does he get this level of enthusiasm after a long-haul flight from London? It's not normal. Who bounces off a plane after being jammed in economy for nineteen hours, smiles through Customs, flirts with the bleary-eyed girl on the car rental counter and then sets off in an unfamiliar sedan in pitch darkness to tackle roads in a country he's never driven in before?

He shoves my shoulder without taking his eyes off the road. 'Come on, *maate*,' he says, imitating the dreadlocked stoner who sat behind us on the plane from Singapore. 'It's one of the world's best surf beaches.'

And that's it: it's his pick. Mine was London. We spent two months hanging out in pubs, trawling through old bookshops, taking trips to the west coast and Scotland. We picked up bits of work in between – me in a cafe, Jude in a bar. But he craves the sun like a lizard, so after a cold month in England it wasn't enough to head to France or even Greece. No. We had to head to the other side of the planet.

'So, I was thinking,' he says, 'seeing as we're already in Australia, I thought we should head north next and check out that place I was telling you about. Pandanus Beach.'

I am so not in the mood for this right now. 'Can't we get where we're going first? I'm tired, I'm hungry for something that doesn't come covered in plastic or foil, and I'd like to stop moving for a few hours.'

'And clearly you've got PMS.'

'Fuck off.'

He laughs. 'That's the spirit, princess. Fire up.' He reaches behind me to rummage around on the backseat. 'I know what you need,' he says, digging in his backpack. 'Something to get the blood pumping.'

I groan. 'It's four in the morning, Jude, I am not listening to Foo Fighters or AC/DC or Led Zeppelin—'

'Trust me, you'll love it.' He pulls his hand back, triumphant, a CD between his fingers.

It's not that I'm not happy to be in Australia. It's not that I'm not looking forward to a few weeks kicking back at the beach. It's not even that I don't like his music. I'm tired and, yes, possibly a little hormonal. And Jude knows me well enough that he should stop needling me.

'You take that CD out and you know where's it's going to end up, don't you?'

His eyes widen with mock fear. 'Where?'

'Up your arse, bro.'

'But that would involve you moving off that seat, and that's not happening any time soon, is it?'

I bite back the urge to laugh. We've had this exchange of insults a thousand times, and the familiarity is disarming. But I'm trying to make a point here.

I snatch it out of his fingers and wind down the window. The sound of the road rushes in. I'm not going to throw it out, but for a second he believes I might. He takes his hands off the wheel and his eyes off the tarmac.

'Give me that before you hurt yourself,' he says, wrestling with me.

'Watch what you're doing.' I'm trying to see past him, but I'm not giving up the CD.

'I'm not joking—'

'Neither am I—'

'Fuck!'

Too late: the car has drifted off the road. We're in soft dirt on the verge, heading straight for the pale trunk of a massive tree. Jude reefs the wheel. For a few seconds we're back on the tarmac, but he's over-corrected. He spins the wheel the opposite way, and the car fishtails all over the road.

'It's okay, it's okay, it's okay.'

I've dropped the CD. I've got one hand on the dash and the other on the car door, bracing myself. For the first time since I woke up, I've got nothing to say.

We're sliding sideways down the middle of the highway, in the middle of nowhere, in the middle of the night. Jude rides the brake. Tyres squeal, burn. And then they grab on the road and the world turns upside down. End over end. Glass shatters, metal twists, the car jolts so hard I scream. Dirt flies in through the window. We keep tumbling. Something smacks into the back of my head. An explosion of white across my vision. The car is crumpling around us. My legs aren't where they should be. Something breaks . . . Something else lets go.

And then everything stops. The engine, my screaming. My head swims from a stabbing pain and petrol fumes. I'm upside down, hanging from my seatbelt. Blood rushes to my head . . . rushes *down* my head, drips in my eyes. I can't feel my legs.

'Jude . . .' My chest is in a vice. I can't get his name out clearly. 'Jude . . .?'

I turn my neck enough to see him hanging there beside me. He's so still, and there's so much blood . . . I check to see if he's breathing, reach out for him. But there's a guidepost through the window, in the way. And it's only then I realise the guidepost is where his head should be.

SAY IT OUT LOUD

I wake up screaming.

'Calm down. Calm DOWN!' Strong hands pin me. I thrash against them, relieved I can still move. And then all at once I know where I am: on an uncomfortable bed in Dubai – not lying broken and bleeding on the side of the road in Australia. Rafa is leaning over me, one knee on the bunk, gripping my arms.

'What the fuck?'

'I'm okay.' I go still beneath him, let out my breath. Try to slow my pulse. 'I'm fine.'

He eases the pressure but doesn't let go of me. 'What the hell was that?'

I close my eyes. 'Nightmare.'

'The nightclub?'

I turn my head to the side so I don't have to look at him. 'The crash.' The words come out thick.

'It wasn't real,' he says. When I don't respond, he leans closer. 'Gaby.' He waits until I face him. 'It didn't happen.'

'I know, but . . .' Tears spill down my cheeks and my throat is swollen. 'It feels so real.'

He sits on the mattress, not taking his eyes from me. 'We're going to find him.'

I bite my lip and turn away again.

'What? What are you so scared of?'

I stare at the scuffed wall. If I look at him, I won't be able to get the words out. And I have to. It's time. I need him to understand.

'What if . . .' I swallow. 'What if he remembers who he is? What if he doesn't want to be found? Or what if he wants Gabe, not me?' As soon as the words are out I feel exposed, hollow.

'Gaby.' His fingers lift to my face, hesitate, and then push a strand of hair out of my eyes. 'How could he not want you?'

'I'm not Gabe.'

'It won't matter, trust me.'

My eyes burn.

'Is this why you've been stalling? Why didn't you say something? Gaby, look at me.'

I wet my lips, force myself to face him.

Rafa is more serious than I've ever seen him. Whatever was in his eyes when we were sparring has gone.

'We're going to deal with this mess in LA and then we're going to get him. I don't care what it takes or who we have to go through. Or how much it scares you.'

'But what if we can't find him?'

His breath is warm against my skin. 'If he's alive, we'll find him.'

'How can you be so sure?' I badly want to believe him, but this is Rafa. The guy who's all action and no plan.

His smile is tired, knowing. An echo of a shared past I don't remember. 'Because I'm not smart enough to give up, and you don't know how to.'

We watch each other, and it's like that moment on Patmos when he found me clutching a photo of Jude, completely undone. The moment I understood my life was a lie and the brother I knew never existed – at least not the way I remembered him. And, just as he was then, Rafa is gentle, thoughtful. I never see this side of him any other time. Only when I'm at my lowest, when I'm the least like the Gabe he remembers. Maybe that's the only time he's willing to drop his guard. Right now I wish he'd drop it a little further and hold me.

Rafa digs into his duffel bag and offers me a towel. I touch my cheeks. They're hot, tear-streaked. I sit up and wipe my face.

'What if Jude remembers you and not me?' Rafa says. 'You ever think of that?'

I blink. I hadn't. I move my legs so we're side by side on the edge of the bed. I half-expect him to make room, but he doesn't and I don't mind. Our shoulders and knees touch. I'm not thinking about Patmos now. I'm thinking about the sand on his back earlier today.

'Were you and Jude always best mates?' I ask. 'From the start?'

He takes the towel from me, tosses it over the bag. 'I don't remember not knowing him. Or you. We were about six the first time we all got into trouble together.' His lips curve. 'Brother Roberto – long gone now – always made these sweet ladies' kisses—'

'Ladies' what?'

'Kisses. Biscuits made from hazelnut meal with chocolate cream in the middle. Brother Roberto called them *biscotti crèma* and we'd tease him until he called them by their real name. Blushed every time.' He gives a small smile at the memory. 'Anyway, you were obsessed with them. Talked Jude and me into sneaking into the kitchen with you.'

I raise my eyebrows at him. 'I talked you and Jude into it?'

'Yeah – you were always the instigator.' He bumps his shoulder against mine, gently. I find myself smiling.

'Naturally, Brother Roberto caught us and gave us a lecture about stealing. Dragged the three of us by our shirts to Nathaniel.'

'And what did he do?' This is the first time I've heard a story about my childhood: about Jude, Rafa and me running around together as kids. It's strange – and comforting.

'Nathaniel turned it into a lesson: made us practise moving about quietly, undetected. For about six hours.'

'Seriously?'

'No time to waste when you're building an army.' Is it sarcasm or bitterness I hear in his voice? Rafa stands up and pulls me to my feet. 'Let's get out of here for a while.'

'Where?'

'I know a decent coffee house down by the Creek.'

We face each other, standing close. He hesitates for a moment. Then his fingertips brush my elbows, guiding me closer to him for the shift. He holds me carefully.

We arrive in an alley as the call to prayer blares out from a nearby mosque. It reverberates in my chest. After the iciness of the shift, the air here is a warm bath. Rafa laces his fingers through mine and leads me along the promenade under a dark purple sky. The sun is almost gone and a few lights are on in the buildings across the water. Beside us, the Dubai Creek is crowded with dozens of flimsy wooden boats ferrying workers. The drivers shout at each other, jostling for space to dock. I breathe in diesel fumes and garlic.

We find a seat at the coffee house and order thick, strong Arabic coffee. It's poured from a traditional coffee pot into tiny bronze cups, and served with bowls of sweet, fat dates and Turkish delight. The first mouthful of sugary dessert brings a vivid memory: of Jude and me in Istanbul, eating so much one afternoon we had to go back to the hostel to sleep it off. Again –it never happened. Right now, I'd kill for something real, something that's mine – that I understand. I thought all this would get easier. I was wrong.

'Anything else I need to know about?' Rafa dusts icing sugar from his fingers.

I watch him over the rim of my cup as I take a sip. It's strong, earthy. Exactly how I want it.

'Like what?'

'Like anything Mya might have said to you.'

Did Ez tell him? No. He knows Mya well enough to know she wouldn't have been able to stay away from me. I glance around the coffee house. Men in crisp white robes are seated at the table next to us, red-chequered head-cloths held in place with twisted black rope. They pay no attention to us. They couldn't care less what Mya said to me. I take a deep breath.

'She wanted to tell me her theory about what happened between you and me before you guys left the Sanctuary.'

There's the smallest twitch in Rafa's jaw. He doesn't speak, so I push on. I wish I hadn't eaten that Turkish delight. The sweetness is cloying now.

'She said I tried to hook up with you and you weren't interested. That's what we fought about: that I didn't take rejection well.' I try to smile as if I'm in on the joke.

Rafa still doesn't say anything and I can't read him.

'Is it true?'

'No.'

'That's it? That's all you have.'

'That's all we've got time for.'

Anger flares. After feeling off-balance for the past few hours, I can't help but embrace it. 'Make time.'

'What, you believe her?'

'Well, you won't tell me what happened between us so what am I supposed to think?'

He rolls his shoulders. 'Can you at least wait until we find out if Jude's alive?'

'No.'

An impatient sigh. He shifts position. 'You know that nothing in our world is simple, right?'

I wait.

'What went down between you and me, it's more than a five-minute conversation. I'm not going to attempt it now, not when we need to focus on what's going to happen in LA.'

He fidgets with his spoon. He's uncomfortable. Good.

'Let's get this job sorted first,' he says.

I put my cup down. 'Do you know how hard it is when everyone else knows more about my past than I do? I had to listen to Mya telling me I humiliated myself with you, and I couldn't defend myself because I don't remember what I did.'

'Gaby . . .' Rafa runs his tongue over his lips. Takes a breath. 'You didn't humiliate yourself. In any way.' He checks I understand what he's saying.

I do. He's saying I didn't throw myself at him. I sit back in my chair, let his words settle around me. Relief seeps through my anger, softens the edges.

Rafa's phone rings. He's not happy when he sees who it is. 'What now?' he says by way of greeting. He listens. 'Perfect – the job's gone to shit before we even get there.' A glance at me. 'We'll be there in a minute.'

'What's happening?'

'We're going in early. Mya's briefing the others now.' He finishes his coffee. 'We need to go.'

Back in the alley, I don't go to him immediately. I should be thinking about LA, but I'm still stuck on our conversation. Rafa says I didn't humiliate myself, but I'm not sure I can believe him. I hope he doesn't think this is over.

'Ready?' He waits for a beat and then closes the space

between us. One arm slips around my waist, the other around my shoulders. 'I'm sorry about the training session,' he says into my hair.

For a second I think he's going to say something else. But then he draws me closer. I sigh, trace his lean muscles through his t-shirt. We stand there longer than we need to. And then Rafa tightens his grip and the ground drops from beneath us.

TIMING IS EVERYTHING

Everyone is in the training room, huddled around Mya. Voices raised.

'About time,' she says when she sees us. I avoid her eye and we join the throng near Ez and Zak and the discussion resumes.

'How many on the streets?'

'A couple of hundred as of ten minutes ago, but the word's out so it will get worse, fast.'

'Armed?'

'Yes.'

'Cops?'

'Arriving as we speak and the riot squad's on the way.'

A pause as everyone takes in that piece of news.

'What happened?' Rafa asks Jones, not Mya.

'Kids,' Jones says. 'Wrong place, wrong time. They got caught in a shoot-out twenty minutes ago. Three are dead. The retaliation was brutal and now it's an all-out war a couple of blocks from our target.'

Rafa catches Mya's eye. 'A street war nearby? You think that's a coincidence?'

'No,' she snaps, 'but it doesn't change the fact we've got a job to do. It means we can't wait until the shift changes. We need to get in now and clean it out before the whole neighbourhood explodes.'

I look from one to the other. So now it's not only child predators and demons we've got to deal with, it's also armed gangs.

Tremendous.

'You sure those kids are still there?' Rafa asks.

'Yes.'

'Confirmed?'

Mya gives him an impatient look. 'Jess called five minutes ago.'

'Does this change the plan?'

'Morning, afternoon – what's the difference? At least now there's a distraction to keep the cops out of our way. Look, I'll go in on my own if I have to,' she says.

Rafa's laugh is harsh. 'Don't be such a martyr. We're all going. But let's not pretend this is anything other than an ambush, okay?'

'Then keep your eyes open.' Mya looks around the group. 'Be ready in five.'

Ez taps my arm. 'We need to change.'

We're shifting as soon as I nod . . . and then we're back at our bunks. Shit. This is really happening. I rifle through my bag for combat clothes. I've pulled off the vest and am standing in my bra and jeans when Rafa and Zak arrive. Zak pretends not to notice I'm half-dressed, but Rafa looks me over. Slowly. I pull on a black t-shirt and by the time I'm covered, he's helping with the weapons.

I tie a hoodie around my waist. 'What am I taking?' I ask Ez. She's wearing regulation Rephaite black jeans and t-shirt, her knives already strapped to her arms.

'This.' She tosses me Jude's training katana. I catch it, easier now. 'And this.' A short dagger in a leather pouch.

I look from the weapon to my body. 'Where am I supposed to put that?'

'Here.' Rafa steps closer and slides the pouch inside the top of my jeans, against my hipbone. The hilt sits up under my t-shirt. We're so close I smell lingering sweetness on his breath. He repositions the knife inside my jeans, the backs of his fingers brushing against my skin.

'Isn't that a little dangerous?' I say, ignoring the heat radiating out from his touch.

'But very handy for in-close fighting.' He strokes my hip one last time.

Ez picks up a katana, spins it by the hilt. 'You two ready, then?'

We shift back to the training room. I step away from Rafa as soon as I've got my legs back. I need to concentrate.

It looks as though everyone's here, armed with knives, swords and a couple of poleaxes. But how effective is all this steel going to be against guns?

Mya has the map out again on the floor.

'Rafa, Ez, Zak, Jones and Gabe – you're with me. We'll go in through the back and downstairs to the kids. You lot' – she points to a cluster of ten Outcasts including the tall blond, Seth – 'cover the streets front and behind, keep anyone from coming in. Everyone else, stay close to the main entrance and be ready to come in on my signal. If all goes to plan, we'll be in and out of the basement before they know what's hit them. No shifting unless absolutely critical.' She's all business now, focused.

'Where's Jess going to be?' Ez asks.

'She's in the club. She'll come downstairs to lead the kids out when she hears from me.' Mya rolls up the map, tosses it behind her, adjusts the sword strapped to her back. Her eyes are bright, fierce. She looks at me. 'Are you ready for this?'

No. But it's a bit late to say it.

She fidgets one last time with her sword hilt. 'Let's go and show how valuable this pack of bastards can be.'

FIRE IN THE BELLY

We arrive behind bars. Beyond them is an empty street and vacant car park. The morning sky is cloudless, hazy. I turn around, confused, and then work it out: the bars form a wrought-iron fence around the back entrance to the club. Cameras perch on top, angled at the street, red lights blinking. We've arrived behind them at the rear door, undetected.

The haze isn't just LA smog – it's smoke. Traffic hums a few blocks away. Nearer is sporadic gunfire, breaking glass. The riot has moved closer already. My hand is slick with sweat, making it hard to grip my katana.

The door into the club is huge: heavy timber with steel bracing, made to withstand a mediaeval siege. It's unlocked. As soon as Mya cracks the door a fraction, a low bass note spills out . . . *doof* . . . *doof* . . . *doof*. We mute our phones, and Ez sends a quick message to the Rephaim covering the other entrances. Mya creeps inside, sword first. Jones is behind her, then Zak, Ez, me and finally Rafa.

I step into the dark corridor, and freeze. I've been here before: almost every night in my dreams until a week ago. Except in my dream the stench of sweat, cheap aftershave and cigar smoke wasn't this foul. The scratched wall panelling is here; so is the faded orange carpet covered in cigarette burns and stains that could be beer or blood or other bodily fluids I don't want to think about. At the end of the corridor is the door to the nightclub. The one Rafa kicked in before we threw ourselves into the fray. Except it wasn't me with Rafa, it was Jude – but I've had the memory of it stuck in a loop in my brain for a year. Mutilated bodies splayed around the club, torn apart by hellions. The smell of death and blood. For a week I've known it wasn't a dream. Now I feel it.

My head spins. I think I'm going to throw up. Men and women died in that room. *Horribly.* The music is so loud it vibrates in my chest, even with the door closed. I shouldn't be here. I'm not equipped to be here.

'Keep moving,' Rafa says. The others have disappeared. He guides me towards concrete steps and we make our way down, hugging the cinderblock wall.

The music from the basement is faster, just as

monotonous. There's a scuffle somewhere below us. A thud. We round the corner in the stairwell. Zak stands over a body on the floor – human, as far as I can tell from this angle. Mya is pulling a keypad apart near the door and Jones holds a surveillance camera in one hand. Wires hang from the wall above his head. Hopefully he was quick enough to disconnect it before anyone saw him.

There's not much light down here; a dull fluorescent tube bolted to the ceiling. I peer at the guy sprawled on the concrete. He's big. Samoan, maybe, wearing a suit and tie like he's the maitre d' of the kind of restaurant I can never afford to eat at. Only someone Zak's size and with his inhuman speed would be able to take him down without a bullet. Blood is trickling from the side of his head. He was hit with something hard: a sword hilt or maybe Zak's fist.

Zak catches me staring. He bends down, puts two fingers against the man's neck and nods at me, which I take to mean the guy is alive. Then he grabs the back of his jacket and drags him under the stairs, out of sight.

Zak clips the guy's phone to his own belt and relieves him of his handgun. 'Happy?' he mouths.

I give him a tight smile.

Mya uses a small pair of pliers on the keypad wiring. There's a click, and a tiny light on the panel flicks from red to green. She sends a message on her phone and we wait under the stairs out of sight.

Less than a minute later, footsteps descend. Bright red stilettos click past our faces. Mya steps out into view, eyes the woman up and down. 'Classy.'

The blonde woman – Jess, I presume – is wearing the world's tiniest nurse's uniform, complete with hat and stethoscope. She's busting out of it in all the right places.

She nods a greeting to the others. Familiar, but wary. I'd still like to know how an undercover LA cop knows the Rephaim.

'Where do you keep your badge?' Rafa asks, deadpan.

Jess slips a hand into a lacy red bra and produces her police ID.

'Impressive.'

I don't know if he means her outfit or the fact she could fit anything else in that bra.

'Where's your back-up?' Zak asks.

'You're it,' Jess says. 'I'm solo until I've got something to report.' She looks at me. Waits.

'This is Gabe,' Ez says when nobody else speaks. I nod hello, feel the pressure of the knife against my hip, the weirdness of all of us crammed into this small space, a sickness in my stomach. Jess stares at me for a long moment before nodding in return.

Mya clicks her fingers. 'Let's do this.' She catches Jess's attention. 'Will you be all right out here?'

Jess nods. 'Just get those kids. You remember what I told

you about the layout and what's in there?'

'Every word.'

Rafa opens the door into the basement. Soft red light and pulsing music spill out into the stairwell. He looks inside, gives the all-clear. We creep forward.

The basement is sectioned off with red curtains, like a garish hospital emergency ward. The air is thick with pine freshener, cigarette smoke and a smell I don't want to name.

Using her blade, Mya lifts back the first curtain. Beyond it is a double bed covered in satin sheets and children's toys. Rafa checks the curtain on the other side. It's empty like the first, though the bed is stripped, the linen crumpled on the floor. There's a break in the music. It lasts only a second, but it's enough to hear a child whimper.

My stomach twists.

Children are bought and sold here. Hurt here. These empty beds are bad enough. I don't want to pull back one of these curtains and see—

Too late.

Mya has found a pale middle-aged man sitting on the edge of a bed holding a stuffed white rabbit. He flinches when he sees us. He mouths something but we can't hear him. The throbbing bass is too loud. My heart hammers in time with it.

Mya is on him, quick and silent. She slams him back

on the bed, one hand around his throat and the other covering his mouth. He thrashes with surprising strength. She lets go long enough to drive a fist into his stomach. I force myself to look around. There's nobody in here with him. I'm so relieved I almost weep.

Mya rolls the man onto his stomach and puts him in a headlock, cuts off his air supply. The others move on. I stay. He goes limp and the white rabbit finally escapes his clutches. Mya drops his head onto the bed and looks up at me, wipes the guy's spit off her arm with disgust. She reaches under the bed and pulls out a length of rope. I help her tie him up. Under the bed again, she finds duct tape, which I roughly plaster over his mouth. Mya uses the tip of her katana to make a small hole for him to breathe through.

I taste bile. We move on.

Rafa and Jones have found two more men. One in his twenties, the other older. Both freshly worked over. The younger one's right eye is already closing up. Rafa's knuckles are red. Jones wipes blood from his hand on the curtain and takes the duct tape I offer.

In the next cubicle, Ez is sitting on her heels in front of a young boy. He can't be more than seven or eight, all bony limbs and pale skin. He's wearing shorts and a Spider-Man t-shirt, both two sizes too big. Thick black hair hangs down over his face; his huge brown eyes are vacant.

Something hot and violent rips through me. Blood pulses in my temples, faster now than the drums pounding in the music.

Ez is trying to get the boy's attention, but he's too far away. Drugged, or catatonic with fear. She smoothes his hair and brushes the back of her fingers against his cheek. The boy closes his eyes, slowly. When she looks up at me I recognise what I see in her face: outrage.

Rafa slips between the curtains, glances at the boy. The muscle in his jaw twitches. Twice.

Mya points to the stairwell where Jess is waiting and Ez scoops up the boy, heads in that direction. The plan is to get the kids upstairs to the portico and wait for our signal. We keep going, checking each cubicle until we reach Zak and Jones. They've found a door behind a curtain of beads. There's no camera in sight: nobody wants to be filmed in this cesspit.

Rafa takes up a position on one side of the door and locks eyes with me. I take the other side and we part the beads. I steady my breathing, brace for whatever might be in the next room. Zak slams the sole of his boot into the door and it flies inwards, smashed off its hinges. Rafa follows its trajectory. I'm right behind him.

Three men scramble backwards, reaching for handguns. The door hits the table they were just sitting at, smashing glasses and sending the whole thing skittering across the tiled floor. A thin girl in a floral dress cringes in the corner, her hands covering her head.

I charge in, register the men are human. Am I capable of killing them? The guy closest to me has chambered a bullet and is about to fire. I need to decide. Now.

He points the gun at my face.

I duck as he fires. It's deafening. I change my grip on the sword and slam the hilt into the side of his head before he can recover from the recoil. A sickening sound. He crumples to the floor. I kick the gun back towards the door, where Mya scoops it up.

Rafa took down the other two before either could get off a shot. One of them has lost a hand: no doubt the one pointing a gun at him. There's a lot of blood and screaming.

I lead the way down a narrow corridor, tracking other terrified voices. There's a door halfway along, locked. I kick it once, twice. It flies open and the screams intensify. It's a bathroom. There must be twenty children huddled on the tiles, crying. Boys and girls. Pale. Underfed.

I block the doorway protectively, forcing Rafa to look over my shoulder

'Get them out,' he says in my ear.

Thumping music comes from above us now as well. I hope it's loud enough to drown out the screams. And the gunshot.

Mya is covering the door we came through. The girl in

the floral dress leans against her now, her face pressed into Mya's shirt.

'Come on.' I gesture wildly for the kids in the bathroom to leave.

Nobody moves. Twenty pairs of eyes are locked on my sword.

'Now!'

They flinch. I hate yelling at them but this is taking too long. I move my sword behind me. 'Come ON!'

A girl with a tear-stained face jumps up. I step out of the way so she can get through. She runs to Mya. One, then another, run past me. And then the rest bolt as a group, jostling and crying.

I take a shaky breath, move on to the next door, yank it open. No kids this time – a staircase and a wall of pounding music. The club's up there. Zak joins me, filling the doorway. His size is reassuring.

Rafa checks the other rooms while Jones fleeces the injured guards. He stomps mobile phones and strips ammunition clips from their guns. The four of us gather at the foot of the steps. Mya materialises a few metres away. Ez must be with Jess and the kids now, upstairs, waiting for the all-clear. As soon as they step outside the portico cage onto the street, they'll be on camera, and we need the place empty of Immundi by the time that happens – before Jess calls for back-up.

'What?' Mya has to shout to be heard over the music.

'No Immundi down here,' Rafa says.

She points to the room above us.

She can't be serious.

The camera outside the basement door has been down for at least five minutes. Where's the security? This isn't right. Even I can tell this is a trap and I've never done this before. We should go. Get the kids to safety.

Mya watches me, waiting for a reaction. Of course she knows it's a trap; they all do. She just wants me to be complicit in the decision to go upstairs. I check Rafa. He's ready. This is what the Outcasts do, right? Hunt demons? And it's clear they're not leaving here if there's a chance Immundi are upstairs. I tighten my grip on my sword. What did Rafa tell me before we went for Maggie? *When it's happening, don't think. Just go with your instincts.* Right now, my instincts are telling me to get the hell out of here. But I can't back out – I won't give Mya the satisfaction. So I nod, and she messages the others.

We climb the stairs two at a time, swords pressed flat against our legs; Rafa in the lead, me right behind him. I can do this. I've killed a hellion, fought a Gatekeeper, been in a brawl at the Imperial . . .

But that was then. This is different: this is me *looking* for trouble.

The music up here is deafening. It's too loud – as if

someone's trying to hide the noise of the riot up the street. The carpet comes into view along with a forest of chairs and table legs. The place stinks of booze and nicotine. Rafa holds up a hand and we wait for his signal. A yellow light flashes over his face. I have another wave of déjà vu. I grab the handrail to steady myself.

Rafa clears the stairs first, nods for us to follow. We're at the back of the club. A dozen men sit around the dance platform, ties loose and shirts untucked, watching a redhead in stilettos and lacy underwear. She's wearing a police hat and has fake police badges placed strategically on her breasts. Right now she's hanging upside down on the pole, her free leg stretched back over her head until it almost touches the platform.

The man behind the bar whistles sharply over his shoulder when he sees us.

We spread out to cover the room. Two guys in expensive suits emerge from a door at the far end of the bar and take up positions near the stripper. They're short and wiry. Their heads are too big for their bodies. They remind me of monkeys . . . except there's nothing playful about them.

'Get those idiots out of here,' Rafa shouts at me over the noise.

I think he means the new arrivals, but then one of them sneers and I realise my mistake. It's not just that his eyes are black: his teeth are pointed and, when he gestures at me, his black lacquered nails are way too long.

Immundi.

How could anyone mistake them for anything other than demons? I know there are some freaky people up the road at Venice Beach. But still.

The Immundi are the same height and build as each other, with the same round faces. One has jet-black hair, the other platinum. Their forearms flick out in an oddly synchronised movement. Straight blades, about half the length of a katana, slide out from their shirtsleeves as they move towards me.

Someone kills the seedy soundtrack. The silence is louder than the music. The demons stop sharply; the dancer – about to take off one of her fake badges – turns herself the right way up and peers at the back of the room. 'Turn that back on!'

Jones is behind a bank of equipment, power lead in one hand. 'There's a riot outside.' His voice comes out too loud in the quiet room. 'You might want to get out of here.'

The lights keep flashing and spinning.

'That's bullshit.' One of the punters stands up, clutching the notes he's been saving for the redhead. His suit is crushed, eyes cloudy. He takes three steps and freezes when there's a burst of gunfire outside. He stumbles back to his seat, downs the dregs in his glass and snatches up the rest of his cash.

An explosion rocks the building.

The two Immundi charge.

Rafa takes them both on. More appear from the doorway, all armed with blades or knives. The dancer screams.

Don't think.

I forget about getting the men out and run at the new arrivals, striking at the first demon I reach. He blocks and I spin away before he can counterattack. More Immundi in black suits stream past. I lunge at the first one again, and again the bobble-headed demon blocks me, crossing the short blades in front of his face. He grins, his mouth full of razor-sharp teeth. I kick him hard between his legs. He grunts, drops to his knees. Good to know that works on demons too. His neck is exposed.

I draw back the katana, tighten my grip. I hesitate. These things almost look human.

But those teeth and claws. And those kids . . .

I bring the sword down. Hard.

Zak, Jones and Mya are all busy with Immundi now. We're outnumbered three to one. And then a dozen more Outcasts are there, leaping into the fray.

The patrons are on their feet, knocking over stools and crashing into tables.

'The back door!' the barman shouts and runs in that direction himself.

The back door. Where Jess and Ez are waiting with

the kids. They'll get trampled. Another round of gunfire outside.

'Rafa!' I race to get ahead of the scrambling men. 'Jess and Ez are out there.'

Mya kicks an Immundi in the chest and runs towards me. 'Go! Go!' She shifts before she finishes yelling.

The fleeing men are panicked, fighting each other as they run. I race ahead down a corridor. Slam a door shut behind me and shove boxes in the way. Not enough of an obstacle to trap them – I need to slow them down until we can get the kids out of the portico.

I burst out of the back door and Ez immediately shuts it behind me. It's complete chaos out here: kids crying and banging on the bars; Jess trying to calm them, carrying the boy we found in the cubicle. His legs are wrapped around her hips, head on her shoulder. Mya is trying to get the gate open. She's ripped the cover from the electronic pad and is pulling out wires, her eyes constantly flicking from Jess to the back door. More gunshots up the road – closer now – followed by shouts and distant sirens. A building is on fire half a block down. The street is choked with smoke. My nostrils burn with it. A neon sign buzzes, then disappears as the smoke drifts closer.

I find a path through the kids, hold my katana over my head out of harm's way. I grip the gate, ready to push it open as soon as Mya gets it unlocked. How far away are the rioters? I press my face against the metal bars. A movement on the street catches my eye. Neon and flames swim in my eyes.

'Well, *this* is an added bonus.' The voice is deep and smoky, and I have to hang on to the gate to stop my legs giving out from beneath me.

NASTY SURPRISE

Oh shit, oh shit.

Bel.

Blood and all the noise of the street and the kids roars in my ears.

The pale demon is standing in the middle of the road, a broadsword at his waist. I vaguely register that he's recovered from the blade Nathaniel buried in his shoulder earlier in the week on the mountain. He looks taller in daylight, his fine features and white hair more startling. His irises are still on fire. My fingers tighten on the bars.

Behind me, the men from the club hit the back door. I hear it open, then sounds of fighting.

More screaming. The kids have seen Bel. Seen his blazing eyes. His sword. He stands there on the street, soaking up the fear and panic roiling behind the gates.

I risk a look over my shoulder. Ez is holding off the men, kicking and punching them back into the corridor, using everything but her sword to slow them down; they're a problem we don't need, but they're still human. She doesn't know we've got a bigger problem outside the gates.

The kids are swarming, frantic, caught between the fighting men and the monster behind the gate. I catch a glimpse of a floral dress and then it's gone, lost in the crush.

Something clicks in the metal under my hands. I freeze.

'Open it!' Mya shouts.

'We've got company.'

Mya straightens, sees Bel. 'Jess, call for back-up.'

Jess's eyes skitter to the white-haired demon. 'I can't! You're not done inside yet!'

'I don't care. We're getting these kids out.'

'But—'

'DO IT!'

Jess pulls a slimline phone from inside her nurse's uniform, taps in the number. Bel strolls back and forth in front of us, his eyes flitting from Mya to me and back again. The children cower away from the bars now, crying.

'I knew you would not be able to stay away from here,' Bel says to Mya. 'All that guilt. All that regret. But you, Gabriella, you are a most delicious surprise. Are you still trying to work out which side you want to die on? Let me give you a tip: Nathaniel will not be turning up to save you this time. Not at this place of the damned.'

Scuffling continues behind us. 'Hey!' Ez shouts. 'Either open that gate or give me a—' She doesn't finish the sentence and I'm not game to take my eyes off Bel again to find out why.

'Bring the bus,' Jess shouts into her phone. 'And bring back-up – uugh!' She slams into me as the men from the club crash into her. Ez isn't holding them back any more. Mya and I lock eyes. We have to open the gates. It's not as if they're keeping Bel out.

'Go on, let the little ones run,' Bel says. 'More Immundi are coming. It will give them something to do when they see their pets fleeing.'

Bodies press against me. I react without thinking. I punch two men and use my knee to push a third away. They stink of bourbon. Mya lays a hand on the gate, looks at me. She's waiting for me to make the call.

Is this more complicity or is she unsure? Right now it doesn't matter – there's no choice.

'Open it.'

Mya turns the handle. As soon as the latch gives, we're pushed onto the street by the crush of men. I clear a path for the kids. They stream out from the portico, all of them instinctively veering away from Bel, which means they run towards the riot. Jess goes with them, her red stilettos the only colour in the grey street. Ez has gone back inside.

Mya glances from Jess and the kids to Bel and me.

Oh shit, don't leave me here with him. Surely nothing I've done to her warrants being thrown to a demon. I can't do this on my own.

She reaches for something behind her, moving backwards. Bel draws the heavy sword from his belt. I grip my katana, my fingers numb.

Two loud pops echo in the street. I flinch with each one.

Mya has fired two rounds into Bel's forehead. He staggers, surprise registering on his angular face. Blood dribbles from the two neat holes. She fires twice more, one in each bicep. He flinches and drops his sword.

'Might slow him down till the cavalry arrives,' Mya says, and then takes off into the smoke.

It's the only break I'm going to get.

I run at Bel, swinging at his long neck. He ducks, then I see a flash of metal coming for my face. I only just manage to block him. He grunts at the impact of steel on steel, his face covered in bright red blood. There's more seeping through his coat sleeves.

He swings again. Quick, brutal – I deflect it. He's driving me towards the fence, backwards. There's a gutter here somewhere. I step carefully, block another strike at my neck. The next step is shorter. I'm over the gutter – more luck than skill. There's a burst of noise behind me in the portico. It sounds like a stampede out of the club. I can't risk looking but Bel is grinning with bloodstained teeth. It's not good news.

I back into the fence. There's nowhere left to go.

Bel takes his sword in both hands, rains down blow after blow until the katana jars from my hand and clatters to the ground. Before I can duck, his bony body is pressed against mine, pinning me against the metal bars. The flat side of his heavy blade is pressed against my throat. It's strangely warm.

He has to lean down to keep his weight against me. There's so much blood on him. How much can he have left? But his irises are still blazing.

'I suspected you could no longer shift.' Bel's breath is hot on my face. I smell sulphur and decay. 'I am so pleased to find it is true. It will make hurting you much more satisfying. You will tell us the truth about what you and your brother did, no matter how long it takes.' He strokes the blade against my throat. 'And this time when I end you, you will not come back.'

The road blurs. I bite the inside of my lip. I need to stay conscious, buy myself some time. He can't force me to shift with him unless he knocks me out.

'Foolish to come alone,' I say between breaths.

'Yes, it would have been. So I did not.'

My chest tightens. That's why Rafa and the others are still in the club. Fighting Gatekeepers. I really am on my own out here.

Sirens – so close they must be out front now. But they're not coming for me. At best they're coming for the kids. I move my foot. I can feel the edge of the sword, but I can't move. Bel smiles, then kicks it away. What sort of fighter am I? I lose my only wea—

The knife.

It's still there, digging into my hip.

'Who did you bring?' I hold his gaze, keep my movements as small as possible. Knowing I can't shift has made him complacent. I reach under my shirt.

'Some old friends, who will be very happy to—'

I jam the knife between his ribs. There's bile in my throat as I push through muscle and sinew. He stumbles back. 'Pestilence!' He sprays spittle and blood on my face and the fence.

I dive for my katana. I take it cleanly and spring back to my feet, just as he jerks the knife out and throws it, straight and true.

It lands cleanly in the top of my thigh. My bad leg.

The force of it drives me backwards. I stagger, hit the tarmac hard. The blade's gone into my leg up to the hilt, which is still quivering. But it's not hurting. Oh, wait . . . shards of white pain radiate down my leg.

'Ah shit.'

Rafa.

He's kneeling next to me, still out of breath from fighting inside. 'Don't pull it out yet.'

Pull it out? Is he insane?

Rafa looks up at Bel, who has moved back into the middle of the road. 'You're not looking so hot yourself.' He stands up and spins his katana. It's dripping with dark blood.

Bel pokes at the wound in his chest as if it's a science experiment. Rafa moves so fast he must have shifted but, even with that speed, Bel's gone by the time he reaches him.

'Chicken shit.' Rafa comes back to where I'm leaning against the fence. He slides an arm around me.

'I stabbed him first.' I don't want Rafa thinking I just let Bel take my knife and stick it in me.

'I told you it would come in handy. Good job dealing with him on your own.'

He helps me to my feet. I grit my teeth and take my weight on the other leg. 'Mya put four bullets in him first.'

'Also handy.'

Jones comes out of the club. 'The police are inside—' He does a double-take at the knife. 'Everyone else has gone.'

Ez and Zak shut the door behind them. Ez takes one look at me and winces. 'Let's go.'

'We need to make sure Jess got the kids out,' I say.

'I'll go,' Ez says.

'I'm coming too.'

Rafa's fingers dig into my side. 'You've got a knife in your leg.'

I face him. His arm around me is hot, overly hot. I'm on fire. The noise that was all around us moves overhead as well. A chopper. 'Then get it out and—'

Mya sprints around the corner before I finish. Her sword's gone, but she's still carrying the handgun. She pulls up when she reaches us, sees the knife.

'Nice catch.'

'The kids?' I ask.

'On their way to a safe house.'

Thank God. 'Is Jess okay?'

'She twisted her ankle in those stupid heels, but otherwise she's fine.'

A burning tyre rolls through the intersection at the end of the street. Two guys are running behind it, tyre irons in their hands, hoods up.

'The rest are coming.' Mya steps through the gate, out of sight from the street. She taps a message into her phone, glances at me. 'You should get her out of here,' she says to Ez. And then she's gone.

Rafa takes my weight and Ez ducks under my other arm to help half-carry me into the portico. They exchange a look. Ez nods.

'Ready?' Rafa says, but he's not asking me.

Ez leans down, yanks the knife from my leg and clamps her hand over the wound. I scream. Loud enough that the cops inside probably heard it.

They take me into welcome blackness.

LINES BLUR

When I come to, I'm back on the bunk in Dubai. I can't have been out long because the rattling air conditioner hasn't had time to take the warmth from the room. My leg throbs.

'You scream like a girl.' Rafa sits on the bed next to me.

'I am a girl.'

He glances down at my bare legs. 'I've noticed.'

I struggle to sit up. All I'm wearing is a t-shirt, my underwear and a bandage around my thigh. My legs are still scarred from the accident – or whatever happened last year. White, ugly marks across my thighs and knees. I'd cover myself up, but with what? My jeans are on the floor, torn up.

Rafa gestures to my leg. 'Better?'

I tentatively probe the bandage, nod. I still ache all over from the aftermath of adrenaline. 'How come Ez pulled out the knife before we shifted?'

'You can't heal with a blade in the wound.'

Oh. Yeah.

'Where is she now?'

'Mya's doing a post-mortem.'

I look around for water, find a bottle by the bed. It's warm, but I don't care. 'We need to make sure Mya gives us that laptop before she disappears from here,' I say.

'And then we're going to Melbourne?'

I look Rafa in the eye. 'Pan Beach first.' I check my watch. 'We've been gone less than twelve hours. It'll show Taya I kept my word, maybe buy us a bit more time. Maybe even some trust. And then Melbourne.' My pulse still skips at the thought.

Rafa rubs his jaw, sighs. He needs a shave and he's got dark circles under his eyes from the shift.

'What happened in the club?'

Rafa loosens the laces on his boots, slides them off.

'We nearly had those monkey pricks,' he says. 'But then, big surprise, Leon and his buddies turned up. Ez came in around the same time, so we held our own, and then the Immundi worked out the kids were gone and took off.'

That must have been what made Bel so happy when he had me pinned to the fence: the thought that the Immundi would run down the kids and drag them back.

'They ran straight into the riot,' Rafa says.

'Can Immundi shift?'

He smiles without humour. 'No.'

'So, Leon and Bel turning up, it was a trap?'

'Yeah. But at least Bel didn't bring hell-turds this time. Or Zarael. I'm surprised he hasn't shown up after all the crap that's gone down this week.'

I pick at the bandage on my leg. 'Is this what Jude used to do – rescue people from demons?'

The question surprises him. 'Yeah. He was always out to save the world.'

'All the time?'

He sighs. 'All the time.'

'Do you guys succeed very often?'

A tired, crooked smile. 'Most of the time, actually – despite what you'll hear from the Sanctuary.'

There's movement by the door. Ez and Zak are back. Mya is with them.

'Are you still talking to me?' Ez asks. She glances at my leg.

'Yeah, just.' I smile. 'Thanks.'

'My pleasure. But maybe dodge next time.'

Mya steps out from behind Zak. Her eyes are still bright.

'So let's hear it, Gabe.'

'What?'

'Tell me the problem with what we just did.'

I use the top bunk to pull myself to my feet, try not to put too much weight on my injured leg. I should thank her for saving my life, but I need to know she's not backing out of our deal.

'I've got a problem with how you got me here, but not with getting those kids out.' I straighten. She's shorter than me, so it forces her to look up. 'And I did what I said I would, so now it's your turn.'

Her lips twist. 'Can't get away from us quick enough?'

'I said one job. I've done it.'

'What's the big rush?'

I point to the tattered denim on the floor. 'I need another pair of jeans for a start.'

She shakes her head. 'If you really had changed, you'd stay with us.'

My fingers dig into the metal on the bunk. 'Why would I stay? I'm not a professional fighter, Mya, I'm a librarian.'

'Oh, come on, you're still good enough to stick a knife into a Gatekeeper.'

'What makes you think I want to fight demons?'

Her vivid eyes bore into me. 'What else are you going to do?'

'*Not* fight demons. Have a life.'

She scowls. We watch each other for a moment. My leg throbs but I'm not sitting down again while she's here.

'I'll have Jude's laptop now, thanks.'

The room is utterly silent. Mya's nostrils flare, and then she's gone.

I ease myself back onto the bed. 'She's gone to get it, right?'

Ez nods. 'If Mya says she'll do something, she'll do it.'

I can't allow myself to think about what might be on that computer. Not yet. Not until it's in my hands, far away from here.

Ez sits on the bunk opposite mine. 'Did you mean what you said before – about being okay with that job?'

'Of course – how could I not be?'

'Well . . . the Sanctuary calls us money-grubbing mercenaries. You came up with the term.'

I press my toes into the rough concrete floor, watch them turn white. No wonder Daniel misses that other version of me: I sounded exactly like him. I lift my head. 'I don't know about past jobs, but that one needed to happen.'

Ez nods. 'Thank you,' she says simply.

Zak sits on the other end of the bunk from Ez and wipes down his sword. Rafa grabs a cloth and goes to work on mine.

'What was going on in that basement, was it—' I stop, think about what I'm trying to ask. 'All the bad shit that happens in the world – are demons behind it?'

'That would be handy for humanity, wouldn't it?' Ez

crosses her legs on the frayed mattress. 'Humans have been living with evil for so long they don't need much encouragement to do unspeakable things to each other. Humans always have a choice. *Always*. Filth like the Immundi tap into appetites that already exist and then feed off the misery those appetites create.'

'Do the Immundi work for the Gatekeepers?'

'It's looking that way. Zarael must be summoning them from the pit and letting them loose, either to distract us or lure us into a fight. But Bel kept a low profile on this one. Jess had no idea there were other demons involved.'

I take a hairbrush from my duffel bag. I don't have to touch my hair to know it's a mess. 'Jess is human, right? How does she know about demons?'

'She was undercover at the Rhythm Palace the first time around, working on a drug bust. Her team had no idea there were girls downstairs, taken from Eastern Europe. When Bel and Leon set the hellions on the crowd, she hid under a table and saw the whole thing go down. We found her and got her out. She was terrified, but she kept it together, even tried to question Mya. Mya told her if she stayed quiet about what had really happened, we'd come back and give her answers. She kept quiet. We went back.'

'And what did you tell her?'

'Enough about demons to keep her safe. We've done a

few jobs with her since – you'd be surprised how much filth from the pit ends up in LA.'

Something doesn't fit.

'Who foots the bill when you work for a cop?'

'Don't worry, you'll get paid. We always do.'

'But . . . does Jess know what you all are?'

'Of course not.'

I don't understand how Jess could accept that demons exist and not question how the Outcasts know so much about them. She's a detective; she's meant to be suspicious – or at least curious.

'But—'

Mya reappears with a computer bag, and Jess and all my questions vanish. I'm fixated on the worn black leather and Mya's possessive grip on it. My fingers are trembling.

Rafa stands up. 'Let's see it.'

She hesitates and then hands it to him. He unzips it, checks inside.

'What's the catch?'

'No catch.'

He gives her a level look.

Mya's eyes are still on the bag. 'It's password protected.'

'Yours or his?'

Her eyes flare. 'His. And I can't crack it.'

PILLOW TALK

I wake in my own bed, Rafa's arm draped over me. I'm still only half-dressed. The sheet is scrunched up at the end of the bed; I must have kicked it off in my sleep.

My room was dark when we arrived, the house in the empty silence that exists only in the small hours of the morning. The last thing I remember is falling into bed, dead tired, and Rafa sitting on the edge to take his boots off. We agreed to wait until the morning to try the laptop. I reach for it on my bedside table. Still there.

Dawn light filters through the window, casting everything in a warm glow. There's bird noise in the jacaranda outside. My pillow smells like vanilla shampoo with a whisper of sandalwood. For a fleeting moment I feel safe.

I should let Maggie know we're back.

Rafa stirs. His arm shifts to rest along my hip and thigh, his fingers spread out on my bare skin. He mumbles something in my hair.

Another minute won't hurt.

Maggie's alarm goes off. A thump silences it about two seconds later.

'Doesn't anybody sleep-in in this house?' Rafa's voice is husky from sleep.

'Only if we're hungover.'

He plays with the edge of the bandage on my thigh. 'I haven't had a hangover in months.'

'You sound disappointed,' I say over my shoulder.

'I miss the oblivion that comes with getting one.' He yawns, taps his finger on my bare leg. 'So, this morning . . .?'

I roll over, expecting him to make room. He doesn't. We lie facing each other, centimetres apart. His fingertips find my leg again. He's still in his jeans, but he's naked from the waist up. The button on his jeans is undone. And he hasn't shifted . . .

I swallow, focus on the question. 'Jude's laptop. Catch up with Maggie and Jason, find Taya, go to Melbourne.'

Rafa is watching my lips while I talk. When I finish, he lifts his eyes. 'How's the leg now?'

'It still throbs a little.'

He gives my uninjured thigh a squeeze.

'Let me see.' He takes his weight on one elbow, rolls me onto my back. He carefully peels back the bandage. The adhesive tears at my skin enough to make me wince.

'Oh, man up.' Rafa smiles. 'You took a knife a few hours ago.'

I make a face at him, and then see the angry scar on my leg for the first time.

'It would have been tidier with stitches,' he says. 'But it's still better than a gaping wound.' He runs the tip of his finger over it, causing goosebumps to spread across my skin. And then he leans down and brushes his lips over the scar. My fingers slide into his hair.

Footsteps thump down the corridor and my door flies open. I sit up so abruptly I almost knee Rafa in the head. It's Maggie, wearing silk pyjama shorts and an oversized t-shirt tied in a knot at her side.

'You're back—' She takes in the scene on my bed. 'Oh . . . is this a good time?'

'Rafa's checking my leg.'

She gives me a knowing smile and crosses the room. Jason follows her in, pulling on a t-shirt. He's got a shocking case of bed-hair.

'Glad to see you finally made it to the bedroom, Goldilocks,' Rafa says.

Jason ignores him, but Maggie glares at him. 'What happened?' she asks.

Rafa makes no effort to create space on the bed, but she climbs on anyway. Jason shifts books and clothes on my desk and props himself on the edge. When they're settled, I give them a run-down on what happened in LA.

'So . . . Mya helped you?' Maggie asks.

'It's not like she took a bullet for me but, yeah, she did.' And I still didn't thank her.

'Well.'

'I know.'

She checks out the scar on my thigh. 'I wish you'd stop getting hurt.'

Rafa sticks the dressing back down. He runs his thumb and forefinger around the edges.

'How were things here?' I ask, trying not to think about his fingertips. Trying not to think about what might have happened if Maggie had slept in a little longer.

Maggie and Jason glance at each other. Her eyes are shining. 'We found your nurse.'

My heart thumps, hard. Rafa stops stroking my leg.

'Her name's Hannah McKenzie. She still works in intensive care.' Maggie reaches for my hand. 'The guy we spoke to on the phone remembers you – he'd never seen anyone survive a neck wound like yours.'

Rafa's hand strays to my thigh again. Almost protectively.

'But was this Hannah the one who told Gaby about the funeral?'

Maggie nods. 'We think so, and we—'

'Didn't you talk to her?'

'She wasn't working. She's been on holiday. *But*,' she says, before he can interrupt again, 'she's on again tomorrow.'

'Nice work, Margaret.' Rafa gives her an appreciative nod.

'Thank you, Rafael.' She gives a meaningful look in Jason's direction.

Rafa sighs, nods. 'Goldilocks.'

Hope flutters in my ribcage like a startled bird. I can't get ahead of myself. Even if this nurse remembers me, it doesn't mean she can point us to Jude. But it's a start.

'So, you can hang around one more day,' Maggie says to me. 'And Jason will be here when you go, so there's nothing more to worry about.'

That's not quite true, but I nod anyway. I reach for my old jeans on the floor. 'You working today?'

'Yeah, are you?'

'What's today?' I've seriously lost track: too many time zones in too few hours.

'Saturday,' Maggie says.

'I suppose I could do a few hours at the library after I check in with Taya.' I ease the jeans over my bandaged thigh.

'I thought the goth was covering for you,' Rafa says.

'Gaz? He is.'

'Then don't worry about working.'

I rummage through the clean washing on my desk. 'I need to work to live, Rafa. I can't afford to pass up a chance to earn a few dollars.'

He lies back and puts his hands behind his head; his abdominal muscles flex. 'You'll get a cut of the job.'

'I didn't do it for the money.'

Something shifts in his eyes. 'You think there's something wrong with getting paid for what we did?'

'That's not what I'm saying.'

'Then take the money when Mya divides it up.'

I run my fingers through my hair, try to subdue it. Accepting that money could tie me to the Outcasts. Not accepting it will look like I'm making a statement. Is anything simple with these people?

'Fine.' It's not like I don't need the cash.

He pauses. 'Seriously? You'll take money from us?' A slow grin. 'I wish I could be there when Pretty Boy finds out.'

Of course: all he's worried about is Daniel's reaction.

Jason has been following the conversation closely. He seems almost as surprised as Rafa that I've agreed to accept the payment. Maybe on some level, he still expects me to act like the old Gabe too.

'What is it with you and Daniel?' Maggie asks Rafa.

Rafa's grin fades. 'He's a prick, pure and simple.'

'Oh, well, that explains it.' Maggie's eyes track to my bedside table. 'Is that what I think it is?'

'Yeah.' I reach out, touch the laptop again. 'We have to figure out Jude's password before we can see what's on it.'

'Then why are we wasting time talking?' Maggie springs off the bed. 'Get cracking on it.'

'We'll go start breakfast,' Jason says.

By the time Maggie and Jason are in the kitchen, I'm on the edge of the bed and Jude's computer is whirring to life on my lap. His name is already in the first field. The cursor below it blinks, prompting for a password.

Rafa looks over my shoulder. 'Thoughts?'

I open my mouth and then stop. 'Maybe what I think isn't helpful. The guy who put the password on here is your Jude, not mine.' There's that clench in my stomach again.

'Forget all that,' Rafa says. 'Stay focused.' He gets up, his mind working.

'Let's start with weapons.' He names a string of deadly instruments: katana, poleaxe, scimitar, something called a sai. I type each into the password field. None unlock the laptop. Next we try books and authors, then bands – even drummers. Twenty minutes later the cursor is still taunting us.

I think about all those books on his shelves in the

cottage on Patmos. 'What about something more . . . theological?'

Rafa rubs his jaw. 'Try two-Peter-two, four-nine-ten.'

'Is that a bible verse?'

'One of Nathaniel's favourites: "For if God did not spare angels when they sinned, but sent them to hell, putting them into gloomy dungeons to be held for judgment . . . if this is so, then the Lord knows how to rescue godly men from trials and to hold the unrighteous until the day of judgment while continuing their punishment. This is especially true of those who follow the corrupt desire of the sinful nature and despise authority."' Rafa delivers it by rote, deadpan.

I lift my eyebrows.

'Trust me, you know that one too. Raised by a fallen angel, remember?'

'Yeah, but why would Jude—'

'He recited it every time he got drunk. Thought it was ironic.'

'Oh.'

But it's not the password. I straighten the doona with my free hand. The sun through the window throws stripes of light onto the bed.

'Maybe it's all numbers.' Rafa snaps his fingers. 'Co-ordinates. Jude was freakishly good at retaining them.'

'Like longitude and latitude?'

'Yeah. Possibly somewhere he's been. Somewhere important to him.'

'What about Monterosso?' Only Jude and I – and Jason and Nathaniel – know that's where we were born.

Rafa is back on the bed beside me now. He finds the co-ordinates for the Italian village on his phone and I type them in. No go. We try the co-ordinates for the Sanctuary. Still nothing.

'What about Patmos?' I ask. 'You said nobody but you two ever went there.'

'Except you that time.'

Rafa knows those co-ordinates by heart. I type them in and hit enter.

The system starts to load.

My fingers tingle. My head swims in the sunlight. The rawness – the night, the hope, the crumpling metal – all of it tangled up. Neither of us speaks.

The directory appears.

'Ready?' I'm not sure if I'm asking Rafa or myself.

I take a deep breath, click on Documents. I stare at the screen. There's only a single folder in it: Research. I open it and find dozens of files with names like Apocalyptic theory, Eschatology, Demonology and Angelic Garrison hierarchy.

'Shouldn't there be more on here?'

'Keep looking,' Rafa says.

I check Jude's photos. My pulse skips: among the dozens of folders is one with my name on it. Well, Gabe's name. Inside is a single image. It's me – that other me – in a hammock. It must be somewhere warm because I'm in shorts and a vest. There's a tattered novel lying face-down on my stomach and my eyes are closed. I look . . . peaceful.

Rafa is still beside me. 'He had a heap more photos of you than that.'

'I guess he deleted them.' The words are ashes in my mouth.

'Check the emails,' Rafa says.

I open the inbox.

Empty.

Web browser history.

Empty.

I stare at the screen, hollow.

'This makes no sense.' Rafa sounds as off-balance as I feel.

We sit in silence for a long moment. The magpies in my tree warble again. The distant surf rolls into the beach. None of it is comforting now. Sweat gathers at the base of my neck under my hair.

Rafa rests his elbows on his knees, his eyes fixed on the worn timber floorboards. 'Maybe he knew he wasn't coming back when he saw you that last time.'

'You think he knew something bad was going to happen?'

'I don't know.'

'Why didn't he tell you what we were doing?'

A sigh, almost too soft for me to hear. 'That's the million-dollar question, isn't it?'

I click on Jude's web browser bookmarks, expecting more disappointment. But the list isn't empty: there are thirteen sites listed. I check each one. They're all for surf beaches: in Hawaii, South Africa, Indonesia, Peru, Australia.

My breath catches on the last one: Pandanus Beach.

'Was Jude planning a trip?' I ask.

Rafa gets off the bed, grabs his t-shirt from the floor and pulls it on. 'Not that he told me.'

'But he would have, right? If he was going somewhere, he'd tell you?'

Rafa gives me a pointed look and jams his foot into a boot.

Idiot.

Jude kept more than one secret from his best friend. Trust me to grind salt in the wound.

Rafa stands up, straightens his shirt. He stares out the window, but I don't think he's really seeing anything.

'I'll be back.'

And he's gone, shifted, before I can speak.

I stare at the space where he was and then flop back onto the bed. My eyes track to a tuft of cobweb suspended from the ceiling.

I don't get it. Any of it.

Jude wiped out all clues of what he was thinking a year ago except for generic information on a handful of the world's best surf beaches – and he put a password on the laptop only Rafa would figure out. But he didn't tell Rafa about it.

What the hell does any of it mean?

THE FALLOUT

I grab a lift when Jason takes Maggie to the Green Bean. I need to think about something other than what's not on Jude's laptop, and the look on Rafa's face when he disappeared.

The esplanade is humming. It's always noisier on Saturday, with the roving calypso band, traffic and fishmongers shouting their specials. The breeze is light today, the surf calmer. A few wispy clouds are stretched thin along the horizon, far out at sea.

I'm going to Rick's in the hope I can talk to Taya without it ending in an argument – or worse.

Simon and Rick live above the bar on a floor that was once guest rooms: back before the resorts and backpacker lodges sprouted up and down the coastline. I climb the back stairs, catch a whiff of stale alcohol. Why is it bars and pubs always smell so much worse in daylight?

I find the dark green door on the second-storey landing, pause, ring the buzzer. A few seconds later Rick is in the doorway, holding a set of keys. The sound of an acoustic guitar drifts out from the apartment.

'Gaby,' he says. 'Enjoy the fun last night?' He's sporting a fat lip. I pretend not to notice.

'Not particularly. How's Simon?'

'Check for yourself.' He gestures behind him, but I can't see past an ornate bamboo screen shielding the rest of the apartment.

'Actually I'm looking for Taya.'

He leans against the doorjamb. 'She's a firecracker, isn't she?'

I manage a tight smile. 'Something like that.'

'You're a bit of a dark horse yourself. You've got some interesting friends.'

'I wouldn't call them friends.' I crack a knuckle and then stop myself. That's one habit I don't need. 'Was there much damage?'

'Enough.'

'I'm sorry.' Someone has to say it.

'I was down there till three this morning, cleaning up. I'm still not done.' He glances at his watch. 'How about you take your mates to the Imperial next time?' He moves past me, not expecting a response, and takes the stairs two at a time.

I scratch at the bandage under my jeans. I'm grateful the wound is healing so quickly, but I could do without the constant itching. The music in the apartment stops. Another song starts. I can't stand out here all day.

Beyond the screen is an airy room: the walls are covered with old posters of retro martial arts films, and sliding glass doors open onto a narrow balcony overlooking the esplanade. The place smells of raisin toast and the sea.

Taya is sitting on the arm of a worn red leather sofa, checking Simon's stitches. He's trying not to look at her breasts while she leans over him. Her black hair is tied loosely at the nape of her neck and hangs over her shoulder. It takes them both a second to notice I'm in the room and, when they do, it's like I've walked in on them undressing each other. Simon jerks away from Taya, and Taya *blushes*.

'I guess Mya's job went bad even quicker than usual,' she says. Is that a hint of relief I hear in her voice? Clearly she wasn't expecting me to come back.

She swings her legs off the sofa and stands up. Her black eye looks way worse than last night, the lid half-closed.

'Why haven't you had that healed?'

Taya gives me a withering look. 'When have I had time?'

I check Simon. 'How's the head?'

'Sore.' He gives me a once-over, probably more out of

habit than any lingering attraction. 'Ten stitches.' Simon glances at Taya. 'Turns out having a psycho behind the bar isn't all bad.' There's no malice in his voice. Wonderful – they've bonded. I think about joining him on the sofa, but stay standing.

'What happened with Mya?' Taya moves Simon's fingers away from the dressing and takes over putting it back in place.

'We went to LA. To the club that used to be the Rhythm Palace.'

Taya goes completely still. 'Tell me you're joking.'

'I'm not.'

'You can't be that stupid.' She stares at me. 'You have no idea what you've done, do you?'

I wait for her to tell me.

'You've been rubbing her nose in the Rhythm Palace massacre for six years – and now she's got you back there to fight *alongside* her. You're going to hate yourself for this when you remember.'

I should have known there'd be a sting in the tail.

'You're probably right,' I say. 'But we saved twenty terrified kids from Immundi.'

'We're not here to involve ourselves with humans.' Taya's hands drop to her sides. 'That's what got the Fallen into trouble in the first place. The Outcasts draw attention to us. We fight demons only when they get in our way—'

'Most of the kids were under twelve, Taya. A couple of them were so drugged up they didn't know what country they were in. You think it's okay for those monkey demons to kidnap them and sell them to perverts?'

'That's what the police are for. You still don't get it, do you? The only reason we've been allowed to exist is so we can find the Fallen and deliver them to the Angelic Garrison. Wasting time doing anything else is an abrogation of our responsibilities.'

'Why? Because Nathaniel says so?' No way did Taya come up with the phrase 'abrogation of our responsibilities' without help.

'Daniel said Rafa's filled your head with lies. I never should have let you go with him.'

'This isn't about Rafa – it's about doing what only the Rephaim can do. The police can't stop the Immundi or the Gatekeepers – they don't even know they exist.'

Except for Jess, but Taya doesn't need to know about her right now.

Taya moves away from the sofa. 'The Gabe I knew would never have fallen for this crap. This world is saturated in evil. If we tried to counter that we'd never have time to do anything else. We can't turn the tide so what would be the point?'

'So you do nothing?'

'It's not up to us.'

'Then who is it up to if not the offspring of angels?'

Simon presses his hand against his head. 'Can you two stop arguing? The balcony doors are open.'

Taya ignores him. 'So that's it, then, you're joining Mya?'

'Not a chance.'

'Then why are you defending her?'

'I'm not. But I'm not going to pretend there's no value in what the Outcasts do' – I hold up a hand – 'I'm not saying Mya's not manipulative or a huge pain in the arse.'

'What *are* you saying?'

'That you might want to see what they do before you write them all off as mercenaries.'

A scowl. 'Did you get Jude's laptop?'

'Yeah.' The breeze coming through the open door blows a strand of hair into my face. I catch it and retie my ponytail, squash my feelings down. 'There's nothing on it. He deleted everything.'

'So Mya got what she wanted and you got nothing? Who could've seen that coming?'

Simon sits forwards and rests his forearms on his knees. 'We should tell her about Mick and Rusty,' he says to Taya.

When did they become 'we'?

'Yeah.' Taya turns to me. 'Those guys Rafa *sorted out*? They're building an army.'

'I heard.'

Simon drags his fingers through his hair and winces.

'Rusty thinks you guys are part of some government experiment with mutants. He said you confirmed it.'

'No,' I say slowly. 'It was their theory, which I didn't correct. You think they would have taken the truth any better than you did? You didn't tell them, did you?'

Simon makes a choked noise. 'I can't get my own head around what's going on. You think I could explain it to Rusty? He only told me what they're doing because he wants me up there with them to back their story.'

'What did you say?'

'That I'd think about it.'

I rub my eyelids. Brilliant.

My phone beeps with a message.

'Give me a sec,' I say to Simon and go out on the balcony to check it.

Ring me. Urgent.

A stab of fear.

Maggie.

WELCOME TO THE REAL WORLD

It's not Maggie who answers; it's Jason. He sounds flat, drained.

I can't get the words out quickly enough. 'Where's Mags?'

'Right here.'

Relief washes over me. 'What is it?'

'Gatekeepers have taken the farmhouse.'

I stare down at the esplanade. I can't grasp the significance of his words. My eyes track to the row of Poinciana trees. A few orange blossoms still cling to them, but the rest are scattered on the road, crushed by passing cars.

'Zarael has control of the iron room.' Jason says it slowly, as though he's heavily medicated. 'The one people like us can't get out of.'

I have a flash of Rafa hurling himself at those walls. 'Does Rafa know?'

'I tried to call. It went straight to voicemail.'

I feel everything slow down around me: the traffic, the drumming of the band. It lasts a beat, then the world returns to normal speed.

'How did they find the house? How did they even know it existed?'

'I don't know.' Jason's voice cracks. 'Sophie and her mother were there. Her aunt, Debra, found what was left of them in the cornfield . . .'

The sun is too bright. I hold up a hand to shield my eyes; my fingers are shaking.

A dead cornfield littered with dead women. Sophie . . . She must have been terrified when the Gatekeepers stormed in. I steady myself in the balcony doorway.

Maggie says something to Jason. Then her voice is in my ear: 'Gaby, it's so awful.'

'When did he find out?'

'Just now. Some woman named Virginia called, hysterical. She's the head of the family, I think. She wants Jason to go there.'

'No, Mags, it's too dangerous.'

'That's why he wants you and Rafa as back-up.'

'Who's going to watch out for you?'

'I'm going back to work now and I've got the necklace. Really. I'll be fine.'

All I can see is the iron room stripped bare, the giant wings powerful enough to contain the children of the Fallen.

'We have to tell the others.' I should have done it before now.

'What others?'

'The Rephaim.' I lower my voice. 'All of them.'

'But then Nathaniel will know about Jason.'

'Micah saw him up the mountain, and Simon knows—'

'But Taya doesn't, not yet.'

'Maggie, she's living with Simon; she'll find out sooner or later. This is too important – we have to warn them. I'll do it; tell Jason to come here to Simon's as soon as he can. And keep trying Rafa. Okay?'

When I go back inside, Taya is on her feet, waiting.

'What now?'

'Hang on.' I move away, call Rafa. Voicemail.

'Rafa, we've got a problem. A big one. Call me as soon as you get this. Let me know you're okay.'

I take a steadying breath, face Taya.

'What problem?' she asks.

I tell her about the farmhouse and what we found under the plaster in that room. And then I tell her about Zarael and the Gatekeepers. By the time I finish, she's pale, furious.

265

'How could you keep something like this from us?'

'I didn't mean to—' I stop myself. She's right. We should have warned them.

'How did Rafa know about the farmhouse?'

'He didn't. Jason did.'

She opens her mouth. Frowns. Closes it.

'He's one of us, Taya.'

I wait for the explosion but she looks at me as though I'm speaking a foreign language. Simon is still on the sofa, watching her.

'I thought you knew,' he says. 'He's the one who got Mags and me out of the cabin.'

'But . . .' Taya looks at him, not really seeing him. 'Is he with the Outcasts?'

'He's not with anyone,' I say. 'He's been on his own all this time. Until now.'

She studies me. The pieces finally fall into place. She snatches her phone off the table and storms into the next room.

One down.

I run my fingers over dry lips, fight the urge to try Rafa's number again. I have to call Ez, but I need a second to get my head around all this.

'You can sit if you want.' Simon gestures to the other half of the sofa.

I don't realise how shaky my legs are until I cross the

room and sit down. I leave plenty of space between us. Taya's voice carries from the other room, but I can't hear what she's saying. Not that I need to. I sink back into the soft leather.

'I'm sorry you got dragged into this,' I say quietly.

'Me too.'

'In my defence, I did try to keep you out of it.'

'I know.' He runs his thumb over a rough patch on the leather seat. 'I wasn't thinking straight that night.'

Does he mean kissing me at the falls or insisting on coming with us up the mountain to get Maggie back?

'Are you scared of me?' I ask him.

'No. Not really.'

'Do you trust me?'

His gaze skitters away.

'Nice.' I turn sideways, find a loose thread on a hand-knitted cushion cover. It looks like something Maggie might have made.

'You don't trust me but you're okay with Taya living under your roof? I guess you've forgotten she's the one who snatched Mags from the party and I'm just the one who got torn up trying to get her back.' I fling the cushion down between us.

He swallows, looks at me. 'What would have happened if we hadn't been interrupted at the party?'

The question surprises me. I remember his hands,

tentative under my shirt; his lips whispering against my neck. I never should have let it get that far – not when it wasn't really him I wanted to kiss.

I shrug off the question. 'You probably would have finished getting my jeans undone.'

'And then what?'

'I don't know, Simon.'

Taya walks back in and for the first time ever I'm happy to see her.

'Daniel's coming,' she says.

'Here? Why?'

'Why do you think? To find out more about this iron room and decide what to do about it – and to have a chat with the Rephaite who's just crawled out from under a rock.'

Jason's going to love me for this. I go back to the balcony doorway, glance at my phone again. Why hasn't Rafa called?

'How come this room is such a big deal?' Simon asks.

Taya sits on the arm of the sofa again. 'We can't be captured or forced to shift – not by each other or by demons – but a room like Gabe describes changes all that.'

Simon frowns. 'Does that mean it could trap demons too?'

Taya looks at me, her mouth slightly open. I hadn't thought of that. Neither had she.

'Is that possible?' I ask.

'Maybe.' She lands a light punch on Simon's arm. 'You're a genius.'

He shrugs, but I catch a small smile.

I check up and down the esplanade. Still no sign of Jason. Damn it. I pull out my phone.

'Who are you calling?' Taya comes out.

'Ez. The Outcasts need to know about this too.'

She doesn't argue: this is bigger than Rephaite politics.

Ez doesn't speak for a few seconds after I give her the news. Then: 'I'll let Mya and the others know.'

'Thanks.'

'She'll want to talk to Jason.'

'Tell her to get in line.' My eyes are drawn to the orange blossom scattered across the road. 'Have you seen Rafa in the last hour? He's not answering his phone.'

'No. I haven't.' There's a long pause, and in that moment the possibilities crowd in. Frightening possibilities. 'He wasn't talking about going back to that farmhouse, was he?' Ez's voice is tight.

The sun beats down. A bead of sweat trickles down my neck. 'No . . .' But I know how much that room shook him up. And how agitated he was after what we didn't find on Jude's laptop. 'He wouldn't go alone. Even Rafa's not that reckless, right?'

'Gaby,' Ez says, quietly, 'reckless is his thing.'

WHEN WORLDS COLLIDE

Simon mutes the music and we wait. Outside, the surf breaks on the beach, again and again.

'I'm making coffee. Anyone want one?' Simon stands, a little shaky on his feet.

'Take it easy.' Taya's fingers go to steady him. 'You're probably still concussed.'

Is that concern in her voice? Neither of them lets go straightaway.

'I stood up too quickly, that's all.'

Her hands linger for a second and then drop to her lap, and he leaves.

A moment later there's a rap on the door. My heart misses, but then I realise it can't be Rafa – he wouldn't knock.

Daniel is waiting on the landing. His eyes go straight to me. When I first saw him earlier in the week, I was disarmed by how unnervingly handsome he was, how immaculately groomed. Now all I see is a half-angel bastard who had no qualms watching me suffer. As usual he's detached, carefully composed. What the hell did that other version of me ever see in him?

'Gabriella.'

'Daniel.'

Given everything that's gone on in the past week, you'd think we'd have moved past formality.

'May I enter or does your threat still stand?'

It takes me a second before I remember: the last time I saw him – after we got Maggie back – I promised to cut off his head if he came near me or my friends again.

'That depends.' I stay in the doorway, don't lower my eyes from his. 'Are you a threat?'

'To you? No.' He glances at Taya behind me. 'What happened?'

Her fingers stray to the bruise blooming around her eye. 'Bar fight last night. I had to step in.'

I try not to react. Does that mean she hasn't told him about Mya being here – or me leaving? I glance at her, but she won't look at me.

'It looks sore. You should get it seen to.'

'I will.'

'Where's the boy who lives here?' Daniel asks.

'In the kitchen, making coffee,' I say. 'And he's not a boy.'

'Taya, would you join him for a moment?'

She leaves the room without arguing – a little too quickly. Still I don't move. Daniel is watching me, waiting.

'Gabriella—'

'Gaby.'

He pauses, looks beyond me into the apartment. 'Can I at least come inside?'

I leave him hanging for a few seconds and then finally step aside. He comes into the main room, spends a moment looking around. I move past him, keeping distance between us. He's never raised a hand to me himself, but that doesn't stop me feeling uneasy. I've seen what he can do with a sword.

He turns to the open balcony door. 'It shouldn't surprise me you are so attached to this village. You've always been drawn to the sea.'

Demons have a Rephaite trap and Daniel opens with small talk. I fold my arms, refuse to be interested in what he knows about my past, about who I used to be. 'I thought you were here to find out about Iowa?'

'I am. But there are things I need to speak to you about first; things I need you to understand.'

'Like what? That you're devoid of emotion? That you'll obey Nathaniel no matter the cost? It's okay, I've got it.'

'That's unfair.' There's the smallest hint of frustration in his voice. He unbuttons his shirtsleeves and rolls them up over toned forearms. 'Your . . . *predicament* is unprecedented. We had to err on the side of caution. Your situation would have been very different if we'd found you first. You must realise how it looked when Taya and Malachi found you with Rafael.'

I blink. 'That's why you ordered me into a cage with a hell-beast – because of how it looked?'

'I didn't order anything. The Five made decisions about how to access your memories. My role was to oversee the actions we agreed to take.'

'Stop talking like a politician – those actions nearly killed me.'

'For God's sake, Gabe, stop being so irrational. Stop being like *him*.'

'Like who, Rafa?'

He gives me a dark look. 'Your brother.'

'What's so bad about being like Jude?'

'The way you are with me, this disrespect for the Five, for the structure at the Sanctuary – it's not you.'

'Yes, it is. This *is* me, Daniel.' I tap my finger on my breastbone. 'It's the only me I know.'

'No; someone has made you think this is who you are – it's not the same.' He rolls his wrist until it cracks, momentarily forgetting himself.

'Can you hear yourself? How do you expect me to react to a statement like that?'

'I expect you to use your considerable intelligence to think for yourself.'

'For fuck's sake – enough.'

I need air. I kick a magazine across the floor and go out to the balcony. I stare at the beach in the distance and wish I was down there with the sand between my toes, burning off this nervous energy.

Footsteps echo on the floorboards. Daniel's not giving me space. He really should.

'The Five made decisions about you, not me alone. There was no pleasure for me in seeing you hurt,' he says.

'You've come to the wrong place if you're looking for forgiveness.'

'Gabe . . .' There's a catch in his voice, enough to cause me to turn around. 'Don't think for a moment any of this is easy for me. You . . . me . . . This isn't us.' His eyes are softer, willing me to understand.

'Really.' I look at him again – still can't see any trace of the 'us' he's talking about.

'We had a life together.' He thinks for a moment. 'A few months before you disappeared, we went up to the Tiger's Nest Monastery in Bhutan. We didn't shift there: you wanted to hike up that mountain. It took us two and a half hours, sidestepping tourists and donkey manure.

We stank by the time we were at the top. And then you made us hike all the way back down again. You made me promise that we'd make the trek every year. And then four months later you were gone . . .' For a moment I see a hint of who he might be with his guard down.

I can't imagine being in a place like that with him. I don't want to think about why he's telling me this. I sigh. 'What do you want from me, Daniel?'

He opens his mouth and I think he's going to say something real. But then he presses his lips together and the moment passes.

'What I want is for you to remember who you are. I want you to tell me if you found the Fallen last year. I want to know how much damage you and your brother have done so we can rectify it before the Angelic Garrison decides we've failed in the single task they've given us.'

Ah, yes, the reason the Rephaim exist: to find and deliver the Fallen to the archangels. To win the favour of the warrior angels Nathaniel served with before he, Semyaza and the rest of the two hundred fell from heaven: warrior angels nobody but Nathaniel has ever seen.

'If I was so loyal before, how can you believe I would have done anything to jeopardise the Sanctuary?'

Daniel gives me a steady look. 'Because you were with your brother.'

Prick.

This conversation is going nowhere.

I go to step past him but Daniel doesn't move from the doorway. 'Are you going to make me fight my way back inside?'

His expression is one I now recognise well: weary condescension. He goes inside and sits on the sofa.

'Regardless of how you feel about me, you're not safe now Zarael has the means to imprison us. It's time to come home.'

'Pan Beach is my home.' I say it without thinking.

'The Sanctuary is your home, and you won't be safe until you accept that.'

I make a noise in my throat. 'Do you seriously believe I could ever feel safe in that place?'

'When you remember who you are, yes.'

'Then I don't want to remember.' I say it to spite him and something flickers in his face, too fast for me to catch. But it's not entirely true – I *do* want to know who I used to be, what I've done. I just don't want to be Gabe. I don't ever want to be the person who chose the Sanctuary over her brother.

He sighs. 'Tell me about Jason and these women in Iowa.'

'Are my friends here safe? My human friends?'

'They're safe from us. I can't speak for the Outcasts or the Gatekeepers. Now, please, can we have an adult conversation?'

I open my mouth, think better of telling him to piss off. 'Fine.' I sit at the far end of the sofa, leaving plenty of space between us. 'What do you want to know about first: Jason or the women?'

'Jason.'

That surprises me. Jason's existence really is big news for the Rephaim. Bigger even than the iron room. I give him the edited version on Jason, the detailed one on the room.

'You and Rafael were trapped in there?' Daniel asks. 'Just the two of you?'

Unbelievable. After everything I've told him, that's what he's most interested in. Still.

'Do you want to see what we found or not?'

He rubs a palm over his jaw, realises what he's doing and drops his hand. 'Yes. Please.'

I take out my phone and he moves closer to get a better look. His knee touches mine. There are faint scars on the back of his hands – a reminder that he wasn't always a politician. And then it hits me: those hands knew my body not so long ago. Is Daniel thinking about that right now? Is that why he's so obsessed about me being with Rafa? I swallow, suddenly self-conscious. I quickly find the image of the wings and hold it out to him. He takes the phone but doesn't move away; studies the photo for what feels like a long time. Finally, he frowns.

'That's—'

Daniel doesn't finish because Rafa and Jason materialise in front of us.

I feel like my whole body breathes out. Whatever Rafa's been up to, he's safe, though in the second it takes him to get his bearings, he looks washed out, hollow. And Jason looks more vulnerable than I've ever seen him. They've arrived in the middle of the room, separately, which means they've both been here before. I'd put money on Rafa's other visit not involving an invite. I don't care: he's here.

I want to go to them. I'm about to get up when something crosses Rafa's face. Anger? Jealousy? Daniel is still sitting close to me.

'I was hoping to go a few more years before I had to see you again,' Rafa says to Daniel. He doesn't meet my eyes.

Daniel stays seated; his knee brushes mine again. 'I see your ability to focus on a task hasn't improved. You told Nathaniel you'd watch out for Gabriella and yet here she is alone.'

'I didn't realise you wanted me by her side every waking moment. She's going to need a bigger shower.'

Always a pissing contest with these two.

Taya emerges from the kitchen at the sound of Rafa's voice; Simon hangs back, watches over her shoulder.

'Did Gaby tell you what we did last night?' Rafa asks Daniel.

Daniel stays still, but his nostrils flare a little. I catch

Rafa's eye, try to warn him off. I don't know why Taya hasn't told Daniel I left Pan Beach, but I'm happy for it to stay that way.

Rafa's eyebrows go up, mocking. 'What, he doesn't know?'

Taya looks ready to tear Rafa's head off with her bare hands. Rafa follows my gaze. He measures Taya – has a fleeting moment of surprise – and laughs.

'Ah, Pretty Boy. I'm just messing with you.'

Daniel is many things. Unobservant is not one of them. 'What happened last night?'

'The brawl at the bar,' I say before Taya can answer. 'Rafa was there.'

Daniel is still focused on Taya. 'You didn't think to mention that?'

'Hey!' It's Jason. His eyes are red and his mouth is set in an uncharacteristic hard line. 'Demons have a way to trap us. Shouldn't that be the priority right now?'

He looks terrible. 'Are you okay?' I ask.

'Not even close,' he says.

Daniel finally registers there's someone other than Rafa in the room. 'You. It was you with Rafa in the infirmary on Tuesday, wasn't it? I didn't notice it up the mountain, but now—'

'Does it matter?'

'Of course it matters. How many times have you been to the Sanctuary?'

Jason's laugh is short, bitter. 'I went to get Gaby back after you let a hellion tear her up. It was my first and last visit. I have no intention of ever going back.'

'Daniel,' I say. 'Let's talk about Iowa or this conversation is over.' I stand up, put my hand on Jason's arm.

Taya says to Rafa, 'Why don't we start with how you and Gaby got out of this iron trap.'

'Jason went to Zak. Zak brought help.'

'And by help, you mean Mya?'

'We didn't ask her to come,' I say. 'Up to that point, she thought I was dead.'

Daniel picks a non-existent piece of fluff from his shirtsleeve. 'And nobody thought to warn us this room existed?'

'We're telling you now,' Jason snaps. 'I'm so sick of you people thinking you're the centre of the universe. Two women died at that farmhouse today; doesn't that matter to anyone?'

For once, Daniel has no response.

'It matters to me,' Jason says. 'I don't care how twisted their theology was, nobody deserves to die like that. Certainly not a sixteen-year-old who isn't old enough to know what she believes. I'm going to see Virginia. I'm leaving in thirty seconds and I could use some back-up. I've already called Ez, and that will mean Mya. So, do you want to play man-in-charge, or can you get over yourself long enough to do something useful?'

I've never seen – or heard – Jason like this. I glance at Rafa; he's a little impressed.

Daniel exhales. 'I need a moment with Taya.'

'Make it quick.'

Their discussion on the balcony is intense. And too low for me to hear.

Jason watches them. He's rigid, resolved. It burns him to ask for their help, I can see that, but he asked anyway. I can't help but feel a stab of admiration for him.

Rafa comes over to me, keeps his back to the others. 'What did Daniel say to you?'

'Nothing I haven't heard before.' Up close, I can see the strain around Rafa's eyes. 'Are you okay?'

He checks on Daniel and Taya, doesn't answer.

'Where were you this morning?'

His attention settles back on me. 'I'll tell you later.'

A gust of breeze blows through the open door, stirs Rafa's hair. His closeness is reassuring; I resist the urge to reach for him.

Behind him, Daniel and Taya end their conversation and turn back towards us. I breathe in, deeper this time.

For the first time since Jason's phone call, I feel close to steady.

YOUR ENEMY'S ENEMY IS NOT YOUR FRIEND

The light is dying when we arrive in the cornfield. It's colder than before, the darkening sky streaked with clouds. Leaves rustle around us; the papery rasp is unsettling now. Taya freezes ahead of me, draws her sword, then realises what the sound is.

'Where's this other house?' Taya whispers.

'Next field over,' Jason says.

Daniel steps between them. 'I want to see the main house first. The one with the iron room.'

Jason hesitates. Then he leads the way along the cornrow, more cautiously than on our last visit. Before we reach the clearing, he crouches and waves Daniel down beside him. They part the corn stalks to see the house. The rest of us hunker down behind them. The dead crop here is mouldy. I peer over Jason's shoulder and my skin prickles.

The farmhouse is crawling with Gatekeeper demons. I count a dozen posted around the front entrance and another five on the roof. They're not hiding. They all have that trademark spindly build and long white hair. From this distance I can't tell if Bel's among them.

Daniel takes in the scene without comment and lets the corn leaves slip from his fingers.

We're halfway back to where we arrived when four figures appear in the cornrow ahead of us in a small cloud of dust: Mya, Ez, Zak and Jones, all armed.

Mya's face looks drawn, her eyes are bloodshot and she's still wearing the same clothes as in LA. I don't know where she was going after the job, but it must have involved a serious bender.

The four of them block the path.

Daniel's face takes on that infuriatingly calm expression. 'This situation requires a delicate approach, Mya, not a sledgehammer.' He keeps his voice low.

I wait for her to tell him about the LA job. But she doesn't speak at all, just gives him a cold, hard stare.

Daniel takes in the others. 'Esther, Zachariah, Jonah.'

'Daniel,' Ez says.

Jason pushes between them. 'Let's keep moving.'

I let everyone walk ahead so I can join Rafa at the back

of the line. His eyes roam from one side of the cornrow to the other. 'Stay close. I've got a bad feeling about this.'

'No shit.'

'I'm serious. Stay within my reach.'

My scalp tightens.

I check the others: they're all tense. But of course they are – they're truly vulnerable for the first time.

Ahead of us, Mya's steps are heavy, stilted. Is she drunk? Her ponytail falls to one side and I glimpse the back of her neck. There's a tattoo of an ornate Celtic cross where her Rephaite mark should be, the ink faded with age. It starts under her hair and disappears below her jacket. No wonder she wears her hair down so much. She spent most of her life not knowing what she was, but did she really think a tattoo would draw less attention than a crescent-shaped mark?

We find the older house, a weatherboard, where Virginia and her surviving daughter Debra are waiting for us, in a shallow gully, hemmed in by dead corn. The roof is pitched low, sagging. Weeds grow up around the front door. A rusty swing set sits off to one side.

'Do they know you're not coming alone?' I ask Jason.

He nods, not taking his eyes from the house. 'I'll go in first. Check they're still here.'

'What if it's a trap?'

'Then I won't come out, and you'll know.'

'Jason, you don't have to prove anything.'

He wipes his palms on his pants. 'Just watch my back, okay?'

Keeping to the shadows, he runs to the front door. The flyscreen screeches when he opens it. He knocks lightly, once, twice. I hold my breath. The door opens almost immediately and Jason steps inside. A few seconds later he materialises back on the porch. No iron trap at least. He waves us over. Ez and Zak take point at one end of the house, Jones the other.

The smell hits me as soon as we're inside: wet feathers and chicken shit. The house is now a makeshift chook-shed. The wallpaper is flaked, the carpet stained and torn. The women waiting for us in the shadowy room look completely out of place: Virginia has a short grey bob, pale blue eyes and is dressed in a tailored suit as though she's off to a board meeting. She's sitting in an armchair covered in stiff plastic, next to a blackened fireplace. Her daughter is beside her, a hand on the chair, barely keeping her feet. Debra is blonde, thirty or so. I feel as if I've seen her before but I can't place her. Both stare at us, blank-eyed, torn between fear and grief.

'I'm so sorry for your loss.' Jason speaks quietly, doesn't move any closer.

But they're looking past him still, at us. We must be familiar to them from their photo collection but Jason introduces us. They're silent at our names.

'What happened, Virginia?' Jason asks.

She doesn't reply.

'How are you two alive?'

Her eyes slowly move to him. 'The silent alarm went off.' Her hand twitches. 'We have a panic button. If it's hit, we all receive a message.'

'Has that happened before?'

The plastic on the chair crackles as she shifts, takes hold of her bracelet. 'Only once; when you brought the unholy offspring here yesterday. When it went off again today we assumed you and your new friends had come back, so we parked at this house and walked over . . .' She can't keep the pain from her eyes now. 'The devils were everywhere, all over the roof like lice. And what they left in the field . . .' She turns her face away.

Debra's grip tightens on the back of the chair. I feel ill. Where did the demons leave the bodies? Did we pass them? I have a quick, sickening flashback of the nightclub in my dream, of torn bodies soaked in blood.

'You're the architect,' I say to Debra, pushing the feeling away. 'You designed that place on the hill. And that room.'

Her black patent leather shoes are covered in dust. Her shoulders shudder, either from the cold or shock. Or both.

Virginia repositions herself in her chair, straightens

her clothes. She looks at each of us again. 'You brought weapons?' Her fingers stray to her necklace: pearls. No pendant.

'You've got a demon infestation,' Rafa says. 'We weren't coming unarmed.'

'I cannot believe the day has come that I must breathe the same air as filth such as you.'

'Careful,' Rafa says.

'Rafa.' Jason turns quickly. 'Show some respect. These women lost family today.'

Virginia's hand is still on her chest. I scan the charms on the bracelet she's wearing. One isn't as shiny as the others: it's round and flat.

'That doesn't change the fact they built a room to trap us,' Rafa says. 'Or explain how the pit scum found out about it.'

Virginia glares at him. 'You tell me. You and that one' – she points a long finger at me – 'were here yesterday, and today we are attacked. You led them here to slaughter our family.' The finger moves to Jason. 'You did this.'

'We didn't lead anyone here,' Rafa says. 'So think harder about how it could have happened.'

He's so cold. That room really shook him up.

Daniel clears his throat. 'Please forgive Rafael,' he says to Virginia and then holds out his hands to show he's unarmed. 'On behalf of Nathaniel and the Rephaim of the Sanctuary, I offer you and your family our deepest condolences for your losses today.'

'I don't want sympathy from your kind,' Virginia says. 'You're an abomination, every last one of you.'

'We are not all alike, madam, I assure you. And you have seen the real enemy today: it is not the Rephaim.' He approaches her slowly, respectfully. He brushes off a dusty kitchen chair, pulls it closer to her and sits down. She moves back in her seat to widen the distance between them. The stiff plastic on her chair crackles again.

'The Fallen and their bastards are no better than the devils who have violated our home this day,' she says. 'Between all of you, you will end the world.'

Daniel folds his hands, a study in self-control. Beside me, Rafa is looking at the walls and the near-dark window. The cold pushes through my jacket. I take a deep breath. God, this place *stinks*. Ask her about the room so we can leave and Jason can take them somewhere safe.

'That sounds like fear talking,' Daniel says.

'It is a revelation from God.'

Daniel dips his head. 'Please, then, share your revelation so we can understand.'

Virginia's pale eyes flare as something stronger than grief takes hold. 'You seek the Fallen. If you find them, you will release the two hundred and they will make war on heaven.'

'No, Virginia, we'll hand them over to the Angelic Garrison. The archangels will decide their fate.'

'You will fail.'

'Then why did you allow Jason to bring us here? Why agree to meet with us?'

'You are the only creatures strong enough to drive the spawn of hell from here.'

'You're asking for our help?'

'No . . .'

'Come now, Virginia. Now's not the time for lies.'

Her eyes roam his face and the hard lines around her mouth soften. It's as if she's only just noticed how beautiful he is. Her hand drops to the armrest and Daniel gently places his over it. Virginia flinches, but doesn't pull away.

'I swear to you, our purposes are the same.' His voice is gentle.

Mya makes a noise that's somewhere between scoffing and clearing her throat. I'm surprised she hasn't had something to say by now.

Virginia breaks eye contact with Daniel to look over at the rest of us. 'Not all of you have the same purpose, though, do you?'

Daniel sighs and slides his hand from hers. 'That is true and a shame. But we can talk about that more later.'

Virginia glances down at her wrist and gasps. In the

space of that sound, Taya is moving across the room. She grabs Virginia's slender arm – Mya shouts – and then Taya and Virginia disappear.

'You bastard!' Mya yells at Daniel.

He holds up the bracelet he slipped from Virginia's wrist. That's why he didn't ask about the room: he never intended to interrogate her here.

'You think Taya didn't notice your girlfriend showing off that necklace?' he says to Jason.

Mya lunges at him but Daniel's already gone.

'Fuck!' Rafa lashes out at a cracked vase on a weather-beaten stand. It hits the fireplace and shatters. I blink at the empty chair. How could I think Taya would miss something as important as that pendant on Maggie? Of course she saw it. It's why she was in Pan Beach in the first place – to watch us. But how did she know what to look for? How did Daniel?

Mya strides towards Debra, who has sunk back against the wall.

'No way.' Jason blocks her but she steps around him. Debra's pale lips are moving in what could be a silent prayer.

Jason grabs Mya's wrist. 'I can take her somewhere safe—'

'There isn't anywhere safe.' She wrenches free, shoves him back. She takes Debra's arm—

They're gone.

'What the . . .?' The flywire door creaks as Ez comes in. 'Debra must have been wearing one of their trinkets, right?' I say. 'How did Mya do that?'

Jason doesn't look at me. He goes to Virginia's chair and sits down, puts his head in his hands.

'Either she wasn't wearing one or she didn't leave against her will,' Ez says, and flicks feathers off a chair with the tip of her sword.

Rafa shrugs. 'Maybe after Pretty Boy snatched up the old girl, she figured she'd be safer with us than trying to get past Zarael on her own.'

'But Jason was still here . . .' I frown. 'Maybe she didn't have hers on. Maybe it was in the other house.' I look to Ez. 'Did Mya come here planning to do that?'

'I don't think so.'

'I can't believe I was naive enough to think you lot came here to help,' Jason says.

'Be fair,' Ez says. 'Daniel made the first move, not us.' She looks to Rafa. 'Mya might have gone to Jess. I'll take Zak and Jones and call when we find her.'

Rafa nods and she goes back outside.

'Come on, let's go,' Rafa says.

Jason doesn't move.

'Goldilocks, are you coming with us or staying in this shit-hole?'

'You don't get it, do you?' Jason doesn't look up. 'Virginia's right: it's my fault. Sophie and her mother are dead; Virginia is a prisoner at the Sanctuary; Debra is at the mercy of the woman who tore the Rephaim apart. That's all on me.'

'We couldn't have led the demons here. They can't feel us or track us.' I look to Rafa.

He goes to the window, checks outside. Shrivelled corn leaves are swirling between the rows, caught on the breeze. 'They have to see us. Unless a hell-turd's had a taste of one of us.'

'See?' I say to Jason.

He stares at the shit-encrusted carpet. 'Do you know how many humans I've watched die?' he asks, as if Rafa and I haven't spoken. 'How many men and women in my mother's family? One after another. Generation after generation. Some of old age, some not. Old men. Young mothers. Babies. Think of a way to die, and I've watched it happen to someone I care about. I've stood beside more graves than I can bear to remember.' He takes a deep, ragged breath. 'Even if I stay away, they die. We're cursed, you know, to live forever. And now this . . . Look at the horror I've brought here.'

My longing for the family Jude and I might have had with Jason evaporates in the room, in the stench of it. One hundred and thirty-nine years of death and loss. I can't imagine the weight of that, or how he's carried it all these decades.

I wish Maggie was here. She'd know how to comfort him. 'I don't know how the demons found out about the iron room, but it's not your fault.'

He looks up at me, his blue eyes almost grey. 'It's my fault you and Jude went missing last year. I brought you back together, took you to Dani after she had the vision. I should have known it would lead to something bad.' His hands ball into fists on his knees. 'I froze when I should have helped Maggie. I let her see demons—'

'She's fine, Jason, she—'

'She's not fine. She has nightmares.'

I pause. I didn't know that.

'Beating yourself up doesn't change that.'

His shoulders fold. 'I don't know what I'm supposed to do, Gaby. I don't know who to believe. What are we, really? Why are we here? Does anything we do even matter?'

'If we knew that, Goldilocks, we'd all be less prone to binge drinking,' Rafa says.

I glance out the dirt-covered windows. The sun is almost gone now, straining through the dead corn.

'Get up and stop feeling sorry for yourself.' Rafa nudges shards of the broken vase with his boot. 'We've all fucked up at one point or another. You can't live as long as we have and not make mistakes.' He glances at me and then away again.

Jason wipes his face. 'So what do I do?'

'Nothing, here,' Rafa says. 'But if you can get your shit together, we could use some help to look for Jude.'

I blink. Did Rafa just throw Jason a lifeline?

'Unless you'd rather stay here and mope,' he says.

I'm still studying Rafa when something flashes behind him outside. Something with flaming eyes.

CATCH YOUR BREATH

Rafa shifts across the room to me. And then we're in the freezing void, stretching and compressing. By the time we find solid ground again, his arms are tight around me. We're back at his shack. It's clean, the bench still bare. But now there's a rucksack on the table.

Jason appears. 'I tried the bungalow first. Is it safe here?'

'Safer than up the hill,' Rafa says and lets go of me.

I look from one to the other. 'You think the demons will come to Pan Beach – into town?'

'They might risk it if they've fixed the door to that room,' Rafa says. 'They only need one of us as leverage.'

'Leverage for what?'

'For you.' He looks at me, serious. 'We can't wait any

longer to go to Melbourne. We need to get out of here right now, and that's as good a place as any.'

'What about the rest of the town?'

'They'll be fine. Zarael's not after them.'

'And what about the Butlers and their militia?'

Rafa shakes his head. 'Not my problem.'

'Let me get Maggie,' Jason says. 'She can't go back to the bungalow, not now. Daniel knows about the iron amulet, so the necklace isn't going to help if the Rephaim want her again.'

'He's right,' I say. It doesn't matter what Daniel said to me – all assurances will go out of the window as soon as Rafa and I disappear from Pan Beach.

'Fine. Get her here in ten minutes or we're going without—' Jason's gone before Rafa finishes.

I turn my phone back on. 'Will Taya come back here?'

Rafa shrugs.

She cared enough about Simon to get involved in the bar fight last night, so maybe she cares enough to keep an eye on him – or at the very least make sure he doesn't join the Butlers up the mountain.

'Why didn't Taya tell Daniel about us going with Mya last night?'

Rafa sits at the table. 'She didn't want to wear the blame if you didn't come back. And then the shit hit the fan over the farm and she lost her chance.'

At the sink, daylight is forcing its way through the grime on the shack windows. It's barely midday here. I stare at the grey wall of the shopping centre.

'Virginia must have thought the Rephaim would charge in and purge the place.'

'Then she doesn't know as much about the Sanctuary as she thinks she does.' Rafa stretches his legs out to one side of the table. 'The Five will take at least a day to debate the merits of an attack.'

I sit opposite him. 'But first they'll interrogate Virginia.'

'Yep, and I guarantee they'll find out more about her family in twenty-four hours than Jason's managed to in seventy years.'

I don't want to think about what that might involve.

'But Nathaniel will attack the farm at some point, won't he? He'll destroy that room?'

'Maybe not. Too many Gatekeepers; Rephaim would die. No, he'll find out how to make his own iron prison.'

'For Rephaim or demons?'

'Both, if it works that way.'

'Could it hold the Fallen too?'

'Maybe.'

We sit with that thought.

'But if Nathaniel didn't know about the iron room, how did Taya and Daniel know about the amulet and what it does?'

'No idea.'

'I think there's something else going on at the Sanctuary. With Malachi.'

Rafa moves his legs again to rest against mine.

'Like what?'

'He was supposed to come with Taya, remember, to keep an eye on me – a direct order from Nathaniel. But he hasn't shown and she was cagey about it, which makes me wonder—'

'If they've got a lead on the Fallen. That's the only thing that would take priority over shadowing you.'

I look up at the water-stained ceiling. 'Maybe Daniel will be so preoccupied with Virginia and the farmhouse and whatever Malachi's up to that he'll forget about us for a few hours.'

Rafa laughs. 'Yeah, right. He's not losing his hard-on for you any time soon.'

I knock my knee against his. 'That's revolting.'

'Speaking of which,' he says, and I really hope he's not still talking about Daniel, 'I grabbed a few things this morning.'

He drags the rucksack closer, pulls out two books and lays them face-up. They're from Jude's collection on angels and demons. I see Jude's laptop wedged in the bag.

'You went to Patmos this morning?'

He nods, glances away.

Rafa was safe in Greece. He was never in danger. That lingering fear finally slides away.

'I thought the books might be useful. You know, if . . .' He flips the pages of the book closest to him. 'They worked for you.'

'No, the photo worked for me.'

He pushes the second book towards me and, when I open it, I see the thirty-year-old shot of Jude and me tucked in the dust jacket, both of us looking no older than eighteen. It still makes me ache.

'Any reason you turned your phone off while you were in Greece?'

Rafa doesn't answer right away; he's prying a splinter from the edge of the table. When he finally speaks he doesn't meet my eyes. 'You think you're the only one who has a hard time seeing Jude's things?'

His voice is quiet and raw.

'Hey.' I lay the photo on the table and tap it. 'That was in my room, not on Patmos. How many drawers did you go through before you found it?'

'A few.' He looks at me, catches the mood shift and goes with it. 'While I was at it, I packed some clothes for you too. You really need to go shopping.'

'You packed – we only just decided to go to Melbourne.'

'I was planning on an early departure.'

There's movement near the front door. Maggie and

Jason. Maggie is toting an overnight bag, which she drops on its wheels, and bolts for the sink. She breathes in and out, slowly. Then she stands up, pours a glass of water and drinks it.

'Oh my God, I *hate* that.' She's changed out of her work clothes and into jeans and a loose-knit jumper. Handmade.

I give her a sympathetic smile. 'Brace yourself. We're going again in a minute.'

She sits at the table, her cheeks still pale.

'What did you tell your mum?'

She gestures to Jason, who gives a tired smile. Being near Maggie has taken some of the tension from his face.

'I said I scored tickets to the ballet in the city,' he says, 'and we had to leave right now so we could check in to the hotel before the show.'

'Nice.' Nothing short of the ballet would get Maggie a free pass from the cafe on a Saturday.

I put the books back in the rucksack and recognise the clothes Rafa has jammed in there, including the only lacy underwear I own. I don't know whether to be annoyed or flattered.

'How come you didn't ask Ez or Zak to come to Melbourne with us?' I ask.

'I didn't want to get their hopes up.'

I study him, wonder if it's more than that.

'Would it have crossed Mya's mind that Jude might be alive?' I ask.

'I doubt it. She's spent the last year blaming you – and me – for the fact he's not here any more. She's not letting go of that too easily.'

Jason pops the handle on Maggie's suitcase. 'Any theories on how Zarael found out about the farmhouse?'

'The only way he could have is if they followed someone who drove there,' Rafa says.

'But that means they'd have to know about the family.'

'Correct.'

'We'll be okay in Melbourne – they can't track us, can they?' Maggie asks.

'No, Margaret.' Rafa smiles at her. 'But we can't do anything stupid to flag where we are. I have no intention of ever seeing the inside of that room again.' He stands up. 'Right then. We're going to need a base in Melbourne. Somewhere we can shift to and from easily without worrying about being seen. Not to mention somewhere to sleep.'

'A hotel?' Jason is sharper now, focused.

'Excellent idea,' Rafa says. 'You paying?'

LAST SEASON'S SCARS

We arrive in a park behind a maintenance shed. The glass and concrete skyline dwarfs the trees around us. It's early afternoon; Hannah McKenzie's next shift at the hospital is tomorrow morning.

The hotel is on Collins Street. We stop for bagels on the way in a cafe so tiny the kitchen is under a flight of stairs. Our room has two double beds, a huge bathroom and dizzying views of the city. I don't ask how much it costs, but I suspect I'd have to shelve books for a month to afford a night here. And Jason's booked for two. Maggie unpacks like we're settling in for the weekend.

Rafa's phone rings. The conversation is short, clipped.

'That was Ez,' he says when he hangs up. 'Mya took the architect to LA.'

Jason looks up from his phone. He's been tapping and studying it for the past five minutes. 'Is Debra all right?'

'She should be happy she's not at the Sanctuary with her mother.'

'Yes, but—'

'Goldilocks, she's fine. She's with a cop. Nothing bad is going to happen to her.'

Jason doesn't seem convinced. 'How long will she have to stay there?'

'Depends how quickly she gives up information.'

'I've met Jess,' I say. 'I can't see her letting Mya hurt Debra.'

He considers this, nods, and goes back to his screen. 'Maggie, I can get tickets to the ballet if you want to go.'

She comes back in from the bathroom, where she's been putting her make-up away. 'Are you sure you're up for it?'

'I am. Really.' He checks Rafa and me. 'I can book for four . . .?'

Rafa looks like Jason's just offered to slip bamboo under his fingernails.

'Thanks,' I say before he can insult Jason. 'But I don't think I could sit still for that long.'

Maggie catches my eye. 'What will you two do while we're out?'

Rafa gives me a lazy smile. 'I'll come up with something.'

'Let's at least have dinner together first,' Maggie says. 'Gaby, did you pack a dress?'

I give her a flat look.

'Of course not,' she says. 'Then that settles it: I'm taking you shopping.'

The afternoon sky is patchy with thin clouds, the breeze like tepid water. Maggie knows every boutique in the city. Our first stop is a tiny shop in a little street packed with cafes and outdoor tables. I know from the limited hanging space that I can't afford anything in here, but Maggie goes in anyway. She chats to the sales assistant about new season lines and colours and then joins me at the back of the store.

'Mags.' I wait until she looks up. 'Why didn't you tell me you were having nightmares?'

'How . . .?' She closes her eyes for a second. 'Jason.' A sigh. 'I had them after Dad died too. It's how I cope.'

'You should have told me.'

'You've got enough going on.'

I flick through a couple of dresses, not really seeing them. 'What are they about?'

'Mostly Mick getting attacked.' She pauses, blinks rapidly a few times. 'But last night I dreamed one of those long-haired demons was in my room. It scared the hell out of me.'

'Oh, Mags.' I reach for her without thinking and hug her

tightly. At least, in my nightmares, I always got to kill the monster.

We stay that way for a while and when I let go she wipes her eyes, laughs. 'If I'd known all it took to get a hug was a few nightmares, I would have told you days ago.'

I smile. 'I'm glad you're not sleeping alone.'

She gives me a half-smile. 'Me too.' She pulls out a few dresses, studies them, puts them back. 'And sorry about the interruption this morning.'

I'm about to ask what she means and then I remember she walked in on Rafa kissing my bare leg. Thinking about his lips on my skin brings a rush of heat to my face. 'Oh, that was . . .' I sigh. 'I don't know what that was.'

'What's going on with you two?'

'Who knows? When we're alone he can be so tender, and when he kisses me, God . . .' I laugh, embarrassed. 'But then he turns into a smartarse around other people, especially Rephaim. And any time I make a decision he doesn't like he takes it as a personal insult.'

'Gaby,' she says carefully. 'You give him just as much of a hard time, you know.' She touches my elbow. 'I don't think there's any doubt about how he feels – and that's what's messing with his head. He fought with the old Gabe; he's attracted to you. Here's a thought: maybe you two could, you know, talk about it.'

'I've asked him repeatedly about what happened at the Sanctuary—'

'I mean talk about how you feel about each other *now*.'

I choke on a laugh. 'I'm pretty confident he feels the same way I do about deep and meaningful conversations.'

Maggie shakes her head, and then: 'Oh my.' She takes a hanger from the rack, shows me a silk, strapless champagne-coloured dress with a fitted bodice and layers that flare out from the hip, delicate and gauzy. 'You need to try this on.'

'I could never afford that.'

'I didn't say buy it, I said try it. Go on. How often do we get to do this?'

She hangs the dress in the changing room and waits outside. I get into it carefully; the material is so thin it feels like I could tear it. Then I open the door so Maggie can zip me up. She stands back to look.

'Wow. That is stunning on you.'

I have to admit the dress is gorgeous. I twirl, making the skirt flare. Maggie takes a photo on her phone.

I study myself in the mirror, surprised at how good it looks; at how good I feel wearing it. What would Rafa think about badass Gabe in an evening dress? I picture him next to me in a suit: tailored jacket and pants, a crisp shirt, tie slightly loose. Could we ever have a moment like that? I let my mind wander . . . And then I see the sales assistant staring at me, horrified. In all my daydreaming I forgot about the hellion bite. My hand comes up to cover it, almost involuntarily, and I duck back into the cubicle.

'Gaby . . .'

'It's okay.' I close the door behind me.

For a moment I stand there, stare at my reflection, at the too-delicate, too-expensive dress and my scar. Ride a brief and fierce wave of anger and regret. Who was I kidding? I've never been the kind of girl who could wear a dress like this. Maybe one day, in a different life, I might have grown into that skin, but now . . . not now.

I reach for the zip and the silk sways against my skin again. I can't undo it. I exhale, open the door a crack. Maggie is waiting, pensive.

'Can you help me, please?'

Her face softens and it takes a second for me to realise: I've never actually asked before.

DANCING IN THE MOONLIGHT

Maggie finds what she's looking for an hour later: a pencil dress in robin's egg blue with cap sleeves and vintage beading around the neckline. On sale.

She doesn't push me to try on anything else. We both know that whatever Rafa has planned for the night won't involve formal wear. At best it'll be a few drinks at a bar. At worst . . . I'm not tempting fate by guessing what that might be.

Back at the hotel, Rafa is propped up on one of the beds, watching a boxing match on TV. Jason has changed into jeans and a shirt. He's at the desk, reading a newspaper. He lays it down as we walk in and I catch a glimpse of a mangled car on the front page.

I flash hot, then cold. Stop moving.

'Are you okay?' Maggie touches my elbow as the heavy door clicks behind us. She follows my gaze to the newspaper. Jason and Rafa look too, at the upside-down car, an accident on a country road somewhere.

'The anniversary,' Maggie says. 'It was today, wasn't it?'

Rafa mutes the boxing commentary, swings his legs over the side of the bed.

I nod. The movement is jerky, forced. 'I nearly forgot.' Something that would have been unthinkable ten days ago.

'It's been a big day.' Maggie rubs my arm.

'Yeah, but . . .' I walk to the window in a daze and sit on the sill, turn my back on the city. How could I forget the defining moment of my life? The moment that's shaped every moment since? Even now, when I know it never happened – that Jude didn't die in a mess of blood and gore and petrol – that moment is so heavy I can still hardly bear it.

Maggie puts her shopping bags on the table and comes over to me.

I take a steadying breath. 'When is this going to end?'

'When we find him.' Rafa's voice is quiet.

I look at him but I can't hold his gaze. There's too much expectation there. Too much hope.

Maggie squeezes my hand. 'How are you feeling about tomorrow?'

'Terrified,' I whisper so only she can hear.

Jason turns in his chair so he's facing us. 'I taught Jude to fish.'

I blink. It's not what I was expecting from him, but he's got my attention. 'When?'

'About a month after your first visit to Monterosso, in the 1890s. Jude wanted to learn something other than fighting. He said all you did at the Sanctuary was eat, sleep and train. He wanted to eat something he'd caught himself.' Jason glances at Rafa; he's got his full attention too. 'You arrived late in the afternoon – unexpected, as always. I'd already cleaned the nets, so I grabbed bait and lines and we took the boat a little way off shore.'

'I came too?'

He nods. 'You didn't fish; you just watched Jude and teased him. He got his line tangled and jabbed himself with the hook. But he took his time and once he got his line set, he was happy to sit there and wait. He had more patience than half the men I fished with. Definitely more patience than you. We made a decent catch and cooked it over a fire on the beach. Honestly, I'd never seen anyone so pleased with themselves over a fish.' He smiles at the memory. 'He was a good guy, Gaby. Smart, caring.' Jason meets my eyes. 'When I saw him again a hundred and twenty years later, he was still that person.'

I swallow. Once, twice. It doesn't shift the lump in my

throat. I turn back to the window, press my fingertips against the thick glass. The sky bleeds purple and orange, the light almost gone. Damn Jason – he's too intuitive for his own good.

'Thank you,' I say finally.

Maggie moves across to him. She squeezes his shoulder and then takes out her new dress and snaps the tags. She's itching to put it on again.

'Go on, go and get ready,' I tell her.

'What about you?'

'I'm not hungry. You two grab dinner before your show; we'll pick up something later.'

'Are you sure?' She hesitates for a moment and then disappears into the bathroom. Rafa goes back to watching the silent fight on the TV, a boxer reeling back in slow-motion, a spray of sweat. Jason has turned back to the paper and is staring at the same page he was five minutes ago. I lean against the window and close my eyes. I think about how high I am above the cars and the people and the pavement; how only a few centimetres of glass stops me from plummeting towards them. I'm suspended in time and space. Waiting. Waiting for Jude.

Maggie emerges from the bathroom, gorgeous. She's wearing the blue dress as if it was custom-made for her.

'Wow,' Jason says.

Maggie dips her chin, accepts the compliment. 'Oh,'

she says to Rafa, her eyes bright. 'You should see this.' She hands her phone to him. 'Recognise this girl?'

He studies the screen without speaking. Maggie turns his hand so I can see the photo. I'm a little startled by it myself: not only the fact I'm in a dress that clings to every dip and curve of my body, but that I'm relaxed. Unguarded.

Rafa takes the phone back, studies it for a while longer. Finally, he looks up and meets my eyes.

'You need to buy that dress.'

Then Jason and Maggie are gone. Off to do something normal. To feel normal. Even before Rafa turned up in Pan Beach, I'd never felt that way. I pull my feet to the sill and rest my chin on my knees, stare out at the lights coming on around and below us.

'What?' Rafa says. 'You wanted to go to the ballet?'

I sigh. 'What's the plan?'

He pulls on his boots and stands up. 'It's a surprise.' If he were anyone else, that might sound like a good thing. 'Come on.' A sly smile. 'Trust me.'

I meet him in the middle of the room. He slides his arm around me and pulls me close, links our fingers. 'Maybe I'm taking you dancing.' His lips are against my hair.

'Is that before or after the bar fight?'

He starts to sway and I can't help it, I move with him. 'Hmm,' he whispers. 'I haven't decided.'

I close my eyes, feel his arms tighten around me, his

hips against mine . . . before the ground drops away.

It's over in less than a second and we're in darkness. Traffic hums in the distance, and I smell damp grass. There's more space around us – a park, maybe. Rafa and I are still locked together. Still swaying. I can't see his face clearly, but his breath warms my cheek.

I find his mouth. The kiss is slow, sweet. Rafa's thumb strokes my collarbone. I kiss him harder.

He breaks away first. 'Keep that up and I'm going to forget what we came here for.'

'Maybe I'd rather do this.'

'Really?' His hand slides down to my hip. 'I was going to give you your first shifting lesson.'

My whole body snaps to attention. 'Okay. Shit. Okay.'

He laughs and lets me go.

I look around us, feel the way my pulse has quickened. City lights wink above a bank of trees. The night sky is mostly clear, the moon bright enough that I can make out the tops of palm trees, a manicured lawn, a large lake.

'Are we still in Melbourne?'

'The Botanic Gardens. It wasn't worth the argument to take you too far from Maggie.'

I walk a few metres from him and take a deep breath, roll my shoulders. If I can travel the way the Rephaim do, I won't be so vulnerable. I'll be more of an equal. I'm going to learn to shift. On my own.

'So, how do I do this?'

Rafa rubs his jaw, thinks for a few seconds. 'What do you do when you walk?'

'I don't know, I just do it.'

He nods. 'Right. Shifting's the same.'

'I'm going to need slightly more specific instructions.'

'Give me a second. I've never taught anyone before.'

'How did you learn?'

'I don't remember – it was a long time ago.'

I shake the tension from my wrists, feel the air against my hands.

'Okay, the key is to visualise where you want to go.'

'But you shift to places you've never been.'

'And I've been doing it for a hundred and twenty years. When you start out, you need to visualise.'

It makes sense; Jason can only shift somewhere on his own if he's been there before or has specific directions. His skills are nowhere near as advanced as the rest of the Rephaim because he only knows as much as Jude and I did when we taught him at the end of the nineteenth century.

'We'll start with something easy. Take your shoes off.'

My bare toes sink into grass damp with dew.

'Feel that? Now look at the trees around you, the sky. Find landmarks. What do you smell?'

I breathe in deeply. 'Mown grass, some sort of flower, ducks . . .'

'You got it all in your memory?'

'I think so.'

'Right. Walk down to the path by the lake.'

I do as he says. I think I know where this is going. When I face him again all I can make out is his silhouette.

'When you're ready, focus and shift back to me.'

'Rafa, the landmarks are exactly the same here.'

'No, they're not. Pay attention. You've walked twenty metres. Everything is different.'

I stare at the point I have to get to.

'Don't focus on it from there. Focus on what it was like when you were here.' His voice is loud under the trees. There's nobody around to hear.

'Wouldn't this be easier when there's more light?'

He laughs. 'This is as easy as it's going to get. It's not your first time. My bet is it'll be exactly like your fighting skills: once you start, muscle memory will kick in.'

'You didn't think that a few days ago when I asked about shifting. You said it would be like teaching a kid to fly a fighter plane.'

'That was before I saw you in action with a sword. Quit stalling.'

I rub my palms together, let out my breath. Jason said the first time the Rephaim shifted they all ended up where they were born – not that they knew it. Technically, this isn't my first shift, so I shouldn't find myself in Italy. Assuming this works at all.

I check my back pocket. Yep, phone's still there, just in case.

'Come on, Gaby. You can do this.'

I nod, close my eyes. Picture faintly-lit skyscrapers above the trees, palm fronds coiling out of shapeless shadows; feel cool blades of grass between my toes, a light breeze on my skin. I sway on my feet, waiting, willing something to happen . . .

Nothing.

'You're thinking too much.'

I open my eyes. 'Shouldn't I, like, imagine myself *projecting* back over there?'

'Whatever works for you.'

I move a few steps to the left. Like that's going to help. 'What happens when we shift? I mean, are we travelling really fast and, if so, why don't we hit planes or mountains or—'

'Does it matter?'

'I think it'll help if I understand how it works.'

He walks down the hill to me. 'Zeb says—'

'Who's Zeb again?'

'One of the Council of Five. He always said we don't hit anything because we're not travelling in this dimension.'

'Say again?'

'We leave one place, end up in another, and in between we go somewhere else. Another dimension.'

My skin prickles. 'What happens if you get stuck there?'

'Nobody ever has.'

'But—'

'Do you want to try this again or obsess about the metaphysics of it?'

I bite my lip, take my weight on both feet. 'Try again.'

'Then less talk and more trying.'

This time when I assemble all the sights and sounds and smells, I imagine myself being drawn towards them; moving without moving; grass replacing the concrete under my bare feet.

Again nothing happens. But I stay focused, sweep the thought fragments back into a neat line, ignore the insects and distant traffic. Try again. This time I imagine stepping through a curtain into nothing: a nothing that will take me to a place that looks and smells like the spot on the hill.

Something pulls at me – something ferocious and wild. I'm sucked forward, stretched. The air turns icy. I can't open my eyes: the pressure's almost unbearable. Noise like a waterfall swells and crashes around me. I can't feel the ground.

God, I'm doing it, I'm shifting—

I slam face-down on concrete.

I groan and roll onto my back. My palms and elbows

sting; my ears are blocked. I can't tell if the stars wheeling against the inky sky are real or not. The path is hard against my spine and there's blood in my mouth.

Warm fingers touch my face. 'You all right?'

I nod and my neck hurts.

Rafa helps me stand. I ache as if I've run for hours; my legs shake, my stomach churns. 'I need to sit down.'

We find a bench and I put my head in my hands, wait for the ground to stop rolling. 'I thought it was working.'

'It was, you just didn't go anywhere. You disappeared for a second, though.'

I turn my head. The moon is clear of the trees. 'Seriously?'

'Didn't you feel it?'

'Oh, I felt it all right.' It was the single most terrifying sensation of my life.

'Do you want to try again?'

I shake my head so vigorously it makes me dizzy. 'Not tonight.'

'Fair enough.'

I lean back against the bench, close my eyes. Rafa settles next to me. Our shoulders touch. We sit like that for a while, listening to the insects, the light rustle of the breeze through the trees.

I like how solid he is. How he lets me lean against him. It should be enough, but it's not. I can't let it go. I have to ask him again. Maybe here in the quiet is where he'll answer.

'Rafa.'

'Mmm?'

'What happened between us before you left the Sanctuary?' Even with the weight of the words, it's still an easier question than the one Maggie wants me to ask him.

He doesn't answer.

I open my eyes. He's staring up at the night sky, as if the question will go away if he can't see me.

'In Dubai, you said we needed time to have the conversation. We've got time now.'

He sits forward, stretches his arms over his head; one shoulder makes a popping noise. He doesn't look at me.

'We had a fight. A really bad one,' he says finally.

'That's not news.'

'It got out of hand. I hurt you.'

'Why? What was it about?'

His arms drop. 'You told me you weren't leaving with us.'

'Did I say why?'

'Yeah.' He's focused on the shapeless trees on the hill. 'You wanted to stay with Daniel.'

I stare at him. 'I chose Daniel over Jude? Bullshit. I thought I didn't hook up with Daniel until after you guys left?'

No response. This makes no sense.

'Why would that piss you off so much you'd hurt me?'

'Because Daniel's a dick,' he snaps.

'Rafa—'

'The thought of you being with him . . .' He stands up, moves away from the bench and into the shadows.

'What, you didn't want him to have the only woman at the Sanctuary you hadn't been with?'

'That's not what I'm talking about.' He keeps his back to me. 'Damn that prick . . .'

'Then what?'

He takes a breath. 'Things were . . . different.'

'Different how?'

He doesn't answer.

'But weren't you with Mya by that point?'

'Fuck, see, this is too hard.'

And just like that, he's gone. Shifted.

I stare at the place where he was standing. I blink a couple of times to make sure he's really not there.

Unbelievable. He'll charge at a pack of demons but he can't face a difficult conversation. He's deluded if he thinks I'm going to forget about it. I need to know. I need to not be stumbling around in the dark all the time. Why is that so fucking difficult for him to understand? What does he think—

Something splashes in the water behind me. I stand up and spin around. A lone swan glides across the lake, moonlight flickering in the ripples behind it. The edge of the water is crowded with dark, hulking shapes.

Shit.

I'm alone in the middle of a huge garden in the dark. Now I have to find a way out on foot, get back to the road without someone seeing me and calling the cops. How high is the fence? And where is the hotel from here?

The trees whisper to each other.

'I'm done having this conversation.'

I flinch, as much from the hardness in Rafa's voice as the fact he's standing a few metres away under a willow tree.

'What the fuck?' I don't mean it to come out so loud. 'I thought we were having a conversation. You don't shift in the middle of a conversation.'

'You need to let this go.' I don't have to see his face to know how angry he is.

'How can I, Rafa? Everywhere I turn, people are punishing me for who I used to be – you included. I'm sick of it. Why can't you tell me what happened?' I'm breathing faster than I need to.

'Because we didn't just beat each other up. We said some really shitty things, tore each other apart. I can't undo that and I don't see the point in giving you a blow-by-blow replay.'

'Don't you think I deserve to know what it was about?'

He throws his head back in exasperation. 'It wasn't you!

If you ever get that other life back we can have it out then, all right? But I'm not ripping the scab off this thing when it's got nothing to do with who you are now.'

'That doesn't help me.' I'm aware that I'm shouting and then a wave of dizziness hits me. I reach for the bench, steady myself. The shadows spin and I have to sit down.

'You all right?' His voice is still tight.

'I'm fine.'

My elbow stings. I touch it and wince; my fingers come away sticky.

Rafa walks over to me. 'You're bleeding.'

'It's just a graze.'

'I can see that.'

We watch each other, getting our frustration under control. Rafa stays standing. An owl hoots in the trees; another answers further away. The breeze shakes the leaves in the dark trees around us. I sink back against the bench, spent.

'What if I do get my memories back, Rafa?' I suddenly sound as tired as I feel. 'What if, by some miracle, I remember all the things you don't want me to?'

He rubs his eyes with his thumb and forefinger. 'I don't know, Gaby. But I can tell you one thing . . .' He picks up a stone and tosses it into the dark. It splashes on the far side of the lake. 'It won't make your life any simpler.'

SOOTHING MENTHOL

'How old is she?'

'I don't remember.'

'Fit or overweight?' Rafa asks.

I shake my head.

We're on the street outside the hospital, a three-storey concrete wall at our backs, studying every woman in a nurse's uniform. The chance Hannah McKenzie comes to work through the main entrance is slim. The likelihood I'm going to recognise her, slimmer.

Rafa is all business this morning, as if our argument in the park didn't happen, as if it was perfectly natural for us to watch TV sitting on separate beds in a hotel room with the lights turned down, while Maggie and Jason were at the ballet.

'You sure you're okay?' Maggie asks for the third time since we left the hotel. 'This must be a little strange for you.'

Strange? That's an understatement. I don't feel like I fit my skin today.

My eyes are constantly drawn to the hospital entrance, opening and closing, swallowing people, spitting them out. I limped out of those doors nine months ago, my brother dead, my body broken, life as I knew it shattered.

My hands shake and I push them into my pockets to steady them. Jason notices and gives me a small, encouraging smile, putting aside his own raw grief. I have a rush of gratitude: that Jude and I met him all those years ago, and that he found me in Pan Beach.

'Maybe we should go in?' Maggie says, shivering against the breeze. It's cooler today, the sky a blanket of grey.

I nod. But then I see her: a fine-boned middle-aged nurse, grinding out a cigarette on the footpath. She drops the butt in a bin and drains what's left of a takeaway coffee. She looks tired. But there's something familiar about the way that she moves, the smile lines around her mouth, and her eyes, which are dark and smudgy.

I approach her as she's dusting off her hands.

'Excuse me.'

She glances up, wary, then looks confused.

'Hannah McKenzie?'

She tries to place me. Her frown deepens.

'I'm Gaby. Gaby Winters. You looked after me about a year ago after a car accident.'

'Sweet Jesus, Mary and Joseph, is that you, love?'

That Scottish accent. It brings a wave of chest-crushing memories. Of a sterile hospital ward, bone-deep pain that was always worse after dark, suffocating grief. Desolation. A warm hand holding mine and a no-nonsense voice telling me I'd make it through the night, no matter how much it hurt.

'Look at you. How's the leg?'

'Better.'

'And the neck?'

'Ugly.'

She spins her index finger. 'Show me.'

I hesitate for a second, and then turn around, covering the hellion bite so she won't see it when she lifts my hair. Hannah studies the year-old scar for a moment before speaking.

'Not pretty, but better than being dead. Trust me, it was a miracle you survived.' She steps back and surveys me. 'I can't believe how well you look. You all right then?'

I nod. The others have moved closer so I introduce them. Hannah glances at her watch and I know we don't have much time.

'Um . . .' I bring my hands out of my pockets, put them

back again. 'This is going to sound strange, but I need to ask you something. Do you remember who told you about' – my voice catches – 'my brother's funeral?'

Hannah's face crumples. 'Ah, love, I wish I hadn't been the one to tell you.'

'I didn't come here to make you feel bad,' I say. 'I'm just trying to put the pieces together.'

Hannah digs in her handbag and pulls out another cigarette. She lights it, takes a long draw.

'It was a woman. She probably told me her name but it's long gone now.' She turns her head and blows smoke away from me. 'Youngish, early thirties maybe. Dark hair, pretty. A little anxious.'

'Anxious how?'

'She didn't want to be there. And she had a bairn with her.'

I blink. 'A child?'

'Cute little thing with blonde curls. Can't have been more than ten or eleven.' Hannah ashes behind her. 'From memory, they sounded American.'

My breath hitches. Maria and Dani. In the corner of my eye I see Jason put a hand on Maggie's shoulder to steady himself.

'I thought they were family.' Hannah frowns at me. 'Are you still not talking to your parents?'

'No.' I pull my hoodie tighter around me.

She takes another draw, studies me. 'Love, life is too short. I know family can be tricky, but—'

'Just out of curiosity,' Rafa says, gesturing to Jason, 'have you seen him before?'

Hannah's sharp eyes register the strangeness of the question but she shakes her head. 'He's got curls like that sweet bairn, though.' She checks her watch again, takes a final puff on the cigarette. 'I'd better get inside. I hope that helps.'

She wraps me up in a smoky menthol hug as I thank her. 'Gaby, love, look after yourself.'

She's barely through the entrance when Rafa turns to Jason. 'What the fuck?'

'I don't understand.' Jason's eyes are distant, confused.

'No wonder they haven't come out of the woodwork,' Rafa says. 'Any ideas on how they happened to know that Gabe was alive in this hospital?'

'No . . .' Jason is far away, his mind working.

'They knew the story about Jude's funeral was bullshit, so why were they there? Who sent them?'

'I don't *know*, Rafa. I have no idea how Maria and Dani could be involved.'

A man in a grey business suit gives us a dirty look as he leaves the footpath to get past us. I move closer to the road. Maggie puts a reassuring hand on Jason's arm as a bus pulls up and passengers pile out. No one speaks until they disappear into the buildings and small streets around us.

'Dani couldn't remember what happened to you and Jude, but she remembered everything else. She knew who you were.' Jason sounds like he's trying to convince himself. 'Something else must have happened.'

'How long after Jude and I disappeared did they take off?'

'About two days.'

I chew on my lip. There's an answer to this, but it's too far away.

Rafa leans back against the grey wall. His eyes are distant, his annoyance fading. He's too busy thinking.

'You know,' he says to me, slowly, 'if they came here to tell you Jude was dead, maybe they gave Jude a similar message. He must have been hurt too. Maybe not as bad as you, but he still might have ended up in hospital—'

'Oh my God, that makes sense, doesn't it?' Maggie touches my arm. 'Someone saved your life, gave you new memories and sent Maria and Dani to reinforce the lie. And if you and Jude each thought the other was dead, it wouldn't matter if you were left in the same city.'

I wait for her to say it.

'Jude might have been here in Melbourne too.'

Is that even possible? Jude, living and breathing in the same city as me. A whole year ago. My breath shortens. I'm still close to the road, leaning against a sign post, vaguely aware of the lights changing at the intersection down the road and traffic moving quickly behind me. The air is thick with fumes.

Jason takes my arm, leads me over to the wall. 'We need to check every hospital with an emergency ward. We can divide them between us, show around your photo of Jude, see if someone remembers him.'

'It's been twelve months,' I say.

Maggie holds out her hand. 'Give me your phone.'

I hand it over and she taps the screen until she finds what she's looking for. She turns the phone to show me the photo of Jude on Patmos. 'Look at him, Gaby. Anyone who laid eyes on your brother will remember him.'

'What do you think?' I ask Rafa.

He looks at Jason, Maggie and then me. Eyes shining with hope.

'I think we have what some people might refer to as a plan.'

LIFE SUPPORT

Every hospital smells the same. It's not only the antiseptic and disinfectant: it's the worn carpet and plastic chairs in the waiting rooms, the limp flowers in the gift shop, the stench of stale nicotine near the entrance.

And the same people shuffle the corridors: the ill, the injured, the worried. The lost. There's no hiding the reality. Lives end here; hopes are destroyed. And after two hours, the hope I felt on the street is borderline anaemic.

After talking to Hannah, we ordered coffees at the hospital cafeteria and Jason went to work on his phone, scribbling down names and addresses on napkins. He and Maggie took half, Rafa and I the others.

Outside our fourth hospital, Rafa's hand slides around my wrist. 'Get that look off your face.' He links his fingers through mine and for a second we're back on the bench in the gardens, leaning into each other. Together. Right before we screwed everything up again.

The glass doors open. Close. We stay outside.

'It's too early to give up,' he says.

'I'm not giving up.' I take back my hand so I can zip up my hoodie. I'm cold again.

'But?' He doesn't move away. He's going to make me say it. I take a slow breath.

'There's a chance Jude might have been in Melbourne a year ago. But there's also a chance he was on the other side of the world.'

And there's the other option: that he's really dead.

'Gaby . . .' Rafa leans in close, his voice soft. 'Harden the fuck up.' He says it gently, kindly.

I laugh, I can't help it. I turn my head so the breeze dries my eyes. I wasn't crying, not really.

'Come on,' he says. 'If this one's a dead end, we'll go to a bar and drown our sorrows. Find something to argue about.'

As we have at every other hospital, we head to the main desk. The young nurse on duty looks as though he came to work straight off a huge night out. He's still buzzing.

'My brother was in a car accident a year ago,' I say. 'I'm trying to find out if he was brought here.'

The eyebrow ring goes up. 'You don't know?'

'I've been away and my parents aren't talking to me.'

His smile is rueful. 'I hear you, babe.' He turns to the computer next to him. 'What's his name?'

'Jude Winters.'

He clicks and taps a few times. 'This time last year? *Judah* Winters, that him?'

My heart forgets to beat. I grip the counter so hard my fingertips go numb. 'Yes.' I try to swallow. Can't.

'Your parents are missionaries or something, right? Who gives a kid a name like that?' He keeps clicking through screens. Rafa takes my hand again, crushes my fingers with his. I can't bear to look at him.

'Yep. Here we go. Came in with broken ribs, lacerations to the neck and chest, punctured lung . . . ended up in the surgical ward.' He smiles at me then scribbles down a ward number and directions on a scrap of paper and slides it across the counter. 'Someone up there should be able to tell you more.'

Rafa takes the directions and steers me along a solid yellow line painted on the floor. Everything fades around us. There's just the line and the sound of our boots on the too-shiny lino. Rafa's arm is tight around me. I feel weightless, as if everything inside of me has dissolved.

Inside the lift, he holds me against him. My heart hammers, or maybe it's his. Neither of us speaks. I don't know that I could make a sound, even if I had the words. The lift jerks to a stop.

We navigate our way to the ward and find an older woman with heavy green eyeshadow at the nurse's station.

I manage to get Jude's name out, the words strange and thick in my mouth. She checks her computer. I fiddle with the plastic out-tray on her counter, stare at a poster about post-operative infection without taking in a single word. None of this feels real. Is this real?

'Yes,' she says, finally. 'Judah Winters was in here for a few weeks last year.'

'Do you remember him?'

'Darling, I can't remember who was here a week ago.'

I take out my phone and show her Jude's photo. Maggie was right: the recognition is almost immediate. 'Oh, *that* sweetheart.' She grins. 'Hang on.'

She picks up the phone, dials. 'Is Mandy with you? Tell her I need her.'

We wait an agonisingly long minute before a blonde nurse turns into the corridor. Her steps are confident, purposeful. She has a healthy, beachy glow, and the hair tied at her neck is sun-bleached.

'Mandy,' the desk nurse says when she's closer. 'I think you can help these two.'

Mandy stops. She checks out Rafa and smiles at me. Her face is open and friendly.

The older nurse repositions her out-tray. 'They're asking about your boyfriend.'

BUZZING

Mandy's smile falters. 'And by boyfriend you mean . . .?'

I hold out my phone, every nerve ending electrified.

Jude is alive. This woman knows him. He might still be here in Melbourne. Oh my God. Oh. My. God.

JUDE IS ALIVE—

I take a shaky breath, try to calm down. It's no good: my heart still gallops and I can't feel my legs.

Mandy looks at the photo, bites her lower lip. She turns away from the desk. 'Let's talk over here.'

She leads us down the corridor and into a waiting room with two sofas, a stack of tattered magazines and a giant poster about heart disease.

She sits on one of the sofas. After a beat, Rafa and I join her.

'You look like him.' Her eyes flicker with sadness, and her fingers stray to a brooch on her uniform, a delicate silver dove.

'They're related,' Rafa says.

Mandy nods, gathers herself. 'I'm so sorry for your loss.'

The poster bleeds into the walls. My fingers dig into Rafa's thigh. 'He's dead . . .?'

Mandy starts. 'Jude? No. No, oh God, sorry, I meant his sister. His twin.'

Rafa puts his arm around me, keeps me upright.

'Jude's alive?' I manage to get my lips to form the words. 'He's really alive?'

'You didn't know?'

'I've been away.'

And it hits me then: this Jude – the one who was here – thinks I'm dead. My eyes sting with tears. Shit, don't lose it now.

Rafa tightens his hold on me. 'You and Jude, you're together?'

'No, not for a while.' She pulls down the sleeves of her cardigan as if she's cold. 'We email occasionally.'

'Do you know where he is?'

'Still in Tassie as far as I know.'

'Tasmania?'

No way is Rafa as calm as he sounds right now.

'We hooked up while I was looking after him here. He

was always talking about the sea and wanting to be on the water, so as soon as he was well enough we went to Hobart for a fortnight. I've got family down there who sail.' She presses her palms together, places them between her knees. 'It didn't work out. He couldn't cope with his sister being gone and he wouldn't talk about it, or see anyone for help. In the end, he stayed there. Got a job as skipper on a charter boat—'

'Is that where he is – Hobart?' I don't mean to cut her off but I need to know.

'He was a month ago. He sent me a message for my birthday.' Mandy's fingers return to the brooch. 'I think he's doing better. It's hard to tell with Jude.'

Rafa is very still. 'Do you know where he is – exactly?'

'I think he lives on the boat he works on. If they're not out on a charter, it'll be at Constitution Dock.' She looks from me to Rafa and back to me again. 'Are you going to go see him?'

We nod without looking at each other. Rafa's hand twitches against my waist. He's going to shift, right here in front of her.

'Is Jude okay?' she asks. 'Someone else was here yesterday asking about him.'

Something cold and heavy settles in my stomach.

'Who?' Rafa asks.

'I don't know; I wasn't working. I overheard a couple of

nurses talking about it this morning.' She sighs. 'Everyone here knows Jude's a bit of a sore point for me . . .'

'What did they tell them?'

'The only thing they could have known was that he was in Hobart. There's nothing else to tell.'

Rafa helps me up.

'Thanks,' I say. And I mean it.

'I need to get back to work.' Mandy hesitates at the door. 'Tell Jude I said hi, okay?'

When she's gone, Rafa and I look at each other for a long moment. And then he picks me up and swings me around. The room spins: a rush of carpet, the cracked beige sofa, the discoloured heart on the poster.

'He's alive,' he says in my ear. His relief and joy flow into mine, fierce and intense. He sets me down, takes an uneven breath, his green eyes vivid.

'Let's go and get your brother.'

WAKING

At the hotel, Maggie hugs me tightly.

'Oh my God, Gaby . . .'

I couldn't tell them; Rafa had to.

Jason sinks to the bed, drops his head. Maggie gives me one last squeeze and sits with him. She puts her arm around his waist, rests her head on his shoulder. Rafa stares out the window, his broad shoulders framed by the dull sky. A pigeon walks along the ledge outside. It cocks its head at its reflection, pecks at the glass. I sit on the other end of the bed, buzzing. Still incapable of forming a coherent sentence.

My thoughts crash over each other: he's alive. Jude, living, breathing, grieving. We could shift and be with him in seconds. But which Jude? And which version of me has he been mourning?

Finally, Jason wipes his face. 'So, we're going to Constitution Dock?'

'You know it?' Rafa asks.

'I was in Hobart ten years ago to meet with a priest who had some unorthodox theories on fallen angels.'

'Think you can guide the shift?'

Jason stands up. 'I'll try.'

'Then let's go. We're already a day behind whoever else is looking for him.'

I stand. It takes a second for feeling to come back into my legs.

'It's always cool in Hobart, even this time of year,' Maggie says. She opens the wardrobe and pulls out a familiar cherry-coloured scarf from her suitcase. It takes me a second to place it: the last time I saw it, it was half-finished, hanging over the chair in her room the night Taya kidnapped her.

'Here.' She loops it around my neck. 'This is for you.'

I stare at her for a moment and then run my fingers over the soft wool. Almost cry at her thoughtfulness. Shit, I'm a mess. Again. 'It's beautiful, Mags.'

I go to the window while she changes from ballet flats into boots. I put my hands in my pockets to steady them. Outside, the pigeon has gone. Far below, the street keeps moving under the murky sky: traffic jostles, lights change, people stream across the intersection.

Rafa looks down at the city, our rucksacks ready at his feet.

'You all right?'

I nod. 'It's just . . .'

He searches my face. 'Yeah, I know.'

And he does. I see it in his eyes. We're close to finding Jude, but only one of us can have the version of him we remember.

'Gaby, I promise you, it's going to be okay.'

A few minutes later we shift into a dark, dusty room in an old church. Maggie recovers quickly and we walk the three blocks to Hobart's main dock, past centuries-old buildings and noisy cafes. The sky is heavy with low, dark clouds and the wind is cold. I pull on my hoodie, tighten my new scarf and brace myself against the gale coming up the wide Derwent River.

The dock is crowded with yachts, fishing trawlers and million-dollar pleasure cruisers. Everything smells like salt water and fish. We know Jude's not on a fishing boat, but a charter could mean a yacht or a cruiser – we didn't think to ask. So we have to check them all. We split up.

My eyes sting as I jog past trawlers stacked with crab pots, raising a few eyebrows from the weary fishermen on deck. I peer into the cabin of a small yacht. No sign of life. I move on to the next one. Then the next, heading further out into the harbour. What if we've missed him? What if he's out on a week-long charter? What if he got bored and moved on? Maybe he's hanging out with mates or he went fishing. Or maybe whoever beat us to the hospital beat us here too.

Rafa catches up with me. 'It's only been ten minutes.' Gulls circle above, crying out to each other. 'Hey.' He pulls me to a stop. 'Jude's lived here a year. This isn't a big place – we'll ask around, find out where he is and when he'll be back. Someone will know.'

I don't want to wait. I want to see him now. I can't separate hope from fear any more: it's a single raging storm under my ribs. Maggie and Jason are halfway along a parallel pier, their blond heads together.

Rafa and I start down the next row. A large yacht motors in, its sails tied down. A group of women in pink spray jackets are clustered on the deck, laughing and shrugging on backpacks. Their voices whip away in the wind. We're still a dozen berths away when a deckhand jumps onto the pier and ties up the boat.

Onboard, a shock of dark hair appears out of a cabin.

The pink jackets are off the yacht, walking down the pier, blocking our view. We step around them, picking up snatches of conversation.

'—best hen party *ever*.'

'How freaking cold was it last night?'

'How hot was the skipper?'

The guy onboard moves across the deck, his back still to us. Rafa and I stop dead.

That hair. That build. The way he rolls his shoulders. I can't take my eyes off him, not even to check Rafa's reaction.

He bends over to pick something up and when he straightens I get a good look at his profile.

It's him.

Everything else fades: the sky, the water, the boats. Rafa. Even Rafa. There is nothing but the figure on that boat. He's winding ropes, talking to the deckhand. His hair is longer than I remember.

And then Jude looks around.

He sees me.

His arms fall to his sides. Rope hits the deck. His lips form my name but he's too far away for me to hear it. I'm moving again, in the cold wind. He steps off the boat, walks towards me, dazed. Then he stops, uncertain.

'Are you real?'

My throat closes over; my heart is too big for my chest. I reach him in three steps, throw myself at him. We nearly stumble off the side of the dock. His arms clamp around me, his face presses into my hair. We collapse to our knees and I don't let go, even when splinters stab through my jeans. He crushes me to him.

He smells of the sea.

Time stops. I have no idea how long we stay like that. My bad knee complains. I ignore it. I can't breathe properly. I don't care.

Eventually, his grip loosens a little. He strokes my hair. Mumbles something I don't catch. He draws back enough to look at me, his chest rising and falling, eyes searching. 'Are you real?' he says again.

I touch his face. 'Are you?'

He drags me back into a hug.

Please let this be real. I'll do anything, just let this be real.

Rafa is sitting on the pier, his back against a pylon, arms folded. Eyes shining, face streaked.

The cold and the wind and the smell of the pier rush back in. Underneath us, the river slaps at the timber. My knee's had enough. I have to stand up. Jude steadies me as we get to our feet. His dark brown eyes – my dark brown eyes – search my face again.

'Princess, what the fuck?' Jude wipes his face, not taking his eyes from me. 'I saw you die.'

LONG STORY SHORT

'I saw *you* die,' I say. 'We were arguing over music—'

'—I lost control of the car and we rolled—'

'And you . . .' I swallow. He's standing right here, so I can say the words. 'You were decapitated by a guidepost.'

He stares at me, hands still on my shoulders. 'No. *You* were.'

My knees almost give out again. It's impossible: this is *my* Jude. I point to both of our heads, still attached to our necks. 'Obviously not.'

'But—'

'It's a long story.' Rafa climbs to his feet, wipes his cheek against his shoulder.

Jude studies him, momentarily distracted. 'I know you.'

'You remember me?' There's no hiding the hope in those three words.

'Not really.' A pause. 'You've kind of been in my dreams.' Jude holds up his palms. 'Not in a gay way.'

Rafa half-smiles. 'Glad to hear it.'

'In that dream, are you fighting hell-beasts in a nightclub?' I ask.

Jude frowns. 'How could you know that?'

'I've been having the same dream for a year.'

Jude narrows one eye like I'm messing with him. How do I explain this?

'That's Rafa,' I say as a place to start.

Jude steps forward and offers his hand. 'Jude.'

Rafa falters, and then he slaps Jude's palm and drags him into a man-hug. When he lets go, Rafa makes a point of taking two steps back. Jude steps back as well, looks awkward. I laugh. Or cry. I can't tell the difference right now.

The deckhand is hovering by the yacht. 'Everything okay, skip?'

'Cody, man . . . I have no idea.'

Cody scratches the tip of his nose. A gust of wind blows his long fringe into his eyes. He waits for an explanation. Doesn't get one.

Jude gestures to the boat. 'We can finish up later. Take off if you want.'

Cody doesn't have to be told twice.

'Come aboard, sit down,' Jude says.

I look around for Maggie and Jason. They're hurrying up the pier towards us, almost running. They get a curious glance from Cody as he passes them.

'Hang on,' I say to Jude. 'These two are with us.'

Maggie is looking from me to Jude and back again.

'Wow, you two are so alike,' she says when she's close.

'Jude, this is my friend Maggie, and that's—' I pause. Too hard. 'That's Jason.'

Maggie is straight in for a hug. Jude looks at me over her shoulder, careful where he puts his hands. She steps back, sees he's a little startled. 'Sorry,' she says and smiles. 'You're so much like Gaby I feel I already know you.'

Jude nods. Frowns. Offers a hand to Jason more out of habit than presence of mind.

Jason shakes it – old-school style – but doesn't speak. He keeps blinking and swallowing, occasionally nodding even though nobody's talking.

We follow Jude onboard. The yacht is huge – the kind that races from Sydney to Hobart. The mast towers above us. We go down into the galley, lush with wall-to-wall gleaming timber and dark green leather. Empty champagne bottles sit in a neat row on the sink and the place smells of pancakes and maple syrup. I wonder if Jude cooked breakfast for the girls. We squeeze around an oval table and Rafa drops our rucksacks at his feet. He's acting as if he's okay with the fact Jude doesn't remember being Rephaite. Maybe for the moment he is: maybe Rafa's happy to have any version of his best friend, as long as he's alive.

I can't stop staring at Jude. He studies each of us, his attention settling back on me. I look to Rafa. He nods for me to start.

Great.

'Right . . . well.' I roll up the linen placemat in front of me. Even on the calm water of the dock the yacht still rocks gently. More than ever, I understand why Daisy and Rafa were in no hurry to attempt to explain the Rephaim to me. I miss Daisy. I wonder how she'd react if she was here now, sitting across from Jude? How she would tell him that life as he knows it is a lie?

Maggie gives me an encouraging smile. 'Start with what you remember.'

It's good advice. So I tell him about waking up in hospital, learning he was dead. And then how our 'parents' came to Melbourne and took his ashes without visiting me.

Jude listens, nods. 'I got the same message about you. Some woman and her kid came to the ward—' He glances at Jason. 'What?'

'We'll get to that,' I say. 'Long story.'

I tell him about the violent nightclub dream and posting the short story about it online. How Rafa turned up at Pan Beach, followed by Taya and Malachi. And then Rafa's bombshell about the Fallen and the Rephaim. I explain it the way he told me. Jude takes it all in. He doesn't ask questions or interrupt. He's always been quick to get his head around new concepts, but this is a tad more complicated than understanding the government structure of a European country we're about to land in.

'Are you doing okay?' I ask.

He nods. 'Keep going.'

I tell him about Patmos, the photo of us in Istanbul. I rush through Maggie's kidnapping and my experience at the Sanctuary – minus my time in the cage. By the time I've told him about the fight up the mountain and meeting Nathaniel, his eyes are distant.

He's overloaded. He sits back and stares up at the wood-panelled ceiling. 'Bloody hell.' His fingers go to his neck. 'I thought this was a birth mark.'

I check under his hair and find raised skin in the shape of crescent moon; a scar through the middle of it. Someone tried to take his head too but with a little more finesse. I take off my scarf and show him my matching scar. His breath comes out in a hiss.

'What the fuck—' He pushes the neckline of my hoodie aside, more interested in the hellion bite. 'What is that?'

I pause. 'You know that monster you kill in your dream? I ended up in a cage with one when I was in Italy.'

'She cut off its head,' Rafa says, as if that's the most important part of the story, 'but not before the pricks let it drink from her.'

Jude stares at him. He's trying hard to absorb this, but he's struggling. 'The people who did this – they're the ones you're saying I walked away from?'

'Yep.'

'And you're telling me I left Gaby with those assholes?'

'In fairness, they only turned on her after you two disappeared last year. Actually, they only turned on her when they thought she'd changed sides. They found her with me last week, put two and two together and got seven.'

Jude's breathing is controlled, his face like stone.

Rafa pulls two books out of the rucksack, slides them across the table. I'm not sure now's the time for show and tell, but it's too late, Jude's already reaching for them. He can't help himself.

The first is leather-bound and embossed. Jude runs his palm over the cover. He flicks through a few pages and then stops when he sees his handwriting scrawled in the margins. He traces a fingertip over the blue ink. I open the second book and hold out the tattered photo of us in front of the Blue Mosque in Istanbul. Jude peers at it, looks from it to me, and back again.

'Bloody hell,' he says again, forcing a smile. 'What's with your hair?'

I touch the edge of the old photo, fight the emotion tugging at me.

'You're taking this better than she did,' Rafa says.

'I'm faking it.' Jude rubs his eyes.

'That's your laptop too,' I say. 'There's not much on there but you should take a look when you're ready.'

Jude studies Rafa. 'We trained and fought together? You used to have my back?'

'Through the good, the bad and the ugly – and I'm not just talking about the women.'

Jude's smile is wry. It takes some of the tension from his jaw. Then, to Jason: 'Am I supposed to know you too?'

'We're related.' Jason explains how. Slowly, patiently. He tells Jude about Dani. When he's done, Jude sits back from the table and runs both hands through his hair. We've been at this for nearly two hours.

'So, just to check I'm understanding all this: there are two groups of half-angel bastards at war with each other, a horde of demons after both sides, and a missing kid who has visions? And Gaby and I might know where two hundred fallen angels are hiding out?'

Yeah, he's the smart one of the family all right.

'The Rephaim aren't really at war with each other,' I say, trying to flatten out the placemat I've been strangling. 'But the demons – that's a whole other matter.'

We haven't mentioned Iowa yet.

'You can accept all that?' Jason asks.

Jude gives him a measured look. 'My sister is sitting next to me. The only way that's possible is if the rest of it's true. If that's the price for getting her back, I'll pay it.'

My eyes burn with fresh tears. I wipe them away.

A seagull cries out on the pier, then another yacht glides past and we rock back and forth in its wake. Jude splays his fingers on the polished table top. I don't remember his knuckles being so scarred.

'I've been told I'm a soulless prick by a few women in the past year,' he says. 'Turns out they were right.'

'Hey, we're not—'

'And we didn't talk for a decade? No fucking way. Who told you that?' He doesn't wait for an answer. He climbs out from the table and pushes past Rafa. 'I need air.'

Jude disappears up the stairs to the deck. Rafa and I are right behind him, bringing our gear with us.

'Give me a minute,' Jude says. 'Let me absorb this.' He steps off the boat.

'Where are you going?' I sound panicked. I am.

His face softens. 'Just there.' He points to the end of the pier, out in the river. There are no boats moored, just open water. 'I'm not leaving your sight.'

Maggie and Jason come up on deck and the four of us wait in silence, huddled against the wind. Fifty metres away, Jude paces back and forth, stops and stares out over the wide river. Glances back at me every few seconds. The wind whips his hair around his face.

Rafa stands close to me to block the breeze. 'He'll be fine,' he says. I'm not sure who he's trying to convince. A gust stirs the river and the yacht rocks under our feet.

My heart is trying to climb out of my throat. I'm a whirlwind of joy and fear, anticipation and anxiety. What's Jude thinking? How does he feel about me now he's had time to himself? What happens now?

They are the longest fifteen minutes of my life.

Finally, my brother comes back to us.

'Jude, listen,' Rafa says. 'I know it's all fucked up right now, but we'll figure it out.'

Jude pauses on the pier, takes in Rafa's proximity to me and then steps on board. 'Figure what out? That some other version of me was a big enough prick that I took off without my sister and didn't speak to her for a decade? And then I nearly get her killed doing God-knows-what, and now demons are after us? Dude, I don't want to figure it out.'

'Then you'll both die. For real this time.'

Rafa is angry with Jude. I wasn't expecting that.

'Some serious shit happened today—'

'I'm not who you want me to be,' Jude says.

Rafa throws his head back. 'Is that the only chorus this family knows? For fuck's sake—'

'Give him a break.' I get between them. 'I got all this in doses – he's just had the whole lot dumped on him in one go. He needs more time.'

'We don't *have* time.'

'You got that right,' a new voice says over the wind.

Malachi.

He's watching us from the pier. How the hell did he find—

Daniel. That bastard. In a rush I get it. The job that kept Malachi away from Pan Beach wasn't some new lead on the Fallen. It was finding Jude. I didn't tell Daniel much about my time in Melbourne, but it was enough to give him the same idea we had.

'You're looking well, Jude,' Malachi says. 'Hello, Maggie, have you missed me?'

Jude eyeballs him. 'And who the fuck are you?'

'Malachi's part of the crew from the Sanctuary,' I say.

Jude's eyes harden. 'Is he one of the bastards who hurt you?'

Malachi's hands come up. 'Hey now, we've moved past that and Gabe's scored a few rounds herself.' His black hair blows across his face. 'You don't know who I am either, do you? What the hell did you two *do*?'

Rafa catches my eye. There's no mistaking what he wants. We have to get Jude out of here before Malachi's reinforcements arrive. He would have called the Sanctuary before he revealed himself. The last thing Jude needs is to get caught up in a Rephaite brawl. The problem is, we haven't actually touched on shifting yet. All the talk of travel has been pretty vague.

'You've been busy,' Rafa says to Malachi. 'How many nurses did you sweet-talk before you found the right hospital?'

'Six.' Malachi watches me get closer to Jude, knowing full well I would have shifted by now if I could.

'Do you trust me?' I say to Jude, quiet enough so the wind catches the words before they carry to Malachi.

'Of course.'

'Whatever happens in the next few seconds, go with it.' I don't look at Jason: he's standing right next to Maggie and he'll know what to do.

Rafa crosses the deck as if he's trying to intimidate Malachi. 'How long have you been sniffing around here?'

Malachi steps back from the boat. 'A couple of days. I should have known Jude would be out on the—'

Rafa disappears. I grab Jude and don't see Rafa materialise before the boat drops away beneath us.

Jude doesn't even have time to swear.

THE ELEPHANT IN THE ROOM

Jude is Rephaite, so if he'd had the slightest hesitation about Rafa he'd still be on the yacht rather than standing in the tiny house in Patmos leaning against the fireplace, recovering.

'We can't be here,' I whisper to Rafa. 'If the Gatekeepers find us—'

'Just let him see his room.'

'Bel's been here, remember? He said he tracked us after the Sanctuary when I was covered in—'

'I *know*.'

Jude straightens and looks up at us, pale. 'What. The. Fuck.'

I step between him and the window, block the view of the harbour. The sun is breaking the eastern horizon;

I have no idea what day it is here.

'The offspring of the Fallen can travel pretty much instantly. Anywhere in the world.'

He looks at me. Blinks. 'You did that?'

'No, but we used to be able to – both of us. Look, we don't have much time here but Rafa's right: you should take a look around. You used to stay here. Some of your things are still in your room.' I try to nudge him along but he stops and stares out the window.

'Where are we?'

'Greece.' I say it like it's no big deal. 'Patmos. Come on.'

Jude stands at the window for a few more seconds and then follows me along the corridor and into the bedroom. He makes his way around the room, just as I did a week ago. He starts at the bookcase, picks out random books and then caresses the first editions of the *Lord of the Rings*. Just like I did. Next, he moves over to the drawers and pulls them out, one at a time.

'We should take the weapons,' Rafa says from the door.

I stop watching Jude long enough to find a bag under the bed. When I look up he's at the wardrobe, both doors open, staring intently at his weapons cache. Rafa steps around him and grabs a handful of knives. He lobs them to me, hilt first, one at a time. I catch them without thinking. Then he uses a leather belt to bundle half a dozen swords together.

Jude needs to process all this but we don't have time. Bel could check the cottage every hour for all we know, in the hope of finding Rafa and me here. I don't want Jude to face a demon today. Or ever. 'Right,' I say, 'let's go.'

'Where?' Rafa holds the sword bundle in one hand.

'Your place in Pan Beach.'

He takes a slow breath. 'We've got safe houses all over the world, Gaby. You can ring Maggie—'

'I don't want to hide out in one of Mya's Third World hovels.'

'What does it matter? We've got Jude. Let's go somewhere safe.'

I zip the duffel bag. 'Pan Beach is my home. I know that doesn't mean anything to you, but it does to me.'

'I'm well aware of how attached you are to that place, but every man and his dog knows that's where you'll be. And once word gets out Jude's there, what do you think will happen? It won't be too hard for Bel or—'

'Hey.'

We stop, look at Jude.

'If Gaby wants to go to Pandanus Beach, that's good enough for me. We can decide on a longer-term plan from there.'

Rafa's nostrils flare. 'You two—' He doesn't finish, shakes his head. 'Fine.'

I narrow my eyes. 'You're not going to take us somewhere else, are you? Or leave me here?'

'Seriously? You still have to ask me that?'

'Sorry.' And I am. 'I'm a little uptight right now.'

'No shit.'

Jude closes the wardrobe loudly. 'Whatever this is' – he points to Rafa and me – 'I assume you can continue it where we're going?'

I swear I see heat in Rafa's neck.

'Good. Can you take me back to Hobart first?'

I change my grip on the weapons bag. It's heavier than I expected. 'Why?'

'To grab my stuff.' He looks to Rafa. 'I'd be right in assuming I won't be going back there again?'

Rafa gives me a triumphant look. 'See? Jude gets it.'

I text Maggie while Rafa checks maps on his phone. She and Jason are at the hotel in Melbourne. I suggest they stay there, make the most of the room. Stay safe.

Jude waits, pensive.

'Man up,' Rafa says. 'You used to do this drunk.'

Jude presses his lips together. 'Screw it. Let's go.'

It's not a gentle arrival.

The floor slams under us so hard I pitch forward. Rafa breaks my fall, his arms locked around me. I lose contact with Jude. He hits somewhere behind me with a dull thud.

'Bloody hell,' he mutters.

My legs are tangled with Rafa's. He's cradling my head.

'You all right?' he asks. He runs a hand down my side. My head swims with sandalwood and cinnamon. And musty carpet.

'Uh huh.' I climb off him, not trusting myself to make eye contact. We're in a tiny room with only a desk and an old vinyl kitchen chair. If I stretched out my hands I could almost touch the white stucco walls either side of me. Beyond the thick glass pane is a sweep of hills and the choppy river.

Jude is against the desk, recovering. It's cluttered with books and newspapers, a large nautical map. 'You always land that rough?'

'Not if I get decent directions.' Rafa sits up. 'The correct height of this hill would have been handy.'

'I thought you said you were good at this.'

'I thought you had a higher pain threshold.' He grins as Jude helps him off the floor.

Jude shakes his head. A small smile. 'You shouldn't have talked yourself up so much.'

God, they're already so easy with each other.

'Is this your place?' I ask.

'It's a mate's. I stay here whenever I'm not on the water.'

On the desk, the newspapers are open to the crossword page. Every puzzle filled in. My eyes skim the spines of the novels: Cormac McCarthy, George R. R. Martin, Ursula

Le Guin. T-shirts, jumpers and jeans, all neatly folded.

Jude grabs a few things and I follow him down a short corridor and into a room at the end, with a bar crammed with spirits, an old-fashioned gas heater and a tartan sofa.

'My bed,' he says, gesturing to the sofa. 'Don't look like that – it folds out. I've slept on worse.'

I run my fingertips over the pilled fabric. 'Remember Peru?'

'In the cave with the llamas?'

'You slept with that ridiculous hat on. The one with the tassels and ear flaps.'

He grabs a backpack from behind the bar and puts clean clothes into it. 'It's called a *chullo*. And it was the warmest thing I had after you pinched the blanket.'

'I won that fair and square. Remember?'

The last word hangs in the air. His smile falters. All the warmth leaches out of the moment. We never slept in a cave with llamas – or maybe we did, but not in the way we remember.

'You already packed?' Rafa asks from the doorway.

Jude tests the straps on his pack. 'Yeah, I always have a bag ready to go.'

'So why did you stay here so long?'

A shrug. 'I couldn't bring myself to leave Australia.' He ties a pair of combat boots to the pack. 'Ready.'

A few seconds later, he's recovering again, this time over

Rafa's sink. I text Maggie to tell her where we are.

By the time I'm done, Jude and Rafa are at the table, beers in hand. I say no when Rafa offers me one. The afternoon sun is behind the shopping centre, casting half the kitchen in shadow. I find a patch of filtered sunlight near the bench and let the warmth seep into my bones.

'My place is nicer,' I say to Jude.

He's already feeling the change in temperature and strips down to a black t-shirt. He's more ripped than I remember.

'So, seriously, are we safe here?' I ask Rafa, peeling off my hoodie.

He gives me a pointed look. 'I doubt it. That's why I didn't want to come back to Pan Beach.'

'I mean are we safe here, in this shack. From Gatekeepers. We never finished that conversation.'

He shrugs. 'Depends.'

'On what?'

'How far the hell-turds tracked us on Tuesday.'

My eyes flick to Jude, make sure he's still here. Still real.

'How's that work?'

Rafa sips his beer. 'Hellions are bonded to the Gatekeepers. The hell-turds get the scent, the demons read what they're thinking and pick up a location.'

'How far away can hellions track Rephaim?'

'If they've had our blood? Generally anywhere on the planet – at least for a couple of days, or as long as they keep the taste.' He puts his bottle down. 'Same goes for hellion blood if it's fresh; if we're covered in enough of it, they'll find us. At least get a general idea of where we are. You had enough on you after the cage for them to track us to Patmos, but Bel was pretty vague about what he found when they got here. He's a smug prick; he would have rubbed it in if he'd found your place or this one. I think they followed us to Pan Beach but then lost the scent.'

My skin crawls. But Bel would have been here waiting for us if he knew about this place . . .

'We're not going to be anywhere near safe until we get the demons out of that farmhouse,' I say.

'Agreed. But it's going to take more than our crew to do it. And no way am I asking Pretty Boy and the Five for help. They can come to us.'

'Isn't this a bit more important than a pissing contest?'

His eyebrows go up. 'You want to see a pissing contest? Wait until Daniel and Mya turn up here to fight over Jude.'

Shit. Mya.

'Does she have to know?'

'Think about it. Malachi's told Daniel about Jude by now and, if Mya finds out you kept her in the dark, she'll think you've sided with the Sanctuary.'

'She can think what she likes. For fuck's sake, I just got my brother back.'

Jude tears a neat strip off his beer label, pastes it on the table. 'Rafa,' he says quietly. 'Any chance Gaby and I could have some time to ourselves?'

'I'm not leaving you unprotected.'

'How about some privacy then?'

Rafa looks from Jude to me, his expression unreadable. Then he stands up, points down the corridor. 'I'll be in my room. Yell if anyone turns up.'

Jude waits until Rafa's door closes.

'Do you trust him?'

I glance down the empty corridor. 'Yeah, I do. Mostly.' Now's not the time to tell Jude all the things I don't know about what happened between Rafa and me in the past.

I pull out the photos I took from the iron room, the ones of him and Rafa. I don't attempt to explain how I got them. 'And so did you.'

He studies each picture. 'This is mental, right?'

I nod and my throat closes over again. I watch him frowning while he thinks, his unruly hair in his eyes. My brother. Alive. Here, with me. And then he comes around the table, pulls me into another hug. He still smells salty. I bury my face in his neck; his stubble is rough against my cheek.

'I'm so sorry,' he whispers, his voice thick.

'Me too.'

We breathe together. In. Out. In. Out. We've never been huggers; we are now.

He lets out a deep sigh. 'You're alive. That's all that matters.'

'But Jude . . .' My words are muffled and he pulls back to look at me. 'What we remember . . . none of it's real. Not Peru, not Italy, not school. Not our parents.'

He frowns again, lets me go.

'What do you remember?' I ask.

We sit on the edge of the table. He stares out the window for a moment, and then he tells me: fighting with our parents; running off backpacking without telling them; the race up the hill at Monterosso; camping in Peru; bungee jumping in Switzerland; getting jobs in London; the crash. Our stories aren't similar – they are exactly the same. *Exactly*. Neither of us has a memory the other doesn't.

'We went to Italy after Switzerland, right?' he asks me. 'Do you remember how we got there – train, bus, car?'

'No, I've got lots of gaps from that trip. Anything before the accident is hazy.'

'But we've both got the same gaps. I guess whoever did this didn't think we'd ever have the chance to compare memories,' Jude says. 'But why? I don't understand why someone would make us think we're different people, make us believe we lost each other. What does it achieve?'

'I don't know.' I pause. 'But Rafa thinks you might have been involved somehow.'

'Based on what?'

'On the fact we still know we're twins; that the way I remember you is apparently not that different to who you used to be – minus the half-angel bit. And the fact I know the words to every Foo Fighters song ever written.'

'You hate Foo Fighters.'

'Yep, especially at six o'clock in the morning. And now I don't.'

'That's bizarre.' A crooked smile. 'And kind of cool.'

'And I've been dreaming about that nightclub massacre, which turns out to be your memory, not mine.'

'But why would I do that? How could I do that?'

Now's not the time to tell him we probably did a deal with demons – and it nearly got us killed. He can come to that conclusion on his own.

'So, how did you find me?' Jude asks, shaking off the too-hard questions.

I tell him about Melbourne. And Mandy.

'How is she?'

'Okay, I guess. Still hung up on you.'

'She's only human.' Jude's smile is ironic until he realises what he's just said. I prod him before he can get too lost in that train of thought.

'I can't believe you were in an actual relationship.'

'I thought it would help, but she wanted more than I could give her. The usual drama, really, it just took a little longer.'

I don't remember Jude being this open with me. We never talked about relationship stuff, or not that I remember anyway. He crosses to the window, listens to the surf.

'I've missed that sound. I thought about coming here when I was in hospital, but then I hooked up with Mandy and we went to Tassie—'

'You were still coming to Pan Beach?'

'Yeah, but it felt wrong. If I hadn't been pushing so hard about coming here, I wouldn't have run off the road.'

I close my eyes for a second, hear squealing tyres.

'Actually, you were thinking about coming to Pan Beach . . . *before*,' I say. 'You'd bookmarked surfing websites on your laptop. One of them was for here.'

Jude comes back to the table. 'It doesn't matter. What's on that laptop, what happened before, the memories, none of it.'

'How can you say that?'

'Because you're my sister. End of story.'

'We didn't speak for ten years, Jude. The past—' I pause. 'It's complicated and messy and it's not going to go away.'

'We'll figure it out.'

I stare past him at a black mark on the window and the way it blocks a fraction of the sun. 'I can't lose you again.'

'That's not going to happen. Ever.'

'I don't want to remember my old life if it's going to tear us apart again.'

'Gaby.' He waits until I look at him. 'I don't care what happened. Nothing is going to tear us apart.' He pulls out a chair. 'All I want now is to keep you safe.'

'I don't think that's an option any more.'

'Why not? We could go to one of those beaches, disappear.' He meets my eyes. 'Get on with our lives without all this other shit hanging over our heads.'

We watch each other. The possibility hangs between us.

'Fucking unbelievable.'

We look up to find Rafa standing in the corridor, his eyes dark, flinty.

Accusing.

CAN YOU HANDLE THE TRUTH?

'You could walk away from us – just like that?' Rafa is gripping his beer bottle so tightly his knuckles are white. He must have shifted to the corridor because we didn't hear him coming.

Jude opens his mouth. Closes it again.

'You're our fucking leader. Everything went to shit when you disappeared. And now you're back and you're going to piss off again?' Rafa's gaze moves to me. 'And you'd go with him, wouldn't you? You two, finally together again, and the rest of us can get fucked.'

'Rafa, ease up,' I say. 'He doesn't remember that life.'

He shakes his head. 'I forgot what it's like when you two are together. Nothing else matters.'

'Mate.' Jude stands up. 'We're not going anywhere.'

'You have no idea, do you? You two lost each other – I lost both of you.' He hurls the bottle at the wall. It smashes against the tiles over the sink and the place instantly reeks of beer. 'Screw this.' He shifts. Two seconds later something hits the wall in his room.

Jude is still staring at the space where Rafa was just standing.

'I'll go,' I say.

'I don't think he's in the mood for talking.'

'I'll be fine.'

He studies me. 'What's the story with you two?'

I pick at the hem of my t-shirt. 'It's complicated.'

Rafa is sitting on the edge of his bed, knees on elbows, head down. The chair is on its side, one steel leg folded back at the wrong angle. There's a hole in the flaking wall above it, plaster dust on the floor. Putting furniture through walls is starting to become a habit.

'Rafa.' I sit next to him on the grey-and-white-striped doona. Sunlight falls through the window onto his pillow.

He doesn't lift his head. I'm close enough to touch him. I don't. From the kitchen come the sound of clinking glass and running water.

'Jude's not going anywhere,' I say.

He doesn't react. I hate it when he's this quiet; it's unnerving.

'And neither am I. Not without you.'

He turns his head towards me, but doesn't look at me. 'Yeah? Why not?'

'Because I don't want to.'

'You could've fooled me.'

'Rafa—'

'You're hot, then you're cold. You trust me, then you don't. You let me get close, then you shut me down. You've got Jude now, you don't need me.'

'I do.' I say it quietly because the words are hard. 'I do need you.'

He stares past me for a few seconds, breathing quietly. 'Why?'

'Do you have to ask?'

When he looks at me, his eyes are clouded. 'Gaby . . .'

I tuck my hands between my knees and wait. Give him space.

Finally Rafa frowns and exhales. 'Jude's right. The safest thing would be for you both to disappear again. Cut contact with all of us.'

'We're not doing that, and you know it.' He doesn't speak again so I lean closer, lower my voice. 'I know things are messy with us, but do you really think I could just walk away from you?'

This time he doesn't look away. 'Do you really think I'd let you?'

We watch each other for a few long seconds.

'We really suck at this, don't we?' he says.

'You don't see Mags and Jason yelling at each other in a deserted park in the middle of the night.'

'Only one of us was yelling.'

'Yeah, well, I didn't expect to suddenly find myself alone.'

'Did the swan scare you?' A smile plays on his lips.

'Shut up.' I say it softly.

He's still watching me, his green eyes looking for something. 'Gaby . . . I'm not going to talk about the past any more, okay? Whatever this is, it starts now.'

Whatever this is.

I take in his long lashes, the strong lines of his face. Everything about him is so familiar now.

'That's okay for now, Rafa. But it's not going away. We'll have to deal with it some time. Can you live with that?'

He hesitates, and then his lips brush mine, tentative. I kiss him back – firmly, purposefully – take a handful of his t-shirt to keep him close. He murmurs his approval and draws my legs across his lap. This kiss is longer, lingering. His hand strays to my thigh. I touch his face, trace his jaw with my thumb. When we break apart, Rafa rests his forehead on mine. 'God, I want you,' he whispers.

Footsteps in the corridor remind us we're not alone.

I swing my legs back around so my feet are on the floor.

Rafa takes a deep breath, still watching me. Jude clears his throat before he steps into the doorway. If he notices the charged air between us he doesn't mention it.

'So you're going to hang around?' Rafa says. I reach down, pretend to retie my boot lace to hide the heat in my neck.

'Yeah.' Jude rubs his shoulder, the one he landed on. 'I need to understand who we are and figure out what happened last year. It's the only way we can stay safe. Until then we're running blind.'

'I thought none of that mattered?'

Jude acknowledges the dig with a dry smile.

'If that's the plan then, buddy, you're going to need help. You need to choose who to trust: the Outcasts or Nathaniel's crew.'

'Why do I have to choose either? You'll do.'

Rafa blinks and then laughs. 'All I've been worried about is finding you. I don't have much of a plan beyond that. You were always the one for strategy.'

Jude picks up the chair, straightens the bent leg. 'Give me time, I'll come up with something.'

Rafa shakes his head, his smile the same as Jude's.

'What?' Jude tests his weight on the chair before sitting down.

'You. You haven't changed. No drama. No bullshit. You're rolling with all this so much quicker than Gaby did.'

He looks at me quickly and I feel the heat in my neck again, the kiss. I push it away. I can't be offended: he's right. In fact, it's a little disconcerting how easily Jude is slipping into this new life.

Jude seems to weigh up something. 'All this . . . it almost makes sense. Ever since I woke up in the hospital, I've felt . . . wrong. Not only because you were gone,' he says to me. 'It's as if there's something I should be doing, but I can't quite remember what it is. And the dreams, they've always felt more like memories.' He shrugs, apologetic. 'The only way I've coped is being on the water. Out in the strait the sky's so big, the ocean so demanding, the rest of the world falls away.'

My phone rings in my back pocket and Jude recognises the Foo Fighters tune and smiles.

It's Maggie.

'Are you still at Rafa's?' she says before I can speak.

'Yeah.'

'We're coming there now.'

'What's going on?'

A pause. 'Jason has heard from Dani. She wants to talk to you.'

FROM THE MOUTHS OF BABES

Maggie and Jason arrive before we're back in the kitchen.

'This place smells like a brewery,' Maggie says.

The remnants of Rafa's bottle are in the sink, the dishcloth rinsed and drying over the tap. I join Maggie at the table.

'Well?' I say to Jason. 'Where is she?'

'I don't know. She's ringing back in a minute.'

'For fuck's sake,' Rafa says. 'Why can't she tell us where she is and we'll go there? We're not going to hurt her.'

Jason sets his phone on the table between us. 'We're not putting her at risk.'

I pick the glass from the sink, take it to the bin. Why now? Has she suddenly remembered something? And do I want to know right this minute?

I've got Jude back. All I want is a bit of time with him without all the other bullshit. Is that too much to ask?

'What did she say?' I ask.

'She's had a vision. She didn't say what it was, only that she needed to talk to you and Rafa. And she knows we found Jude . . .'

Jude sits across from Maggie and me. 'This is our, what – distant cousin? The girl who sees angels and demons, and . . . us?'

'She doesn't see the Fallen – except for Nathaniel,' I say. 'And she hasn't been able to see either of us for a year.'

'But she was there when we were hurt?'

'If she was she doesn't remember it. But it was her vision that led to us doing whatever it was we did.'

Jason's phone rings and he puts it straight to speaker.

'Dani?'

'Are you with them?' She's on speaker too. Her voice is soft, with a hint of a New York accent. It's hard to believe it belongs to a seer gifted enough to be a threat to the Rephaim. She sounds even younger than twelve. 'Gabe and Jude, are they there?'

'We're here.' I nod for Jude to say something.

'Hey, kid.'

For a few seconds, nothing. And then a sob. 'I'm so sorry.' Dani's voice breaks up. 'I wish I knew what happened but

I can't remember. I can't see it, no matter how hard I try. I don't know what I did wrong—'

'Dani, Dani,' Jason says. 'It's okay. Isn't it, Gaby?' He looks at me, pleading.

'Yeah, don't beat yourself up. We don't remember it either.' And please stop crying.

Dani sniffles, hiccoughs. We give her a moment.

'I still can't see you unless you're with other Rephaim,' she says. 'I don't know what that means. Maybe if I could—'

'Do you remember visiting two hospitals in Melbourne last year?'

'Rafa.' Jason catches his eye. 'Not now.'

'When would be the time, given she and her mother never talk to you?' Rafa leans over the phone. 'We know what you and your mother did.'

Another sniffle. 'What did we do?'

'You visited Gabe and Jude when they were in hospital. You left messages to reinforce that bullshit story planted in their heads.'

'That's a lie.' A new voice, older. Angry. 'Jason, what's this about?'

'Maria . . .' Jason pauses. 'One of Gaby's nurses told us a woman and girl visited the ward and left a message that Jude was dead. She described you and Dani. Jude got the same story about Gaby.'

'When?' Maria asks.

Jason looks at me.

'A couple of days after I was admitted.'

The phone goes quiet again.

'Maria?' Jason says. 'Dani?'

There's a crackling noise at the other end, possibly a hand covering the mouthpiece. We wait.

The crackling stops. 'I don't know if it was us or not,' Maria finally says. 'It's possible.'

'Meaning?' Rafa asks.

'Meaning, I don't know. Dani disappeared with Gabe and Jude and then somehow came back to me safe. They didn't. We knew that whatever had happened to them wasn't good, and Dani was connected to it. As soon as Jason left the house we packed the car and took off. We drove for a day and booked into a motel. We only meant to stay overnight, but it ended up being for a few days.'

'And?' Rafa pushes her.

'And, we lost a day. I mean, literally lost it. We went to bed and when we woke up, it was the next night. Neither of us could remember what we did, but we weren't asleep for twenty-four hours. We had on different clothes for a start, and we didn't wake up starving. It shook us. We didn't know what to do so we kept moving. We *keep* moving. And we've cut ties with anyone who knows what Dani can do, including our own family . . . including Jason.'

'Where were you when this happened?' I ask.

'A few hours out of New York.'

'You lost just that one day?'

'Yes.'

I do the maths and my mouth dries out. 'But that's not enough time to fly to Melbourne and back.'

I meet Rafa's eyes. Whoever brought Maria and Dani to Australia did so by shifting. And then erased the memory of it.

'What about a way to trap Rephaim? Do you know anything about that, Dani?' Rafa asks.

She comes back on the phone. 'Only what I saw on Friday, when you and Gaby were in that room.'

'You saw that?' I ask.

'Bits of it. Where were you?'

'In a farmhouse in Iowa. Did you know Zarael took control of it yesterday?'

A small gasp on the other end of the phone. Obviously not. 'Jason, you need to be very careful. You all do.'

Jason repositions the phone on the table. 'What did you want to tell us, Dani?'

'Oh.' She takes a deep breath. 'I had a vision. It was awful. I was meditating – trying to find you, actually. I do that a lot when I miss you. But I got glimpses of something else. I don't often see the white-haired demons, but it was definitely them and they were in Pandanus Beach.'

Maggie covers her mouth with her hand.

'What were they doing?' Jason asks.

Dani pauses. 'Killing people.'

THE HIGH ROAD

'I think it was in a forest, a campsite maybe? The demons were everywhere. They were attacking men I didn't know, chopping them up with swords. It was . . . horrible. I threw up afterwards.'

I stare at the phone. Coldness is creeping over me. 'Did these men have tattoos and guns?'

'Umm . . . tattoos, yes. I'm not sure about guns. Zarael was there.'

'Zarael?' Rafa breaks in. 'How do you know it was him – have you seen him before?'

'He had black hair. All the others have white, don't they?'

'Fuck.'

'Rafa.' Maggie points to the phone.

'Shit, sorry.' He goes to the sink, leans against the bench.

'How do you know it was Pan Beach?' Jason asks.

'I just do. Sometimes it's like that. I don't know how the visions work – I don't get that many.'

'But did you see something that *has* happened or something that will happen?' I ask.

'I only got bits and pieces but I'm fairly sure it hasn't happened yet,' Dani says.

'How can you tell?'

There's a pause and I imagine her shrugging. 'I just know.'

'Okay . . . So is it definitely going to happen, or is it just a possibility? I mean, if we get them off the mountain—'

'I don't know, Gabe.' Dani sounds upset again. 'I wish I did. Sorry.'

'You don't have to apologise, baby,' Maria says. 'And you've told them what you needed to, so say goodbye now.'

'Wait.' Jason picks up the phone, cradles it close to his mouth, but doesn't turn the speaker function off. 'When can I see you?'

'I don't know,' Maria says.

'I miss you both.'

'We miss you too.' It's Dani, closer to the phone.

'Will you at least take my calls? We'll have more of a chance of figuring out what happened to Gaby and Jude if we stay in contact.'

'Dani's not CNN, Jason. She's not a constant source of news.'

'I know, but—'

'We'll tell you if she sees something you need to know about.'

'I know. Just . . . look after yourselves.'

'You too,' Dani says. 'Bye-bye, Jason.'

'Bye, blossom.'

The call disconnects and Jason looks up, self-conscious. Maggie laces her fingers through his.

Shit. This is bad – and it's our fault. I look to Rafa. 'We have to warn the Butlers.'

'Those morons deserve everything they get.'

'They don't deserve to get torn apart by demons. We at least owe them the truth so they know what's coming.'

'If they'd stayed out of it, like they were told, this wouldn't be a problem.'

'You'd let them die to make a point?'

He gives me a level look. 'No. But don't expect me to be happy about having to save their sorry arses. I'd rather be getting you two well away from here. Did you not hear the part about Zarael coming?'

Jude pushes his chair back from the table and rests his boot on his knee. 'Who are the Butlers?'

I give him a quick run-down.

'Do you know where they've set up camp?'

God, he's straight down to business. Rafa's right: he's so much quicker than I was in coming to grips with the reality that demons and hellions are real. Of course, he hasn't seen them in the flesh yet. Maybe we can still avoid that.

'There's a guy, Simon. He's a friend of' – I catch myself – 'Maggie's. He can contact them, get directions.'

Rafa clicks his tongue. 'The barman? Seriously?'

'Rusty asked him to join them.'

'What about his babysitter? You want to invite her too?'

'We don't even know if Taya's back in town. If she is, we'll deal with it.'

'And who's this "we" you keep talking about?'

What's he so prickly about now? 'You, me and Jude. Maybe Ez and Zak if they're free.'

Maggie gets up from the table and fills the kettle. Her hands aren't steady.

'Do you remember how to fight?' Rafa asks Jude.

He shrugs. 'I can hold my own.'

'When was the last time you got your knuckles bloody?'

'There was a brawl at my local bar about a month ago. Hobby sailors over from the mainland who couldn't handle their piss. It got out of control. I ended up cornered and one of them pulled a knife.'

'What happened?'

'I took him down.'

Rafa raises his eyebrows. 'One guy?'

Jude glances at me. 'No. Six.'

'Have you picked up a sword yet?'

'Not much use for one on a yacht. But' – another quick glance in my direction – 'I was thinking about getting my hands on a katana. It feels like I should know how to use one.'

And again he's ahead of me. I didn't even know what they were called until after I'd used one to kill a hellion.

'You know how to use a katana, buddy, don't worry about that,' Rafa says. 'You're not as good as Gabe when she's firing, but very few are.'

Jude looks at me, a crease between his eyebrows.

The kettle boils. Maggie flicks it off, sets out five cups.

'Right then,' Rafa says, his mood greatly improved. 'You'd better call the barman.'

'Me?' I catch Maggie's eye, give her a pleading look.

'Fine,' she says. 'I'll do it. And I know you need to warn them, but do you really think Mick's going to be happy to see you after what happened on Friday?'

'He'll get over it,' Rafa says.

Steam billows from the cups as she finishes pouring.

'Remember how your last conversation with him ended.' She puts the kettle down, steadier now. 'And this time, he'll have guns.'

ROUGH SEAS

We walk along the esplanade so Jude can see the surf. There's not much action so late in the day, but a few guys are paddling out to tackle what's left of the swell. The sun slips through patchy cloud cover, casting long shadows across the water.

I shouldn't feel happy. Our lives are a lie. Demons are coming to Pan Beach. The Rephaim will come for Jude. And yet . . . I am. I feel strangely settled with Rafa on one side of me and Jude on the other. This is the brother I remember – or close to it. He's more protective, more serious. But maybe that's come from a year of grief. I glance at him. Am I the way he remembers?

'Tomorrow, I'm getting a board.' Jude's eyes are on the

water; the AC/DC t-shirt he's wearing is faded, close to threadbare.

'How long has it been?' I ask.

'A year.'

This from the guy who could barely go a week without catching a wave.

'A punctured lung kept me out of the water for the first month and then I was in Hobart – not a lot of surf down there and I was too rusty to tackle Shipstern Bluff.' Jude turns to Rafa. 'I did surf, right?'

'Every chance you got. Even when there was good beer to be drunk.'

Jude smiles, relieved. We leave the boardwalk and head along the sand. He stops to pull off his combat boots, digs his toes into the sand.

We're on our way to Rick's. Simon agreed to help – but only because it was Maggie asking. She and Jason are back in Melbourne again. It's more important they're safe, and they're safer there than here right now. Maggie doesn't need any more nightmares. Which reminds me . . .

'Did you say you have dreams, plural?' I ask Jude. 'Not just the nightclub fight?'

Jude nods. 'There's one with a giant dude and a gorgeous woman with scars on her face. You're there too,' he says to Rafa, 'and a smoking-hot blonde who yells at me a lot.'

'What happens?'

'I save the blonde from a hell-beast.'

Rafa puts out a hand and we stop. 'Did it have her pinned against a wall in the cabin of a ship?'

Jude's eyes brighten. 'A ship, that makes sense.'

'Is he talking about Mya?'

'Who else would be reckless enough to get trapped in a cabin with a hell-turd?' Rafa says.

'What were you doing on a ship?' I ask.

'A job – what else? We'd heard rumours of weird shit happening off the coast of Oman – huge water spouts, boats disappearing, crazy storms. We were on our way to check it out but Zarael beat us to it. He hijacked a food aid ship headed for Kenya. He took some of his horde and a hellion along for the ride, thought it'd be fun to torture the crew and aid workers.'

A cloud passes over the sun. I can't help it – I shiver.

'At least we knew they were there before we went in,' Rafa says, more to Jude than me. 'If the Rhythm Palace was our biggest cock-up – which it was – then the take-down of that ship was one of our finer moments. Precision shifting in the middle of the ocean, no human casualties, and we took out a Gatekeeper as well.'

'They can die?' I ask.

'The same as us.' He demonstrates a slicing action across his throat. 'Tough though, because the sneaky bastards don't like to stay put. I got lucky on the ship—'

'You killed one of them?'

'Don't sound so surprised.' He grins, turns back to Jude. 'It was a big win for us. Something we could throw in Nathaniel's face. If I'm right, and you were involved in changing your memories, it stands to reason you'd have more dreams about the past than Gaby. And it makes sense you'd remember those two jobs if nothing else.'

Jude takes this in, moves off again. His bare feet leave deep impressions in the sand. 'You really think I did this to us?'

'Not on your own,' Rafa says. 'And I don't know how, but I think you managed to influence the way your memories were messed with. Nothing else makes sense. Gaby only has one dream about the past and it's your memory – and it probably saved her life at the Sanctuary.'

Jude puts his hands in his pockets. 'I need to read the files on that laptop, maybe grab some more books from Patmos.'

'The answer's not in books, Jude, it's in your head. You need your memory back.'

'True. But there must be things Nathaniel can tell us. He's an angel, isn't he? Connected with the archangels?'

Rafa clenches his jaw. 'You didn't get answers from him after a hundred and twenty-nine years. He's not going to give them to you now.'

'But—'

'He doesn't know what you two did. The only people who know are you, Gabe and Dani – and whoever wiped your memories.'

'That can't be a long list.'

'It's not: it's a blank one. I don't know anyone who could have done that.'

Jude turns back to the water; I see the pull of it on his face. 'Well, someone did. We just have to figure out who.'

The sun is almost behind the headland when we reach the car park out the back of Rick's. It's empty except for his jeep and an old hatchback with a flat tyre. I text Simon and he comes downstairs a few minutes later. His eyes sweep over Rafa and me and lock on Jude – who Maggie failed to mention.

'This is my brother Jude.'

Simon looks at me, confused. 'I thought he was dead.'

'Me too.'

'That's . . . how is that possible?'

'He's Rephaite.'

Simon steps back, bumps his hip on the jeep.

'Don't panic, he doesn't remember that life either. He thought I was dead too.'

Jude holds out his hand to Simon. Simon hesitates and then shakes it, awkward.

'Where's Mags?' he asks, not acknowledging Rafa.

'With Jason. They're safe in Melbourne.'

His eyes narrow.

'Ring her if you don't believe me.'

For a second, I think he's going to. 'What about Taya?'

'Who cares?' Oh, that's right. He does. 'She's tormenting another unfortunate soul at the moment. Don't worry, she's not done with me. She'll be back.'

'Can we move this along?' Rafa says. 'Today would be good.'

Simon produces a folded piece of paper from his back pocket. 'The boys are in a valley not far from where we ran into them the other night.'

It's a hand-drawn map, and not a good one.

'What the fuck is that supposed to be?' Rafa points to a bunch of circles near the top of the page.

Simon glowers at him. 'Boulders. Here—' He takes the map and lays it on the jeep bonnet; Jude looks over my shoulder. 'This is the main road.' Simon runs his finger along the thickest pencil line, and then traces a series of finer squiggly lines, pointing out landmarks and finally the camp.

'Sounds like it's on a goat track off a goat track,' Rafa mutters. 'We don't have all night to search the mountain.'

'Could you take us there?' Jude asks Simon.

'No.' Rafa and I say it simultaneously.

'He'll get in the way,' Rafa says. 'Again.'

'I don't want Simon there if demons turn up,' I add.

Simon blanches. 'Mags didn't mention demons.'

Jude picks up the map, folds it over. 'They're your friends up there, aren't they?'

Simon doesn't answer. His eyes are distant. What's he seeing? Bel and Leon coming out of the darkness? The moment when the yellow-eyed hellion savaged Mick?

'Simon,' Jude says.

Simon's eyes clear. 'No, not really. I went to school with Rusty, that's all. But if those things are coming back . . . The boys need to know.'

'Rafa can't tell them if we can't find them.'

Simon leans against the car bonnet. He stares across the car park for a moment and then rubs his arms as if he's cold. 'Okay.' He holds up a set of keys. 'We can take the jeep.'

I look to Rafa. He and Jude have gone to the passenger side of the car. 'Maybe we should have Zak and Ez along.'

Rafa catches Simon's eye. 'How much firepower do those meat-heads have stockpiled up there?'

Simon fiddles with the keys, directs his answer to me. 'From the sound of it, a few dozen assault rifles. Possibly grenades. Knowing Mick, there'll be more than Rusty's told me.' He gestures to Rafa. 'I thought he was invincible?'

Rafa smirks. 'How many trigger-happy morons in the camp?'

'About a dozen.'

'I can sort them out on my own if you don't care how

badly they're hurt. But if you want to minimise the damage, then it'll take a more finessed approach. And on my own, that means there's a chance someone will wear a bullet. Maybe even you. I'm okay with that if you are.'

Simon doesn't bother answering. He gets in the car.

'Right, so you'll call Ez and Zak?' I ask.

Rafa pauses, a hand on the jeep. 'If you want them we'll have to tell Mya about Jude. It's one thing for them to keep the truth about you from her. But if they don't tell her Jude's alive—'

'Can't they tell her in a few hours?'

'Not if they ever want her to speak to them again. Which,' he says, when he sees my expression, 'they do. They'll help us either way, but she'll make their life a misery if she finds out he's alive and they've seen him.'

Shit. Mick's got an army up there, and Jude and I can't dodge bullets. I climb in the back next to Jude. His eyes track from Rafa to me.

'Fine,' I say. 'But this time she stays away from town.'

Simon backs out of the car park, then glances at me in the rear-view mirror. He's just worked out who Mya is.

'You're missing the point, Gaby,' Rafa says. 'She's not going to sit around when she finds out Jude's with us. If you want back-up, she'll have to be part of it.'

'You want her along?'

'No, but I don't want the drama it'll create for Zak

and Ez if we leave her out of this.'

'Fine. They can tell her.'

'It should come from me.' I catch something in his eyes and remember there was a time when the Outcasts were a tight-knit group. That history still carries weight with him.

I push aside empty protein-bar wrappers on the floor of the car. 'Make the call.' Maybe she'll be too busy with Debra from Iowa to answer her phone.

No such luck.

'It's me—' Rafa drums the dashboard. 'Don't start. You should have told us what you were going to do at the farm . . . That's not the point—' He stares through the windscreen. 'Mya, I don't care what you do with that iron-loving bitch. I'm ringing to tell you Jude's alive.' He has to tell her twice more before the news sinks in. 'It's not bullshit. He doesn't remember who he is, but he's here with me. And Gaby.' A drawn-out pause. 'It's a long story and I don't have time to explain. We've got a situation here we need to sort out . . . No, bring Zak and Ez. I'm about to call them. I'll tell them where to meet us . . . Yes, I rang you first.' He turns in his seat to face Jude, listens to the voice on the other end. 'Yeah, Mya, he's really alive.'

He ends the call.

'Don't look so put out,' Rafa says to me. And then, to Jude: 'You might want to brace yourself, buddy; this could get a little intense.'

BACK TO NATURE

Ez, Zak and Mya are waiting on the side of the dirt road that leads up the mountain, straining to see inside the jeep as soon as we pull over.

We're doing the right thing coming up here, no question. But I'd still rather be at Rafa's shack having a beer with Jude. I wish we'd had more time alone. I'm nowhere near ready to share him.

'Bloody hell . . .' Jude says. The three of them would be a startling enough sight at the best of times. But he's seen them in his dreams and now here they are in the flesh, in the falling light. Carrying swords.

Rafa twists around in his seat. 'You should probably get out before Zak wrenches the door off.'

Simon pulls on the handbrake. Rafa jumps out and

opens Jude's door. Jude looks to me.

'I've got your back,' I say.

Jude takes a slow breath, climbs out. He stops before he reaches them. 'Hey,' he says.

Mya is tense, but she walks to him without hesitation, drops her sword and throws her arms around his neck. Jude looks around at me, alarmed. And then Zak and Ez crowd in, their arms enveloping Jude and Mya.

I can't help but remember their wary reaction to me in my kitchen and the animosity from the rest of the Outcasts in Dubai. This is the complete opposite: they love Jude. They don't care what he's done; they're overjoyed to have him back from the dead. They're his people.

I had people too. And what did they do when they found out I was alive? Hug me? Weep? Hardly. I guess I don't inspire the same sort of loyalty as Jude. I feel my chest tightening and the contentment I felt walking on the beach with Jude and Rafa fades. What if Jude ends up preferring the Outcasts to me? Again.

'Don't take it personally,' Rafa says, his arm resting on the top of the open car door.

I glance up, startled. Can he read me that well?

'I must have really pissed some people off.'

He shrugs. 'Our crew just wanted you on our side.'

'It was obviously more than that.'

His eyes stray to the group hug. There's no sign of Zak, Ez or Mya letting go.

'You were pretty unforgiving whenever our paths crossed, but that was probably unavoidable. Under the circumstances.'

He pushes off from the car before I can clarify what those circumstances were.

'Enough, or you'll crush the poor bastard.' Rafa prises the three of them from Jude. Ez wipes her eyes and Zak turns away to brush his face against his shoulder.

Mya steps back from Jude, her cheeks streaked with mascara. 'You really don't remember me?'

'Only from dreams.'

'Dreams about me?'

'About all of you.'

'What do you remember?'

Jude gives her an apologetic half-smile. 'Nothing that relates to being the offspring of a fallen angel.'

She wipes her face, looks to Rafa and her expression hardens. 'You knew he was alive?'

'It was a theory.'

'Based on what?'

'On a few things that happened this past week.'

'And you didn't think to mention it?'

'I wanted to be sure first.'

I study Rafa. There was something in his tone.

Mya snaps, 'Sure of what? That Jude was alive or that he hadn't intentionally dropped off the radar?'

Rafa doesn't answer.

Mya fumes at him. 'I can't believe you went to Gabe with this and not us. She's the reason he doesn't remember who he is. And how convenient he's forgotten all the stuff about her that pisses him off.'

My stomach lurches. Did Jude talk to her about me – tell her all the things he didn't like about me? Simon catches my eye in the rear-view mirror, doesn't speak.

'She doesn't remember any of that, Mya.'

'I don't care! This is what she's wanted from the day we walked out of the Sanctuary. To have him back all to herself, to turn him against the rest of—'

'That's enough.' Jude's voice is hard. 'Nobody knows what Gaby and I did a year ago. But, whatever it was, I was obviously up to my neck in it, so you can stop blaming her right now or this reunion is over.'

Mya stares at him as if he's slapped her.

Shadows fall across Ez's face and across the road. As we stand there, a cockatoo screeches in the tree above us, harsh, piercing. A truck rumbles along the main road a kilometre away.

Jude's chest falls as he exhales. 'Look, it's been a big day. A few hours ago I was winding ropes on a yacht in Hobart, thinking my sister was dead. I'm still getting a grip on all this.'

Mya watches him for a few more seconds and then she turns to Ez. 'Did you know he was alive?'

'No.'

'Then how can you be so calm about this? You and Zak jump whenever Rafa snaps his fingers – you do whatever he asks without question – and he still didn't see fit to tell you about this.'

'Whatever Rafa's done has been to protect Jude,' Ez says. 'How can any of us take that personally?'

'Mya,' Rafa says, stepping between them to get their attention. 'We need to keep moving.'

Zak picks up the katanas and heads for the car. He puts a hand on Jude's shoulder as he passes. 'Good to have you back, brother.'

I slide into the middle again. Simon's fingers are clenched around the steering wheel, watching Mya. She finally notices who's driving but says nothing. She slides in on the other side of Jude and completely ignores me. Ez and Zak take the extra seat in the back.

Simon puts the car in gear and we head up the mountain. The track narrows and the forest crowds in: eucalypt branches scrape against the jeep and vines slap the windscreen. The engine revs harder as we climb. The dusk fills the car with flickering shadows. For a long while, nobody talks. The weight of Jude's presence is too heavy. My hip and shoulder touch his, a constant reassurance he's still there.

'Ez told me about these guys we're going to see,' Mya says after we bounce over yet another rise. 'So we're not going up here to fight, we're coming out to them?'

'Something like that,' Rafa says.

'Explain to me why they need to know about demons and hellions.'

Rafa turns to answer. 'The Gatekeepers lost a hell-turd because of them. Bel's not going to let that go and they're still on the mountain, so we need these boys to be less conspicuous or we'll have another bloodbath on our hands.'

I catch Rafa's eye, silently thank him for not mentioning Dani or her vision. He nods at me and for a split second we're back in the bedroom, and the door is closed and Jude doesn't come in. Warmth flares again and I break eye contact.

Another kilometre and Simon pulls up in a clearing and kills the engine. The light up here is hazy purple – still enough to see by. We climb out and stretch our legs. The rainforest hums with cicadas and is punctuated by the sharp crack of a whipbird. I breathe in deeply, smell damp soil and leaves.

'We're going to have to do this on foot,' Rafa says. 'In case Daniel comes sniffing around.'

Good point. If any other Rephaim scour the mountain looking for us tonight, they'll sense where we've shifted.

'Here.' Rafa unzips one of the two weapons bags Zak brought along and hands Jude a katana. 'It's one of yours.'

It's the sword I've been using. Jude takes it carefully, almost reverently. He steps away, grips it with both hands and swings it back and forth, testing its weight, as if he's done it a thousand times before.

'Now, there's a sight that makes me happy,' Zak says. Jude smiles despite himself.

Rafa nudges my shoulder. He's holding another sword. 'This is for you.'

The hilt is strapped more heavily than Jude's, but the curved blade gleams, even in the mottled light of the rainforest. I don't know much about katanas, but it looks as though someone's taken a lot of care of it.

'Consider it yours.'

I feel my cheeks warm. Anyone would think he'd given me flowers.

We gather around and Rafa lays out his plan. By the time he finishes, Simon looks ill.

'If you throw up and give away our position before we're ready I'll choke you unconscious,' Rafa says.

Simon glowers and sets off without speaking. We follow him under the rainforest canopy through ferns and bushes covered in tiny purple flowers. Ten minutes in we reach a fast-flowing creek. Simon signals for us to move slower across it, and leads us to a cluster of large boulders. We crouch behind them.

My fingers brush dry, rough moss. I find a gap between the boulders and scan the forest twice before I see them: two men leaning against trees a few metres apart, smoking. Rifles over their shoulders. Not sawn-offs; assault rifles. Both have full-sleeve tatts and buzz-cropped hair. Neither was at the Imperial yesterday.

'Sentries?' Ez whispers. Her knives are strapped to her arms, katana poised over the grass.

'You're generous,' Rafa says.

'They're covering the gully. It must be the only way in.'

'The camp should be at the other end,' Simon says.

Rafa nods to Ez. She moves off quietly, using the shrubs for cover. We wait. The creek flows behind us; a bird cries higher in the trees. Rafa and Zak watch the sentries. Mya watches Jude. Jude watches me. I try to work out how the Rephaim can disarm a small army without shifting.

Ez is back less than a minute later, a leaf sticking out from her plait. 'There are at least ten of them in the camp. All armed. No other sentries.'

'Good. Let's sort these two first.' Rafa nods to me, points to the smokers.

I shake my head. A pub brawl is one thing. I'm not

confident I can deal with the assault rifles without getting shot.

'You and me, then,' Rafa says to Ez.

They leave their swords behind and head off in opposite directions, crouched low, moving almost without sound. I lose track of them in the foliage. Beside me, Jude holds his breath. For a minute, nothing happens. And then Rafa and Ez silently appear from the ferns, attacking simultaneously.

The guy closest to Rafa doesn't get his cigarette out of his mouth, let alone his rifle raised. Rafa wrenches the weapon from him and slams the butt into the side of his head. By the time I look across at Ez, her man is slumped at her feet, his rifle in her hands.

'Holy shit,' Jude whispers. 'They're quick.'

'That's nothing,' I say. 'Wait till you see them against demons and—' I stop. What am I saying? The whole idea is for us to avoid demons. Mya looks at me with an expression I can't quite name. It's the first time she's made eye contact with me. It doesn't last.

Simon is trying to get a better look at the unconscious men. Zak's huge hand clamps his shoulder, making him flinch.

'Don't panic. They'll live.'

Rafa and Ez reappear through the trees. Ez hands her rifle to Mya.

'AK-47,' she says, barely glancing at it.

Mya slings it across her chest. The handgun in LA, an assault rifle here: I guess she's okay with guns. Rafa hands his to Zak.

'Seriously?' I say.

'It's the only language these idiots understand.'

Fantastic; Rephaim with firearms.

This is not going to end well.

JUST IN THE NEIGHBOURHOOD

Ez leads us into the gully, which is bordered by granite walls on both sides. Water trickles down the smooth rock and it's damp underfoot. Simon stays close to me – I must seem the least threatening in this company. The breeze picks up, carries eucalyptus, petrol and marijuana. Voices come through the trees. Scuffling. An occasional popping noise.

We crouch behind a thick clump of ferns, take in the camp not far below us.

The Butlers aren't messing around here.

There are tarps strung between palm trees, a trestle table covered with semi-automatics, boxes of ammunition and tinned food. Targets hammered into tree trunks riddled with bullet holes. Sleeping bags laid out under a massive banyan tree and canvas chairs scattered around a fire-pit stacked with kindling. A keg sits to one side in a tub of slushy ice.

Thick roots sprout down from the branches of the banyan tree, creating a natural barrier on the far side of one of the tarps. Beyond it are two wheel ruts that must be the goat track Simon was trying to show us. Trucks and mud-splattered four-wheel drives form a ring around the rest of the camp, all mounted with decks of spotlights. The camp is bathed in a harsh white glare. Above the trees, there's still a smudge of light in the dusk sky.

Mick is at the weapons table cleaning a handgun, his neck and shoulder bandaged. Tank is next to him, doing his best to pull a rifle apart with one hand; the other hangs in a sling.

Oh yeah, they're going to be thrilled to see Rafa and me.

Beyond the tarp, two bare-chested men wrestle on the ground, their mates in a circle around them. I recognise a couple from the Imperial. The guy dominating the scuffle has a gleaming shaved head and his back is covered with a tattoo of snakes coiled around each other; they writhe as he twists and turns.

'Choke him out, Joffa.' It's Rusty, coaching from the sidelines. 'Get your legs around him. These pricks have claws. If you have to go hand-to-hand, don't fuck around. End it quick.'

Unbelievable. These guys think they can take out a hellion by hand.

The bandage is gone from Rusty's head, but even from where we're hiding I can see the welt where I clocked him with the pool cue. Woosha is next to him shadowing the moves on the ground, his busted nose still taped.

Next to me, Rafa scans the camp. After a few seconds, he holds up ten fingers to Ez. She nods, which I take to mean the ten men we can see are the same she saw before. Rafa gives us silent instructions. Ez melts into the ferns in one direction; Rafa, Jude and I creep off in the other, circling around so we can come at the camp from the other side. Mya, Simon and Zak stay behind.

Jude touches my wrist. 'You okay?' he mouths.

I nod. 'You?'

'Yep.'

He's wired. He wants to do this – see what he's capable of. This is how he gets before he tackles something for the first time.

We find a gap between two four-wheel drives, one with monster wheels and half a dozen aerials. It's still radiating heat under the bonnet and stinks of hot diesel. We don't have to wait long.

'Don't shoot, boys,' Mya calls out.

The two guys scuffling in the leaves beyond the cars stop immediately. All eyes turn to Mya and Simon, walking out from behind the boulders. Simon moves hesitantly, his hands in the air. Mya is using him as a shield, her rifle barrel wedged under his chin. My stomach quivers. I hope there's a safety on that thing – and it's on. Zak is a step behind, his semi-automatic trained on Mick. The older Butler leaps to his feet, kicking his chair out of the way.

'What the fuck do you want?'

'Nobody do anything stupid now. We've come to talk.' Mya sounds almost bored. We've got about three seconds to make our move. I swallow, grip my sword. Steady my pulse. I can do this – it's only the Butler crew.

'Now,' Rafa says.

He, Jude and I launch out from between the cars. I kick out the knee of the first guy I reach before he can react, smash my sword hilt above his ear. He hits the ground with a lazy thud. A meaty fist swings at me. One of the wrestlers is up, grass and leaves plastered to his chest. I duck and punch his sweaty stomach. He drops to his knees. Another of Mick's men falls to my right. Was that Jude's handiwork? Someone's shouting now. A gun goes off. I spin around, trying to find Jude in the mêlée. Thick arms clamp around me, pinning mine. Hot breath warms the side of my face, thick with beer and tobacco.

Don't think.

I use my head, connect with his nose.

He grunts, doesn't loosen his grip. I throw my head back

again and feel the bone break. I slam my heel on his foot and the impact jars – he's wearing steel-capped boots. He twists me around and I see another fist coming at my face, a blond mullet behind it. I jerk sideways. The blow glances off my cheek. An explosion of white clouds my vision. *That's it.* I lift my katana, show the mullet I can wield it with my arms pinned. I don't have the breath to threaten him, but he gets the message, jumping out of range . . . and straight into Jude's fist.

Jude's eyes meet mine. So sharp. So alive. He dodges a charge from Rusty, elbows the younger Butler in the back of the head as he passes. Rusty sprawls forward.

I need to worry about myself: I'm being crushed in a bear hug. My rib cage is about to collapse. I turn the katana blade inward and jab it into something solid.

'Ow, *fuck*.' The strong arms let go.

I stumble forward, check over my shoulder. It's the guy with the snake tattoo and shaved head. Joffa. He's on the ground, clutching his leg.

'You *stabbed* me.'

Blood streams down from his nose, over his mouth and chin. He's staying down for the moment, so I chance a quick look around the rest of the camp.

The fight's finished.

Jude stands over Rusty, barely out of breath. Rafa is on his way to the tarp area, a trail of crumpled men in his wake. Ez presses Mick's face against the weapons table, pins his arms behind his back; Tank is unconscious on the grass at her feet.

'Mick, tell them to stay down.' It's Simon, keeping his distance.

'I'm going to rip out your fuckin' throats.' Mick grinds the words out, tries to lift his head.

'Mick,' Simon says, 'they're here to help.'

Mick squirms under Ez's grip. 'And you, you little prick. You're first.'

'Mate, you need to know what you're up against before you get yourselves killed.'

'You've been played, dickwad.'

'No, dickwad, you have.' Rafa steps into Mick's line of sight. 'There's no government conspiracy. No men in black. No mutants.'

'What the fuck are you talking about? You were there.'

I catch a movement to my left. I turn to see Joffa pulling a knife out of his boot. I point my blade at him, raise my eyebrows. I don't want to stab him again, but I'm not taking a knife in the back either.

'Toss it.'

He spits a mouthful of blood at my feet, eyes me, and then lobs the knife into the ferns.

Rafa has been watching my short exchange with Joffa and now turns back to Mick.

'The thing that bit you was a hellion. And those overdressed arse clowns with fire in their eyes? Demons.'

Ez allows Mick to stand up.

'Bullshit.'

'Join the dots,' Rafa says. 'Prove to me you're not a complete moron.'

Mick's eyes narrow. 'If they're demons, what does that make you lot?'

Rafa taps his sword hilt. 'The bastards who know how to kill them.'

YOU AND WHAT ARMY?

'Where are the guns?'

Mick tries to stare down Rafa. 'You blind?'

'I'm not talking about these.' Rafa waves his sword at the row on the table. 'I mean the ones you've got stashed in case you get ambushed. Like this.'

Silence.

'The quicker you tell me, the quicker your boys can get up.'

Mick grunts. 'In the banyan tree. And the rock clump behind the tarp.'

'And?'

Another sound of disgust. 'Back of the yellow truck.'

Mya and Zak head off in opposite directions. Mya comes back with two rifles, two handguns and a sawn-off shotgun.

'Check this out.' Zak holds up his find with one hand – anyone else would need two.

'Is that a bazooka?' Simon asks. I can't tell if he's impressed or horrified.

Zak lies the rocket launcher on the table.

'Shit, Mick,' Simon says. 'How the hell did you get that into the country?'

'All right,' Rafa says to Mick. 'Tell your lads to pull up a chair, hands where we can see them. Then we'll talk.'

Rusty and the rest of Mick's crew pick themselves off the ground, dust off dirt and leaves. One by one they limp to the fire-pit and pull up a folding chair. Jude, Mya and I stand behind them. She stays close to Jude, but I catch her watching me more than once. Zak hauls Tank by the scruff of his shirt and drops him next to Rusty. Simon sits on the bullbar of a battered yellow truck, still fixated on the rocket launcher.

The shadows in the forest bleed together now. The camp smells of sweat and nicotine. I wish Rafa would hurry things along. I want this over and done with so I can talk to Jude again. Alone.

Ez frogmarches Mick across the clearing, deposits him in a tattered chair. She and Rafa pull up seats either side of him.

Rafa nods at Jude. 'Good to see you're still sharp, and you' – he turns to me – 'nice work.'

I try to ignore the small flush of pride at the rare praise.

'I'm lighting the fire,' Rusty says.

Rafa glances at the shadowy forest. 'Knock yourself out.'

Rusty brushes a clump of grass from his shirt and pulls out a plastic lighter. He sits on his heels, sets the flame to a wad of newspaper under the kindling. It catches quickly. In seconds, the grimy faces around the fire are lit with a bright orange glow.

'Beer?' he offers, nods in the direction of the keg.

Rafa ignores him, looks around the fire. 'I told you boys to keep out of this. You've had your fun, now get out of the way before you get yourselves killed.'

Rusty stands up, repositions the kindling with his boot. He finds Simon sitting on the truck. 'You believe what he's saying – that they're demons?'

Simon nods.

'Like, from hell?'

'No,' Rafa says, 'from Comic-Con.' He shakes his head. 'Yes, from hell.'

Mick pulls out a crushed packet of smokes, finds one that's only slightly bent in the middle. He takes a flaming branch from the fire to light it, careful to keep it away from the remnant of his beard. He takes a long, slow drag.

'Let's say you're not completely full of shit. What do these demons want?' He blows smoke through his nose in two steady streams.

'Not important.'

'They want her, don't they?' Rusty looks at me across the fire.

The air turns colder as he speaks. In the firelight, Rafa tenses. He sees me notice and tries to hide it.

'Not your problem,' Rafa says. 'All you need to worry about is packing up your toys and keeping your heads down. You don't have the weapons or the skill to handle what's coming.'

'Mutants, demons – I don't give a flying fuck what they are,' Mick says. 'If we fill 'em full of enough lead they won't get up.'

'You'd be surprised.'

Rusty puts a branch on the fire, sending sparks spiralling up through the canopy. The evening light is deep purple now. Low clouds cover the darkening sky beyond the trees.

'How do you kill them, then?' Mick asks.

'Cut off their heads.' Rafa says it as if he's giving instructions to jump-start a car. 'It's the only way to take out anything from hell.' Or us – which he doesn't mention.

Mick scratches the bandaging on his neck. The fire pops and hisses. 'Bullshit,' he says at last.

'Why do you think we use these?' Rafa rolls his wrist from side to side, making the blade of his sword glint in the firelight. 'Bullets will slow a hell-turd, the thing that savaged you' – he nods at Mick – 'but you need a sword to finish one off.'

'What about the tall guys with the crazy eyes and all the hair?'

'Demons are usually too quick to get shot. They'll have a blade through your heart before you can lift your rifle.'

Jude taps his sword absently against his calf, taking in everything Rafa says. He doesn't seem as keen as me to wrap this visit up.

Mick rolls his cigarette between his thumb and forefinger. 'How come they look so human?'

'Because they can.' It's Ez who answers, sitting next to Mick. 'They're trapped in that form for as long as they're on earth. The only thing they can't hide is their eyes.'

Rusty puts another log on the fire. 'How many are there?'

'We don't know for sure.' She pops out the ammunition clip from the handgun she's still holding. 'We've never seen them all in one place.'

'Best guess is around fifty,' Rafa says. 'We're not sure how many hellions are left – but there's two less than there were a week ago.'

The fire shimmers into a solid ball of light. I blink. Dig my heels into the soil until I feel steady again. Fifty Gatekeepers. Stronger, faster than the Rephaim. Able to shift. If they all attacked at once . . .

'Are you okay?' Jude asks, his voice low.

My eyes stray to the flickering shadows beyond the chairs. Why haven't they attacked the Sanctuary if they've got those sorts of numbers? But then I remember Bel and the other demons cowering before shining wings and know the answer: Nathaniel.

'Where are these demons now?' Rusty asks.

Rafa checks the line of his sword again in the firelight. 'Coming.'

Rusty blinks and stares off towards the gloomy curtain of tree roots. 'We're fucked then.'

Mick glares at him. 'You want to grow some stones, or you just gonna pull your pants down and bend over?'

'Ease up. I'm here to fight, but let's be real.' He gestures to the men around the fire. 'We got good blokes here—'

'Who want to fight.'

'Yeah, they want to fight. Not get eaten by friggin' hell-beasts. Nobody signed up for this.'

'Speak for yourself,' Joffa says. He's still bare-chested, a t-shirt tied around the stab wound in his thigh. 'I'll have a crack at anything that comes out of those trees.'

Murmurs of agreement.

'Fine.' Rusty sits back in his chair. 'Anyone here got a sword?'

No answer.

'Anyone ever use one?'

'Doesn't matter,' Mick snaps. 'We're not running away with our tails between our legs because ninja boy here tells us to. We're staying and fighting.'

'You got a death wish, *mate*?' Rafa says, repeating Mick's threat to him on Friday morning.

'Nah, mate, but I'm not hiding in the pub while demons stroll around my town.'

'You couldn't defend yourselves against us,' Ez points out. 'How do you expect to—'

'You ambushed us!'

'You think demons are going to give you a heads-up?' Mick scowls at her.

'You think you know what you're up against,' she says. 'You don't. You and your friends will die up here, horribly. Get yourselves to safety. Please.'

Mick picks a piece of tobacco from his tongue. Doesn't bother answering.

'Hey,' Rusty says to Rafa. 'Instead of taking the piss, you could help us.'

'We're not babysitting you.'

'Lend us some swords. Show us what to do.'

Rafa gestures to Mick. 'He doesn't look too teachable.'

'Fuck you,' Mick says.

Rafa looks around the fire at the rest of Mick's crew. They're all watching him, waiting. 'It's a bad idea.'

'Of course it's a bad idea.' The voice comes from the

shadows. 'But that's never stopped you from making bad choices in the past.'

I turn to see two figures step out from the trees. Shit. How the hell did they find us?

OLD HABITS DIE HARD

Daniel and Taya. Armed and dressed for battle. Have they come to fight us?

'What the fuck do you two want?' Mick looks to Rafa. 'Are they with you?'

'No chance,' Rafa says. 'What now, Daniel?'

Daniel doesn't answer. He's too busy looking at Jude, as is Taya. 'I see the band's back together.'

Jude steps forward with his katana. 'You're the asshole who locked my sister in a cage with a hell-beast, right?'

'Yes.'

'You don't seem too sorry about it.'

'What I feel is none of your business.' Daniel sounds slightly out of breath.

It's then I realise I didn't feel them arrive. 'Did you hike in? How did you find us?'

Taya nods at Simon, who hasn't stopped looking at her.

I stare at him. 'You told her we were here?'

He frowns, confused.

'Don't blame him. I put a tracker in his phone.'

'What?' Simon says at the same time I say, 'Are you kidding me?'

'What did you expect?' Taya says. 'It's not as if we could get one in yours. And anyway, it was for his own protection. You know Bel and Leon would recognise him if they found him. He'd be the first one they'd grab.'

Simon swallows. 'Is that true?'

Taya points to my side of the fire. 'Look at the company you keep.'

Mya, Ez and Zak flank me and Jude. Our six against Daniel and Taya: not good odds for them. So either they didn't come to fight or they're not the only Rephaim who hiked here in the dark.

'Where's Virginia?' Mya asks, her elbow on the rifle butt.

'Where's Debra?' Daniel counters.

'Somewhere she's not being tortured.'

'You don't honestly believe we'd hurt humans, Mya?'

'Everything's gone to hell, Daniel. I don't know what the Five are willing to do.'

420

'We're more interested in what Gabe and Jude were doing a year ago.' He hasn't come closer but it doesn't make me feel any better about him being here – things never end well when Daniel's around. 'I don't suppose you remember?' he asks Jude.

'No, mate, I don't,' Jude says. 'And when I do, you'll be the last person I tell.'

Daniel's lips twitch almost imperceptibly. Two minutes in Jude's company and he's already pissed off.

Rafa brushes ash from the campfire off his arm. 'What do you want?'

'I wanted to see Jude with my own eyes,' Daniel says. 'I have to say I'm surprised you brought him back here. A little obvious, don't you think?'

Rafa's glance at me is pointed, but he can't hold it. He's enjoying Jude's antagonism towards Daniel too much.

'We don't have time for this,' I say to Rafa. 'We need to get these guys off the mountain, remember?'

Daniel is watching Jude again. 'Is it true that you don't remember who you are?'

'Don't worry about who I am, mate.' Jude spins his sword hilt. 'Worry about what's going to happen the next time you come near my sister.'

'Jude . . .' I think about that cage, about how far Daniel was prepared to go to access my memories. Having him near Jude has set me back behind that wire, white pain bursting across my vision. I try to swallow. My mouth is dry.

'Have you got anything to drink here other than beer?' I ask Rusty.

'Try the coolbox.' He points to the tarped area under the banyan tree.

Jude comes with me. The coolbox is behind the table outside the ring of spotlights. I pull out two bottles of water, hand one to him. We keep our backs to the wall of the banyan tree, our eyes on the others. Rafa and Daniel are bickering across the fire about me and Jude and how irresponsible Rafa is. Mick and his boys have settled back for the show. Ez, Zak and Mya are watching them, and the argument. On edge.

'This is too weird, all these people knowing us,' Jude says. We stay under the tree in darkness. It's the closest we've been to alone since Rafa's shack. 'Does any of this get any easier?'

'No, you just get used to things not making sense.'

'Shit, Gaby, how have you coped?'

'It's only been a week. And I've had help.'

He looks over at Rafa, now on Daniel's side of the fire. Any second and they're going to start throwing punches. Honestly, he and Daniel can argue anywhere. We need to get these guys out of here. *We* need to get out of here.

'So, you and Rafa. It doesn't look that complicated to me.'

I'm watching Rafa. His hair is messy and his eyes are dark and alive. My mind wanders for a second. I want to be alone with him too. Rafa's right: whatever this is between us, it starts now. I want answers about the past. But I want this too. 'There's . . . stuff.'

Across the fire, Daniel is staring at Rafa. He looks stunned. What did I miss?

'You heard me,' Rafa says. 'We cleaned out the Rhythm Palace. Paying job. Gaby came along.'

'Yeah,' Mya says, 'she was a real natural.'

Oh shit.

'Taya knew all about it.' Rafa smiles at her.

She can't meet Daniel's eyes. 'There were circum-stances—'

'Not here.' Daniel cuts her off. He glances in my direction, but I can't tell if he can see me in the shadows. 'That's a low move, Rafa, even for you.' His words come out slow, furious. He puts distance between himself and Rafa, as if he can't stand to be near him. 'Gabe will rip you apart when she remembers who she is.'

'You're an asshole,' Taya says to Rafa.

He laughs. 'What are you so upset about – that you finally thought for yourself or that you got caught out?'

They've both got their backs to the inky forest. They're

so preoccupied with each other they've forgotten the rest of us are here. Rafa really shouldn't drop his guard—

My stomach plummets as though the ground has been torn out from underneath me.

Then Rafa's whole body jerks and a sword emerges from his stomach.

NO—

Everything happens at once.

Rafa looks around, disoriented, to where Jude and I were standing before we left the firelight. His face changes when he doesn't find us there. Taya collapses to her knees, a blade buried in her shoulder.

Gatekeeper demons stand behind them. Eyes blazing. There are more than I can count. I vaguely register a hellion with a stump for an arm.

I want to scream. I can't.

Jude drags me down behind the keg, but I push him away; I need to see.

The swords are ripped out of Rafa and Taya with lightning speed; the hilts slammed against their heads before they can react.

'No—' Ez shifts mid-shout. She and Zak arrive on the other side of the fire at the same time.

They find nothing but empty air.

The dark canopy presses down on me. The walls of the gully crowd in. Nothing is in focus. Not the fire. Not the figures scrambling around the campsite. People are shouting. I can't make out the words.

Rafa and Taya are gone.

Rafa. Gone.

Someone is shaking me. Jude. I can't understand what he's saying. He drags me deeper into the darkness. Pushes me to the ground. My fingers latch around thick bars. No, wait. What I'm holding is rough, alive. The hanging roots of the banyan tree.

Jude says, 'They're everywhere.' His words come and go.

Gunfire. Screaming. Clashing swords.

Rafa is gone.

'Gaby. *Gab.*' Jude shakes me again. His face swims into focus, pale in the spotlights of the camp. 'Are they demons?'

I nod. I can't feel my legs. Am I sitting down? Yes. I bury my fingers in the damp soil.

A movement behind us.

Jude scrambles to put himself between me and whatever it is.

'We have to go.' It's Daniel. He's bleeding from his ear.

'Did you do this?' My voice is flat. 'Did you bring them here?'

I see his eyes. He didn't do this.

Ez, Zak and Mya materialise, almost on top of him.

'Thank God,' Ez says when she sees us. She's out of breath, possibly crying.

More gunfire.

'Where is she?' The voice is loud, smoky and angry. It can only belong to a demon. The Gatekeepers are still here. Everything snaps back into sharp focus: the trees, the harsh lights, the seeping rock walls, the wetness under Ez's eyes. The screams.

'We have to go.' Daniel's voice is urgent. 'Now.' He leans towards Jude.

'Don't touch him,' I hiss.

'Gabe, listen to me.' Daniel grabs my arm, his fingers gouge my skin. 'Nathaniel is the only one who can protect us now.'

'I don't trust you.' I push him away, reach for Ez. 'Will you take us?'

She clasps my hand. 'To the Sanctuary?'

'Where *is* she?' the demon shouts.

'Please,' I say to Ez. 'Don't separate us.'

Mya crawls closer. 'Yes, yes, come on. The chapterhouse will do.'

I lace my fingers through Jude's. His grip is crushing.

My stomach lurches again.

A demon I haven't seen before appears in the middle of the camp. Taller than Bel, his face deeply scarred. His eyes blaze like the others' but his long hair is jet black. His nails are dark too, overgrown talons, holding a mediaeval sword that is shiny with blood.

Ez's hand tightens around mine as the fiery eyes lock on me. He can see me, even in the darkness. His lips curl into a smile. He disappears.

I see a flare of orange, feel hot breath on my face, but the scream is ripped out of me as I'm pulled into nothing and nowhere.

HOME SWEET HOME

Jude's hand is still in mine when we stop moving. For a few seconds, it's enough.

'Get Nathaniel.' Whoever Daniel gives the order to leaves before I open my eyes.

When I do, I'm vaguely aware of towering arches, white marble columns, a pale stone floor. The smell of ancient dust and damp mortar. And cold, cold air.

'Gaby . . . you're shaking.' Ez's arm is around me. She leads me to one of the pews along an alabaster wall. Arched windows with heavy panes let in muted light. The white is so different from where we were. I have no idea what time it is here. It doesn't matter.

'Rafa.' His name comes out like I've dragged it over sandpaper.

'He's alive, Gaby.' Ez and Jude sit either side of me. 'If Zarael wanted them dead he would have taken their heads in front of us.'

I close my eyes, see the blade of the sword coming out of Rafa's body, see him searching the shadows for me.

'They came for you,' Daniel says. 'Or to take prisoners to trade for you. That only works if they're alive.' His tone is calm, focused, but he can't hide the distress in his eyes.

Jude moves closer so our shoulders are touching. Neither of us speaks.

Rafa is alive. But he'll be trapped in the iron room now. Zarael wouldn't have attacked unless he could hold Rephaim in there. God knows what they'll do to him and Taya. I can't shake the image of Rafa hurling himself against the wall, unable to get out—

Mya materialises in the middle of the chapterhouse, drops two men on the stone floor and disappears. One of them is Simon, who moans, rolls over and throws up. Beside him, Rusty scrambles backwards on his hands and feet, eyes wild. His shirt is soaked with blood and he's gulping in air.

Zak appears with Mick and Joffa, bringing pain and noise into the quiet room. Joffa's screaming; his jeans are on fire.

Ez moves to his side, smacks his legs with cupped hands, tells him to calm down. Mick gags – either from the shift or the stench of Joffa's smoking flesh.

'Get the medics,' Daniel orders. There's a flicker in the shadows at the back of the room. Doors open and close.

'I need to get this under running water,' Ez says. A second later they're both gone.

Mya and Zak return within half a second of each other bringing more men, Woosha among them, and the smell of blood and cordite.

'That's it,' Mya says to nobody in particular.

'What do you mean?' Simon sits back on his heels, his face mottled.

'No one else survived.'

Simon drops his head. Above him, on the opposite wall, an enormous oil painting hangs: a chaotic battle scene in muted reds and browns, shining warrior angels slaughtering sinewy demons with black wings. My stomach roils. I lean back against Jude.

'How did they find us?'

Daniel walks in front of us, back and forth. His eyes are distant. 'They shouldn't have been able to track us.'

It takes a few seconds for his words to sink through the fog. And then I understand: Taya was bitten by a hellion up the mountain the night we got Maggie back – a hellion that then lost half an arm when I got in a lucky blow.

'The hell-beast . . .'

'What?' Jude says. 'Gab?'

It must have still had Taya's taste.

'How could you not think of that?' I'm aware that I'm speaking loudly, that my voice is thin, shrill. All the Gatekeepers had to do was wait for her to turn up in Pan Beach and then put the beast on the scent when she left town tonight. Rafa telling me that Pan Beach wasn't safe slides into my mind, drags through my body.

'It was four days ago.' Daniel's voice is bleak now. 'They've never tracked us past three.'

That's how they knew we were at the farmhouse earlier today too. The hellion must have caught Taya's scent across the cornfield.

Heavy doors beyond the marble columns open and men in brown robes hurry in, carrying stretchers and black leather bags with white crosses stitched into them. Their heads are shaved, their faces calm. They surround the men on the floor, wordlessly check their wounds.

'What the fuck . . .?' Mick rasps when a monk kneels beside him.

'Don't speak to the brothers,' Zak says.

'Where are they taking them?' I can't stop shaking. It could be the cold or shock. Or both.

'The infirmary,' Daniel says.

I have a flash of sterile white walls, blinding pain.

'We have trained medical staff. They're in good hands.'

'And then what?'

'That's for the Council of Five to discuss.'

Another monk comes in, carrying a stack of blankets. Jude meets him halfway across the room. The monk stares at him – shocked – and allows him to take two.

Jude wraps one around my shoulders, takes the other for himself. The wool smells of incense and jasmine. It should be comforting. It's not.

And then my skin begins to tingle. Jude looks at his hands, confused.

The doors fall closed again and Nathaniel steps into the chapterhouse. His cold gaze sweeps over me. Then he sees Jude. His chest rises and falls, once, twice. Jude stands up, lets his blanket slide to the floor.

Jude stares at the fallen angel. Was this what he was expecting? Someone who doesn't look much older than us? Who could have been another backpacker – albeit better dressed and with eyes that don't belong to this world?

Nathaniel crosses the expansive room but stops before he reaches us. He looks from Jude to me, back to Jude.

'Gatekeepers ambushed us,' Daniel says. 'Rafa and Taya were taken.'

'Dead or alive?'

Nathaniel's calm. How can he be so fucking calm? I want to scream at him, slap him until he's as horrified as the rest of us.

'Badly injured but still alive. Zarael was there.'

Nathaniel nods. 'Call the Council together.' He turns to the Outcasts. 'Mya, Zachariah. Gather your people and come home. Gabriella, call the lost Rephaite here.'

Oh God, Jason and Maggie.

Woosha moans as the monks lift him onto a stretcher. His shoulder is dislocated and the bandage around his hand is already soaked dark. I'm not sure he has all his fingers. Simon is up from the floor, being led out. He looks at me over his shoulder on his way out, needing reassurance. I've got none to give him.

Mick finds me as Rusty helps him to his feet. 'You fucking people . . .' A monk tries to steer him towards the door but Mick knocks the pale hand away. 'I can walk.' He takes a step and his legs buckle. Rusty grabs him before his knees hit the stones.

'Come on,' Rusty says. 'We need to stay with the boys.' He catches my eye as he turns. 'Your man's the toughest prick I've ever seen. If anyone can survive those mongrels, it's him.'

Ez reappears, tired and drained. She nods at Nathaniel but doesn't speak.

Mya moves into the space between them.

'We don't need your protection, Nathaniel,' she says. 'Zarael has never come close to finding our safe houses and we've managed to hide from *you* for a decade.'

Nathaniel remains impassive. 'Zarael will torture Rafael

and Taya for information. We need to prepare for the possibility one or both might break.'

'That won't happen.' I say it without thinking.

Everyone turns to me.

'Rafa's too strong and Taya's too loyal. But you know that.' It's an effort to keep my voice steady. 'You need to do something, Nathaniel. We know where they are – we can take you there right now.'

'I am not invincible, Gabriella.'

'With enough of us storming the farmhouse, we'd get to Rafa and Taya before—'

'Gabriella.'

I stop, wipe my eyes. I hadn't even realised I was crying.

'This is the first time in a hundred and forty years we have known exactly where Zarael is. It may be the first time his entire horde has been in a single location. We may never get another opportunity—'

'You just said they'd be tortured!' My voice echoes off the ancient walls. 'I know you're angry at Rafa, but' – my voice breaks – 'what about Taya?'

'I care about both of them more than you could ever comprehend. But if we rush in and fail, Zarael will kill them. Any attack must be meticulously planned. We will only get one chance.'

'This is so typical.' The arches loom over Mya. She looks so much smaller in here. 'We can't sit on our hands here while you and the Five work up a battle plan. I know how long that takes. We'll go in on our own if we have to.'

I stand up, shaky. 'Count me in.'

'Me too,' Jude says.

Nathaniel's eyes flash. He's angry. About time.

'Before you do anything reckless, bring the others here.'

'Why?' Mya asks.

'Because this is the only place safe for any of you right now.'

'This place is no safer than anywhere else and you know it.'

'Mya—'

'Stop manipulating us! You haven't learned a thing—'

'The Sanctuary is protected.'

She falters. 'What?'

'There is a reason it has that name,' Nathaniel says. 'Demons cannot come here.'

For a few seconds, the chapterhouse is silent.

'How is that possible?' Zak moves next to Mya.

'There are ways to ward against demons.'

A storm builds under my ribs. 'You knew about the iron, didn't you?'

Nathaniel doesn't respond and I look to Daniel. For a second his mask slips and I see his confusion. This is news to him too.

'Nathaniel.' Sound moves strangely in here; it's stretched thin, echoey.

'It is true, Gabriella.' Nathaniel looks only at me, avoiding the others. Even Daniel. 'The Garrison has always known how to bless ancient metals to prevent demon manifestation. Until today, I was not aware a similar ward could be used to inhibit Rephaite movement. We have barely started questioning Virginia of Iowa, but we must assume her trap uses such powers and bindings. I do not yet understand how she and her family could know of these things.'

'But Daniel knew to look for the amulet on Virginia.'

Outside, a bell tolls once, twice. I lose count after nine.

Mya waits for the reverberation to fade. 'You've kept this to yourself all these years, and now you want us to trust you?'

'This division has gone on long enough, Mya. It has made us weak. Call the others here.'

'As guests or hostiles?'

Nathaniel frowns, as though the question offends him. 'As Rephaim. This place exists for all of you. Nothing that has happened in the past decade changes that.'

Mya turns to Jude. 'Are you hearing this? Damn it, I wish you remembered. I could really do with you being *you* right now.' There's more than frustration in her voice; there's a longing too.

Jude thinks for a moment. 'Nathaniel.'

'Yes, Judah.'

'It's Jude.'

'I prefer the name I gave you.'

Jude stiffens. Recovers. 'I prefer Jude.' A steadying breath. 'We need time to discuss this.'

'No.' It's Daniel who says it. 'These three will convince you and Gabriella to leave with them.'

'Daniel,' Ez says, exasperated. 'This isn't a game. Jude's right – we need to talk about this without you breathing down our necks.'

Nathaniel studies her and then nods. 'It is not an unreasonable request, Esther. We will return shortly.'

Daniel looks as though he wants to argue, but doesn't. He and Nathaniel leave the room without speaking to each other. The door scrapes over the stones, the latch clicks shut.

'He can't honestly think we're going to stay here,' Mya says to Ez.

Ez rubs her eyes. 'Do you have a plan?'

'I'll have one quicker than anyone here.'

'Mya,' Zak says. 'Answer the question.'

She avoids his gaze. 'Not yet.'

Jude walks to the centre of the room, skirting the remnants of blood and vomit on the stones. He cranes his neck to look up at the ornate timber arches overhead.

'What do you think we should do, Gaby?'

I lean back against the hard pew. I can't settle my mind enough to know. Images of Rafa tumble over each other: of him fighting demons at the Retreat . . . racing ahead of me on the beach . . . walking through the crowd at Rick's carrying beers . . . undressing me on his bed . . . his lips on my skin. And then that last, horrible moment, before the Gatekeepers took him. The sword. Blood. The look in his eyes.

Then Jude's arms are around me, pulling me to him. I breathe in the sea and wood smoke, bury my face in the blanket he tightens around me.

'Tell me what you want to do,' he whispers.

'We stay here.' I mumble it into the blanket. Then I raise my head, say it again, stronger. 'We stay here for now.'

'What a surprise.' Mya's voice is bitter. 'You want to obey Nathaniel.'

I pull away from Jude, find the strength to sit up on my own. 'I want Rafa and Taya back.'

'We all want that.'

'Then use your head. The more swords we have with us, the more chance we'll have of succeeding, especially if Nathaniel fights with us.'

'Gabe's right,' Zak says. 'Let's bring everyone here first. Then work up a plan.'

Mya closes her eyes, seems to wrestle with something.

Finally she lets out a frustrated breath, takes out her phone and goes to the other side of the room. Her ponytail swings across her neck and I catch another glimpse of the Celtic cross over her Rephaite mark.

'Jones—' I hear.

Jude leans closer. 'We'll get Rafa back.'

How can he sound so certain? I'm not even certain I could cross the room right now. Darkness drags at me.

I stare up at the painting on the wall. A tangle of limbs and swords, darkness and light, blood and halos. Now, though, I see more detail. Not all the angels are victorious: some lie bleeding among broken Corinthian columns, wings torn, limbs missing – butchered demons scattered around them. Why would Nathaniel want that in here? A reminder that victory comes only with suffering?

I tear my eyes away from the image, find Ez and Zak standing together in the middle of the room.

'You two still with us?' Ez asks.

Jude and I look at each other, nod.

'Well, then,' she says. 'I guess there's only one thing left to say . . .' She holds out her arms, her eyes sad, exhausted. 'Welcome home.'

ACKNOWLEDGMENTS

Writing a second book in a series – especially one featuring Gaby and Rafa – is definitely fun, but it's not without its challenges. Fortunately, I've had my editor, Alison Arnold, along again for the ride. I know you've heard it before, Ali, but I love working on these books with you. Thank you. For everything.

Huge thanks again to the rest of the amazing team at Text Publishing for the ongoing support and enthusiasm for the Rephaim series. Special mentions go to publicist Stephanie Stepan (miss you already) and rights manager Anne Beilby (love your work).

Thanks to my agent Lyn Tranter, who's always there when I need her, and Jane Finigan at Lutyens & Rubinstein Literary Agency for her amazing support.

Thanks to the team at Orion/Indigo Books in the United Kingdom, especially my editor, Jenny Glencross, and senior publicity manager, Nina Douglas. Thanks, too, to the Tundra Books team in Canada, who will soon be officially introducing the Rephaim to North America.

A chunk of *Haze* was written during the inaugural three-day writing frenzy that is the Queensland Writers' Centre Rabbit Hole. It's a fantastic initiative – up there with National Novel Writing Month for first-draft motivation. Speaking of first drafts, thanks to my test readers, especially Rebecca Cram (Place) and Michelle Reid. And to my writer friends, old and new: thanks for the friendship, advice and inspiration.

Thanks to my niece, Kelly Minerds, who actually did that insane bungee jump in the second chapter, and whose Facebook clip I used as research. (I certainly wasn't diving out of a cable car.)

To my wonderful friends and family: thanks for your support and understanding when I seem a little vague. I'm probably thinking about sword fights or kissing scenes. Or food.

And Murray . . . what can I say? This is some adventure we're on. Love you.

Finally, to all the readers, bloggers, reviewers, librarians and booksellers who so kindly embraced *Shadows* . . . I hope you enjoy this next instalment.